London, Where It All Began

The Bavarian Airship Regatta

THE ADVENTURES OF
DRAKE & McTROWELL

Perils in a Postulated Past

LONDON, WHERE IT ALL BEGAN

•

THE BAVARIAN AIRSHIP REGATTA

By
DAVID L. DRAKE & KATHERINE L. MORSE

Drake & McTrowell
San Diego, CA

Cover design by David L. Drake
Front cover art by Mike Maihack
Back cover art by David L. Drake
Book layout by Katherine L. Morse

Published by Drake & McTrowell <www.drakeandmctrowell.com>

Print edition ISBN 978-1-950849-00-0
Printed in the United States of America.

FOREWORD TO <u>LONDON, WHERE IT ALL BEGAN,</u>
HARDCOVER EDITION
By Professor Elemental

Is there anything better than a rip-roaring adventure? Is there a better way to spend an afternoon, than in the company of two fearless and eccentric heroes? Is there anything better than joyfully written, steampunk-flavoured, mystery fiction?

Well, yes, in this case there is — because you hold in your hands something that is all those things and much more. The first adventure of Chief Inspector Erasmus Drake and Dr. Sparky McTrowell is a rare treat.

You also get to enjoy the duelling, but always complementary styles of two very talented authors, who passed the writing of this book back and forth eagerly like a plate of cakes between two gluttons. Or a full pot of tea between two ladies. Or...well, you get the idea. This unique approach works to keep the story utterly vibrant, and moving at full pace. It allows for the fiery, feisty McTrowell and the decisive cool of the Chief Inspector to speak with their own voices and together, create a dynamic that is rather special.

Be prepared to meet pompous Lords, mad professors and a few odd fellows who might not be exactly as they first appear. Brace yourself to head through Victorian streets at breakneck pace, in pursuit of justice, answers and a most curious brew. You'll assuredly encounter exotic weapons, derring-do and even the odd sarcophagus. But unlike some steampunk fiction, these aspects never bog down the story. In the adventures of Sparky and Drake, all the elements are used wisely to enhance the world we're in, not just burden it with cogs and rust.

As a story, it's a delight and as a world it feels new and familiar all at once. And if you're anything like me, you'll long to return to as soon as you get to the last page. So, here's to Chief Inspector Drake and Dr. McTrowell, and here's hoping that this is just the first of many exploits. Because really, there's isn't anything better than rip roaring adventure, not when it's as splendid as this.

INTRODUCTION TO <u>LONDON, WHERE IT ALL BEGAN</u>, HARDCOVER EDITION

By David L. Drake

It started as a bet. Not the type of bet one makes with a friend to help them with their ill-fated plans to stick to their exercise routine. That kind of bet is made in the hopes that it is lost. No, this was one of those bets where the bettor was trying to make a point — and to save us from ourselves.

I'll never forget that moment. John Schloman leaned back and wryly smiled. "You'll give up in a month. Six posts, tops." He gave his beer another sip, arched a single eyebrow, and added, "I'll bet you'll give up." He was trying to warn us that we should not waste our time starting such an ambitious endeavor.

Katherine immediately answered, "You're on!" She emphasized the galvanization of her will with a small jab of her pointed finger at John, as if to make it clear with whom in the group she was entering the wager.

That was how it started, but the story goes back to when our friend and colleague, Mike Newkirk, wondered if we wanted to join him at the Nova Albion Steampunk Exhibition, held in Emeryville, California, in March of 2010. He had planned to extend a business trip to the town of Livermore out over the weekend, and Katherine and I would drive up from San Diego. It looked like good fun, so we innocently committed to going.

It was a wonderful convention. An eye-opening event. It was our first experience with any convention where practically everyone was sporting steampunk garb. While there, we excitedly purchased approximately forty pounds of leather in the form of a duster and cape coat. I suggested to Katherine that we should think of characters to go with our outfits, which would help us in assembling consistent ensembles. Katherine immediately wanted to pilot airships, but be a medical doctor to boot. I saw a bobby's whistle and thought the cape coat would make a grand detective outfit. By the end of the weekend, we had acquired a flying cap for the budding pilot and a brown bowler that went well with the cape coat.

A few weeks later, we made a trip to the main office at work. We were sitting through one of those work meetings where multitasking on electronic communication devices was seriously discouraged, leaving Katherine in a state she hates: scribbling notes on paper, knowing that they'll just have to be transcribed to the digital world later, carving even more time out of her life for no real good reason.

She dreamed of what her plucky pilot would have done in that situation. Perhaps she would have jumped up on the table and kicked the projector into the hall to make it clear that there are better ways for humans to interact. In that moment, she began writing the single paragraph that constituted our first Drake & McTrowell episode.

As we do on business trips, at the day's end we met with friends at a local microbrewery. Ryan Brunton, John Schloman, Jon Labin, and Mike Newkirk, were there with us. With beers in hand, toasting to the completion of the day, Mike regaled the merry troop with stories of shared experiences at the Nova Albion Steampunk Exhibition, and Katherine and I recounted our commitment to the steampunk genre. That's when Katherine confessed.

"Don't tell anyone, but I spent the meeting writing the beginning of a story about my character."

I offered, "We could take turns writing bits of it, like they used to do for serialized fiction in magazines. Like Dickens and Dumas did for their stories."

Katherine scooted to the edge of her seat, her interest piqued. "That would be great!"

Ryan and John shared a glance that indicated that they thought this was one of those ideas that wouldn't survive after leaving the pub.

I rubbed my chin. "I could set up a web site and we could push each of the posts out. If we alternate weeks, that wouldn't be too bad."

John made the – now famous – bet that we'd give up, trying to prevent us from a preposterous commitment of time and energy. Katherine sealed the deal by taking the challenge.

After a year, fifty posts on-line, and a web site with a following, we sat in the same circle of friends and John brought us a very nice bottle of wine to celebrate our first "Adventures of Drake and McTrowell" anniversary.

We hope you, dear reader, enjoy these stories as much as our faithful readers do, and have as much fun with them as we do writing them. Keep in mind that we employ what we call the "Hot Potato School of Writing™," where we give each other free reign to continue the story as they see fit on a weekly basis, leaving a few "hot potatoes," unresolved story components, that the next writer has to pick up and run with. Sometimes these are cliffhangers; other times they are unexpected plot twists. Being aware that this is going on makes the reading of the stories more interesting, knowing that there are two pair of hands in this crazy hot potato juggling act.

So please join us as we step into an alternative world of 1851, in London, where it all began.

ACKNOWLEDGEMENTS

We could neither have written nor published this book without our friends, audience, and supporters. Our friends supplied us with generous amounts of encouragement. Our audience gave us the passion to sustain us in our writing. Our supporters gave us the capability to get the book to print. All of these people became our friends in the end. And for that we are truly thankful.

Some of these friends deserve to be called out individually, and sincerely thanked, for their contribution:

- Mike Newkirk - for tempting us to board the proverbial airship to steampunk adventure
- John Schloman – for daring us to put our stories out there
- Ashok Pathi – for inspiring one of our characters, and for legal support
- Ed Pogue – for his ability with flying gizmos
- Kim Hutsell & the other Starburner Galactic Courier Service members – for inspiring us with their vision of and enthusiasm for steampunk
- Bev Gelfand – for her editing of the published versions of <u>London, Where It All Began</u>
- Gene Turnbow & everyone at Kyrpton Radio – for their encouragement and support during the making of the <u>London, Where It All Began</u> radio show
- All of our author friends from Clockwork Alchemy – you have been the wind beneath our wings regarding inspiration and publication knowhow
- All or our San Diego and Arizona steampunk friends – for being genuinely and profoundly inviting and supportive

A special thanks to Katherine's mother, Marjorie, who taught Katherine that she could be anything she dreamed.

TABLE OF CONTENTS
LONDON, WHERE IT ALL BEGAN

THE BAVARIAN AIRSHIP REGATTA

London, Where It All Began

DR. MCTROWELL ALIGHTS

BY DR. KATHERINE L. MORSE

In the hustle and bustle of the London airship port, she was hardly noticed, though the ground-sweeping leather duster would look out of place on the Marylebone high street. It was only slightly unusual among the international air travelers owing to its being worn by a woman, and a slight one at that. One or two of the air stevedores took note of the wisps of blonde hair poking out from under her aviator's cap and the well-turned ankle barely concealed by buttoned ankle boots, but the icy look in her eyes when she removed her goggles suggested more trouble than such a small morsel might be worth. She signaled one of the air stevedores with a whistle and pointed to several travel-worn trunks. From a pocket concealed inside the duster, she produced an engraved calling card and an elaborately enameled pen. She flipped over the card and rapidly scrawled an address on the back. Pulling a florin from another hidden pocket, she handed both card and coin to the stevedore, turned on the heel of her boot, and strode off into the melee of the airship port, completely trusting that the generous tip would be sufficient to ensure the safe delivery of her belongings. The stunned stevedore bit into the coin to verify its authenticity and checked the address. He heaved the trunks onto his cart. Only then did he turn over the calling card. It read simply, *Dr. Sparky McTrowell.*

CURIOUS TO A FAULT, IN WHICH CHIEF INSPECTOR DRAKE IS INTRODUCED

BY MR. DAVID L. DRAKE

The furniture wasn't actually new. The desk showed signs of wear, and one of the drawers didn't operate smoothly. The springs in the chair that allowed it to rock back a bit squeaked, and the wheels had seen better days. But for Chief Inspector Erasmus Drake, the office felt new. With his recently appointed title, and the office that went with it, Erasmus sat and looked out at the teams of constables, taking on the myriad of minor cases that had popped up today. Compared to the last major case, all of these were standard procedure, run of the mill crimes. The perpetrator was most likely known, in most cases already in lock up, and if protocol were followed properly, going to be tried and sentenced without incident. Three such cases had been turned over to the magistrate this morning; Scotland Yard was running in its usual efficient manner.

Erasmus was taking all of this in. He was in his den of quiet reflection while the workers buzzed in the hive. He had been rewarded for a job well done, after months of grueling police work, and here he sat.

The comfort of success lasted less than five minutes. The leftover details, mostly unrelated to the closed case, were gnawing at his penchant to resolve loose ends. *"Hmm."* There was that eyewitness who mentioned the unexpected overwhelming smell of freshly ground coffee in the back of a temporary exhibit room at the grand pavilion. Or was it cocoa? The room was for electrical apparatus, not the dispensing of food, nor entertaining. What was the name of that witness? Mr. Hampstead? It would be in his notes, he knew, but why ferret them back out? They were filed away with the closed case.

And this wasn't the only remaining unturned stone. Why was Mr. Hampstead—if that was his name—who was of questionable character, running errands for the likes of Professor Farnsworth? The Professor had many students who could perform these manual tasks for him, and with greater clarity of purpose.

These questions not only nagged at Erasmus, but set up shop in the back of his mind and went about tinkering in such a manner as to bring to life more questions, which then joined in with their shop-mates.

"Enough," he thought. He sprung up from his chair, grabbed his cane and bowler, slipped his leather cape coat on, and verified that his ever-present note- and sketchbook was secured in his pocket. Swinging open his office door, he headed out into the bustle of the precinct and toward the street. "This curiousness will not stand unsolved."

BLOOMSBURY

BY DR. KATHERINE L. MORSE

Toting only her commodious flight surgeon's bag, Dr. McTrowell headed toward the line of hansom cabs. While such a mode of transportation was unseemly and "racy" for a lady of quality, it wouldn't be her most inappropriate activity of the day. As she approached the first cab in the line, the driver gave her attire a quizzical look. Surely a lone woman wasn't going to hire his cab. She strode up to his vehicle smartly. He gave her another quizzical look as it became apparent that she indeed intended to hire his services, but he kept his mouth shut since money is money, after all. "University College, please," she said to the driver as she stepped up into the hansom without hesitation. He was beyond astonishment as he mumbled, "Yes, Mum."

The scene in Bloomsbury was incongruous to say the least. While most of the streets reflected their usual quiet, residential nature, if one turned off the busy thoroughfare of Euston Road onto Gower Street, one would have been greeted by the site of a melee of cabs and private carriages disgorging a motley crew of variously attired characters. Some would have appeared normal if rendered in a broadside illustration, but only because such an illustration would not reflect the garish colors of the living soul; perhaps the wearers were colorblind. Others wore more restrained hues, but combined contemporary attire with recognizably anachronistic articles of clothing as if they were time travelers lacking effective research skills. One such individual, a strikingly handsome and exotic young man, appeared Indian to Dr. McTrowell. Many carried parcels of varying sizes or contraptions and mechanisms of unfathomable function. And then there were those truly remarkable individuals who exhibited the totality of these anomalies, including some who appeared to be wearing their inventions.

Dr. McTrowell observed the maelstrom from her cab while she waited for the driver to maneuver her closer to the curb in front of University College, London. Certainly there was no guessing what was in the closed parcels, but she could divine the intent of some of the openly carried contraptions. The wood box with the miniature steam engine attached to the outlet valve of a glass sphere of ether was probably an ether compressor. The oxygen depriving facility of such a device could be very dangerous in an enclosed space. As she was contemplating the sort of mind that could devise such a dastardly contrivance, her mood was lifted by the arrival of an individual riding rather than carrying his contrivance, or rather, conveyance. It was a spider-like walking machine that chugged and lurched toward the building, its "driver" smiling triumphantly. Until he attempted to surmount the stairs. The spider tottered and the gears ground as he shifted them. Trying to stabilize the machine, he grabbed and adjusted several levers. The steam engine on the back wheezed and strained, and the spider toppled, unceremoniously dumping its inventor on the ground. Dr. McTrowell did her best to suppress an uncharitable smile.

Just as she was turning around from paying the cab driver, she spotted a couple just entering the building. No, not a couple per se, but a man and a woman simply walking together. Seeing them from the back and at a distance, she couldn't be sure, but they looked like Mr. Babbage and the Countess Lovelace. Well, they would certainly lend an air of respectability to the proceedings. With her attention diverted to the pair, she didn't turn quite in time to get a fix on something just at the edge of her vision, something of a brown shadow…and a bowler. She shook her head to try to erase the tingling in the back of her neck. As she entered the building, she passed a sign on an easel with elaborate lettering, **Annual Symposium of the Occidental Inventors' Society.**

The Lucid Dreams of Professor Farnsworth

By Mr. David L. Drake

Erasmus strode through the precinct with conviction, hoping to make daylight without disruption. He was not to be so fortunate. Having spied Erasmus' appearance from his office and his beeline for the door, Sergeant Tate Parseval took it upon himself to see if he could intercept Erasmus and find out what would make the newly appointed

Chief Inspector head out so early in the morning. This required the sergeant to make more haste than usual, shoving his chair back with an audible squeak and making his way between the desks at a pace unusual for an office setting.

"Mind if I join you? It looks as if something has caught your attention. If you need a second man I can make myself available," Tate sputtered, trying his best to hop on the coattails of one of Erasmus' interesting adventures.

The Chief Inspector replied without a break in his step, "That is very kind of you, Sergeant Parseval, but this is a minor matter, and does not warrant the attention of two from Scotland Yard. It is simply a matter of clearing up a detail or two. I will give you a full account when I return."

Given the distinct difference between ordinary day-to-day police work and venturing out, Tate now felt that he could have done a better job with his request to join Erasmus. With a nod of his head, Tate retreated to his desk while his posture gave away his disappointment. Erasmus headed for the door.

Erasmus tugged his bowler down enough to block the morning sun, turned right, and started in earnest stride down the sidewalk, the tip of his cane tapping out a strident cadence as he contemplated his tactical approach. Professor Farnsworth was most likely going to be at pre-opening preparations at The Great Exhibition. Erasmus' goal was to find his low-life errand man first. He would be able to get the truth from him long before he could get the Professor to admit to whatever he was concocting. The half-hour walk would give him time to figure out a way to chat up the ne'er-do-well.

Erasmus was not more than a block down the street when a figure in the shadows of an alleyway made herself known to him. Erasmus made a slight change in his trajectory and headed straight for her, greeting her by name. "Abigail, as always, a pleasure."

Abigail Schopenhauer was dressed plainly, with a long scarf that covered her head and wrapped about her shoulders. She was a sturdy woman with the shape of a grandmother who hailed from the continent, providing that odd cross between sturdiness, gentleness, and strength. Abigail stayed in the shadows given that she was traditionally a creature of the night. Although daytime afforded her the ability for panhandling and picking pockets, it more importantly permitted the gathering of minor daily news.

As Erasmus neared her, she looked at him with her toothy grin and revealed her cataract-plagued eyes. "Erasmus, I was hoping, or rather, expecting to see you this morning," she answered, using her lyrical but raspy whisper. "Is there anything new you can tell me to help me with my sessions tonight?" She produced an arthritic hand and laid it gently on his forearm, which he accepted. Erasmus enjoyed their arrangement. Abigail would supply news of activities in the underworld, and Erasmus would bestow upon her upcoming events that would be known only within the precinct. When Abigail would perform her gypsy soothsayer act for the working class at night, she would be able to predict actual events such as the delayed arrival of a passenger ship, or the closing of a business. These simple touches added a great deal to the believability of her predictions.

Erasmus proceeded to inform her about a delayed coal shipment that may affect the output of a number of factories in the area. Additionally, a small band of drunken scientists reveling in Regents Park struck an infant with a diminutive flying gizmo, doing minor harm, but raising a significant kerfuffle. Although this kind of detailed information would be provided tomorrow in the *Times* or the *Daily News*, tonight it would be unknown to the public at large.

However, the news that Abigail provided was vexing. "Erasmus, be very wary of the activities of the student artists. There is something amiss within that community; I can't put my finger on it. Strange goings-on. Check out the pubs and private meeting halls when you can. I know they're a strange bunch, but this is different. Mark my words, it's worth looking into." She gave Erasmus a quick smile and patted his arm, as shorthand for an acceptable exchange of information, a confirmation of trust, and goodbye. She knew his time was valuable and by respecting it, their relationship would endure. Abigail turned back into the shadows. Erasmus proceeded on his journey, putting Abigail's bizarre declaration in the back of his mind to be assessed at some future time.

The work on the Crystal Palace in Hyde Park was underway, and the site was bustling with activity. Cranes, which were a very rare sight, were lifting metal girders for placement within the structure that was to be the magnificent spectacle housing the majority of The Great Exhibition. There were hundreds of people, mostly laborers, going about their duties. Tents were set up on the outskirts in which some of the more complex exhibitions were being prepared, particularly those where heavy machinery or articles from faraway places needed to be assembled.

Erasmus was familiar with the future layout of the Great Exhibition and headed directly to where Dr. Farnsworth had set up a tent in which to piece together his contrivances. As he had hoped, Erasmus recognized the man he recalled as Mr. Hampstead sitting nearby on a crate, his well-worn bowler pushed back in an almost comical manner, whittling a stick with no more of a goal than to simply shorten it. His clothes showed signs of wear and exposure to enough dust and dirt that it allowed his ensemble to match, despite whatever the original colors of the individual pieces had been. Erasmus approached him in the manner of a man with a mission.

The Chief Inspector led with "My good man, I hope you recognize me from before, as I do you. But I must admit I have forgotten your name. I do wish to see your employer, Dr. Farnsworth; if you can be so kind as to let me know where I can find him, I would be very grateful."

The reply was simple and short. "The name's Raleigh Hampstead, but everybody calls me Red. The Professor's not here." He went back to his whittling.

"Why, thank you, Red. Actually, I am willing to meet the Professor where he is currently located. I have some news he may be interested in. It is worth the price of a pint if you know where he is."

This bit of information woke Red up. "Yes, sir, I do happen to know. He's at some meeting of inventors that's held every year. It's going on now over at University College in Bloomsbury."

"This is going well," Erasmus thought, and replied, "Excellent, and thank you again. Let me reward you for your knowledge." Erasmus dug some coins out of one of his front pockets and started counting through them. Red gave this a great deal of attention.

Erasmus took advantage of this opportunity to ask, "Please pardon my curiosity. What does the good Professor have you do for him?"

"This and that, finding parts that no one else can, but mainly I track down Green Fantasy for him. It's hard to find, and I'm good at locating it." Erasmus' puzzled look caused Red to continue, "Oh, forgive me. Green Fantasy is new, but totally on the up-and-up, mind you. It's a combination of a number of things, but mainly absinthe. Someplace local mixes it up, not sure where, but the Professor loves it. It gives him what he calls 'lucid dreams,' and helps him with his work. I'm not an inventor type, so I'm not interested in the stuff. I'm more of a beer man myself, if you get my meaning." Red let all of these words flow out without impediment, as he watched Erasmus finger the coins.

"You have been more than helpful, my good man. Well worth the cost of a beer." Erasmus placed a few coins into Red's outstretched hand. Without looking back, Erasmus turned on his heel and set out for Bloomsbury. *"Well,"* he thought, *"this is getting to be as complicated as I feared. Excellent!"*

KULACHNIY BOY

BY DR. KATHERINE L. MORSE

The scene inside was even more chaotic than outside. Dr. McTrowell was thankful she hadn't removed her duster when she entered the building because it protected her from being poked by elbows, wildly gesticulating hands, and the various pointed protuberances of the inventions of other attendees. She was so busy wading through the crowd that she very nearly knocked over a colleague she hadn't seen in some time, the French mathematician, Jean-Michel Petit of the Université Toulouse.

Several years previously, she and Dr. Petit had collaborated on a mathematical analysis of the flow of pure oxygen through airship baffles. While he often tended toward being a bit fussy, his acute attention to detail had been invaluable in preparing the final mathematical calculations that had enabled Dr. McTrowell to improve the stability of her employer's airships, and subsequently, the comfort of her employer's first-class passengers, who were only too happy to pay handsomely for such comfort. Her employer had rewarded her generously, although not as generously as his first-class passengers had rewarded him, but at least he had seen fit to share a small portion of his good fortune. The windfall had afforded Dr. McTrowell the opportunity to pursue some personal lines of inquiry, one of which had brought her back to London for the symposium, among other things. In contrast, Dr. Petit was simply quite pleased to report the exemplary results in his curriculum vitae.

"Madame…er Mademoiselle…Dr. McTrowell, how very pleasant to see you again."

"Monsieur Dr. Petit, the pleasure is all mine. How are your work and your lovely family?"

Dr. Petit could never get used to the bluntness of Americans, especially those from the wild frontiers of the West. But he chose to ignore this bluntness from Dr. McTrowell because he knew from his previous association with her that she only asked such personal questions out of a sincere affection and interest, and not simple impudence.

"My family is quite well; thank you for asking. Sandrine's mother is again visiting," in spite of himself, he pursed his lips slightly, "as we will be six in another month."

"They would be six? Oh, six people! He must have welcomed a third child since our last encounter and now be expecting a fourth," she thought. "A fourth little Petit, or is that petite Petit?" She smiled and grasped his hand enthusiastically.

"Again the bluntness and excessive familiarity!" he thought. "Yes, we are blessed. Are you perhaps here to share a new invention or procedure with the Society? Perhaps an advancement of your mechanical surgeon's assistant for the small spaces of airship infirmaries?"

"Very kind of you to ask, but no. I am here only as an observer this time, Dr. Petit. And your work?"

"Ah, yes. How providential that we should meet at this time. I believe I have arrived at a proof of Fermat's little theorem. I would very much like to have the benefit of your review of my proof."

She was prepared to answer with an excited affirmative when she once again felt the tingling in the back of her neck and looked

9

around quickly to see if she could identify the source of her disquiet. Nothing again!

When she turned her attention back to Dr. Petit, she was confronted by a very large and unpleasant Englishman who also appeared to be quite drunk. He was slurring his very loud words and spraying Dr. Petit with spittle, much to the horror of the fastidious Frenchman. "Fermat was a pompous, posturing liar like all Frenchmen." He jabbed Jean-Michel hard in the lapel with his portly index finger. Jean-Michel attempted to maintain his polite composure. "And you think you can come here, prancing about with your fancy mathematical proofs and supplant solid English craftsmanship!" He planted his meaty palm on Jean-Michel's shoulder and shoved. The Frenchman staggered back a pace before regaining his balance. While he stared at the Englishman with an absolutely stunned look on his face, Dr. McTrowell's temper boiled over. She had come here to be a silent, unobtrusive observer and this oaf had assaulted her dear friend. Enough was enough!

She tapped the bully on the shoulder. He rounded on her and looked down. Before he could prepare for it, she struck him squarely in the face with a practiced blow. He too staggered backward, but she didn't give him time to recover. She advanced on him again, delivering several rapid, sharp blows to his face, neck and solar plexus. On the sixth or seventh blow he toppled over. Dr. McTrowell relaxed and flexed her fingers to confirm that she had done no damage to herself.

Just then the exotically handsome young man she had seen outside stepped in close. He was carrying a very fine, inlaid cane. He raised his cane as if to strike the now-unconscious miscreant. She stayed his hand. "The rules do not permit hitting one who is already down."

He wrinkled his smooth brow quizzically. "Rules?"

In that single word, she detected the refinement of nobility and the lilting silkiness of the exotic Indians. "The rules do not permit hitting one who is already down. Nor may you kick nor keep iron up your sleeves." She glanced at the unnecessarily elaborate decorations on the cane. "I suspect you were about to violate one, or maybe two, of those rules."

"Of what sport or martial art are these the rules?"

"Кулачный бой."

THE ENLIGHTENING WALK

BY MR. DAVID L. DRAKE

Chief Inspector Drake was off at his usual fast pace. As was his tradition, he avoided the cabriolets and any of the other wheeled conveyances when simply walking through London was an option. He felt that the walk kept him sharp, and kept him tuned to life on the London streets. This was one of the few philosophical points that he was quick to share with others.

The trek up Oxford Street gave him time to ponder what he knew so far. Professor Farnsworth was using connections to the underworld to get access to something. If Red was being totally honest, a major part of the activity was to procure what must have been cases of spiked drink. Was it for use in some peculiar experiment or invention? Absinthe was popular enough in Paris over the past decade, and as a liqueur, was known for its ability to allow writers to loosen their imaginations. Was the Professor plying his students with drink? Erasmus then asked himself the question that he had dared not ask: was this loose end even worth a brisk morning walk to investigate? Or should he be back overseeing his subordinates at Scotland Yard? He had gone this far, what could it hurt to have a conversation with the Professor and mentally close the book on this?

The Annual Symposium of the Occidental Inventors' Society was in full swing. The busyness of Gower Street was a minor distraction to Erasmus, even though he otherwise would have found it entertaining. Every odd character in London seemed to be here playing inventor, dressed outlandishly, and putting on erudite airs. Erasmus was already distracted from his primary job as Chief Inspector, and he didn't need an additional distraction from that. Erasmus entered the main university building, working his way through the cacophonous assembly, many of whom were holding

11

contraptions of brass, glass, and polished wood. Three of the smaller hand-held devices were even running with non-harmonious sputtering sounds, releasing fine pulsating mists of steam that caused some gestures of avoidance by those nearby. Erasmus wouldn't have been able to conceal himself in this crowd; his brown topcoat, trousers, and bowler were too subdued and color-coordinated for this gathering. On the other hand, he noticed they seemed far too absorbed in themselves and each other to notice him. His understated dress and demeanor became his camouflage.

While Erasmus was sizing up the various symposium attendees to see who looked like they had enough clout to know where the Professor might be, a rumpus broke out in the next room. The clamor shifted from elevated intellectual blather to directed chatter about a man who had been pummeled. To add to the normal excitement at such violence in an academic setting, the babbling seemed to indicate that a woman had downed the sizable gent. Erasmus changed roles in a flash, and started the process of elbowing his way through the throng. "Scotland Yard! Step aside! Let me through."

JONATHAN LORD ASHLEIGH

BY DR. KATHERINE L. MORSE

Sparky continued her explanation. "Kulachniy boy. Russian fist fighting." She turned her attention back to Jean-Michel. "Are you all right? What was that about?"

The look on his face was pure horror, although McTrowell couldn't divine whether it was from being assaulted himself or from seeing her beat his abuser into unconsciousness. "*Mon dieu!* It is a scandal!"

"I am terribly sorry Jean-Michel, but I feared that he would do you real harm."

"My apologies, Dr. McTrowell. I did not intend to insult your actions, although I am unaccustomed to being protected by a woman. I meant it is a scandal that this oaf is allowed to remain a member of this respectable Society."

"Who is he?"

"He is the Duke of Milton. Many years ago, he invented a small and insignificant device for the kitchen. It was not an effort worthy of this Society, but he is wealthy and his family has served the royal family for hundreds of years. And so he was admitted. He is a dullard and a bully." Jean-Michel removed a handkerchief from his jacket and wiped his brow.

"Jean-Michel, I would dearly love to hear your proof of Monsieur le Fermat's little theorem, but I had hoped to attend this event discreetly. Clearly that cannot happen now. And I probably should not be here when the Duke awakes. I apologize. We must share a libation before we leave London, and you must present your proof to me. My deepest apologies."

"Of course, I understand. I look forward to our next meeting." He took her hand and kissed it. *"Bon jour."*

As she turned to leave, she came face to face with the young man with the interesting cane.

"Jonathan Lord Ashleigh, at your service madam."

"Charmed, Lord Ashleigh, but I really must be leaving."

"Then I shall aid in your expeditious departure." He rotated smoothly 90 degrees as if he were turning a partner on the dance floor and gestured with an open hand for her to pass him to the doors. His perfectly tailored, but surprisingly deep green colored, frock coat lifted open slightly as he did so, revealing a knife at his hip. Although it was ornately decorated like his cane, in fact like many of his accoutrements, it looked entirely functional.

She paused for a beat to wonder if it were wise to accept his offer. Milton stirred on the floor and moaned. "Thank you, Lord Ashleigh." As she strode out, he pivoted gracefully again and followed closely behind.

When they reached the street where several hansoms and private coaches awaited, he said simply, "To the left, if you please." They had taken only a couple of steps when another Indian appeared by the door of one of the private coaches. Like Ashleigh's coat, it was of exceptionally fine quality, but a little more colorful than was fashionable. The silent servant opened the door and held out his hand to assist McTrowell into the coach, taking her flight surgeon's bag with the other. She was perfectly capable of boarding unaided, but had long since given up arguing against the unnecessary courtesy. This time, however, was unusual. Unlike every other coachman or gentleman who had offered his hand in this manner, the Indian's face gave absolutely no indication that her attire or manner was distasteful or inappropriate. Lord Ashleigh slid into the seat opposite her, simultaneously doffing his richly indigo top hat and sliding his cane into a bracket immediately by his left hand. Did this man glide through his entire life as if the whole world were a fancy-dress ball arranged for his entertainment?

"Please put your mind at ease, Dr. McTrowell. My offer of assistance was genuine and no harm will come to you while in my company."

Perhaps this was a fancy-dress ball arranged for the pleasure of Lord Ashleigh? "You have told me your name, but how do you know mine?"

"The only woman in that company of men and dressed thusly? How could you be anyone but Dr. Sparky McTrowell, aviatrix, adventuress, inventor, and flight surgeon for Western & Transatlantic Airship Lines? May I say, if somewhat belatedly, that it is my august pleasure to make your acquaintance?"

This young man was one surprise after another. She managed to say "thank you," but was otherwise speechless. And that was a rare thing indeed.

The coach rolled along past the corner of Regents' Park and stopped a few minutes later in front of a brownstone in Berkley Square. The silent servant appeared again to open the door. Ashleigh exited with the same grace and composure with which he had embarked and performed another of his smooth dance steps to offer his own arm this time. Unlike his servant, he had an expression on his face; his slightly almond eyes were crinkled at the corners and perhaps one corner of his mouth was turned up under his finely trimmed moustache. The front door of the brownstone opened as soon as they began to ascend the stairs. She had a quick glance around as he handed his hat and cane to the young woman in a bright blue cotton sari who opened the door. The furnishings were beautiful, obviously expensive, and many were unusually colorful and exotic. Well, no surprises there.

"If you would care to refresh yourself from the day's unexpected exertions, you will find suitable facilities at the end of this hall where Virat will have placed your bag. Anu will show you to the sitting room when you are ready. Virat will prepare some chai that I hope you will find to your taste."

As promised, there was a small powder room at the end of the hall. The cabinet beside the sink supported a crystal dish containing a bar of French lavender soap and a boar bristle brush with not a single stray hair in it. *"No sense in letting all this fine hospitality go to waste,"* she thought, and hung her duster on the hook and cleaned up. When she exited, Anu was standing exactly where she had been when Sparky entered. She turned silently and led Sparky to the sitting room.

Lord Ashleigh was ensconced in a large leather wing chair. He had exchanged his frock coat for an even more brightly colored smoking jacket of silk brocade. Although he wasn't smoking when she entered, the lingering aroma in the room indicated that he was in the habit of smoking cigars, and expensive ones at that. How polite of him to have spared her.

He stood when she entered, gesturing to a chair to his left, "Please." She had barely settled into the matching wing chair when the servant she had taken for a coachman appeared dressed in a tunic, loose fitting pants and slippers, and carrying a silver tray with a silver tea set. He set the tray on the table and poured her a cup without asking. It already had milk in it and there was no sugar on the tray. He handed her the cup, poured another just like it for Ashleigh, and left without a word.

"Virat makes the finest chai I have ever drunk, and I have drunk quite a large number of cups of chai in my life."

"Чай?"

"Yes, chai."

"I have had chai before, but it does not have milk in it," Sparky said, looking at the tawny color of the tea.

"It is traditional for masala chai to have milk and sugar in it."

"Masala chai? I thought you meant чай, Russian tea."

"Ah, I see. We have the same word for tea."

"Ah." She took a sip; the spices were unexpected, but delightful. Virat reappeared carrying a fanned stack of freshly ironed newspapers. The top paper was The Californian. All the pleasantness of the last half hour drained out of Dr. McTrowell's body as she read the headline:

49er Collapses and Dies on Sansome Street

MEETING FARNSWORTH AGAIN

BY MR. DAVID L. DRAKE

Erasmus made his way through the crowd arriving at the nexus of the activity. There he found a large man sprawled on the carpeted floor, clearly recovering from being knocked out cold. Erasmus didn't need to look closely to see the red lump on the injured party's left cheek, which was continuing to rise. The man's eyes were just starting to adjust to focusing again, and he raised his head. Erasmus extended a hand and bent over slightly in a formal gesture to help the man to his feet.

"I do not need help from some commoner!" the victim sputtered as he worked one of his legs under his overweight torso. He added a complex punctuation to his utterance with a combination burp and hiccup. The smell of Scotch whisky was in the air due to this, and a few of the scientists took an involuntary step back.

A fellow inventor, who was aghast at this interchange, stepped forward to offer sympathetic assistance, exclaiming "My dear Duke! Do you not recognize this gentleman?"

The Duke of Milton waved off his support with a quick hand gesture. The Duke gave Erasmus a quick once over as he stood unsteadily on his own, and sneered "I do not recognize this man as a member of the Inventor's Society, and he is therefore a commoner. As such, he should not be here."

The sympathetic inventor gasped. He knew where this exchange was likely headed, and given that he recognized the Chief Inspector from the illustration featured in the *Times* a week ago, thought it a bad way to start the Inventor's Symposium by insulting a decorated and newly promoted member of Scotland Yard.

16

Erasmus easily transitioned from concerned to noncommittal regarding the Duke's state of welfare. His hand withdrawn, he was now concerned about the person that took this oaf down and the fact that she—as he had heard from the whispers that it had been a woman—might still be in the area and terrorizing academics.

Erasmus tilted his head and opened with "My dear Duke, I am Chief Inspector Drake of Scotland Yard. What do you remember of the person who struck you?"

"She was a vixen! Tiny fists that came at me for no reason! She was wearing a long leather duster and only stood this tall." The Duke extended a corpulent hand about shoulder height, and continued with a grumbled rant that included few intelligible words, but "quarrelsome" and "witch" were two that could be understood clearly.

Erasmus took a quarter turn, and with a commanding voice, took over the room. "Has anyone seen this woman? Is she still in the vicinity?" Five or more scientists instantly pointed toward the door and stammered that she had left with a gentleman in an expensive private coach. A scientist with thick glasses indicated that the gentleman was Lord Ashleigh.

The Chief Inspector summed all of it up in his mind that a strong-willed woman knocked this buffoon on his rump for good reason, and justice had been served. He filed away the details of the incident in the back of his mind to ponder later and determined it was time to move on, given his task as an administrator of justice was unneeded.

"I need to speak with Professor Farnsworth on another matter. Who knows where he is?" Erasmus queried. This question seemed to shock the gathering. Some turned away as if to pretend they didn't want to assist. Others swallowed hard and fumbled to discover ways not to answer. The thick-glassed scientist stammered out that Professor Farnsworth was in the physics laboratory down the main hall, the one that was, logically enough, named after Newton. He also mentioned that his graduate students were with him, and that he was quite busy.

Erasmus nodded in thanks, and turned to leave. The Duke of Milton boomed out, "What about my attacker? Is Scotland Yard no longer doing their job?"

Erasmus looked back with a quirky grin, and retorted "Not when others do our job for us first!" combined with a "we're done here" nod. The Duke's plump face showed his shock at the Chief Inspector's indifference with wide-open eyes and gaping mouth. Erasmus was down the hall before the Duke's mouth was fully closed again.

The sign above the laboratory entrance simply declared **Newton** to be its nomenclature. The double doors had windows in them that were clearly to make sure the other side was free of people when entering. It was through these windows that Erasmus observed the scene within.

The Professor and his graduate students were gathered around a large lab table working on the parts to various apparatuses. All had on some form of laboratory apron: some were white cloth while others were brown leather, depending on their wearer's task. Most students had goggles over their eyes to better protect against the sprays of sparks being generated from several tools at the table. Whatever they were working on, it was rather small, and they were building more than one of them. The Professor's goggles were temporarily placed at the top of his forehead, and he was frenetic in his movements.

Although the Chief Inspector had talked with Professor Farnsworth just two months ago, he looked like he had aged five or ten years. From the information taken at the previous investigation, Erasmus knew the professor was thirty-nine years of age, but he looked to be about fifty now. His skin had lost some color, his hair was grayer and unwieldy, and his posture was in decline. Another significant transformation was that his eyes were wild, shifting rapidly and looking about randomly, unwilling to relax. When he talked to one of his students, he leaned in and fixed a bore-drilling stare at them. He spoke with an air of desperation to get his point across, combined with an elevated critical-broadcast volume and tone. This was not the pensive, soft-spoken educator Erasmus met before. This change was clear and devastating, and anyone that had known the Professor over the last year would have seen this.

Someone trying to make sense of this transformation would think that the Professor had taken ill for the entire intervening two months. Or that he had suffered a great personal loss, which he wore like a weighted overcoat for an extended period of time.

After a few minutes of surveying the scene, Erasmus entered in the manner in which he walked into any investigation: chest high and with an air of command. A red-headed, be-goggled graduate student looked up and straightforwardly remarked "Chief Inspector, we were not expecting..."

Professor Farnsworth leapt back, brandishing the vaguely pistol-shaped contraption that he had been working on. Wild-eyed and wild-haired, he took trembling aim at the Chief Inspector, shouting "police!" The handgun, if that is what it was, had a number of brass and glass components affixed to it, and thick insulated wires that ran down to the table and off to other contraptions. In the split second that the Professor steadied his aim, two graduate students jumped toward him to stop him, four jumped away in fear, and one ducked under the table. Erasmus saw a small bolt fall out of the side of the gun just as the professor pulled the trigger.

A sound not unlike an explosively building drumroll emitted from the contraption followed by a blindingly white-blue lighting arc that discharged perpendicularly to where the Professor was aiming. The room was lit to such an extent that only those with their goggles in place were able to see immediately after the flash of light faded. The arc had caused great damage to the wall to Erasmus' left, knocking out a two-foot crater in the brick wall at eye level. The room was instantly filled with the pungent odor of ozone and rock dust.

No one was injured, which was a true miracle. Students were slowly looking around to both readjust their eyes and to see if each of their personages were still intact. The Professor stood in amazement at his own actions. He slowly lowered the pistol device, laying it on the table. The large knob at the front of it was still glowing red hot and quietly hissing as it cooled.

He stammered out a bizarrely-timed apology. "I am so sorry, Chief Inspector Drake. I do not know what came over me. Goodness. I have blasted a cavity out of the Newton Laboratory. I hope this calamity does not detour our development." His voice trailed off.

The red-headed student approached Erasmus to calm the obviously shaken officer. He pushed his goggles up, giving him a raccoon-like look from the dust that coated the previously unprotected parts of his face. "My apologies for our reckless behavior. We were just putting some finishing touches on our electrical discharge pistols, and the time pressure to be ready for our demonstration tomorrow has made us jumpy. I pray you are not distressed by our mishap."

Erasmus prided himself in not being shaken in many circumstances, but this went well beyond the normal unnerving situation. He moved his bowler and cane from his slightly shaking right hand to his left and extended his right to the lad for shaking, in an attempt to thank him for his warm reception. It was met with a firm and friendly grasp. Erasmus thought to himself, *"I did seek this out, so I probably deserve this state of affairs."*

MRS. MCCREARY'S BOARDING HOUSE

BY DR. KATHERINE L. MORSE

"Pardon me, Dr. McTrowell, but is the chai not to your liking?"

"Oh, no, it is delightful. The newspaper headline startled me. My mother's place of business is on Sansome Street. It's not much more than a small row, and this is the second time this year a miner has died suddenly on Sansome. Miners are not known for having the finest of health, but they do not usually die suddenly in the middle of the street, either."

"I was not aware that you originated in the California territory," Lord Ashleigh prompted.

"Yes, I was born there although I have spent much of my life elsewhere. Sadly, I missed the statehood celebrations because my vocation and avocations required me to be away. My mother still lives in San Francisco where she has a small, but respectable, assayer's office."

"Your mother is a gold assayer?"

"Yes, among other things."

"What a remarkable occupation for a woman." And then it was Lord Ashleigh's turn to be at a loss for words.

Dr. McTrowell turned the news of the 49er's death over in her head a couple of times and examined it from several angles. The only conclusion she could draw immediately was that she needed to extricate herself from the company of her charming new friend as quickly as was politely possible and rejoin her luggage. In order to do that, the conversation must be concluded, and the only way to finish the conversation was to restart it.

"So, what brought you to the Inventor's Symposium?"

"Although I am yet a student of law at Oxford, I am keenly interested in the patentability of inventions and their potential impacts on the rights of individuals."

"I see." But really, she didn't.

"Should a man be allowed to patent a device that deprives another of his livelihood?"

"I myself have invented a mechanical surgeon's assistant. Would you challenge my right to patent my invention and benefit from its sale?" she retorted.

"Well, I certainly hope that you and I should not find ourselves on opposite sides of the law on this point. I harbor the keen hope that you and I should become fast friends."

McTrowell raised her teacup to her lips so he wouldn't see the faint blush that warmed her cheeks.

"Please, tell me more of your invention."

McTrowell was thankful for the diversion to the more comfortable topic of her work. "Please pardon me if I make this sound like a mathematical equation. The infirmary in an airship is a very small space with really only enough room for a single individual to work. Airships travel slowly over mostly uninhabited areas. Airship passengers are wealthy and spoiled. Should a passenger require emergency surgery while en route, there is only one person aboard who can perform the surgery and she must do so within the confines of the infirmary. Passengers dying are bad for business."

The corners of Ashleigh's moustache curled up slightly above the rim of his teacup at the last comment.

Dr. McTrowell continued, "The device is actually worn, so to speak, by the surgeon. It is powered through a mechanical connection to the airship's engine. A pair of auxiliary arms that are strong, steady, and minutely manipulated is operated by the surgeon's feet and knees." Ashleigh's eyes opened wider and wider as she described the device. His teacup froze halfway to his lips. "I suppose it does sound horrifying as I describe it. I assure you that it is actually a very capable and useful device, and intended only for the benefit of humanity. I used it to save the life of the Ambassador from Hungary after a rather spirited altercation with his mistress who had the most impressive collection of hatpins one can imagine. I cannot say what happened to him after the incident was reported to his wife, as I was not there to repair any subsequent damage." She attempted to hold her smile in check, but was not entirely successful.

"Indeed."

"Lord Ashleigh, I am deeply indebted to you for both your assistance and your hospitality, but the hour is getting late and I should get to my lodgings before I incur the wrath of the landlady. She is a little testy and strict with her rules."

"I shall have Virat bring the coach around."

"You are far too kind Lord Ashleigh. Much as I would enjoy another comfortable ride in your fine coach, I think it would be best if I were to continue more discreetly from this point."

"You make an excellent point. Virat, please call a cab for Dr. McTrowell." She hadn't even heard Virat enter the room, but there he was, nodding his head in obeisance. And then he disappeared as quietly as he had appeared.

"I have truly enjoyed making your acquaintance, and hope that we will see each other again soon," she said, rising from her chair.

"The pleasure has been all mine," he said as he stood up. "Please understand that I am absolutely sincere when I say that if there is any way in which I may be of service, any way at all, do not hesitate to call upon me. My home is always open to you as a refuge no matter the hour nor whether I am present myself."

"Lord Ashleigh, you are a great soul. Good evening." He kissed her hand, and she turned to leave. The thought of staying here in the company of her new friend and his very comfortable home almost made her stop, but the next part of her journey needed to be solitary.

When she reached the front door, Anu was there to open it. Virat stood at the curb holding the door of a cab. As she approached, she could see that he had placed her flight surgeon's bag inside already. She repeated the address she had given to the stevedore to the cab driver and climbed in without any further discussion. She tossed the leather duster on the seat next to her, adding her goggles and cap to the pile. By the time the cab had lurched into motion, she had retrieved a brush from the surgeon's bag and proceeded to turn her hair into a more acceptable coiffure, pinning it up with a tortoise shell comb. She returned the brush to the bag and extracted a canvas tote. The duster, cap, and goggles disappeared into the tote. By the time the cab delivered her in front of a plain row house a few minutes later, she looked the part of a respectable, albeit somewhat tweedy and plain, lady. A tidy little sign next to the bell read: **McCreary's Boarding House for Respectable Single Ladies.**

An Encounter with Ruffians

By Mr. David L. Drake

At the completion of the handshake, the tone in the room seemed lighter, and students went back to their tasks. Erasmus re-engaged the conversation with the redheaded student. "I appreciate your concern for my safety and composure. Whose acquaintance do I have the pleasure of making?"

"I am Alistair Bennington Rutherford, son of Baron Rutherford of Oxford. I am the principal graduate student of Professor Farnsworth's cadre."

"I wish that..." Erasmus was interrupted by half a dozen or so scientists barging through the double doors, obviously reacting to the thunderclap and the dust ejected into the hall a mere minute before.

As a group, they understood immediately what had happened, and Erasmus could tell that, to a man, they had somewhat expected a catastrophe from Professor Farnsworth and his band of students. A syncopated murmur of "Well, I never!" and "I knew he would ruin the symposium!" filled the room, and it was clear that the Chief Inspector needed to act, if for no other reason than to protect the Professor. As Erasmus stepped forward to address the professor, he had another one of those "file this away" feelings that Mister Rutherford was far too calm in the middle of this storm, and that didn't sit well. He would think about this later.

"Professor Farnsworth, we meet again. I would like you to come with me to Scotland Yard, so we can sort out this business."

The Professor was beside himself. "Chief Inspector! Rutherford explained it all! It was a mishap, nothing more. We have work to do, and I need to lead my team to a successful demonstration of a number of inventions. I do not have time for this." He then stepped forward to re-initiate tinkering with the pistol-like contraption.

Erasmus found it comical that Professor Farnsworth was ignoring all of the signs of the recent catastrophe. The Chief Inspector looked about at the cough-inducing dust in the air, the multiple versions of dangerous weaponry on the laboratory table, and the grime on the Professor's face and hair, which looked like it was shot there by a cannon. Behind him he could hear the unruly mob of fellow scientists that was ready to throw the Professor out on his backside.

Erasmus took an insistent step toward Professor Farnsworth, took him by one of his thin arms, and said in a loud and clear voice "Professor, I am taking you into Scotland Yard! An officer of the Yard was nearly injured just a minute ago, and I plan to report the incident. You *are* coming with me!" The professor looked beside himself as he was being marched toward the double doors, his loose arm flailing and his eyes wild. The students moaned in complaint. The two of them parted the group of scientists, passed through the doors, and pushed their way through the onlooking crowd in the hall. After a few hundred feet, they were free of people.

"Professor, I need to get you out of here and talk. I need to understand how you got into this state, and why you took that 'shot' at me."

The professor was still wiggling like a child threatened with a spoonful of castor oil. "I cannot go with you! I cannot tell you why! Let me go! I have to be there tomorrow! Let me go, I say!"

"Well, I hate to use these, but restraints it is." The Chief Inspector pulled a pair of handcuffs out of his hip pocket and, using a key from his front pocket, secured the Professor's hands in front of himself. This was mainly for show, and to indicate to the inventors, the few who were now spying on them out of various doorways, that he was coping with this troublemaker. The Professor kept up his twitching and squabbling.

The gathering in the entrance hall showed the reaction that Erasmus expected. They mainly spoke *to* Erasmus and *at* the Professor, showing their displeasure regarding assembling hazardous gadgets on the premises. Erasmus recognized the renowned Charles Babbage and the Countess Lovelace. Mister Babbage huffed with discontent. The Countess, however, sniffed with disapproval at the Professor, but also quietly thanked Erasmus, showing her appreciation for the completion of his last case, the retrieval of her stolen jewelry and capture of the perpetrator. The scientist next to them introduced himself as Michael Faraday and suggested that Professor Farnsworth should have been working within one of the insulated rooms he had invented, which would have eliminated the dangers. Countess Lovelace quietly complained to her companions of feeling ill again and asked Charles to escort her to her carriage.

Erasmus led the Professor to Upper Gower Street, turned left, and headed south. He found the bright afternoon sunshine and the fresh air a refreshing change after the chaos of the laboratory.

"Chief Inspector, I have a most urgent engagement tomorrow! We can discuss whatever you need to address right now, and then you can release me. I implore you!"

Drake ignored his pleas and, still steering the professor by his arm, led him on.

After a few blocks, Drake spied a young man sporting an unkempt beaver top hat peering around the corner of a row house.

The lad spotted Erasmus and his charge and smiled. The tall teen stepped gingerly onto the walk and waved on two mates who were behind him.

They walked toward Erasmus with the energy of evil intent. All were dressed in a slightly odd manner, too dressy for young men, but too gaudy for individuals trying to impress. They all wore brocade vests without jackets, long trousers, and black top hats. They all had hair that was much too long and poorly cut for the current fashion. Although each had his own flair, they clearly were an organized troop.

Erasmus gave an imperceptible nod and wink to the leader as if to acknowledge his audaciousness. The lad didn't appear to react to it and instead walked directly to the Chief Inspector, grabbed him by the lapels, and dragged him to an alley, with his two comrades doing the same to Professor Farnsworth. Erasmus appeared surprised but stoic despite being pinned to a wall in a back lane.

"What have we got 'ere? An officer and his captive?" The lad's enunciation was uncouth but served him well for intimidation. "Let me state the obvious, Chief Inspector. We are just here for a simple business transaction. Spike, offer a deal to this unfortunate prisoner."

The lad nicknamed Spike spoke roughly to Professor Farnsworth, "Five florins and we help set you free. Say 'yes,' and we're outta here."

The primary thing on Professor Farnsworth's mind was not to be detained, so he struck an immediate deal with an exaggerated head nod and an enthusiastic "Yes! Yes!" reply. Spike produced a key for the shackles from his pocket, unbound the Professor, and dropped the handcuffs on the ground. The lead ruffian continued to pin Erasmus to the wall while Spike and the third silent accomplice spirited the Professor off to freedom.

Once the other two were out of sight, the gang leader released Erasmus. Straightening his jacket, he turned to his attacker and said, "I think that went well," and they both smiled.

LICORICE ROOT

BY DR. KATHERINE L. MORSE

Dr. McTrowell rang the bell and the door was answered very promptly. So promptly that she had the sense that the matron of the establishment had been loitering near the peephole spying on Dr. McTrowell's arrival, which was almost certainly the case.

Mrs. McCreary precisely looked the part of a woman who would run such a self-righteous establishment: middle-aged, matronly, plain, and overwhelmingly stern. Her hair was drawn up in a severe bun, accentuating the pinched look of her face. Dr. McTrowell had only ever seen one range of expressions on Mrs. McCreary's face, all in the category of sour, distasteful, umbrageous, and scornful. There were competing myths about Mrs. McCreary's circumstances. The first was that her husband had died of nagging and left her a tidy sum of money, and she ran the boarding house out of need to have a steady stream of victims to nag in his absence. The other story was that her husband had died of drink, probably also fueled by nagging, and had left her nearly penniless, making it necessary for her to run the boarding house to sustain herself. In either case, she was a widow, allowing her to wear nothing but cheap, well-worn black dresses. Sparky was certain that she had only seen the woman attired in two different dresses. The other point on which there was no quibble was that Mrs. McCreary was cheap.

"Well, Miss Llewellyn, I see you have not cultivated the habit of punctuality since I saw you last."

"I am terribly sorry, Mrs. McCreary. I stopped to pay a visit to my ailing maiden aunt. She has so few callers that she begged me to stay longer and I could not bear to disappoint her." Sparky did her best to appear demure as she entered the dark foyer. Mrs. McCreary sniffed at her hair as she passed.

"A Dr. McTrowell sent along several large trunks for you. Is that his cigar smoke I smell on you? You know I have very strict prohibitions against gentlemen visitors. In fact, if you are keeping the company of a gentleman, it may not be appropriate for you to be staying in this respectable establishment." And then she shut up quickly because she realized that her self-righteousness was just about to lose her a paying boarder. Sparky turned her head toward the trunks stacked in the adjacent parlor to hide the smile spreading across her face. Mrs. McCreary's was a suitably discreet place to stay in London when she didn't want anyone meddling in her affairs, but it was sorely tempting to tell Mrs. McCreary what she thought of her.

"You need not worry, Mrs. McCreary. Dr. McTrowell is an old friend of my parents'. And the cigar smoke is from a rather rude gentlemen, I hesitate to use the term, on the train from Holyhead. He declined my request to extinguish his cigar in the train car."

Mrs. McCreary sniffed dismissively. "You will have to carry the trunks upstairs yourself. Mind that you do not damage the walls along the way. You will be in the lavender room as usual."

Of course, Mrs. McCreary had been too cheap to pay the stevedore to carry the trunks upstairs. Sparky would gladly have repaid Mrs. McCreary, but she was trying to maintain the fiction that she was a schoolteacher of modest means from Wales. As for the "lavender room," the only thing vaguely lavender about it was a very faded old cross stitch of a sprig of the flower on the wall, no hope that the room would actually be that color or smell of the lovely flower itself. At least the room was larger than the others and had a large window that opened, which McTrowell found convenient for concealing the fact that she occasionally performed experiments in the room. She slung the canvas tote over one shoulder, picked up the first of the trunks, and marched upstairs.

ॐ౿ౖ౿ౖ౿ౖ౿ 🙂 ଷ౿ଷ౿ଷ౿

She was well and truly exhausted by the time she had hauled all the trunks upstairs. It didn't help that her hands and wrists were a little tender from her encounter with the Duke of Milton. Had that really only been a few hours earlier? It had been a long and eventful day. She poured some water from the jug into the washbasin and washed her face and hands. No indoor plumbing and French lavender soap like those at Lord Ashleigh's. She felt another tinge of regret at not accepting his invitation, but there was no helping it given her plans for the next few days.

There was neither time nor energy to start her experiments tonight, so she retrieved her portfolio of research and notes from one of the trunks. She pulled her flight surgeon's bag out of the canvas tote to retrieve the notes she had made during the flight. Carefully folded on the top of the rest of the contents of the bag was The Californian. Lord Ashleigh was just one surprise after another. She smiled in spite of herself. She retrieved a small pair of silver scissors from the bag and clipped the article out of the paper, placing it at the bottom of the stack of her other clippings along with her notes from the flight.

She returned the scissors to the bag and retrieved a bundle of letters tied in a satin ribbon of deep rose. Wherever her adventures took her, she always kept this bundle close. It contained all the letters her mother, Elizabeth Llewellyn, had written to her since she left home more than a decade before. She often wished that the bundle were bigger, but her frequent and unpredictable movements created a barrier to more regular communication. Her work on the mechanical surgeon's assistant had kept her in New York for a longer than usual period of time, so there were a few recent letters. Unfortunately, the joy of this wealth of letters from her mother was dimmed somewhat by their contents. Her mother's optimism was comforting, but McTrowell's own realism was born of years of watching others take advantage of her mother's good nature, including McTrowell's own father (the less said about him the better). The recent batch of letters induced that sense of impending heartbreak that Sparky had come to know and dread.

Dearest C.,

Business is fairly booming. My competition on Beale Street, Mr. Abusir, insists that we must drive a hard bargain with the miners, but I think many of them prefer to do business with me because I am fair and honest with them. Perhaps Mr. Abusir earns more in his business transactions, but I could not live with myself if I treated these poor men unfairly. They all dream of striking it rich, but they are truly the most destitute of souls. One can hardly imagine how they keep body and soul together. Just last week one such poor soul collapsed just outside my door. I hurried to his aid as he was obviously suffering from some form of extreme digestive distress, but unfortunately, I am not you, my darling accomplished

daughter. Sadly, he expired before medical assistance arrived. A curious thing happened. Just before he expired, he looked at me and said, 'Why are you so blue, Mrs. Llewellyn?' Whatever could he have meant by that? I shall never know. I hope you are well and happy, my dear.
Love, Mother.

Dearest C.,
I was pleased to read in your latest letter of your success with your surgical contraption. I feel certain it will win you international acclaim and respect. A mother has such dreams for her only child. I have some good news of my own to share. I have paid off the loan on my small establishment. I was just leaving the bank after making the last payment when I encountered Mr. Abusir whom I have previously mentioned. When I shared my happy news, he insisted on buying me lunch as he was on his way to celebrate some good fortune of his own. He has recently come into some money unexpectedly and is building himself a fine house. He was quite gracious at lunch, insisting on pouring tea for me and ordering sweets for dessert. Perhaps I have misjudged him.
Love, Mother.

A knot formed in the pit of her stomach. She couldn't bear to read the next several letters again. Although her mother's optimistic tone was throughout them all, the narrative thread was ever darker. Mr. Abusir appearing, apparently coincidentally, with increasing frequency. His showering her mother with excessive courtesies and lamenting how empty his fine new house would be without a wife to give it the warmth of a woman's touch. Her mother seeing Mr. Abusir entering or leaving the mining claims office several times, an odd place for a gold assayer who lived in the city to go. Two more of her mother's regular clients mysteriously dropping dead. And then the last letter Sparky received just before she left for London.

Dearest C.,
I hope this letter reaches you before your departure. I had hoped your travels would bring you back west rather than farther east. Although I have paid off the loan on my business, business itself has dropped off unexpectedly, and I fear I will have to sell the building. Mr. Abusir has graciously offered me a position in his business. He has also formally requested my hand in marriage. I haven't given him an answer, but I feel

fortunate to have such a fine suitor, especially at my age. I wish you could meet him. I know that London is a much busier city than our cozy little San Francisco, but Mr. Abusir is also traveling to London. Perhaps you will chance to meet. He was very mysterious about his business there, but he mentioned a wedding gift fit for a pharaoh's wife. He is leaving next week and has asked for my answer when he returns in a month. I feel almost certain I will accept his offer.

Love, Mother.

McTrowell had learned over the years that there were certain problems that could be solved with money, and information acquisition was one of them. A small portion of her bonus from Western & Transatlantic Airship Lines became a "charitable" donation to the medical support of an elderly woman in San Francisco whose only daughter fortuitously worked in the claims office. Among the clippings was a letter from the reliable and discreet daughter, Miss Constance Mackay, of the claims office. Copied out in her tiny, neat hand was a list of claims recently filed by Mr. Abusir.

Sparky laid the list below the clippings of the three sudden deaths of miners before the one she had just clipped. There were more items on the list than just the three, but there was a claim on the list precisely two days after each death. No doubt such a list from today would contain another unfortunate entry, and there were probably other bodies in a potter's field whose deaths that had not been deemed newsworthy. Building himself a fine house indeed!

Based on the date on the letter, Abusir had probably already arrived in London. That meant whatever he was planning to do, he was going to do within the next two weeks. There was no time to equivocate or do more research; she would have to act now. She moved to the only trunk that was locked. She removed the key from the fine chain hanging around her neck, hidden by her high-necked blouse, and unlocked the trunk. It swung open easily to reveal rows of tightly sealed apothecary jars carefully packed between bags of straw. She retrieved two jars, one labeled **licorice root** and one labeled **foxglove**.

A Tale for Sergeant Parseval

By Mr. David L. Drake

"Happy to see you, William. Fortuitous that you were here on Upper Gower Street," Erasmus stated. "I really did not want to walk Professor Farnsworth all the way back down to Whitehall Place and have him in lock-up. All of his flailing around was unseemly. Much better to find out what he is up to."

"So, what's the old man's game? What do you suspect?" the lad asked.

"He has gotten himself into a bad spot. I am undecided if he is doing something illegal or just plain stupid. Or some extraordinary mixture of both. I do not have time to get into the details. Have the lads follow him until midday tomorrow. We will rendezvous in the usual manner, around 8 a.m. Railway Time. You can let me know what he has done at that point. I need to get back to Scotland Yard."

William chuckled, and half seriously asked, "Is the Yard not going to figure what we're up to? This springing of 'criminals' to see what they're really concocting is working all too well."

"As long as they remain an unorganized and selfish lot, there is not much to worry about. No 'criminal' has ever complained to the Yard that they got away." They both gave a short laugh. Erasmus then added in a serious tone, "What you and the lads are doing is of great benefit to the Yard, as you know. When you finish your training, I will be mindful of your placement."

"Much obliged, Sir."

With tips of their hats, they parted company, and the Chief Inspector made good time heading back to 4 Whitehall Place. He strode into the door marked **Scotland Yard** and proceeded toward his office, hoping to make himself a few cryptic notes on the day's proceedings. He was intercepted by Sergeant Tate Parseval who was trying to appear stalwart while begging for information.

"Chief Inspector, how did your exploration proceed? Did the loose end develop into a case?"

"So glad you asked, Tate. Come sit with me and I will give you the details." Erasmus truly enjoyed these discussions. However, this one would be special – it was the first such conversation in the privacy of his new office.

With door closed, the seated gentlemen leaned slightly toward each other from across the desk, Tate in "full receive" mode. The Chief Inspector kept his voice down, as if to keep secretive what he was about to disclose.

"It all started as I was tracking the whereabouts of an unsavory gent that was a leftover detail from the last case; I thought I might have an easy collar for the day. Nothing could be further from the truth. I finally cornered him at one of the tents near the unfinished Crystal Palace, but why he was there, I have no idea. With the restraints out, I told him to come along nicely, but he pulled a knife, took a slash at me, which I avoided by a mere whisker. Then he ducked past my attempt to tackle him and led me on a chase all the way over to University College on Gower Road. I followed as he ran inside one of the buildings, but I was waylaid by a gathered crowd of scientists for some symposium of sorts. In a search from room to room to find the villain, I happened upon a crazed scientist who tried to take my life with an electrical discharge contraption. Fear of authority, or some such motive. Having a 'bird in hand,' I arrested the deranged maniac."

"Chief Inspector, that is incredible! Such a day! So where is the madman now?"

"That is the sad part of my tale. In the street, we were assaulted by a throng of ruffians taking advantage of the fact that I was dealing with a lunatic by myself. I was able to defend myself, but my poor charge was carried off, no doubt to be cleaned of his wallet. There were too many for me to pursue alone, so I returned straight away to the Yard to make a plan for tomorrow to address these misdeeds."

"I say! Sounds like we need another round of arrests like back during the Chartist demonstration in '48! What is happening in our streets, I ask you?" Tate followed his exclamation with a bowing and shaking of his head that silently said, "oh, no, not again."

Erasmus gave a warm, comforting smile, stood up, rounded the table, and patted Tate's back twice. "We will handle this all in the morning, my good man. I am off to dinner. Tomorrow is another day."

Grabbing bowler and cane, the Chief Inspector was out the door and headed back to the street, chuckling to himself, *"In three minutes that story will have grown ten times its size and be known by everyone on the floor. I can always count on the Sergeant to do his part."*

FADE TO BLACK

BY DR. KATHERINE L. MORSE

From another trunk she withdrew a small brass teakettle with its matching alcohol burner, the latter more elaborately scrolled than Dr. McTrowell would have purchased for herself. But it had been a gift from her mother when she first left home, so it was sentimentally dear. Besides, it had proven to be quite durable and reliable; excellent qualities considering all the times it had been abused in the pursuit of adventure and science. While the use of the alcohol burner was quite safe, at least compared to many of the activities McTrowell had previously carried out in the lavender room, it was best to complete the next few steps while she was sure Mrs. McCreary was asleep and wouldn't interrupt her preparations.

She filled the kettle with water from the jug and the alcohol burner from a tightly stoppered vessel from the same trunk. After she lit the burner and set the kettle on to boil, she began rummaging in the trunk for an expendable drinking vessel. Whatever she used for this experiment would probably have to be destroyed for safety's sake, so she didn't want to use anything cherished. She found a small glass beaker with a chipped rim. Just the thing. She hadn't thrown it out when she damaged it, but she would when she was finished with it this time. She turned back to the notes and clippings on the bed. Her eyes fell on the latest clipping.

> Mr. John Redshirt, lately of Sutter's Mill, passed from this world unexpectedly yesterday along Sansome Street. Witnesses to the unfortunate event reported that Mr. Redshirt had previously had business with Llewellyn's Assay Office, which appears to have been

> his destination on the day of his demise.
> Mr. Redshirt is reported to have been
> staggering and ranting incoherently
> about the band playing too loudly before
> he collapsed. Although no witnesses
> reported smelling alcohol, Mr. Redshirt
> almost certainly died of drink as is so
> often the case with individuals of his
> standing and vocation.

"Almost certainly died of drink," indeed! As if her mother would ever have done business with such an individual. Oh well, no sense dwelling on the stupidity of so-called journalists; she had work to do. She peered at the measurements in her notes before turning to extract a small pair of tongs and set of scales from the still-open chest. She carefully measured quantities of the licorice root and foxglove and transferred them to the beaker. By then the water in the kettle had come to a boil, and she snuffed out the flame. She poured boiling water into the beaker, swirling the beaker to ensure the contents were completely soaked and would steep thoroughly. She placed the beaker on the worn old doily on the bureau and returned her equipment to its designated locations in the trunks, carefully locking the apothecary trunk and returning the key to its chain around her neck.

She would need to be rested for the next step. She changed into a simple nightgown. Before finally resting after her very long and too exciting day, she pulled a very small clock from her surgeon's bag, a gift from Monsieur Antoine Redier. She set the alarm for 5 a.m. It wouldn't be as much sleep as she would have liked, but she needed to be awake and working before Mrs. McCreary arose, and absolutely no one beat that woman to the market in the morning to haggle for the cheapest prices on the meanest bits of supposedly edible items.

When the alarm awakened her, she felt as if she'd only just drifted off to sleep. Despite her foggy-headedness, she grappled with the clock to silence the alarm before it awoke the landlady as well. Her carefully laid plans would all be wasted if Mrs. McCreary came nosing around now. She hastily dressed, splashed some more water on her face, and firmly affixed her hair out of her way on the back of her head.

She picked the beaker up from the bureau and lifted it to her lips. Her hands had been steadier when she had repaired the perforated Hungarian ambassador. And the smell was something she would never forget. If it weren't for their potentially hallucinogenic effects, the vapors might have been an effective cure for congestion of the head. And the smell did remind her faintly of that time in Crete she sat up all night drinking ouzo with Stavros Theodoropolous, but now she was just stalling. She took a deep breath to steady her nerves and swallowed the contents of the beaker in two gulps. Oh horrors, the taste was even worse than the smell! How could one ever disguise it?

She sat down on the bed, opened the notebook from her portfolio, and began writing notes. First, she took her pulse: 85, a little high, but not unexpected considering the state of her nerves. She waited. When she felt her heart rate rise, she took her pulse again: 100, the licorice root taking affect. And then she felt strangely calm…and heard faint distant singing. She took her pulse again: 50. She started writing her observations in the notebook when the ink from her pen turned from black to blue. No, the page was blue…as was everything she had written before. As her consciousness slipped away, she scrawled illegibly in her notebook, "blue."

THE THREE DRESSMAKER DUMMIES

BY MR. DAVID L. DRAKE

London cooled as the sun disappeared behind city buildings giving a soft orange glow to the rooftops in the west. The streets were crowded with the working and professional classes bustling off to whatever they did after the completion of their workday. For many, their destination was a simple apartment and a plain supper. Others were off to pubs and eateries, and for those with the means, private clubs. London took on an interesting mood during this transformation. Pedestrians took a bit more haste in their step. The hansom drivers were more insistent when their way was hindered and urged their horses to move along more smartly than usual when not. Despite the fact that it was dusk, London seemed to wake up a bit at this hour. It was if every Londoner wanted to be someplace other than where they were currently.

Erasmus enjoyed this hour of day and the additional liveliness that it brought. For him, it was as if the day started anew. He headed east away from Scotland Yard, over to Wine Office Court. Near there was Ye Olde Cheshire Cheese located at 145 Fleet Street. It had been rebuilt back in 1666 after London's Great Fire and provided a traditional coziness that only a centuries-old pub could. By the time Erasmus neared the establishment, it was near capacity with patrons enjoying their bitters and bar food.

Erasmus rented the flat directly above the establishment, one that few would want. True, it had easy access to the pub itself, indoor facilities, and a sizable room, but the din from below would have driven most inhabitants mad. For Erasmus, this was a benefit. Since he didn't fall to sleep until late, it gave him phenomenal cover for his evening studies and training.

Once inside the pub, Erasmus worked his way through the crowd to the bar. The proprietor, James Crocker, noted him, gave him a nod, and made his way over to within shouting distance. Pleasantries were not needed and couldn't be heard anyway. Erasmus leaned past the edge of the bar and raised his voice. "Mutton stew," and indicated that it could be delivered to his flat by a minor pointing of his walking stick handle and a quick glance up the stairs. James nodded his acknowledgement and whistled for one of the waiters.

Erasmus made his way over to the stairs, which involved skirting at least three circles of standing customers, all waiting for tables and so engrossed in their discussions that they didn't notice they were blocking easy passage through the main pub area.

Once upstairs in his flat, Erasmus set his bowler onto a small table, leaned his walking stick on the chair nearby, and shed and hung up his leather cape coat. He then removed his jacket, also hanging it on one of the coat hooks near the door. As he lit the gas lamp over the table, his eyes panned the room quickly to verify that nothing had been disturbed. It was a simple single room, but was quite large. On the far end from the door was a bed and dresser. A small bookshelf stood nearby, completely full of various bound volumes and notebooks. The remainder of the room was empty save three leather dressmaker dummies in various corners of the room, each of them scarred in a fashion that implied that someone had punished them for simply existing.

A light knock on the door was followed by a lad entering with a small stew-pot that he handled with two dishcloths. "Beg your pardon, sir. Your mutton stew. It is just off the fire, so be careful of the pot." He used the two dishtowels to protect the small table from the stew-pot's heat.

"I will. Did you happen to know if there is a glass of red wine that would go nicely with that?"

The lad smiled and produced a bottle from one deep apron pocket and a red wine glass from the other. "I was expecting your request, sir. Hope this will do," and he placed the two on the table.

Erasmus placed a few coins into the boy's hand and bid him a good night as he retreated out of the door. Erasmus gave the bottle label a quick glance and a smile. He tested the stew-pot with a quick touch and verified that it was generously warm. Rather than digging into supper, he instead stripped off his waistcoat and shirt.

Taking his cane, he gave it a knowing push-twist motion with his two hands and unsheathed the hidden shining blade. With the sword in his left hand and the scabbard in his right, he turned and addressed the nearest dressmaker's dummy with a stance that was practiced and intimidating.

If the patrons downstairs knew what to listen for, they would have heard the rhythmic footwork and sounds of strikes. Instead, they only heard their own conversation and laughter.

Erasmus met with William at 8 a.m. the next day at the small peninsula in the lake in St. James' Park. It was close enough to Scotland Yard to be convenient, but far enough away and sufficiently hidden to allow private discussions.

William started the conversation as he approached Erasmus. "A good morning to you, and I hope you had a better night than the lads and me. That Professor is a bit of work! If he slept at all, I will be amazed. Pacing and ranting, pacing and ranting. We told him to hide with us until daybreak, just like we normally do. We stayed over in one of the grain storage warehouses. Normally fairly quiet. But not with Professor Blaa-blaa-blaa."

"Did he indicate where he would go today?"

"Oh, yes. I'm *sure* we have it memorized, given that he mentioned it so many times. He's going to the Egyptian Court in the Crystal Palace at the Great Exhibition. Said he absolutely has to be there at noon. He didn't mention if he was meeting anyone, but he indicated the timing was critical. We asked him what he was going there for, and he just indicated that it was a very secretive mission. At that point we figured we didn't need to follow him anymore, since we knew where he was headed. We were very glad to give him his liberty this morning."

"Good. I have some minor work that I need to do at the Yard this morning, but I will plan to be at the Egyptian Court a bit after 11 a.m. and see if I can figure out what he is trying to accomplish. I know his students are planning an invention demonstration today at University College, and so Professor Farnsworth's activity at the Crystal Palace is completely independent of that. This whole thing just does not sit well with me."

"Best of luck, Chief Inspector. Let me know if you need us again." The two shook hands and they parted.

The Crystal Palace would not be open to the public for a few months. Nonetheless, the Chief Inspector's credentials got him through the checkpoints without much bother.

The Egyptian Court was opulent. Even without all of the furnishings and statues in place, it took one's breath away. Much of the impressiveness was the size and quantity of artifacts; only the best pieces had been brought in to the Great Exhibition. Like many, Chief Inspector Drake had a great interest in ancient Egyptian culture, handiwork, and accomplishments. He had dallied with setting their rulers and gods to memory and tried his hand at remembering a few sequences of hieroglyphics.

The curator of the Egyptian Court was Mr. Joseph Bonomi. Erasmus knew him well from his intervention with an Egyptian man who claimed rightful ownership of a small gold statue that Mr. Bonomi had on display as one of his museum pieces. It was naught but a misunderstanding, given that the specimen was on loan from an Egyptian museum, but it gave Erasmus a few days of interaction with Mr. Bonomi, and they formed a bit of a passing friendship.

Erasmus walked around the multiple sphinxes and mummies, some of the displays completed, others still needing some finishing touches. All and all, very impressive. Erasmus saw the signs of Mr. Bonomi's sense of history combined with showmanship and felt that the future visitors would be awe struck.

As much as he was enjoying the exhibit, the Chief Inspector reminded himself that he had a mission. If Professor Farnsworth did show up, Erasmus needed to watch him without drawing attention. The best way to do that was to look nonchalant, but be very aware of his surroundings. There were many nooks to conceal his presence, and he took to that task. Erasmus thought to himself, *"I am quite ready for the next piece to this puzzle."*

OSIRIS

BY DR. KATHERINE L. MORSE

There was an intolerably foul taste in her mouth. Where had she tasted that before? Oh yes, the tisane she brewed. When was that? She struggled to sit up on the bed. Where was she? When was she? Her eyes fell on her open notebook beside her on the bed. The last thing she had written, if one could call it that and if she could believe she had actually written it, was followed by a large blot of black ink. Wait, why wasn't it blue? Blue! That's what she had written that she could barely read. It was starting to come back to her. The sun was high in the sky outside the window. Was it later the same day? Had she lost a day? No, Mrs. McCreary was far too nosy to have let her lie here for more than a day without making an appearance. She stumbled to the bureau, rinsed her face, and brushed her hair back into some semblance of order. A cup of water did nothing to eradicate the taste in her mouth. She would need to venture out to solve that problem. And now that she was certain foxglove had been used to poison her mother's clients, and nearly as certain that Mr. Abusir was behind it, she would need to venture out to find Mr. Abusir himself.

She had to brace herself more than usual on the banister on the way to the dining room. Mrs. McCreary was already standing in the doorway to the kitchen by the time Sparky made it to the dining room. No surprise there, considering the way the stairs creaked. Mrs. McCreary's fists were firmly embedded in her substantial hips and she was wearing her umbrageous face. No surprise there either.

"Miss Llewellyn, it is very nearly noon. Civilized people are long since out of bed and about honest work. I certainly hope this lying about of yours does not indicate a drinking problem." No doubt Mrs. McCreary had idiot cousins who wrote "news" for The Californian.

"Certainly not, Mrs. McCreary. I am feeling somewhat poorly, no doubt as a result of the long train ride and breathing the cigar smoke on the train. I believe a strong cup of tea and a constitutional walk in the fresh air will put me to rights." As if the air of London would ever be described as fresh or Mrs. McCreary would ever serve a cup of tea anyone would describe as strong. The landlady huffed out of the room, obviously unconvinced, but blessedly, she said nothing more as she delivered a meager cup of weak tea with one, small, very stale biscuit. There was just enough milk in the milk pitcher to make the tea a muddy gray. The "tea" tasted like it had been brewed from tree bark and Thames water. Bark, ah, wouldn't a cup of willow bark tea be just the thing right now? She washed down the biscuit with the tea and headed back upstairs.

She fetched the willow bark out of her field kit and brewed herself some tea while she dressed for the day's explorations. No telling what she would need to do today, so more serviceable clothing was in order. She eschewed the tweed skirt and ankle boots in favor of a more functional pair of knee-high riding boots and a well-worn pair of canvas work pants she tucked into the boots. She would have to sneak out to avoid a row with Mrs. McCreary about her decidedly unladylike attire. She looked out the window just in time to see the landlady cross the back courtyard to the laundry. She gulped down the willow bark tea, grabbed her flight surgeon's bag and duster, and flew down the stairs and out the front door.

By the time she was safely a couple of blocks away where Mrs. McCreary wouldn't see her, the willow bark tea had worked miracles on her pounding head, and she could think more clearly. More than anything, she needed to divine what was so important to the obviously avaricious Mr. Abusir that he would spend the large sum of money necessary to travel all the way to London in person. What was drawing the Egyptian businessman to London now? Well, if one wanted to know the mind of an Egyptian, perhaps one should ask an Egyptologist. She was only a few blocks from Hyde Park. Perhaps she would be fortunate enough to find Mr. Joseph Bonomi engaged in preparations for the Great Exhibition. Although they had never been introduced, she knew the English expected Americans to ignore the conventions of polite society. She formulated a plan for introducing herself and walked briskly toward the Crystal Palace, ignoring the peculiar looks her attire drew.

೫೮೫೨೫೨೫ ⚙ ೧೨೧೮೧೨೧೮೧

The preparatory drawings she had seen in the newspapers did not prepare her for the breathtaking edifice of the Crystal Palace. It was truly an astonishing accomplishment. She was still gaping as she approached the entrance and was almost caught unawares by a burly fellow guarding the entrance.

"Ma'am?" He was a little unclear on her gender. "The Exhibition is not yet open to the public."

She had to think fast if she were going to get in. "I am not the public. I am Dr. McTrowell of Western & Transatlantic Airship Lines. I am here to supervise the installation of my mechanical surgeon's assistant in the exhibit of medical apparatus." She struck what she hoped was an authoritative pose. She was still not quite up to snuff after the morning's exertions.

"Oh. Very well, Ma'am." And just like that, he let her pass. Never underestimate astonishment as a tactical weapon.

42

She picked a direction at random and set off smartly, hoping that she appeared to know where she was going. And then she had her second bit of luck in only a few minutes. She spotted a crew of workers hauling an enormous statue of a seated pharaoh. Her eyes tracked the direction they were hauling and she spotted the Egyptian Court.

When she entered the Court, there were several workmen industriously preparing for the statue that would arrive shortly. A matching statue was already in place. None of these men could be Mr. Bonomi, as he would undoubtedly be dressed as a gentleman. There was only one gentleman in the Court, and he was decidedly unengaged in the workmen's activity. He was staring at a gold statue on a pedestal and his posture indicated acute focus. He was wearing a cape coat that was not in itself unusual, but this one was leather. Dr. McTrowell knew from personal experience that one didn't wear a leather coat as a matter of fashion, but rather as protection from extreme circumstances. To be fair, this particular coat was well cut and flattered the wearer with a short cape that would not interfere with the action of the wearer's arms. Clearly this man was not the architect and Egyptologist she was seeking.

And then there was the brown bowler, a rather fashionable appointment for a man practical enough to wear a leather cape coat. Brown bowler? Hadn't she seen this unusual headwear somewhere else recently? Well, she needed to find Mr. Bonomi, and perhaps the mysterious gentleman could provide a clue.

"I beg your pardon. I am trying to locate Mr. Joseph Bonomi. Have you perhaps seen him in the vicinity today?"

When he turned to address her, she had the distinct impression that he had known she was there despite the fact that his attention had been fixed on the statue for the entirety of her approach, and the noise of the workmen had covered the sound of her boots on the wood floor.

"Mr. Bonomi has completed his preparations for the day and has departed. I expect he will not return until tomorrow," the gentleman replied.

There was neither surprise nor curiosity in his voice. However, his eyes took in every detail of her appearance and demeanor without betraying his assessment thereof. And what eyes they were! In sharp contrast to the various shades of brown of his entire ensemble, his eyes were a striking blue. She felt slightly unsteady for a moment, no doubt the lingering effects of the foxglove and licorice.

"I see. How unfortunate. Are you perhaps a colleague of his?"

"I have been on occasion." What a peculiar answer. "Perhaps I might be of assistance?"

"I wished to ask him about a Mr. Abusir."

"So, naturally, you have come here." He indicated the gold statue he had been examining as she approached. There was a small placard on the pedestal containing symbols.

"I am sorry. I speak several languages passably, but I am afraid hieroglyphics is not one of them. How does this relate to Mr. Abusir?"

"Abusir, the temple of the god of the dead." And he pointed just below the hieroglyphics on the placard to a word she hadn't noticed at first, **Osiris**.

INFANT OF A NIGHTMARE

BY MR. DAVID L. DRAKE

As it turned out, the gold statue that the Egyptian man had thought he had ownership of was now on display at the Egyptian Court. Erasmus walked over and pondered it and its inscription. Despite the clamor of workmen moving a statue of Ramses II, Erasmus felt the presence of a woman approaching him from behind.

He shifted his bowler to his left hand, in case he needed to greet her. She greeted him and asked about Mr. Bonomi. He turned to see a most interesting woman. Her hair was golden in color, but pinned back in a way that was not in fashion in London, but rather of the wildernesses of the Americas. And her coat! A full-length leather duster, better suited to rough weather or hard work, although well-maintained. Given her height and dress, she fit the description of the woman who downed the Duke of Milton at University College. She was not one to be taken lightly.

Erasmus actually didn't know where Mr. Bonomi was, but he wanted to appear knowledgeable, so he gave her his best guess. "Mr. Bonomi has completed his preparations for the day and has departed.

I expect he will not return until tomorrow." She continued her inquiry, not being one willing to wait, and asked Erasmus if he was a colleague of Mr. Bonomi. "I have been on occasion." It was the only truthful way to put it without revealing his association with Scotland Yard, which might have made her more hesitant to continue their conversation.

She then asked about a Mr. Abusir. Odd, "Abusir" was the name of temple associated with Osiris, the same Egyptian god that the statue represented, and Erasmus pointed that fact out on the placard below the statue.

"Ah, I see," she paused, "quite clearly for the first time. I am Dr. Sparky McTrowell." Well, with her name revealed, he was more comfortable confessing his profession.

"Chief Inspector Erasmus Drake of Scotland Yard." Erasmus produced his card and handed it to the lady with the odd nickname. She pondered it just for a split second. In the same action that she pocketed his card into an interior pocket of the leather duster, she produced her own, and proffered it to Erasmus, saying, "I am indebted to you for this very valuable information, sir. You may inquire after me at the offices of Western & Transatlantic Airship Lines at the airship port if I may ever be of assistance to you."

The Chief Inspector smiled and reached for the card just as out of the corner of his eye he glimpsed a figure moving near one of the large archways allowing access to the Egyptian Court. Unexpectedly, it was Professor Farnsworth, and he was quickly backing into the room while peeking around the edge of the archway at something in the next display area. Professor Farnsworth was clearly tickled with glee at what was around that corner. Erasmus stopped and gave the scene his full attention. He had expected the Professor to be meeting someone, not sneaking around.

Professor Farnsworth turned and rushed along the wall of the Egyptian Court. When he reached one of the sizable crates along the wall, he flung off the top, reached inside, and threw a sizable electrical switch. Erasmus had turned to face the clamor and was only able to take a few steps in the direction of the Professor when he heard the now-familiar rapidly swelling electrical hum. Erasmus shouted "Professor, no!" but realized it was too late. An arc of blue-white lightening sprung out of the crate, apparently arcing between two terminals hidden within the wooden box.

The professor glanced back, saw the Chief Inspector, and showed shock at being in the same room with the man that he had escaped just yesterday. But Professor Farnsworth immediately turned back to his task, cackling, not heeding Erasmus' command to terminate whatever he had initiated.

Erasmus instinctively turned toward Sparky and put up his arms to allow his leather coat to shield her from whatever was to follow. He shouted, "Brace yourself!" but she was a step ahead of him. Sparky turned her back to the blinding arc and the earsplitting electrical crackle, momentarily looking back at the workmen. Her quick reflexes got her behind the statue podium in the wink of an eye.

The large electrical discharge instrument unleashed its directed force, arcing through the wall into the adjacent room through the gaping incinerated hole that it had just created. But the arc also ricocheted back toward Farnsworth who had his hands up defensively to protect himself from the light and heat. Farnsworth screamed, and then the blue-white arc was gone, finished with its horrible deed.

The aftermath had its own style of cacophony. Shouts and commotion could be heard from the adjacent room. Erasmus blew his ever-present policeman's whistle twice, loud and long. The contraption in the crate gave a menacing hiss that faded slowly. Farnsworth was on the floor, whimpering over his badly burned hands, but his moans where interspersed with short bursts of ecstatic laughter over his success.

Erasmus was most concerned over the situation in the adjacent room, a chamber that he had not visited, which he now considered a huge oversight on his part. To control the situation, Erasmus had no choice but to scoop the Professor up and carry him to the adjacent room to address the damage there while keeping an eye on the person who had caused it.

Erasmus rounded the corner lugging the Professor in his arms. He seemed lighter than the Chief Inspector expected. *"There is nothing like an electrical blast cannon creating a two-foot diameter hole in a solid wooden wall to get one's heart pumping,"* Erasmus thought. A number of scientists were there, many on the ground, downed by the blast, but not visibly injured. The room was being used to assemble sophisticated machinery, and had various constructions of polished brass, glass, and wood.

One of the downed scientists was the immediately-recognizable Charles Babbage, and he was outraged. But it was for good reason: the blast was aimed at the current prototype of Babbage's Analytical Engine, which now had one molten brass side. A decade of work on precision gears and machinery destroyed in less than a second.

Erasmus set the Professor down, surveyed the situation, and determined that life and limb of the scientists were intact. That was good, and he figured the rest of this chaos could be sorted out after the Professor received medical attention.

Erasmus' police whistle had its usual effect: from multiple directions came three Crystal Palace watchmen, two nearby constables, a *Times* reporter who just happened to be in the building, and five gawking onlookers. Erasmus ordered the constables to tend to the blast victims and to come back to take the Professor to the hospital when they were satisfied that the downed men were in acceptable condition.

Erasmus bent down to Professor Farnsworth and asked the obvious. "Why?"

The answer was unexpected. "He is building a thinking machine. Do you not see? It cannot only do complex manipulation of numbers, it can make decisions! Yes, yes! Decisions! And it is big and robust. Imagine large, self-directed machines operating their own conveyances that are impossible to stop or control! Look right there!" the Professor cried, and gestured with a burnt hand at the sizable contraption, "He is making the infant of a nightmare!"

Erasmus was shocked. How could a man who previously had such rational thoughts be changed into this state in such a short period? And such a waste of Mr. Babbage's years of work. Erasmus broke his usual professionalism, and blurted out, "Professor! That is your reason? Are you *mad*? You have ruined this man's life's work!" The *Times* reporter, pad in hand, was scribbling furiously.

The constables returned to fetch Professor Farnsworth for medical attention, and Erasmus helped with getting him to his feet.

"Make sure you stand guard at the hospital. We will want to make sure he answers for this destruction."

Erasmus suddenly remembered that he had lost track of Dr. McTrowell. Was she gone? He looked around the Egyptian Court, and she was nowhere to be found. But on the floor at the place of their parting, he found a calling card under a thin layer of dust. He bent over and retrieved it, despite that it was visibly burnt on its right-side corners. He pocketed it carefully.

"An amazing young woman, this Dr. Sparky McTrowell," he thought. *"I hope she does not think this is an everyday occurrence for me."*

MAHARAJA DEVA

BY DR. KATHERINE L. MORSE

McTrowell hauled herself up off the floor. It seemed that today was going to be as eventful as yesterday, unfortunately. The recently vanquished headache had returned, accompanied by a sore elbow and hip from where she had hit the ground during the blast. *"There is only so much from which a leather coat can protect you,"* she thought wryly. She turned toward the melee into which her would-be protector had charged. Interesting fellow; where others run away, he rushes in. Others were now rushing toward the chaos in the next room, everyone except for a single workman who was staring at her. No, he was staring at the statue of Osiris. No, he was switching his focus rapidly between her and the statue. Her stomach felt queasy again. Licorice and foxglove again…or something else? The workman realized she was staring as hard at him as he was at her, and the look of vexation on his face turned to something far darker. She hadn't yet decided what action to take when the workman turned and headed toward the activity in the next room. She turned the opposite direction to exit the building. It seemed she would have need of Lord Ashleigh's offer of assistance much sooner than she anticipated.

⁊⁊⁊⁊⁊ ⚙ ⟨⟨⟨⟨⟨

There was no point in finding a cab. Once she reached the edge of the park, it was only a few blocks to his house on Berkeley

Square and the walk would allow her a few minutes to formulate a plan. It was clear that whatever was going to happen was going to happen in conjunction with the Great Exhibition. She would need a plausible reason for her persistent presence at the Crystal Palace. Of course! She had already manufactured just such a reason without even intending to.

Arriving at Lord Ashleigh's residence, she had not yet set her foot down on the bottom step than Virat opened the door. Attempting to look nonplussed, she climbed the stairs and entered the foyer where she was met by Anu who silently ushered her into the powder room down the hall where she freshened up as she had the day before. She had a strange feeling of déjà vu as she hung her duster on the hook and turned to wash her face and hands. The process was proceeding just as it had the day before with Anu leading her to the sitting room, but this time Lord Ashleigh wasn't sitting calmly in his chair. He was pacing tensely when she entered. His face was etched with concern when he turned to face her.

"Dr. McTrowell, you are well!"

"Um, yes, thank you." Curious that he said it as a statement rather than as a question and an exclamation at that. "Why would I not be?"

"The blast in the Great Exhibition did quite a bit of damage."

"How do you know about that and how did you know I had been there?" There was an awkward silence while he obviously contemplated how to answer the question. He was granted a momentary reprieve by the arrival of Virat with the silver tea service that proved to be stocked once again with chai. They sat, sipping their tea, while she waited for an answer. She maintained her "poker face," practically the only useful thing she had learned from her father in the very little time she had ever spent with him. Apparently something in Lord Ashleigh's background also entailed political bluffing because they sat for several minutes with the silence broken only by sipping and the delicate chime of bone china teacups on saucers.

"Very well. I have certain resources at my disposal," he conceded.

"Resources?"

49

"No doubt you have deduced that I have considerable financial resources. My father, Maharaja Lakshmipathi Deva, died when I was young. My older half-brother Vijay Deva is the current ruling Maharaja of Talkad. I have no official power since my older brother is ruling. However, I am the first son of my father's favorite wife, which makes me the heir apparent until my brother has a son. As you might imagine, my brother is not happy about this, so he persuaded me, none too subtly, to reside in my mother's country, England. Lest you doubt me, please be assured that I am indeed studying law at Oxford. The circumstances of my mother's estate, with which I will not belabor this conversation, lead me to believe that a clear understanding of English law may be of use to me in the future. My upbringing in my father's court taught me to be alert for spies and conspirators behind every door and curtain."

"And so you think me to be a spy? Then why invite me into your home?"

"Oh, no, certainly not! Yesterday's events led me to conclude that you are at grave risk of being the target of spies. I have applied some of my resources to ensure that no harm befalls you."

"You and that Chief Inspector from Scotland Yard, both thinking that I am incapable of taking care of myself! Somehow without the assistance of either of you I managed to get myself nearly all the way around the world more than once while earning a medical degree and learning to fly an airship. And lest you did not notice, I was nearly blasted to pieces while under the watchful eye of your 'resources.'"

"My dear Dr. McTrowell, I assure you I meant you no offense, and I certainly never meant to imply that you are incapable of caring for yourself. I am a great admirer of your accomplishments. I just believe there is more intrigue afoot than you might realize. Despite my youth, I fancy I know quite a bit more about intrigue than you. As for my 'resources,' some of them are now in search of new employment as the outcome of today's events at the Crystal Palace was not at all up to my expectations. You should also know that Chief Inspector Drake is quite a bit more than he seems and is not to be taken lightly." He smiled very brightly at this last comment and seemed on the verge of winking.

"I am terribly sorry, Lord Ashleigh. I am forgetting my manners. I am considerably overtaxed by all the unexpected excitement of the last day. And after all this, I actually came to beg a very large favor."

"Nothing would please me more than to grant you a favor."

"You are an amazing man, but it really is a very large favor."

"Please, just ask."

"The matter that brought me to London has taken an interesting turn, to say the least. It seems I am going to need to establish a presence at the Great Exhibition. I believe I can convince the Occidental Inventors' Society to support the entry of my mechanical surgeon's assistant into the exhibition. However, it was designed to be driven by an airship's engine and I cannot very well park an airship in the Great Exhibition. I will need a rather large, but preferably quiet, steam engine to drive it."

"Oh, this is most excellent! I am so looking forward to seeing your invention in operation. I would be only too pleased to acquire a suitable steam engine to drive it. I will require one stipulation. Your exhibit will properly require a human assistant whom I will provide."

"Another of your 'resources?'"

"Yes. After today's events I am even more concerned about the 'matter' that has brought you to London."

"I am forced to admit that you are probably justified in your concern, so I accept your terms. Thank you again. I truly hope someday I will be able to repay all the favors you have done for me."

"I hope that we should both live long enough and our friendship should endure so this should come to pass."

"I am very tired and should get back to my lodgings before dark. I will be at the Crystal Palace on a regular basis beginning the day after tomorrow, but I imagine you know how to find me whenever you want."

This time he did wink when he smiled at her. "Virat will drive you to an inconspicuous location a discreet distance from your lodgings. I will see you at the Crystal Palace within a few days with the steam engine and accompanying 'resource.' Good evening, Dr. McTrowell."

When she entered the foyer to await Virat, Anu materialized with her duster. She turned to slide her arms into the sleeves when her eyes fell on a thick envelope in a silver tray on the console table. The address was Lord Ashleigh's, but the name on it was Maharaja Deva Raya III.

A STOUT-HEARTED MAN

BY MR. DAVID L. DRAKE

As he walked, Erasmus' cane tapped out a cadence that bespoke his determination to return to his flat. He thought back on his last five hours: organizing a team to seize Professor Farnsworth's electrical discharge device at the Egyptian Court; traveling with Farnsworth to the hospital; getting constables to volunteer to guard him; scratching out the details of the day's events on a commandeered hospital notebook; and requesting the Yard find a scientist who could determine the nature and safety of the professor's contraption for storage. Quite the ordeal.

Erasmus also thought back on the hospital report on their odd patient. As a result of his own actions, Professor Farnsworth took a great deal of damage. He lost his middle and ring fingers on his left hand, and his right hand and arm were badly burned. The doctor indicated that Farnsworth's right arm should be operable in a few months, but that his scarring would be permanent.

Erasmus was walking from the Westminster Hospital where the Professor was cared for, located just cater-corner across from Westminster Abbey, to his flat. He spent his walking time contemplating two very different subjects: a stiffer drink than usual to compensate for the day's labors and the very interesting woman he met at the Egyptian Court.

The drink would help him justify to himself that freeing Professor Farnsworth the day before was defensible despite the damage the Professor caused in the Egyptian Court. If he had just brought him in to the Yard, all of this would have been circumvented. He was being his own harshest critic, and no one at the Yard could have predicted this outcome to yesterday's actions, but it still ate at him. The solution for tonight was simply some strong spirits, shake it off, and get some sleep.

As for the woman, that was a different matter. Like many things that Erasmus couldn't help but ponder, she generated more questions than answers. He wanted to call on her simply to find out why she had flattened the Duke of Milton. Or how she learned to move so quickly and deliberately in the presence of unexpected peril. And more importantly, why she felt it necessary to leave the scene so quickly when she clearly had no part in the cause of the blast.

Erasmus pulled out her card, singed as it was. This was the seventh time he had done so over the past five hours as if by inspecting it again, it would reveal some new truth. It was a calling card with her name on it, but using her peculiar nickname of "Sparky." Most unusual for a formal calling card. Perhaps she was known by this name better than her given name, and as such, it opened more doors. She had indicated that he could enquire after her at the offices of Western & Transatlantic Airship Lines. The way she said this made it sound as if she was well-known enough that her name alone would allow discovery of her within an international company. Well, ironically, he did need to contact her because she was a witness to the Professor's misdeed, so visiting the London airship port would go on the agenda for tomorrow. Or was that merely an excuse to call on her? *"Well, back to considering that stiff drink,"* he thought, pocketing the card carefully. The cane continued heralding his journey. Tock, tock, tock.

The crowd was light at Ye Olde Cheshire Cheese. Upon arriving, Erasmus didn't have time to even sit at the bar before James Crocker stopped him. "Your friend is here! Great chap."

"My friend?"

"Yes! I let him in upstairs. He said that you were expecting him. He said his name was...oh, you know. I cannot remember! You know the chap. While waiting, he told some hilarious stories, oh my."

"Ah, yes. Of course. It just slipped my mind. Been waiting to see him all day. Thank you for taking care of him." Since this was quite unexpected news, Erasmus took just a second to determine the best way to proceed. "Do not bother sending supper up. We may come down. Or go out." Erasmus ascended the stairs carefully.

While in the upstairs hallway, Erasmus placed his bowler back on his head to free his hands and prepared his cane. He twisted the handle and exposed just a glimmer of blade. Holding the scabbard in his right hand, his right thumb restraining the handle, he cautiously tried the door handle of his flat with his left hand. It was unlocked. *"Now is as good a time as any,"* he thought, and squeezed his eyes shut for a good number of seconds for them adjust to darkness and then stepped into the room in a lively fashion.

His eyes surveyed the room rapidly, looking for any movement or signs of danger. Instead he saw a figure sitting in the dark in his chair, which had been moved to the far side of the room near his bed, along with his table. The individual's calmness oozed though the room, causing Erasmus to relax despite himself. It was not the reaction Erasmus expected or wanted of himself.

"Alistair Bennington Rutherford, as you may have deduced. You may re-fasten your sword stick, if you wish. There is no danger here, as I will explain." His voice was smooth and unwavering. It had an air of command. He made no sudden movement. In fact, he moved not at all during his strange introduction. "Please, light your lamp."

Erasmus did secure his cane, as suggested, but kept it with him. He lit the lamp with cautious, measured actions. He placed his bowler on one of the coat hooks and walked, watchfully, over toward Alistair. The nature of his cane was known to almost no one, so the request to re-fasten it did not give comfort to Erasmus.

Alistair spoke as if he owned the flat. "I wish I could offer you a chair, but since there's only this one, please sit on the bed."

Erasmus nodded and sat, placing the cane on the bed. He didn't want it too far away. Erasmus thought it was time to break his silence. "Thank you." Erasmus kept his right hand on the cane, mentally measuring the time and movement it would take to unsheathe the sword and reach Alistair with a cutting blow. Over the next few seconds, he mentally practiced this several times.

Alistair began, "Mind if I start the conversation?" Pause. "Good. First, I wanted to talk to you privately. There are those I work with who would not understand my motivations in speaking to an officer of Scotland Yard. They may take it incorrectly. Please do not be off-put by my meeting you in this manner."

"Fair enough."

"Glad you can see my point of view. Second, I was not fully honest with you at University College. Professor Farnsworth and I have an understanding where I pose as his principal graduate student to stay close to him. He needed a great deal of oversight, and I was helping him. This ruse is not even known to his other students. His affliction is due, at least partially, to me."

"Alistair is far too familiar with me," Erasmus thought. *"He knows my place of lodging, the details of my life, even about my cane. If he knows all this, what of the things he knows, but has not said yet?"* There is a set of circumstances that permits a keeper of the peace to feel that they are in charge of a situation, but Erasmus knew these were being eroded. This should have put Erasmus' guard up, but instead, the tone of Alistair's voice and his demeanor kept putting Erasmus strangely at ease. He found himself trying to stay sharp, but it just wasn't working.

"How so?" Erasmus replied.

"A bit of my history is needed to understand that. I was raised in the manner of the upper-class as you may have deduced by my clothes and my manner of speech. I was very interested in the nature of science, and six years ago I was accepted as a graduate student at University College as a chemist, although I had interests in a great many other things. I worked in the various laboratories for many hours, driving myself to find the results I was seeking. One weekend while taking a much-needed hiatus, I took an extended recess with my non-scientific friends, students of philosophy, art, and history. We gathered at one of their 'clubs,' which was actually a collection of wrought-iron chairs and tables in the greenhouse of one of their spinster aunt's house.

"They filled the air with pipe smoke and the sounds of bawdy songs while they introduced me to absinthe. Later that night, full of energy, I re-entered the laboratory. I was able to complete experiments that would have taken me weeks to work through, simply because I was thinking through the issues of the experiments more precisely. I realized that my new-found clarity gave me the ability to concentrate, precisely imagine things I had not before, and remove all distractions and inner doubt. I saw this as a solution to my long laboratory hours, eliminating my previous experimental trial and error. You see, the alcohol relaxed me, the wormwood opened my mind, and my scientific imagination was allowed to operate."

Alistair continued. "But I wanted to enhance absinthe's facility, heighten the effect. So I spent a year or so adding various compounds that heighten awareness, yet relax the brain's desire to be cautious. I was quite successful. And I shared my elixir with my colleagues and friends. For most, it was just as effective for them. So, I started a side business mixing and selling it. Initially, manufacturing was an ordeal. Some of the ingredients are pharmaceutical substances, and others can only be created in a laboratory. I had to be diligent in improving the production process, which I was able to do. In the last few years, this has become a reasonably lucrative business. Although I believe that my elixir could be sold through more normal distribution channels, I do not want to stop the flow of sales to set up such a system."

Erasmus wasn't completely trustful of this reasoning and wasn't quite sure if Alistair's confession to him that he had a questionable business going on was really the reason for this chat. "Please go on," he urged.

"Unfortunately, some of my customers have a reaction to my elixir that I am trying to understand and eliminate. Professor Farnsworth is one of them. He wished to continue consuming the elixir, but as you could see by both his physical change and his mental state, some modification of the elixir is needed for him so that it gives him only the positive effects. That is what I was trying to provide him. So, please do not think of him as a criminal or a lunatic, but rather as a man who is ill. I need to find him the correct balance of substances that will help him recover."

"I would like to believe that you are trying to help the Professor, but how do I know that you have not simply created a pleasant-tasting poison, one that affects its imbibers like opium affects its smokers?"

"Because I am a testament to its positive effects. Are you a stout-hearted man, Chief Inspector? Can you handle a strong drink?"

"Of course, my good man. What did you have in mind?"

"First, fetch your revolver."

This was the last thing that Erasmus expected at this point in the conversation. But his trust in Alistair grew as he listened, and his curiosity was overflowing. Deep in the pocket of his leather overcoat was a revolver that he carried infrequently. It was heavy and slow to reload. It was often more scary than deadly, and the chance of hitting what one was shooting at was proportional to the frequency of practice, which Erasmus didn't do enough of. He wanted to see how this played out.

Erasmus produced the revolver and placed it on the table.

"Excellent," exclaimed Alistair. He produced a bottle of Green Fantasy from a deep coat pocket and a tumbler glass from another. He poured only a small quantity into the glass. "That should do it," he stated.

Alistair looked Erasmus in the eye and said without faltering, "Drink this, look at your revolver, and tell me what you see."

Erasmus thought, *"In for a penny, in for a pound."*

A MUTUALLY BENEFICIAL AGREEMENT

BY DR. KATHERINE L. MORSE

Anu handed Sparky a small, colorful tin just as she was stepping out the door. She opened it in the coach. Amazing! Lord Ashleigh thought of everything. There was no way he could have known that she had eaten nothing all day except for the stale biscuit, but here in her lap was a perfect little snack to revive her: a few slices of bread with sharp cheese, a small jar of something that appeared to be pickled, and some nuts dusted with pungent spices. She was so famished, she ate one of slices of bread and cheese while Virat drove her to within a few blocks of Mrs. McCreary's. He deposited her without so much as saying a word. Sparky was bone-tired as she walked the last few blocks, thinking only of finishing her repast with a little tea and sleeping until her body was well and truly to awake.

But, of course, it just wasn't going to be that easy. Mrs. McCreary was standing at the top of the steps when Sparky arrived, and the expression on her face was truly horrible to behold. *"Ah yes, my attire,"* thought McTrowell dourly. She was still wearing her leather duster, work pants, and knee-high boots. This was going to require some very creative storytelling.

"Miss Llewellyn, what is the meaning of this horrible, shameless attire?"

"Oh, Mrs. McCreary, you cannot imagine the unspeakable horror to which I have been subjected today! I must get inside before other decent folk see me." Sparky rushed up the steps and squeezed past the rotund landlady before she could raise an objection. At least she was inside. "I was having a quiet, reviving stroll through Hyde Park. I stopped to admire the construction of the Crystal Palace. As I was walking around the building, there was a horrible blast and I was thrown to the ground. I must have fainted from the shock because I awoke to find myself covered by the coat of a chief inspector of Scotland Yard, quite a polite and chivalrous fellow I might add. My clothing was so damaged by the blast that I was not decent. I was quite fortunate that the Chief Inspector happened upon me in my state of distress rather than some ruffian or heaven knows what other unspeakable misfortune might have befallen me! Well, I certainly could not wander about in that state, so the clever Chief Inspector procured some bits of clothing for me from the workers at the site. So, as you can see, I really must get cleaned up and dressed in more appropriate attire. Good evening, Mrs. McCreary."

With that, she dashed up the stairs to her room. She could tell Mrs. McCreary didn't believe any of her far-fetched story, but wouldn't stoop to calling her a liar outright, particularly given the mention of the presence of the Chief Inspector. It seemed Sparky was going to have to find new lodgings on her next trip to London because she could tell her level of impropriety exceeded even Mrs. McCreary's greed. It was all she could do to change into a nightgown and eat Lord Ashleigh's generous little snack, which proved to be quite fiery, requiring quite a bit of herbal tea to wash down. The sun was only setting when she collapsed into a sound slumber.

The sun was well up the next morning when she awoke, but it was still earlier than the day before when she recovered from her "experiment." She selected her most demure ensemble for the day and pinned her hair up in a tight, sensible bun. There was no sense incurring any more of Mrs. McCreary's wrath. It proved to be unnecessary because her landlady was nowhere to be found when Sparky arrived downstairs, nor was there tea waiting for her. She must have really irritated Mrs. McCreary this time! Nevertheless, she walked several blocks before hailing a cab to take her to the London airship port just to be safe, as a cab was a luxury a poor Welsh schoolteacher couldn't have afforded. She tried not to focus on the events of the last couple of days as she rode to the port in silence.

ഊഊഊഊഊ 🙰 ଔଔଔଔଔ

As usual, there was no silence to be had at the port with the comings and goings of passengers and cargo. Even the usually business-like offices of Western & Transatlantic Airship Lines seemed to be enveloped in a flurry of activity. The guard let her in past the ticket booths to the offices in the back where she discovered the source of the perturbations: Reginald Wallace, the president of Western & Transatlantic was in the manager's office.

Wallace was the sort of man who filled a room both figuratively and literally, a state of affairs aided by his propensity for wearing red and lots of it. This sartorial selection had a way of setting off the slightly red cast of his complexion, particularly when he was in high dudgeon over the failings of a subordinate, whether real or merely perceived.

At the moment he was stabbing his stout finger at a garishly decorated broadsheet on the manager's desk and bellowing about the importance of some opportunity to show what Western & Transatlantic was made of, causing the manager to cower lower and lower in his chair behind the desk. Sparky tried to sneak a peek around Wallace's belly at the broadsheet without being noticed, but to no avail. Surely the man had eyes in the back of his head.

"Dr. McTrowell, just the bold adventuress I was looking for!" She didn't like the direction this was going. She glanced down at the

59

broadsheet and saw a physically unbelievable rendering of airships tilted at alarming angles sailing improbably over high mountain peaks. No, she didn't like the direction this was taking at all! "I was just trying to get it through Mr. Littleton's thick head the importance of demonstrating the technical superiority and airworthiness of our airships by entering and winning this race. It will be a huge boon for our continental routes!"

"Yes, well, it would certainly be impressive and newsworthy." She was far too tired to be thinking as fast as the circumstances clearly required. "I am sure I do not know a thing about the impacts of such an event on commerce. I will just be off to the Lewis & Clark now."

"Why are you going to the Lewis & Clark? It is not setting sail again for several days."

"I am just going to arrange to have the mechanical surgical assistant sent to the Great Exhibition. I should think a demonstration of the exceptional medical services aboard Western & Transatlantic should be good for commerce as well." She hoped the smile she was putting on was winning.

"Possibly, but I did not give permission for the surgical assistant to be moved."

"Of course not, Mr. Wallace, since I built it from materials I purchased. Therefore, it belongs to me and does not require your permission for me to move it."

"And yet, it is bolted into my airship." The "cat that ate the canary" smile he was now wearing was not having a positive effect on her recently abused stomach. "Since we were discussing commerce, I believe you and I may be able to negotiate a mutually beneficial agreement."

She was quite sure that "mutually" didn't mean "equally," and that she was going to be on the unequal end of the agreement. "And what 'mutually beneficial agreement' did you have in mind?"

"Quite simply, you may take the surgical assistant to the Great Exhibition in exchange for agreeing to pilot the Burke & Hare in the race."

"Mr. Wallace, you have far more capable pilots than myself who would dearly love an opportunity to flaunt their expertise in such a prestigious event."

"Yes, but none so colorful and newsworthy as you, Dr. McTrowell. Who can forget the Pecos incident?" There it was. Reginald Wallace never missed an opportunity to trumpet the flamboyant exploits of his ships and pilots for the benefit of his own enlargement. He probably would have been a circus ringmaster, but owning an airship line was so much more profitable.

"Very well, Mr. Wallace, you have yourself an agreement." She shook his hand ostentatiously, ensuring that everyone in the office saw it. She knew from painful experience that he never went back on a handshake, but without the handshake, no agreement existed.

"Littleton, have the surgical assistant trucked to the Great Exhibition immediately. And get this broadsheet up on the wall." He smiled magnanimously upon everyone in the room as if he were doing Sparky a great favor. "Dr. McTrowell, the Burke & Hare sails for Munich in a week. I will see you at my table for dinner that night." It wasn't a question.

"Yes sir." She got a better look at the broadsheet as Littleton was tacking it to the wall. Emblazoned in an arc across the top of the broadsheet were the brightly illuminated words **Bavarian Airship Regatta.**

COLT POCKET 1849

BY MR. DAVID L. DRAKE

Erasmus lifted the glass and gave the contents a sniff. Licorice, well, anise to be precise. Other unique aromatic spices came through too, but not ones that he could discern. He asked Alistair, "I understand why you would want me to experience your elixir, but why the revolver?"

"Do you have any background in engineering or the hard sciences, Chief Inspector? Chemistry or physics?"

"No, not formally. I have learned this and that through my life, particularly in investigating cases where I have worked with experts. But certainly not university study."

"Then I am suggesting that you think of the revolver as a non-trivial object that you are familiar with. One that you have operated, in this instance, fired, as I gather from the newspaper's accounts of your last major case. Trust me on this; it will become clear."

Erasmus was not a man who was known for hesitation when action was called for. He saw this situation in that manner. He could either shoo out this intruder or see this through and answer many of the questions that had arisen over the past two days. He decided that the latter was the way forward.

As he raised the glass to his lips, Alistair interjected, "Given the small quantity I poured, drink it all at once, but let it roll around in your mouth for a bit, even under your tongue. It will expedite the process." Erasmus raised one eyebrow at this, and then mentally committed to consuming the libation.

Erasmus tipped the glass up and let the liquid flow into his mouth. It was like drinking any strong liqueur: slightly syrupy, pungent, and aromatic. As instructed, he let it linger in his mouth as if savoring it. After a few seconds, he swallowed. The bouquet lingered, and there was a slight bitter aftertaste, but it was short lived.

Erasmus looked back at Alistair. Was that a slight smile Erasmus perceived? Perhaps. Alistair's eyes went down to the revolver, and Erasmus' followed. The firearm lay on the table with its handle toward Erasmus, its barrel toward Alistair. Erasmus remembered the last time he'd fired it, which had been just a few weeks ago. It was fired in haste, in the heat of the moment. The report of the gun and the smoke it issued seemed to come back to him as if it were happening both rapidly and slowly as memories of the past often do when regarding life and death decisions. The recollection focused in on pulling the trigger, the exertion to pull it, the concentration to get the shot to hit the intended target, and where it went instead.

His mind then jumped to cleaning the revolver. The parts on the table. The smell of solvent and oil. The small squares of cleaning rags that he used. Being a good steward of the gun, he cleaned it after every use, so he was familiar with each of the major components: handle, hammer, cylinder, barrel, trigger, and loading lever. But, the smaller components also started to become perceptible. Moreover, he could see how those parts fit together in the revolver itself. It was as if the parts were somewhat translucent, and their interactions were apparent. The hammer had to be cocked manually, of course, rotating the cylinder into place. And as the trigger was pulled, it would press against the combination bifurcated trigger and bolt spring before releasing the hammer. What? Where did he get that terminology? Oh, yes. He remembered scanning through the manual for the revolver when he received it from the armory at Scotland Yard. It was a Colt Pocket 1849 with a four-inch barrel for easy carrying and concealment. The parts list was easy for him to remember now with its 50-plus components and instructions on how to care for each one. Disassembly and reassembly were both obvious.

The process of the revolver's inner-workings continued to be revealed. As the hammer struck the cap, it acted as a very small fuse, igniting the black powder, and the subsequent explosion forced the shot down the cylinder out toward the barrel. The criticality of having the hammer stay in place after striking became apparent: so that the expanding gasses wouldn't eject backwards or upwards out of the gun, which would reduce the force expressed on the shot. That explained the shape of the hammer head, its weight, its fulcrum location, as well as the shape of the hole for the cap.

As the shot left the cylinder, it entered the barrel. Erasmus noted that a good portion of the gas from the explosion escaped at the point where there was a small gap between the cylinder and barrel. And with the rifling within the barrel, what little pressure was left would leak out around the shot. It now became apparent to Erasmus that whatever punch the black powder gave the shot while in the cylinder was all it was going to get. After that, the barrel only provided some semblance of aim, gave the shot some spin, and slowed the projectile down. If the action of pushing the shot forward also forced a newly added lever back, causing the cylinder forward until it met the barrel, it would significantly improve the velocity of the shot. But that would also complicate the revolver. The rifling could also be improved through the use of flat sides of the barrel rather than raised grooves. All of this additional velocity of the shot would actually improve the consistency of its flight, making the revolver more accurate.

Erasmus continued to stare at the revolver. Alistair sat calmly in his chair, with a faint but controlled smugness. He finally decided to break the silence. "Talk to me."

Erasmus suddenly realized that he had been silent for the entire time. He also hadn't touched the revolver, although in his mind he had felt its weight in his hands, fired it, reloaded it, and walked his way through each component and mechanism.

"Well, it is obvious to me that I have been oiling it too much after I clean it," Erasmus chuckled.

Alistair smiled, and added, "Go on."

"The trigger and bolt spring could be adjusted to allow the trigger to move smoothly for a slight distance farther before the hammer is released; this would prevent a jerking of the pistol when firing, which I am currently prone to. There is also a problem with the loss of gas thrust after the initial detonation of the powder, reducing the consistency of the shot's flight. The issue could be addressed by creating a container of sorts for the cap, powder, and shot, which in turn would allow easy loading from the breach. I would need to know more about alloys and manufacturing processes to have a full explanation, but I certainly could draw it and explain how it can be ignited by the hammer and allow the revolver to be rapidly loaded. The container could also seal off the gases that are leaked between the chamber and the barrel. Another explainable improvement is the automatic cocking of the gun by the trigger or by the recoil. This would greatly aid constables that need rapid firing pistols and may even allow a sizable rack of the aforementioned containers to be automatically fed into the line of the hammer-cylinder-barrel. The challenge is ejecting the empty containers without injuring the shooter, but I could illustrate how it would work. But these suggestions all seem obvious now. The real improvement is to sidestep the issues of powder completely, given the noise, heat, and procurement, and instead pull the bullet out of the barrel using electrically controlled magnets. It may take some doing, but it would be a greatly improved system altogether."

Alistair allowed himself to smile to the point of dimples. This seemed to be exactly what he had hoped for. "I am impressed with how far you got on such a small amount of the elixir. Bravo. You should think about sending Mr. Samuel Colt a letter on these improvements."

Erasmus suddenly seemed more aware of his surroundings as if coming out of a trance. "I am amazed I did not actually pick up the revolver. It feels like I turned it over in my hands hundreds of times. Taking it apart. Reconstructing it. Even modifying it and shooting the modified version."

"No looking at your watch," Alistair challenged. "Tell me how long you have been contemplating your pistol."

"Twenty minutes at least. No...closer to twenty-five."

Alistair held up the pocket watch that he had been holding under the table. "Five minutes and twenty seconds. Incredible, yes? And you will remember it all. The effect will fade over the next few minutes since I did not tender you with that much. I should also mention that your mind has now had a taste of running at a higher tempo. You will remember that, too."

"I am impressed. Your little demonstration worked. Scientific advancement could be greatly aided by your elixir, I gather. Am I missing something?"

Alistair smiled. "It is not a panacea. Good ideas need to be followed by hard work. But my experience is that the elixir has the same effect on manufacturers and tradesmen. They see how to improve their processes and the generation of products. There are not that many people aware of it yet, but its use is growing," Alistair said, with a bit of pride showing.

"However," he continued, "it does not play well with physicians. All they do is feel their internal organs operating at the most detailed degree, and they panic. Not a pretty sight, as you can imagine. I and my distributers dissuade medical practitioners from partaking." Erasmus realized that this might be one of the reasons that Alistair hadn't tried to get pharmaceutical approval for distribution; physicians would think that the elixir drove people insane. "Not a very good endorsement," he mused.

Alistair looked at his watch again, but this time in an almost theatrical way, to make sure Erasmus understood the gesture. "I must be going. My main goal here was to have you fully understand Professor Farnsworth's plight. Please keep this in mind as you go forward." Alistair rose and extended his hand for shaking. Erasmus took this to be more of an "agreement on particulars" rather than a "parting on good terms" gesture. Erasmus shook his hand despite the subtle implication.

After the handshake, Alistair went straight for the door, and left. The whole of his exit seemed abrupt and calculated.

Erasmus' mind was still running at its new-found speed. What could he do to take advantage of this? He looked around his room. Of course, it was obvious. He flung off his waistcoat and shirt, grabbed his cane, and prepared to practice. If a deeper insight into his defensive arts were possible, it would make the evening complete. Erasmus felt rejuvenated from his day, had mentally organized tomorrow's timetable, and prepared himself for a complex attack to the nearest dressmaker's dummy. *"Before I sleep,"* he thought, *"perhaps I can also scratch out a quick letter to Mr. Colt!"*

Monsieur de Fermat's Little Theorem

By Dr. Katherine L. Morse

McTrowell was quite certain it was time for a bite of food and something refreshing to wash it down. She glanced at the ornate street clock in the center of the airship port. She marveled at both its beauty and its accuracy; she stood for several minutes, watching the hands click around the face. When she came out of her reverie, she remembered her need for sustenance. It was half past noon, and if history were any indication, Jean-Michel would be having a light lunch and a pint at Ye Olde Cheshire Cheese in about half an hour. For a Frenchman, he had an unusual taste for strong English beer, and Ye Olde Cheshire Cheese was his favorite source. She secretly suspected it was the reason he always accepted the annual invitation to the Inventors' Symposium. Not only did a pint sound truly delightful, but the promised proof of Fermat's theorem seemed just the invigorating, intellectual diversion she needed from all the unpleasant excitement of Abusir and Wallace.

She started walking and thinking. She would need to spend all day tomorrow setting up the surgeon's assistant and connecting it to the steam engine Lord Ashleigh had promised, or should she start thinking of him as Maharaja Raya? She would need some sort of enclosure around the engine to reduce the noise. She would need a surgical table. What about a mannequin to simulate a patient? And then there was the question of whether this whole ruse would cause Abusir to reveal himself and his plan. She sighed; she didn't like days with more questions than answers.

It was crowded and noisy when she entered Ye Olde Cheshire Cheese, as usual. Although she personally preferred quieter venues, this particular one had the advantage of being so full of "eccentrics" that she was never cause for particular interest. She threaded her way through the clutches of other patrons, searching the corners of the room looking for Petit. She was just about to give up when she spotted him in a corner by himself. He had a nearly-drained pint in front of him and was observing the crowd as if he were trying to divine the equation for its movement, shifting and coalescing through some hidden motivation.

"Jean-Michel, may I join you?"

"My dear friend, what an unexpected pleasure! I have just ordered *le déjeuner*. Please join me. To what do I owe this visit?"

"I needed lunch and I was hoping to hear your proof of Monsieur de Fermat's little theorem."

"But of course. However, it is not to be heard without a fine, English beer." He raised his hand to signal a tap boy, a mop-headed lad in otherwise drab clothes except for a green vest. "A pint of bitters for my good friend, please. And another porter for me as well." He turned back to McTrowell with a slight smile on his face. "I should tell you that the gendarmes arrived at the Symposium after your fisticuffs with the unpleasant Duke."

"Oh, dear. Are they looking for me?"

"Oh no, I believe the Chief Inspector felt the Duke got, how do you say, his comeuppance. A very sensible gentleman, the Chief Inspector, not like so many you meet."

"A gentleman inspector, you say?"

"Yes, a rather polite and well-groomed fellow with luxurious mustachios of the type that would make any Frenchman proud." He smiled again.

The tap boy in the green vest returned with a pint glass filled with an impenetrably dark liquid with a dense, foamy head that he put in front of Petit and a much lighter brew that he placed in front of McTrowell.

"*A votre santé.*"

"And to the health of the new petite Petit, may it be a girl as lovely as her mother whose charms her father will not be able to resist." She thought Petit's cheeks turned a little rosy at her toast, but it was hard to be certain in the dark of the corner.

The bitters were true to their name; the first swallow made her screw up her face. She set the glass back down. Rather than let Petit know that she didn't really care for his choice of beverage, she returned to the reason for seeking out Jean-Michel's company.

"Before we were interrupted at the Symposium, you were going to share a proof with me."

"Ah, yes, Monsieur de Fermat's last theorem. As you know, Monsieur de Fermat asserted that no three positive integers a, b, and c can satisfy the equation $a^n + b^n = c^n$ for any integer value of n greater than two. And then he died without revealing the general case of the proof! I believe I have rediscovered the general proof!"

In her excitement at the prospect of hearing the proof, Sparky forgot her first reaction to the bitters and took another swallow. It was no better than her first taste, and that clearly showed on her face. This time, Jean-Michel noticed.

"My dear friend, I think this peculiar type of English beer is not to your liking. Please accept mine instead. I have not yet tasted it." Without waiting to hear her answer, he took her bitters and slid his porter over in front of her. He took a swallow. "*Mon dieu*, this is truly bitters." She took a swallow of the porter. She had to admit she found it more approachable. Jean-Michel reached for his valise to retrieve some papers, but was interrupted by the tap boy bringing his lunch. She had been hungry when she arrived, but the sight of the bread and cheese platter was not appetizing and she was feeling unsteady again. A trip to the loo felt in order.

"Pardon me, Jean-Michel. I will just be a moment. Enjoy your lunch." He smiled and nodded, taking a bite of bread and cheese and washing it down with a couple more swallows of the bitters. She was searching for the appropriate exit when she spotted a tap boy and thought to ask for directions. He was wearing a vest too, but this one was blue rather than green. Why were all the tap boys in Ye Olde Cheshire Cheese wearing vests? No wait, this was the same one who brought their beers. Why would he have multiple vests and why would he change in the middle of working? No, it wasn't just his vest that was now blue. His dirty blonde hair and fair skin were now bluish too. Oh no, could she be having a relapse? She staggered around in a wobbly circle and faces blurred past her. She thought she saw an unpleasantly familiar, dark, malicious face. She turned around again. It was gone.

And then, despite her delirium, she had the most terrible moment of absolute clarity of her entire life. The bitters had hidden a taste even more bitter that she hadn't recognized without the licorice root. The face had been the workman from the Grand Exhibition. Abusir!

Jean-Michel! She staggered around in another circle searching for the direction back to the table. She stumbled into other patrons, spilling their beers but ignoring their curses.

"Noooooo! Jean-Michel!"

THE SMELL OF COCOA

BY MR. DAVID L. DRAKE

Erasmus awoke with a start. Something just wasn't right, and he had to figure out what it was. He decided that he would rush through his morning routine, which was not his usual manner. Early rising and being the first to work were not his style; it went against his natural tendencies and clashed with his philosophy. But this morning was different. And to make it worse, it was his gut that drove him forward, and so he needed to figure out the particulars of this instinctual response.

As he approached his table to pour a basin of water, he saw it. A clean square of cloth had been laid out on his table, and his revolver had been lovingly disassembled until every possible removable piece of his pistol was placed in a most orderly fashion. It looked so tidy an effort that it gave the appearance that he was planning to lead a private instruction on the construction of the Colt Pocket 1849.

Erasmus didn't have time to concern himself with this. He typically didn't carry it with him, given the hassles of a cap and ball pistol, and he would need to take the time to reassemble it in the evening. Today needed to get started; the revolver would have to wait.

He made it out of Ye Olde Cheshire Cheese building in half the time it normally took him. Bowler on head and cane in hand, he started his usual serious stride toward Scotland Yard. Erasmus' young friend, William, popped out from around a corner and caught up from behind. William was uncharacteristically agitated, and he started the conversation before he was alongside Erasmus. "You are up early. You must have heard the news then."

"Actually, no. But I suspected something happened. Do tell."

"Well, the first part of it is that you're the main subject of the front-page article of the *Times*, at least the law-abiding side of the story. The article details the explosion at the Great Exhibition site and the chatty Professor's success at ruining Babbage's machine. The second part is what you probably don't know. Farnsworth escaped from Westminster Hospital last night! The headline's rather interesting. The reporters quoted you after the explosion..."

William held up a copy of the *Times* and jabbed a finger at a midpoint in the frontpage article. Sure enough, there was Erasmus' exclamation at Professor Farnsworth's rantings. Erasmus took the paper into his hands and, by unfolding it, revealed the headline:

Mad Scientist Escapes!

"Oh, great," he thought out loud. "That will stick in the minds of citizens everywhere."

As he walked, he scanned down the article. "The Professor escaped at 8 p.m. yesterday. Do you know any more about how it happened?"

"No, I'm afraid I don't. I just saw the article and thought," William paused, "well, Sir, I thought that I could help you in some way."

"Good man. Your aid would be appreciated. I must get to Scotland Yard to follow up on yesterday's activities. But I feel that there may have been a link between an unexpected visitor I had last night and the Professor's escape. My gut is telling me that he was there to detain me while others were freeing the Professor. I need you to look into it."

"What is his name, Sir, if you know it?"

"He is one of the Professor's students, per se, but no time to explain the particulars. His name is Alistair Bennington Rutherford, and he operates a manufacturing plant that distributes a variation of absinthe that goes by the name Green Fantasy. He has been..."

"Sir! Sir!" William interrupted, "I know where that may be. The manufacturing plant. It's buried in the textile mills, I believe. I have seen the chemistry students that loiter outside of a particular warehouse. Many cases of clinking full bottles that go both in and out. It caught my eye, it did. I could investigate there. Undercover, and all that. Maybe ask for a job and get a quick tour or something."

"Jolly good! What luck! The critical item is that I need to find out where to find Mr. Rutherford. If I am correct, he may be dodging me, and I need to confront him." Erasmus gave William's shoulder a solid two pats. But before sending him off, he added, "Stay low and in character. We do not want to give away that we may know the location of the plant or Alistair if you find out. Our association should also be kept hidden. Best of luck, lad, best of luck. Oh, yes, and feel free to use the other fellows! Relay the same goals and cautions if they join you." He added one last pat to William's back, and William was off, clearly excited to be part of the hunt.

When Erasmus entered Scotland Yard, it was abuzz with activity. Bartholomew Horner, Erasmus' superior, met him at the door. "Early today. Good. I am sure by now that you are aware of Professor Farnsworth's escape. I want to have you organize and brief a team of constables I have assembled for recapturing him. After that, I would like you to brief the metropolitan area constables on what to look for so they can provide additional coverage. After that, work with one of our printers to get out a public notification broadsheet to report sightings of the Professor. Given the nature of his crime, I want to have him back in our control as quickly as we can."

"Excellent plan. However, I would first like to talk to the constable who was guarding the professor. Is he about?"

"Higgins is here. Ducking the reporters, I am sure. He is outside the briefing room since he has volunteered to be part of the search team. Oh, that reminds me. Expect more reporters to want to discuss the investigation with you. Especially with this 'mad scientist' headline. I am sure that will haunt you awhile. I will get the rest of the search team lined up to be briefed by you at the top of the hour. If there is anything else you need my support on, let me know."

"Thank you, Sir." Erasmus did a quick visit to his office to drop off his leather cape coat, bowler, and cane, and then headed straight to speak to Constable Zachary Higgins.

Constable Higgins was well respected within the Yard, or had been until last night. He had been a stand-up constable for four or so years, but letting a criminal of such recent notoriety escape wasn't good for one's reputation. Erasmus knew this and felt that if he wanted to get the constable to give him the full story of what happened the night before, he needed to be as positive as possible.

"Higgins. How are you holding up?" Erasmus queried. Higgins was standing outside of the briefing room, looking a bit lost and alone. He was clearly trying to keep his chin up, but only slightly hid his feelings of defeat. "Well, Drake, it has been a rough morning. You are the first to talk to me, to be honest. I have actually been up all night running around the streets near the hospital trying to find him. Have not slept a wink, and I want to get back out there to catch this clown. Volunteered for the search team, I did."

Erasmus smiled, and said, "The Professor may be a lunatic, but he is a smart one. He built that electrical contraption that can conjure up the equivalent of a lightning bolt. He is not your average criminal." Erasmus paused to see if Higgins offered more details, but the constable just shook his head and shuffled his feet for a second. Erasmus didn't have time for delays of this sort.

"Higgins, the newspaper said that Professor Farnsworth escaped out the window. I know they almost never get the details right. What is your account of the events?"

"Well, he did leave through the window. But it had been secured from the outside, and he was in restraints in the hospital bed. I was outside the door, and the lights were off in his room so he could sleep."

"Was the time of escape accurate? 8 p.m.?"

"I do think so. I was checking in on him once an hour. At the eight o'clock check, I observed the window was open, and there was no sign of the Professor. The restraints looked like they had been picked, but I did not see any tool that could have performed the deed."

"Higgins, I have my suspicions that someone was aiding Professor Farnsworth. The newspaper report did not mention anyone else. Be straight with me. Was there anyone else there?" Given the hour, Erasmus thought that Alistair might have gone straight to the hospital after visiting his apartment. That would make sense given his relationship with the Professor.

"Your suspicions are justified, Drake. I did not pass this along since it would have made me look like I had shirked my duties, which, looking back, perhaps I did. At around 7:30, a fellow came along all happy like and told me his wife had just given birth to twins. He was dancing around and offered me a touch of drink from his flask. I refused, of course. So he said just a drop. 'Symbolic,' he said. 'It is just symbolic.' So he poured no more than a few drops of liquid into the flasks top, we clinked the two like glasses, I just had a taste of the stuff, and he took a swig from his flask. I gave him his cap back, wished him the best, and he was on his merry way. The drink was absinthe, I think. Tasted like a child's licorice drop. But then the strangest thing happened. My mind wandered far and wide, and I was thinking how this guy's dancing around reminded me of a prancing street juggler I once saw, and then I realized that I do not know how to juggle. But then I suddenly realized that I was sure I could figure it out. Next thing I know I am outside the hospital juggling three small rocks like I had been doing it all my life. And then it hits me that I am neglecting my guarding duties. I rushed back in, and that was when I saw that the Professor was gone, a little after 8:00."

"I will keep this quiet. The one detail that is important to me is what the man with the flask looked like."

"Oh, there is no mistaking this one. He had on those puffy pants and long vests that are so popular with the student artists. Shaggy black hair and a little pointy beard, also black. Looked harmless enough, despite being about a hand taller than myself. Could not have been any older than twenty-two or twenty-three." These were exactly the specifics Erasmus had hoped to hear. He hurriedly thanked Zachary for the details, mentally filed them away, and got his busy morning underway.

The briefings went well. During them, he listed the places he thought the Professor might return to, his colleagues, and the nature of the electrical apparatuses he used as far as he thought the team needed. The search team consisted of eight good men, and they were to work in teams of two, starting their investigations at the locations Erasmus listed. The metropolitan constables were just to keep a wary eye out for any sign of the Professor and to be quick with the sound of alarm.

By noon, Erasmus felt like he had put in a full day. It was at this time that William stopped by with news. Since William was in training as a constable, it wasn't odd for him to be at the Yard. Erasmus felt that keeping William's "additional support" quiet would be for the best, and his coming directly to Erasmus' office today was warranted.

As Erasmus looked up from his desk, William burst through his office door. "Sir, I did it! I was in character throughout! Did it on me own, too. You should have seen me!" Erasmus gave a friendly "come on out with it" hand gesture as William grabbed a chair, plopped in it at a speed only a teenager can, and burst into his story.

"I acted as if I was looking for work and went in alone. I figured that it would look odd if there was a group of us. I was on the right track with my original hunch. The warehouse I originally thought of is a distribution point. Mr. Rutherford rarely goes there, but where they mix the stuff is where he spends his time. I got to be friendly with one of the case haulers who gave me the address of the mixing plant. He knew Mr. Rutherford personally and said that he spends most his time talking with future customers. Scientists and musicians and the like. This afternoon he said Mr. Rutherford will probably be at a private club for artists. The Blue Cat over on St. James' Street. I stopped by the place on my way here. Not much of a private club. More of a dive with tables and bad art on the walls. May I join you?" It seemed to Erasmus that William had said all of that in one breath.

"Hmm, this could get messy, or even rough. But you could be my back up. Let us make haste." They both stood at the same time, Erasmus pausing long enough to grab his walking attire, and out they went.

The sky had clouded over, giving the city of London a stark grayness despite being midday. William took the lead with a bounce in his step. His enthusiasm was a tad infectious, and Erasmus smiled at his puppy-on-a-leash mannerisms.

Suddenly William turned around. "Lunch? Have you eaten, Sir?"

At the question, it occurred to Erasmus the effect the elixir had had on him the evening before. He hadn't eaten since midday yesterday—he hadn't been hungry or even thirsty for a full twenty-four hours. That just wasn't right. He filed that away for later consideration. "No, lad, I have not. We should stop for a quick pot pie."

The Blue Cat was near the corner of St. James' Street and Pall Mall, hidden among the type of shops that have small friendly storefronts that obscure repair and light fabrication rooms in the rear. Its entrance was down a set of stone steps leading to a heavy blue door with a small brass knocker. Once close enough, Erasmus could see that the knocker had the face of a hissing cat encircled by a hinged ring. Erasmus and William looked silently at the door for a few seconds, and then Erasmus gave a sweeping gesture to William to take the lead. He backed up the stone stairs one step. William gave Erasmus a "here goes" eyebrow raise, turned to the door, and clinked the knocker twice.

Shuffling sounds could be heard from within, a muffled request to hold on, and a young man wearing a beige poet's shirt and baggy pants opened the door. "Huh," is all he said at first and gave both William and Erasmus a quick look over, followed by, "I see you came by again. Still looking for work?"

William began, "Yes. I wanted to see if Mr. Alistair Bennington Rutherford had come by so we could talk. May we come in?"

"What's with him?" he asked, gesturing to Erasmus with a quick jab of his chin.

William smiled and retorted, "Oh, my father? He is just along for the walk. Thought he might make a good reference, if needed." William actually winked with this, and Erasmus looked around, as if uninterested, to play along with the ruse.

"Well, there's not much going on here now, being the middle of the day, and all. I don't know when Mr. Rutherford will be by. Might as well come in."

William and Erasmus went in and let their eyes adjust to the dimness. It was as William had described. A few tables and chairs. A crude bar was set up with a limited selection of drinks. The place was empty.

"You can wait here if you like. I can't really offer you a drink. It's a private club." He smiled with the knowledge that calling this room a private club was dripping with irony. He continued, "I'm working on a piece in the back, so if you'll excuse me..."

Erasmus spoke up, seeing an opportunity to explore further. "Do you mind if I look? I am very interested in art. We have a good deal of it in the house. Always looking for new pieces."

"Fine by me. Everything in the back here is a work in progress, so don't be too hasty to judge. Watch your step. Our floor's a mess."

To the left of the bar was a draped doorway. As the artist pulled back the drape, a low-ceilinged work area was revealed. It was better lit and had a few easels, a stool, and a paint-splashed table crowded with the tools and supplies of the craft of painting. The workroom had two additional archways leading to similar rooms. The artist went straight away to an easel and pulled back a cloth protecting his work in progress. The image he revealed was quite experimental, a rolling landscape dotted with cows—or were they horses?—but using larger and heavier strokes than one would see in paintings in most sitting rooms. Erasmus thought the effect was interesting, but not anything he would ever buy. He turned his interest back to exploring the premises.

Without explanation, Erasmus ducked through the archway on the left, which led to another work area. This one had the trappings of a student of clay sculpture: a table with a number of terra cotta colored pieces on it that appeared to have been fired, various scraping and smoothing tools, and small bits of clay everywhere. A bag of powdered clay was on the floor next to a tin bucket that was sadly unmaintained. Erasmus' ears could now detect that the basement was a rabbit warren of a dozen or so rooms with voices coming from one of them buried in the back. If Alistair was such a busy man, this seemed an odd place for him to frequent. The answer lay in the people here, most likely. He started to make his way back through the gas lit rooms, toward the voices, just as he could hear William making small talk with the baggy-shirted painter.

As he got closer, Erasmus could tell that two artists were having a bit of a celebration after completion of a difficult task. He hung back in the shadows of the room adjacent to theirs to determine what success they were discussing. The two were dressed in leather aprons and goggles, the latter currently draped around their necks. In the room sat a bathtub-sized pan with high sides and two wires running out to what looked like an electrical generator. Erasmus recognized this as electroplating equipment, but more sophisticated than he had seen before. Two gold bars lay on the floor next to the pan. One looked as if its surface had been melted away. A clay cast on the table had been used for creating the underlying metal sculpture. The cast was broken, obviously removed from around with artwork. Shiny silver-color castoff metal was still stuck to the bottom of the cast.

The two leather-clad artists were beside themselves. They were drinking and carrying on as if they had just won some grand fortune at a betting table. Erasmus realized that the far one had the black hair and pointy beard described by Constable Higgins.

Erasmus' left elbow touched something that shifted as if it were going to tip over. He carefully turned his head to see what was on the table next to him as he slowly backed his elbow away. Hidden by the darkness was a bottle, but no ordinary bottle. It was a half-full stoppered bottle of Green Fantasy. A glass stood next to it.

Erasmus froze. He flirted with the idea that with just a taste of it, he could solve this entire circumstance in five minutes. He knew he could. He could still hear the conversation in the next room, but his attention was now on the bottle. Erasmus forced himself to look back into the next room to hear the black bearded one say how overjoyed he was that the twins were healthy and his wife was fine. As he turned back, he had apparently picked the bottle up in his now slightly shaky hand. *Just a sip, perhaps. No, not a good plan.* He remembered he was on duty and all that rot. A look back at the artists and he recognized the cast. It was the statue of Osiris, the same one that was in the Egyptian Hall. He looked at his hands. He had somehow taken up the glass and poured about twice as much as he had had the night before. He could smell it. He could imagine the unique taste. The glass moved halfway to his mouth and stopped. A constable blew his whistle outside in the street, twice, loud and long, but it seemed miles away and muffled, as if Erasmus had pillows over his ears.

He slammed the bottle and glass back onto the table and sprinted through the warren, past William and Mr. Baggy Shirt. He threw open the door and bolted up the steps to find a most curious scene.

Across the street was the well-known Lobb shoe store. In their doorway stood Professor Farnsworth brandishing one of the electrical discharge pistols in his burnt right hand, his blackened finger nervously twitching on the trigger. The cable that attached to the pistol now ran to a backpack apparatus, which most likely supplied power to the pistol while allowing the Professor complete mobility. Clutched in the professor's left arm was a panicked young lady employed as both a shield and hostage. Her arms pinned and her eyes wide, she appeared to have witnessed the incredible capability of the pistol, stunning her into silence. At that particular moment, she was looking with horror at the Professor's damaged left hand was grasping her right arm as well as it could with its remaining three fingers. Incredibly, the Professor had a leather holster strapped to his right leg that was obviously made to accommodate the pistol, but looked a good deal like a repurposed fine gentleman's shoe.

Erasmus noted more details. The window of the shop was slightly melted from the inside, causing the gilded-paint signage to run. The pistol had obviously been discharged inside the store. The street had been cleared of people. Erasmus noticed that the constable who blew the alarm was either hiding or had left the vicinity completely. Apparently, Erasmus' description of the power of the pistols had been heeded. No one from Scotland Yard was on scene except Erasmus.

The Professor was in full-tilt maniacal mode—twitching, wild-eyed, and grinning at his circumstance. But now the Chief Inspector was there. *"I have become someone for him to point his pistol at,"* Erasmus thought, and the Professor obliged his thought and leveled the pistol at Erasmus. As the electrical firearm moved it made a humming sound not that unlike the sound of a dragonfly on the wing. *"It must be partially powered,"* thought Erasmus.

William charged up the stone steps, breathless. Erasmus instinctively held out his right arm with a "stay behind me" wave. William slowly backed down the steps, but not to the extent that he couldn't watch what was about to happen.

"Chief Inspector Drake, how nice of you to show up again. Would you like to see how I have improved the electrical discharge pistol? I gave the owners of the Lobb shop a little demonstration!" He chuckled to himself and grabbed his young hostage tighter.

Erasmus' new goal was to keep the Professor pinned down until more firepower showed up. *"Try to continue his little dialog,"* he thought. "And a good day to you, Professor. I see you got free of the hospital room."

"My friend Red came to the rescue, of course. Easy to break into a room that is meant to keep someone in. Red told me of your little chat. What prompted your initial visit? You have thrown quite a spanner into my plans."

"Well, it all started with the smell of cocoa in the temporary exhibit room at the grand pavilion. It did not make sense. That is why I visited Red."

As he said this, Erasmus took a nonchalant step forward hoping to get a tad closer to the Professor. The motion incensed the Professor, and his pistol quivered with his anger. "All of this over the smell of cocoa?" He turned the quietly humming pistol to the young lady's head, which made her long blond hair stand on end out to her left, directly away from the pistol like a comet's tail points away from the sun. It gave the impression that it was a still picture of the pistol blowing her head off. The young lady produced an audible whimper indicating that she understood her predicament.

"One step closer and her head disappears," the Professor said through an evil smile. As he minutely moved his right hand, the young lady's blond hair instantly jerked about to remain as distant as possible from the bulbous end of pistol.

Through gritted teeth, Professor Farnsworth growled, "We had just finished celebrating a critical technical breakthrough relating to electrical reservoiring. The day before you showed up, we had a troupe of dancers and jugglers entertain the graduate students. They used cocoa on the floor to prevent slipping on the smooth marble." By this point, the professor's growl had built to a shout. "You bumbled in and interrupted my life's work, Chief Inspector!"

No backup yet. Erasmus needed more time, and wanted to change the direction of the conversation, and fast. "Young lady, are you all right?"

She stuttered something and then froze again. The Professor rolled his eyes and hissed, "Oh, answer him!"

She slowly stammered out, "I am...fine, Sir. Just my nerves are rattled."

Erasmus decided to continue this conversation to keep the Professor from getting more excited. "What is your name, dear?"

"Margret. Margret O'Malley. I work at Lobb's. At the till."

Professor Farnsworth rolled his eyes at the banality of the exchange. "Enough of this jibber-jabber! I must take my leave. Good day, Chief Inspector." At this, the professor lifted Margret until her legs dangled and he took a few steps to his left toward Pall Mall. At that second, the search team of half a dozen blue-coated constables rushed in from the far end of the street. *"Finally,"* thought Erasmus, *"more firepower."*

The Professor reacted to their arrival by cursing and sweeping his aim across in a wide arc, causing Margret's hair to hang down naturally again and the constables to dive for cover with the exception of one very determined Constable Zachary Higgins, who stood his ground. The other constables brought out their firearms. From Erasmus' perspective, it was as if the buildings had all grown blue arms with revolvers.

The constables all understood the situation and the odds. The electrical discharge pistol probably took a while to fire, if the Professor hadn't modified it to fire immediately. Whoever was in its line of fire might be killed, but the others could bring the professor down. However, they had no knowledge that he had used the weapon to kill anyone, so preemptively firing on him was unjustified.

Erasmus took a small step forward saying, "Professor, we have no proof that you have injured anyone. If you lower your pistol, and give yourself over to our constables quietly, the magistrate will be lenient."

The Professor was infuriated further. Waving the pistol through a few more arcs, he shouted, "Enough! I made this pistol for blasting my way out of situations just like this. Watch this!" He locked his aim onto Erasmus.

Erasmus instinctively reached into the inside pocket of his cape coat where his revolver would be and found something unexpected. It was a short cylinder with a long nozzle or barrel and a button-like trigger near his index finger. It fit well in his hand. Was this the magnetic gun that he had mentally invented? Had he built it overnight, as some sort of sleepwalking inventor? And surely if he had, it would fire instantly rather than taking time to charge up.

Upon thinking this, Erasmus pulled out his new-found weapon and, in a single motion, leveled it at the professor and pulled the trigger. The sight and sound of the empty oilcan made Professor Farnsworth rear back with laughter. The first thought Erasmus had in

81

that split second was that he'd placed the oilcan there to remind himself to buy more oil for the reassembly of his revolver. How ironic.

The second thought was his grand luck, and he shouted, "Now!"

Zachary sprinted toward the Professor, who lowered his pistol again at the poorly armed Erasmus and pulled the trigger. The sound of the pistol's warming up began—an ugly high-pitched whine. Margret screamed a soprano note that created a strange harmonic with the pistol's electronic screech.

Erasmus took two steps forward and lunged, counting correctly on Zachary's success. Zachary wrapped his arms around the Professor's thin legs, causing the Professor to spin around, landing on his back in the street with Margret thrown free, off-balance. Erasmus caught Margret in the middle of her fall, saving her from a hard landing. The electrical discharge pistol fired straight up, loosing a thunderous crack and a blue-white flash that looked like lightning straightened out into a rod. The immediate effect was a perfect hole augured into the clouds above, as if some deity had decided to drill a hole so he or she could spy on these earthly shenanigans.

Zachary moved like man on a mission, deftly knocking the pistol out of the Professor's hand, sending the pistol skittering away as far as its tether allowed. And then, with an enormous splash, the entire condensed contents of the vaporized cloud segment rained down onto the block in a perfect ring the size of the hole bored in the clouds, drenching those in its path. The strange meteorological phenomenon was short-lived, but it made everyone, including the Professor, look up at the blue sunshiny hole in the sky in awe.

The next half hour contained the usual steps back to normalcy: the constables came out from hiding and returned their revolvers back to their holsters; Professor Farnsworth was placed in restraints while he ranted about his mission to stop the use of thinking machines; Margret thanked Erasmus at least three times; the Lobb shoe shop owners were released from their bindings of shoelace string; a Scotland Yard cabriolet was brought around to transfer Professor

Farnsworth back to the Westminster Hospital; and the constables all thanked Zachary and Erasmus for their actions and preventing bloodshed. There was nothing that could be done regarding the Lobb's cash register that Professor Farnsworth had reduced to a molten blob. As well, no one wanted to touch any of the knobs or switches on the electrical discharge pistol's backpack for fear that it would cause some additional catastrophe, so Erasmus requested a special team to be called in to address the issue of the dangerous technical device. The hole in the clouds started to fade, but a gathering crowd of pedestrians all stood around looking at it as if they had never seen blue sky before. Reporters showed up, of course, but they were mainly taking the reaction of the crowd; they would get the story from the members of the Yard later.

By the time Erasmus reached the hospital, where he planned to verify that the Professor was properly restrained and guarded, multiple reporters from each of the London newspapers and a few reporters from out-of-town and foreign papers met him at the steps. He gave them short versions of how he distracted Professor Farnsworth with an oilcan, of Constable Higgins' heroics, the recapture of the Professor, the rescue of Margret O'Malley, the freeing of the Lobbs, and the effects of the odd, cloud-clearing pistol. He joked that the Mad Scientist's invention now had a "good use" after all. But secretly, he was glad that the electrical discharge pistol didn't fire straight the first time he encountered it, or he wouldn't have been there giving the interview.

Once he was finished with the reporters, he went in to talk with the guards. All three of them were in place, their rotation plan was well understood, and they were briefed on the possibility that someone might try to free the prisoner.

Erasmus decided to talk to the professor, to see if his normal side had returned, still keeping in mind Alistair's request for leniency for the poor man. As he neared the Professor's room, he saw Alistair kneeling by his bed. Erasmus held back, curious as to what exchange they were having.

Alistair was beside himself. "I have failed you, Professor. I have created this problem for you, and I swear I will do whatever it takes to save you. You have my word on it."

The professor responded, but his lucidity was only temporary. "Be gentle with yourself, Alistair. I am what I am by my own hand. But...please help me escape! I must stop the machines! Please, I beg of you!" A tear silently ran down Alistair's face.

Erasmus turned and walked down the hall alone, until he heard a cry for help. As he moved down the hall toward the shouting, he thought, *"I am needed again; once more into the breach."*

Sandrine, Je T'aime

By Dr. Katherine L. Morse

By the time she stumbled back to the table, Jean-Michel was lying on the floor, clutching his hands to his chest. The other patrons were ignoring him, probably interpreting his fall as mere drunkenness. She clouted the nearest large patron in the shoulder with her fist. "This man needs to get to the hospital! Help me get him to the street!" The patron prepared to take offense at the assault and tell her to piss off, but the mixture of delirium and desperation on her face was truly terrible to behold, so he just picked up Petit under the arms and helped McTrowell carry him to the curb. She dropped Petit's feet and ran into the street right in front of the nearest hansom cab. If the cabbie had looked away for an instant, the horse would have trampled her. She grabbed Petit's feet again and hauled him into the cab with the aid of the still-dazed patron. "Westminster Hospital!" she screamed frantically at the cabbie. Being a fairly astute man, the cabbie whipped the horses into a gallop, dousing the helpful patron in muck from the street. Sparky held Jean-Michel propped up against her, taking his pulse. His heart was pounding sluggishly. He mumbled deliriously, *"Sandrine, Je t'aime, Je t'aime."*

As the horses rounded the last corner toward the hospital, she propped Petit up in the seat and leapt out of the cab before it had even come to a halt. She flew up the stairs into the hospital, shouting at the top of her lungs, "Help! I am a doctor. I need licorice root immediately." The passersby in the hallway all looked at her as if she were mad, which was not too far from the truth at the moment. All of them save one – the one sporting the familiar brown bowler, Chief

Inspector Drake. "Chief Inspector Drake! My friend, Monsieur Jean-Michel Petit, has been poisoned!"

"Where is he?"

"He is outside in a hansom." Drake dashed out of the hospital without hesitation with McTrowell close on his heels. He leapt up into the cab, tossing the cabbie some change and hoisting up Petit. McTrowell grabbed Petit's feet again, the two of them reversing the procedure performed with the assistance of the pub patron. They hauled Petit inside the hospital. He went into convulsions as they laid him on the floor.

"Fetch me some licorice root," McTrowell commanded, and Drake dashed off again without question while she held Petit.

"Sandrine, mon amor, Je t'aime." He shuddered again and Sparky felt his pulse stop.

"Nooooo!" She dropped her head on Petit's chest and began sobbing. The front of Petit's shirt was soaked in her tears when Drake came running back down the hall moments later, a small apothecary jar in his hand. The look on his face was crestfallen. "I fear I am too late."

"It was probably too late before we left Ye Olde Cheshire Cheese. At least Sandrine will not have to hear that her husband died in a pub."

Drake took notice of the mention of Ye Olde Cheshire Cheese. "You said your friend was poisoned. Who was he and why do you think he was poisoned?" The commotion had attracted considerable attention by now. He motioned for a pair of orderlies with a stretcher. They lifted Petit gently onto the stretcher and carried him away. Drake helped McTrowell to her feet and proffered his handkerchief. She wiped her eyes and cheeks, struggling to catch her breath.

"He was a professor of mathematics at the Université Toulouse and without an enemy in the world. He was not the intended victim; I was," she sobbed. Drake raised his eyebrows slightly in an expression of interest. "A Mr. Abusir has been courting my mother very aggressively. At the same time, my mother's gold assaying business has been suffering as her patrons have been dying unexpectedly, exhibiting symptoms of foxglove poisoning. I have tested my theory of the poison by trying it on myself. This is how I knew what had befallen Monsieur Petit and why I sent you for licorice. It was the antidote I used on myself."

"Astounding, pray continue."

"Mr. Abusir has been stealing the claims of the gold miners he murders. I have a spy in the claims office who has reported as much to me." The Chief Inspector again raised his eyebrows. "My mother wrote that Abusir was coming to London on some mysterious business, something to do with a wedding gift for a pharaoh's wife, and I have had the sense that I was being followed ever since I arrived. Recall that you and I were standing at the statue of Osiris yesterday when the blast occurred. After you left, a workman stayed behind. He was somewhat swarthy, but more importantly, he stared maliciously at me and covetously at the statue of Osiris for quite some time before leaving. I saw his face again just moments ago in Ye Olde Cheshire Cheese! Jean Michel ordered me a pint of bitters, but I did not care for its extreme bitterness, so he drank it! It was Abusir at the Great Exhibition and at Ye Olde Cheshire Cheese. He is trying to kill me!"

He smiled knowingly and added, "Why would Abusir wish to kill you?"

"Because I've written to my mother opposing the marriage. I love my mother and wish her every happiness, but she's not a very good judge of character in men..." and then she added under her breath "...including my father."

"Fortuitously, I may be able to fill in some details. Just today I saw two artists who had just finished crafting a replica of the Osiris statue that we discussed. I also saw the electroplating equipment to put a finish of gold on it. They were having quite a celebration of this accomplishment."

"Abusir must have gold from the miners' claims—that must be the source of the gold for the electroplating. But why would he come all the way to London to create the replica if he had the gold in San Francisco? If he were here to steal the original, he could have stolen it after I left the Great Exhibition yesterday. Is it missing?"

"If the original were missing, Scotland Yard would have been notified. I will return to Ye Olde Cheshire Cheese in search of evidence of the poisoning. If you could stay here to make arrangements for the body of Dr. Petit, we should meet tomorrow at the Great Exhibition where we may find more evidence."

"I have made arrangements for my mechanical surgical assistant to be installed at the Great Exhibition. You may find me there."

Drake held his bowler over his heart and bowed slightly before departing. McTrowell walked slowly to the basement of the hospital and wandered dejectedly along the hall until she found the door with the small brass plaque with the single word, **Morgue**.

COUNTERBALANCING A SARCOPHAGUS

BY MR. DAVID L. DRAKE

Erasmus made his way through the morning fog toward Hyde Park, the day's copy of the *Times* in hand, mulling over the previous day's excitements. Erasmus' scan of the first few pages over his morning's Earl Grey revealed that the Professor's recapture didn't get the lead article, but it was prominent enough to keep the good work of Scotland Yard in the minds of the readers. Constable Higgins had redeemed himself, which was an excellent turn of events, and Erasmus was heralded as a master tactician who had foiled the mad scientist with an empty oilcan. *"Well,"* thought Erasmus, *"it was somewhere between hogwash and the truth, but the important thing was that it wasn't dead wrong."*

The poisoning of Monsieur Petit had its own article. It read as if it were rushed to press, which made sense given the hour of the day that the newspaper found out about the deed. The paper had a great deal more detail on Monsieur Petit's accomplishments, and clearly his loss was going to be felt in a number of academic and industrial circles. The man seemed to have had the rare gift of being able to work in both theoretical realms as well as mechanical engineering disciplines.

Erasmus' findings at Ye Olde Cheshire Cheese didn't turn up as much as he would have liked. Once Dr. McTrowell and Monsieur Petit left in a hurry without paying, their beer glasses had been drained and washed. Most of the patrons were paying attention to their friends, and so Abusir, if he had been there, didn't leave an impression on any of the patrons. The one interesting point was that the tap boy that delivered the two beers had set them down and turned his attention elsewhere for a few moments, leaving ample time for someone familiar with administering poison to spike Dr. McTrowell's beer. For someone to do that, he would have to have known which beer she ordered, or make an educated guess, or maybe not even have cared whom he killed. There was just a good chance that the assailant may have been within earshot of the two when they ordered.

Arriving at the Crystal Palace, Erasmus went about the process of finding the hall in which the surgical assistant had been installed. He was informed that it was in a unique location: the actual harness was situated in the Industrial Applications room, adjacent to the Mechanical Engines room where the steam engine that powered it was located. A long shaft connecting the engine and the harness ran between the two rooms, housed within a ventilated pipe, which was fashioned for both safety and noise reasons.

Erasmus found Dr. McTrowell in work clothes and leather gloves, sitting on the floor, wielding two wrenches, putting the final touches on reassembling the surgical assistant.

It was an impressive device. Unlike many of the contraptions that Erasmus saw at the Annual Symposium of the Occidental Inventors' Society, which were heavy brass and wood, this was more delicate, more precise, and more refined. Almost the opposite of what one might have expected from an inventor from the wilds of California.

"Good morning, Dr. McTrowell. I see your mechanical surgical assistant arrived."

Looking up from her labors, Dr. McTrowell replied, "Ah, a good morning to you! And please, call me Sparky, all of my enemies do. I am sorry, it is a bit too early in the morning for dark humor. But still, I prefer Sparky."

"Sparky it is then, but please pardon my British manners, I am sure I will slip up. I see you are close to completing the reassembly. Fascinating! If you have the time to give me a tour, it would..."

"I would be glad to! I will try to keep the boasting to a minimum." She then pointed out and described each major part and its function.

The primary component was worn like a backpack, with extensions to the floor via attachments to the wearer's legs. It provided two brass foot-plates that the wearer stood on to give stability to both the wearer and the apparatus itself. There were some other fixtures on the foot-plates to fasten it to a specially-made floor plate for even more stability, but it was only needed for an unsteady or unleveled airship. Erasmus noted there were also small foot pedals, or rather buttons, that could be stepped on, but they went unexplained for the moment.

For Erasmus, it was its arms that gave him pause. It had two pair that extended from the backpack, one set that attached to the wearer's arms, the other pair free-standing. The pair worn on the arms were principally for controlling, although they also could aid in steadying by dampening or eliminating small extraneous motion. The free-standing pair of arms were substantially sturdier. They were attached in such a manner that they worked outside of the swing of the wearer's natural arms, so they could be above, outside, or below the wearer. They could be used simply for holding, like an extra pair of hands, but could also perform lifting, pushing, or pulling motions, guided by the wearer, but with greater force. It was for this latter function that the surgical assistant required a connection to a steam engine. With this, explained Sparky, she could lift an overweight man onto a surgical table, perform a delicate operation, and then place the man back onto a nearby bed.

On the side of the backpack were additional tools for the sturdier arms, Sparky explained. What surprised Erasmus was that Sparky had designed and built the mechanical surgical assistant so that all of the components that fit onto the wearer were adjustable, with brass winged thumb screws for setting the length between joints. She had not only made this for herself, but for a wide range of doctors, he reasoned. It was apparent that with a change of tools, this apparatus could be used for any number of medical applications, from dentistry to autopsy.

The long shaft from the steam engine connected low to the mechanical surgical assistant, near the foot pads, with an adjustable length linkage that went up into the backpack. Sparky finished bolting this shaft and declared the apparatus ready for demonstration.

"It's a shame I won't be able to demonstrate it during the Great Exhibition," Sparky sighed.

"Why is that?"

"I have been 'requested' to pilot an airship in an upcoming regatta. I will be leaving within the week. The plan is to display a mannequin in the place of a physician, and not have it actually running."

"You are a pilot, too?"

"It started as mandatory training for all crew members, but turned into one of my side passions. Airships, like seafaring ships, require anticipation and early- but not over-reaction. The truth is, Chief Inspector, it's fun." At that, Sparky smiled, despite the seriousness of the true reason they were at the Great Exhibition today.

A crash from the Egyptian Court echoed throughout the halls, followed quickly by shouting from a desperate man, "Help! Help! Oh, Lord, give me strength!"

Erasmus rounded the corner to see a disheartening scene. Two of the workers had been trying to rotate a large wooden sarcophagus on a shoulder-high stone dais when it must have shifted off-balance and fallen, the high end still on the dais, the other pinning one of the workers to the floor. The second worker was desperately trying to lift the sarcophagus with all his might. Erasmus was the first to join him in the effort, and Sparky immediately followed.

Within seconds, the room had half a dozen helping workers. The angle of the weight made it difficult to get a grip. Sparky yelled, "You there, and you, climb up and counterbalance it! Pull down on the far end. Hard!" Two workers scrambled up and did as she bid, causing the sarcophagus to right itself with the effort on each end.

The poor workman, not much older than a teen, had taken the full weight on his chest. Although he had youth and strength, the weight had clearly taken its toll, and even to one not medically trained, Erasmus could tell that serious structural damage had been inflicted on the lad's chest. He was not moving, and if breathing, it wasn't obvious.

Sparky was on him in a flash, ripping open his shirt to examine the injury. It was not a pretty sight. The skin was torn. A deep, red gash ran full across his chest, and his chest was dented in on his left side. Sparky barked out instructions as she took control of the situation. "Lift this man and follow me!" She sprinted to the room with her equipment, flinging off her leather gloves as she went. Erasmus and three other men carried the lad into the next room as requested. "On the table. Gently, now, he has at least one broken rib."

Sparky gingerly stepped into her mechanical surgical assistant, buckled both straps of the leather harness and cinched the belt about her waist, while commanding, "Chief Inspector, start the steam engine. Immediately!"

Erasmus led the sprint, with the three other men close behind. "Is there one of you familiar with starting a steam engine?"

"Yes, Sir," said the oldest of the three, "but pray that the boiler is going, or it will take a while for it to turn over."

The Mechanical Room had a number of running steam engines, but not the single trestle German steam engine attached to the mechanical surgical assistant. Erasmus turned to the mechanic, asking, "Move the shaft to a working machine, or stoke this one?" pointing to the one connected to Sparky's apparatus.

"Stoke it! Use the embers from the other engines!" the mechanic yelled as he verified that there was water in the boiler. The four of them stole hot coals from the various surrounding engines with the wide flat shovels available.

The engine for the surgical assistant was smaller and more compact than the rest and, within moments, the furnace was red hot, the water starting to boil. Erasmus left the starting to the experts while he ran back to tell Sparky that she would soon have power. Rounding the corner, Erasmus shouted, "power is on its way," to which she replied, "the sooner the better, I need to carefully retract this rib from his lung." Sparky was working strenuously to move the outside arms and attach the instruments she needed.

It was an interesting process. With her fingers in the brass ring controllers, she was reaching back with her right hand to her own right side, which caused the outer arms to reach back to the tool selection compartments on the side of the backpack. She indicated that she needed the mechanical arms to pull up on the cracked rib once she had gotten access to it within his chest and had power. Just then the shaft began to turn. Erasmus breathed a sigh of relief, and thought, *"it is all in her hands now."*

The Surgical Assistant Under Steam

By Dr. Katherine L. Morse

Sparky slipped her fingers into the controllers for the outer arms and stepped on the left foot pedal, rotating the left arm with a large pair of forceps around so it was close to the chest wound. She switched feet and rotated the right arm around to brace the workman by his right shoulder with a padded clamp. She slipped her fingers out of the controllers and reached up to loosen the winged screws at her elbows, releasing the inner arms, which she also swung into place over the chest wound. She tightened them back down, grabbing two more pairs of forceps out of loops in the chest harness and snapping them into the "arms." She extracted a scalpel from the harness, took a deep breath, exhaled purposefully, and started cutting. She opened the chest wound cleanly with her own hands, snapped the forceps in the inner arms to the edges of the wound, and then gently pulled back the flaps of skin by gently pushing back with the backs of her hands against a pair of paddles just below the controllers for the outer arms.

Having established clear access to the broken rib, she stepped on the left pedal again to bring the forceps on the left outer arm down to clamp onto the broken rib. With her foot still on the pedal, she eased the rib back up until the broken ends dovetailed back together. The workman groaned slightly as if he was coming to, and Sparky realized she would have to move fast. She had no anesthesia available, and if he came to now, his pain would send him into wild thrashing, making it impossible to finish the delicate operation.

She pulled a length of silk from a spool in the belt, cutting it off with the notched cutter next to the spool. She selected a needle from what could only be described as a pincushion on the belt beside the spool. Drake marveled that she seemed to thread the needle even as she was making the first stitch to the flesh under the rib. She stabbed the needle back into the pincushion when she finished stitching while simultaneously releasing the forceps on the rib. She unclipped the forceps holding the skin and waved the inner arms out of the way with the backs of her hands. Another length of silk and she stitched his chest closed.

Drake was struck by the way that McTrowell's operation of the surgical assistant made her look like a giant, dancing praying mantis, or a steam-powered Shiva…except that she was bringing life rather than death. She danced a bit of a jig on the pedals to get the outer arms under the workman so she could lift him off the table. From the other side of the belt she produced a large roll of gauze and a pair of scissors from the harness. She snipped off the remains of his shirt and wrapped his chest with gauze. She hadn't yet finished wrapping when she began shouting orders to the other workmen who were standing by anxiously.

"Rig up a litter and bring sandbags!" The workmen snapped out of their stupor and did as ordered while she slowly lowered their injured fellow back onto the table. She swung the outer arms out of the way so they could get to him.

"Put him on the litter on his right side, gently! Use the sandbags to prop him up. Take him to Westminster Hospital as fast as you can without dropping him and tell them to give him as much morphine as he can stand! If they argue, tell them it's an order from Chief Inspector Erasmus Drake of Scotland Yard!"

The workmen hustled to do her bidding and departed with such haste that one would have thought the devil himself was on their tails. McTrowell slumped forward in the harness, breathing rapidly and shallowly. Drake noticed that she was drenched in sweat. He stepped up to the opposite side of the table and pulled a clean handkerchief out of his waistcoat pocket. He began gently dabbing the sweat off her face and she revived slightly.

Looking up at him she said, "I hope you don't mind that I gave the order in your name, but I thought the hospital would take orders from you better than from me."

"Quite all right. You have done a miraculous thing today and I think that young man will have you to thank for the rest of his life. Would you care to extricate yourself, and if I may suggest, have a cup of tea and a biscuit?"

"Yes, I think I would. If you be so kind as to shut down the steam engine, I will get out of this contraption."

Drake rounded the corner into the Mechanical Engines room while McTrowell began putting her equipment back in order. She used the pedals to release the outer arms and swing them completely overhead before she lost power. She was collecting the instruments she had left strewn around the operating table when she heard movement at the far edge of the room. When she looked up, her heart almost stopped. It was Abusir! He was sneaking through the room toward the Egyptian room carrying a sack with something heavy in it. Their eyes locked. It would have been hard for an observer to say which of them bore a more ferocious look on their face.

McTrowell came back to her senses. "Drake! It's Abusir!" McTrowell had seen quite a few angry faces in her adventures, but none to compare to the truly murderous look on Abusir's face when she called for Drake. The sound that came out of Abusir's mouth was not so much a shout as the growl of a cornered, feral animal. He dropped the bag and charged toward her. Where was Drake? He must not have heard her!

She tried to get out of the harness, but her hands were sweaty and shaking from the exertion of the operation. She couldn't operate the buckles! The mechanical surgical assistant was powering down, leaving her trapped and at the mercy of the madman charging across the room.

She screamed with the volume and terror of a woman certain she was facing death, "Drake, re-engage the steam engine!" She had just an instant to marvel at the wits of a man who wouldn't question such an order, but recognized that executing it meant the difference between life and death. *"Truly he must be Scotland Yard's finest,"* she thought.

The mechanical surgical assistant came back to life just as Abusir closed on her. She tipped back onto her heels so she could engage both foot pedals at once while jamming her fingers into the controllers for the outer arms. She tried to block his advance with the outer arms, but the engine wasn't quite back up to full power and Abusir had the strength of insanity on his side. His arms waved frantically, trying to grasp at her neck. She waved desperately at the counter-controlling paddles for the inner arms, bringing them back in front of herself and jabbing at Abusir with the forceps that were still locked into them. Useless! The forceps poked at him, making tiny wounds, but doing nothing to actually stop him from getting his hands around her throat.

Drake sprinted in from the Mechanical Engines room just in time to see Abusir begin to choke the life out of McTrowell. She was trapped in the harness and he was too far away to reach her in time. He watched helplessly as her hands dropped to the operating table...where they landed on the scalpel she had just used to save the young workman's life. With her last bit of strength, she clenched it in her fist and brought it straight up into Abusir's throat with a surgeon's accuracy. Blood sprayed everywhere. Abusir barely gurgled as he dropped to the floor. When Sparky collapsed into the harness exhausted, the mechanical surgical assistant was truly holding her up.

Drake leapt the pool of blood forming around Abusir and pressed two fingers to her throat where a bruise was already starting to form; he put his cheek so close to her mouth that the tips of his moustache brushed her face. He felt a faint pulse and a tiny puff of breath. She was alive! He uncinched the belt and unbuckled the shoulder straps of the harness. She collapsed into his arms and took a proper breath, "Behold, I am become Death."

QUITE THE GENTLEMAN

BY MR. DAVID L. DRAKE

"Catching women, that is my job this week," thought Erasmus. Sparky was fairly light in his arms, and fading in and out of consciousness. He placed her delicately on the operating table where she had just performed a life-saving operation. And what was that she said about death? It sounded like a quote, but not one that he was familiar with. But first things first. There was a dead body. Abusir, he assumed. But wait; hello! Look at his face! Was he not the Egyptian

man trying to wrangle the statue of Osiris from Mr. Joseph Bonomi a few years back? Here he had correctly associated the name Abusir with the temple of the god of the dead, but hadn't made the link to the name of the man who was hounding Sparky.

"Time to get some help from the boys from the Yard," Erasmus thought. Erasmus raised his whistle to his lips, turned toward the heart of the room to be heard as well as possible, and blew it twice, loud and long. By the time three constables arrived, Sparky was up and walking off her attack. Her throat was in incredible pain, and she had had a few short spasms of coughing over the last few minutes.

Erasmus had a short conversation with the constables, letting them deal with the matter of Abusir's body, while he took on the task of "interviewing" Sparky.

"This is the second time I have come to this building to investigate, and violence resulted. Strange." Erasmus paused, and then queried, "From your description, Mr. Abusir has previously been furtive and clandestine in his actions. What could have sent him into such a rage?"

Sparky took a break from rubbing her throat and pointed off to a corner entrance of the Egyptian Court. A plain cloth sack lay on the floor.

"Do you want to clean up while I take a look?" Erasmus offered.

Sparky looked down and realized that she was covered with blood splatters from both the operation and the attack. "No," she said grimly, "it's more important we figure this out. When he saw me, he dropped that sack, flew into a rage, and charged me."

Erasmus strode over to the satchel. It was still gaping open where it had fallen, the chipped base of a statue sticking out of it, a result of the bag being dropped. Erasmus hefted the effigy; it was the statue of Osiris! But rather, a counterfeit of the statue. He inspected the broken off fragments. It was an excellent imitation, but it was clearly not solid gold, but rather a heavy base metal, perhaps lead, coated with silver, and over that a thin layer of gold. Clearly the work of the artists who were at the Blue Cat. He carefully set it on the marble floor after they had both inspected it. Sparky dug into the bag and came up with two letters and some notes.

One letter was from Sparky's mother, Elizabeth Llewellyn. It stated that she was hesitant to marry Mr. Abusir, on the advice of her daughter. The letter went on to mention that her daughter was currently in London, displaying and demonstrating her invention, and how proud she was of her. She was planning to wait for her to reply before giving him a definite answer.

The second letter was by Mr. Abusir himself, unfinished and unsent. It stated that he would give her the best wedding present that had not been bestowed on a loved one in 2000 years, and he would be returning to the Americas with it. His final sentence read: "A gift fit for the wife of a pharaoh will be bestowed upon you, and further description will only lessen the wonderment."

The notes were the greatest of the finds within the satchel. It had a great number of pages, full of detailed illustrations: hieroglyphics on some pages, maps of San Francisco complete with X's and notes regarding mine locations and their owners, and finally a rather improbable multi-page family tree that claimed that Mr. Abusir was a direct descendant of Osiris, the Egyptian god of resurrection. He even wrote multiple passages to himself within the notes, as if to bolster his confidence, that he had the right to the statue and all things Egyptian. The last page of his notes concluded that he, like Osiris, needed a wife to bring his body back to life after death. It was complete with grisly details of how it was to be accomplished with a combination of salts, flower petals, and gauze, and included pseudo-medical descriptions that made even Sparky queasy.

"This is rather disturbing," Sparky said solemnly. "I'm not sure my mother was aware of what he had in mind for her. I now see why he was so upset with my interference."

"Actually, there is a bright side to this," Erasmus mused aloud, rubbing his chin in thought. "Since the only information the Yard has on Mr. Abusir are these letters and notes, it shows no living relatives in his family tree, at least based on the small skulls next to these initial family names. Since your mother is mentioned as a future bride, the Yard will send all of his effects to her, including the bars of gold the artists received from him for the plating and this replica statue. It is the least we could do."

Sparky eyes welled up, and she stepped toward Erasmus with outstretched arms for an instinctive hug, but she stopped short, suddenly realizing her unvarnished show of appreciation. Her eyes looked up to see his smiling face. Erasmus took her right hand, retreated the tiniest but most precise distance, bent low, and kissed it. "Glad to be of service," he added.

Sparky did her best to curtsy for the Chief Inspector and looked away to hide an oncoming blush. To Erasmus, it was an interesting sight, this accomplished woman in work clothes, including britches, splattered with blood drops, attempting this most feminine of gestures. He continued to hold her hand a bit longer than he had intended, while he looked into her eyes, wishing there was an additional reason to linger in conversation.

"Chief Inspector, Sir!" a voice interrupted. "We are ready to go here. May we corroborate our accounts?"

While holding his gaze with Sparky, Erasmus answered. "Of course, my good man, of course." Still holding her hand delicately, Erasmus said in a gentle voice, "You have my card. Do not ever hesitate to contact me for any reason. It has been a pleasure."

Sparky turned to leave, but there was an atypical hesitation in her step. About halfway to the exit, she turned to look back, and caught a glimpse of the Chief Inspector, bowler in hand, still standing guard over the scene with the satchel, body, and pool of blood.

For Erasmus, the next few hours were a haze of activities associated with Scotland Yard: transporting Mr. Abusir's body to the morgue; creating detailed notes regarding the attack by Mr. Abusir upon Dr. McTrowell and Dr. McTrowell's harrowing self-defense; organizing a cleaning team to address the bloodied floor and askew sarcophagus at the Egyptian Court; sending a constable to visit the artists at the Blue Cat to retrieve the unused gold bars; and checking on the health of the injured workman.

As the sun was setting, Erasmus found himself at Ye Olde Cheshire Cheese with both William and Constable Higgins, sitting at a table nestled in the back. "Is it really Friday?" he asked, knowing the answer.

Zachary answered in an officious and slightly mocking tone, "Friday the 23rd of May, 1851, to be exact." And raising his pint, "Time has come for the work-week to end." They all joined him in a toast.

But after the glasses were safely back on the tabletop, William and Zachary looked at Erasmus knowingly. Erasmus, tipped his head slightly, and looked back at them. "What is all this about?"

"Well, you have spent a major part of the week with this Dr. McTrowell," William said, "and we have heard you have been quite the gentleman, kissing hands and all. Word travels fast at the Yard. What do you have to say for yourself?"

"The doctor had been through quite an ordeal. I *was* being the gentleman, I suppose."

William and Zachary looked at each other and each gave a single chuckle. William echoed, "I suppose. I suppose."

"Judge me if you wish. I had hoped to cross paths with her again. Perhaps she will see fit to visit London another time."

Zachary chimed in, "Well, sir, if that happens, I hope it will be a less hazardous event to those around you. And may I add, welcome to your first week as Chief Inspector."

They raised their glasses again, and, while sipping, Erasmus considered that he might have missed an opportunity to perhaps see Sparky off on her flight, or contact her to resolve some last detail of shipping Mr. Abusir's effects. He thought to himself, *"There is a tide in the affairs of men, and we must take the current when it serves or lose our ventures."*

THREE PIECES OF PAPER

BY DR. KATHERINE L. MORSE

Sparky was feeling terribly dazed as she stumbled out of the Crystal Palace and made her way to Oxford Street. She had saved a man's life today. She had nearly died today. She had avenged the death of her dear friend today. She had killed her mother's fiancé today. Today she had had an encounter with a man with the potential to turn her life upside down. She was startled by a dark brown hand gently grasping her arm as she trudged along the street. Virat. As soon as she looked up at him, he released her arm and motioned toward Lord Ashleigh's carriage that was waiting at the curb. She hadn't even noticed it in her self-absorbed reverie. He held the door for her without so much as flinching at her blood-spattered work clothes. And then, as if there were no limit to the surprises today had to offer, he spoke!

"Where shall I take you, Madam?"

She gaped with an open mouth for a moment. More than anything, she wanted to get cleaned up and change her clothes, but she wasn't sure she had the strength to deal with Mrs. McCreary. *"Oh, to hell with the old bat! It's not like I'm ever going to stay there again,"* she retorted to herself. "Virat, please take me to Mrs. McCreary's boarding house. Thank you."

He closed the door without another word and drove her straight there, stopping at the curb directly in front of the boarding house. Of course, when he opened the door for her, Mrs. McCreary was standing at the top of the landing, and the look on her face was like none that Sparky had ever seen. Her eyes were swinging back and forth between McTrowell's blood-stained work clothes, the "strange" brown coachman, and the obviously expensive carriage. She was huffing and puffing, her corpulent face was scarlet, and her head looked like it might actually explode.

Sparky turned to Virat and said loudly enough that she was sure Mrs. McCreary would hear, "Please thank Lord Ashleigh for his immeasurable assistance. I will endeavor to pay him a visit before I depart for Paris and the Bavarian Airship Regatta." Virat nodded slightly, mounted the carriage, and drove off.

Sparky summoned the last of her strength and strode up the stairs, the heels of her knee-high work boots ringing with each step. She turned slightly sideways to squeeze by Mrs. McCreary who was still huffing in astonishment, but was blessedly struck dumb, at least for the moment. When she got to her room, she slid one of her trunks in front of the door to ensure some privacy and put some water on to boil for tea. She stripped off the bloody clothes, turned them inside out, and rolled them up. There was not time to deal with them now. By the time she'd washed up, had some tea, and put on her traveling clothes, her head had cleared somewhat. She methodically repacked all her trunks.

She pulled some paper from her flight surgeon's bag and the enameled pen from the inside pocket of her duster. Before she could put pen to paper, she remembered that she had bought the pen in Toulouse when she had visited with Jean-Michel and Sandrine just after the joyous birth of their second child. And she started crying again. This was no good! She would have to pull herself together to write a note to Sandrine. She had to dry her eyes three more times before she made it through the simple note. She expressed her deepest condolences, but she couldn't bring herself to admit to Sandrine that Jean-Michel had died for the mistake of being her friend. She closed by telling Sandrine that Jean-Michel's last words had been of his love for her.

She sealed the letter and pulled out another sheet of paper. On it she wrote a bank transfer for the paymaster at Western & Transatlantic, who also served as the banker for the highly transient staff of the Airship Lines. It was a draft for 1,000 francs to Sandrine Petit of Toulouse, France. She signed it with a flourish that didn't match her mood. Nothing would mend Sandrine's heart except time, but McTrowell could ensure that she didn't struggle to support their children until that time had passed. She folded the draft in quarters and placed it on top of the letter to Sandrine.

Finally, she took a third sheet of paper upon which she wrote the contents of a telegram in block letters.

MOTHER STOP CHIEF INSPECTOR OF SCOTLAND YARD REPORTS MR ABUSIR KILLED IN ACCIDENT AT GREAT EXHIBITION STOP SCOTLAND YARD FORWARDING HIS BELONGINGS TO YOU STOP LEAVING FOR PARIS STOP WILL WRITE WHEN I ARRIVE STOP LOVE C STOP

She had tried to formulate a sentence that could explain to her mother that it hadn't been an accident, that Abusir had died by her own hand. But then she would have had to explain that he had tried to kill her…twice, and had almost succeeded twice. And then there was the whole matter of the poisoned miners to force her mother into marriage and the insane criminal enterprise with the statue. The brevity of a telegram might have been an act of cowardice, but she was all out of bravery. She folded the paper in half and wrote on the back, "Elizabeth Llewellyn, Sansome Street, San Francisco, California, United States of America."

She tucked all three pieces of paper into her flight surgeon's bag, rolled the trunk away from the door and into line with the others, put on her leather duster, aviator's cap, goggles and four-button red flight gloves, and stepped smartly out the door. As she expected, Mrs. McCreary was stationed at the bottom of the stairs, her arms crossed ferociously over her formidable bosom, and her feet planted uncharacteristically far apart. There was clearly not going to be any sliding by her this time. Unfortunately, there was also no divining what she thought of the vision of Dr. Sparky McTrowell swooping down the stairs in full flight gear.

"Miss Llewellyn, this is absolutely the end of sanity! I can no longer countenance your outrageous behavior in this respectable establishment!"

McTrowell stopped two steps from the bottom so she towered over Mrs. McCreary. She swept the leather duster back with her free left hand, planting her scarlet-encased fist on her hip. "My name is Dr. Czarina Llewellyn McTrowell. I am a decorated pilot and the chief flight surgeon of Western & Transatlantic Airship Lines. I am an internationally famed inventor and today I have used one of my inventions to take a man's life before he could take mine." She waited a moment for her words to sink in. "And while we are on the subject of things you can't countenance, I should think you would include color and fun. Buy a bright green dress. Go to the theater. Drink too much in the company of a man whose intentions may not be entirely proper. Just do not die in this dreadful, cheap, gray mausoleum without enjoying a moment of the pleasure you have earned for yourself."

Mrs. McCreary's arms dropped to her sides and her mouth opened and closed, giving her the appearance of a fish dying on the deck of a ship.

"By the way, those who fear me, among whom I imagine you now number yourself, call me Sparky. A carter will come for my trunks. In the strongest possible terms, I advise against meddling with them." She reached out with open palm of her gloved hand and bodily moved Mrs. McCreary out of her path. She was out the door and down the street without a glance back. Once she was out of sight of the boarding house, she spread her arms and spun around, the tails of the leather duster rising around her like a dust devil. The boarding house had been like a weight on her shoulders, and she was glad to be rid of it.

She walked all the way to the airship port for the invigorating exercise of it. As fortune would have it, she spotted the same air stevedore who had carted her trunks to Mrs. McCreary's. Had it really only been three days earlier? He smiled as she approached, possibly in memory of her as a story told to his mates or the generous tip. No matter. He tipped his cap slightly. "Good day, Ma'am. Pleasure to see you again."

"Good day. Do you remember the boarding house to which you carted my trunks?" To make her point, she produced another florin from her duster.

"Surely, Ma'am." She handed him the florin that disappeared into his pocket so quickly she wondered if he had previously made his living as a fingersmith.

"Please retrieve them and deliver them to the Burke & Hare."

"Right away, Ma'am." She didn't see him shaking his head in bemusement as she walked away toward the business office of Western & Transatlantic.

It was quieter in Littleton's office than it had been the last time she'd been there. "Hello, Dr. McTrowell."

"Hello, Mr. Littleton. Has the casket of Dr. Jean-Michel Petit arrived from Westminster Hospital?"

"Just an hour ago."

She handed him the sealed letter. "Please see that this letter accompanies the casket and charge the freight fee to my account."

"It is going to be quite expensive."

She just glared at him. Littleton was an efficient manager, but had never acquired the sense not to argue with her when she was in a mood. He mumbled, "Done," and went back to his ledgers and schedules.

She was beginning to run out of words for the day. When she arrived at the paymaster's window, she didn't even greet him before sliding the bank draft under the grating. "Dr. Jean-Michel Petit's casket will be departing for the continent tomorrow morning aboard the Lewis & Clark. Please see to it that the funds are in the Lewis & Clark's safe when it departs."

The paymaster unfolded the draft and gasped. "Dr. McTrowell, this is a large sum of money." She fixed him with an even more withering glance than she had given Littleton. "Yes, Ma'am."

Her final stop was the telegraph office. Fortunately, the telegraph operator was one of those taciturn, all-business sorts of fellows, so he didn't ask any questions when she handed him the third piece of paper. But he did cock a quizzical eyebrow at her after reading the contents twice to make sure he had understood it.

Business concluded, Sparky walked across the yard to a tall, square, open tower with a large '3' painted on the side. It was really just a half-encased stairwell several stories tall. A workman with a tool belt exited the bottom of the stairs just as she arrived. An airship was tethered to the top of the tower at a height of about four stories. She started climbing, watching more of London reveal itself at each turning of the flights of stairs. When she reached the top of the stairs, she stopped and gazed down on the Crystal Palace. She wondered if Chief Inspector Drake was still there cleaning up the day's monstrous mess. She wondered if she would ever see him again. She wondered what would happen if she did. With a small smile that barely curled up the corners of her mouth, she turned to enter the airship. Over the door was an engraved, arched sign, **Burke & Hare**.

The Bavarian Airship Regatta

A SERIOUS KNOCK

BY MR. DAVID L. DRAKE

"You like?"

Scotland Yard's Chief Inspector Erasmus Drake answered uncharacteristically with his mouth half full. "I like!"

The new French bakery had opened near Trafalgar Square, about midpoint in Erasmus' morning walk from his apartment above Ye Olde Cheshire Cheese to 4 Whitehall Place. Erasmus was trying one of their freshly baked croissants after the proprietor, Jacques, had dunked one end into an open jar of strawberry jam. Erasmus had only stopped by to see the new store and possibly get something reasonably small to eat on his commute. Instead, Jacques has started him on tasting the pain au chocolat, followed by a cream puff, and then half an almond horn. Erasmus liked them all, but politely informed Jacques that they were a bit too sweet for his English palette. The croissant was the baker's response, despite the added jam.

Erasmus held up two fingers and redundantly requested *"deux"* verbally. Jacques smiled. "No French needed. My English iz good, Chief Inspector Drake."

"Oh, you recognize me?" Erasmus asked, a bit surprised.

"But of course! You are in zee paper twice zees week! A very good illustration!" Jacque pressed a paper bag with the croissants inside into Erasmus' hands. "New store! Samples of our goods for you. Enjoy them, *s'il vous plait.*"

Erasmus' initial response was to force some payment on him, but Jacques looked so happy to have him there. A mother and her child had been peeking in the window and finally got up the courage to enter the newly-opened shop. The bell over the door gave a cheerful ring as they entered. Erasmus finished thanking Jacques, turned, and gave the young mother a nod combined with bringing his bowler halfway up to his head and tipping it from there. He eased the bowler back to its rightful place on his head as he exited the bakery.

Tock...tock...tock. Erasmus' cane made its distinctive sound on the sidewalk. Erasmus took in the scenes of early morning London while he mentally listed the minutia he needed to address at work.

Mondays always had a feeling of new beginnings and new challenges, particularly at the Yard.

Erasmus entered the rear door on Great Scotland Yard; the office had an atypically calm atmosphere. He settled into his office chair, pulled out his latest notes to see if there were any additional details that he had forgotten to include, filled his pen with ink, and started the process of verification.

Erasmus' door opened just far enough to allow Superintendent Bartholomew Horner to jut his head through. "Minute of your time?"

Erasmus motioned him in. "Good morning, Superintendent. How can I assist you?"

Bartholomew strode in with a rolled-up broadsheet in his hand. He placed it on Erasmus' desk and unfurled it, anchoring it to the desk at top and bottom with his burly hands. "Seen these around?" Bartholomew asked.

"Yes, I have, but I haven't had time this week to read it in detail. I heard about the airship regatta, but I hadn't noticed the particulars." This was not true. Dr. Sparky McTrowell mentioned the regatta, and Erasmus had looked over the broadsheets posted around London many times over the intervening weekend.

"I need to place a member of the Yard on the Burke & Hare. The airship is assuming the role of Britain's international participant in the regatta. Due to the nature of the voyage, Her Majesty requested that we provide guardianship of the crew and passengers. Normally I would ask for volunteers, but I thought you might want a bit of a breather from last week's excitement. Didn't you get to meet this doctor who's piloting the craft? What was he like?"

Erasmus knew he was being played. Bartholomew read over investigation notes with enthusiasm, and he had had access to Drake's notes all weekend. Erasmus knew that Bartholomew was aware that Dr. McTrowell was a woman. Erasmus also knew that this was a bit of a test, to see if he would bite at the chance to join the voyage. But all of that didn't really matter, now did it? Getting a chance to be on that airship would just fulfill the aspiration he had toyed with all weekend.

"Interesting offer, I do say. I see by the date on the poster that it sails today. I would have to get a number of personal and occupational things in order. Do you have word on when it launches?"

"Erasmus, what about the doctor?"

"Oh, yes, yes. Dr. McTrowell turns out to be a woman. Hails from the Americas. Known for a number of things, including inventing. She was in the process of displaying a contraption at the Great Exhibit when she was attacked. Upstanding character, she is. That said, do we know the launch time? Can I still board?"

"There will be a dinner on the Burke & Hare itself tonight, seven o'clock, just after launch. Can I count on you to shoulder this?"

"You can. I will put my things in order straightaway," Erasmus replied, employing his best straight face.

"One more thing," Bartholomew added, "I want you to carry arms. I know you have a revolver. Take it. I also want you to have a sword from the armory. Some of it is for show, I know. But you can always count on a sword to let others know who's in charge."

It took an entire hour for Erasmus to get out of Scotland Yard. He kept the broadsheet, procured a saber from the armory, and arranged to have Sergeant Tate Parseval take over command of his cases for the duration of his absence. The Sergeant had his flaws, but he was a good administrator.

Upon leaving, Erasmus turned the corner to head back to his apartment, when he saw Abigail Schopenhauer in the shadows. She was wrapped, as usual, in a shawl that covered her shoulders and head, leaving her grandmotherly face peeking out. She was "looking" in Erasmus' direction with her cataract-filled eyes and smiling to the extent that it made her entire face rounder than usual. As Erasmus approached, she started in with, "I was right, wasn't I? Eh? The artist's den. That's where you had to look." Her voice was cheerful but raspy, with a bit of kindness coming through.

"You were spot on, my dear. Spot on."

As he got close, she took his arm. Her smile didn't lessen a bit. She queried, "Anything new for me?"

"Hmm. Word at the Yard is that the cold weather in the north means less wheat coming into the mills. Expect the price of bread to go up."

"Thank you, thank you. Are you off to travel or a formal ball? Oh, don't look at me like that. You don't usually have a sword at your side. You're off to play bodyguard, I bet."

Erasmus realized that she was better at detective work than some of his own officers. He replied, "Why, yes. I have been called to duty, of a sort. I will not be around for a few weeks."

Abigail's smile lessened. She didn't like the idea of Erasmus playing hero somewhere. Good way to end up as a statue in a London park. *"No use being gloomy,"* she thought. "Well, safe travels, then!"

Normally Abigail had some dire warning that she passed along. Odd that she didn't this time. Perhaps it was because of his travel, and not wanting to worry him. The truth was that she was very concerned about the growing number of cholera victims in the city and that something needed to be done soon. No one knew what was causing the sickness, and since it struck the poor the most, it didn't get as much notice as it should.

As usual, they parted and Erasmus made good speed back to his apartment. Within two hours, he had his trunk packed, and informed James Crocker, the proprietor of Ye Olde Cheshire Cheese, that he would be away for the duration of the regatta. James agreed to let Erasmus' laundry service know about his absence and forward his mail to him. Erasmus scribbled a few quick missives to friends, including William, about his journey, and provided them to James for posting.

Erasmus hired a carriage to transport himself and his trunk to the London Airship Port. The short ride was uneventful for the most part, but Erasmus had time to think about the fact that it had been a long time since he had been outside of London. It had played a safe haven for him, and the idea of leaving was one of exiting a protective bubble. But that stirred a memory of a long ago past. He shook it off, and prepared himself to look forward to the things to come.

At the Airship Port, Erasmus procured his ticket with a few simple words describing Scotland Yard's request for him to join the crew. He released his trunk to the porters for storage in his cabin on the Burke & Hare and lingered a bit in the station, looking at the posted broadsheets and pamphlets for visiting foreign lands. He then strode across the flight yard to tower number three that tethered the airship, and climbed the stairs. He stopped at the top and took a minute to look back at London. It was a grand view from that height. And this was the city where he had made his mark. The sun was just setting, an orange glow adding a little extra warmth to the city of gray.

Erasmus took an extra look at his ticket, which directed him to cabin number seven. Once inside the airship's gondola, it was clear that the craft was made for speed more than comfort. The passageways were compact, with handholds for when the airship was used in an athletic fashion. The decor was of oiled teak, brass fixtures, and nautical rope.

There were a few other people on board that Erasmus saw on his way to his cabin. Most were dressed in the attire of the crew, making prelaunch examinations of all of the various mechanical systems on board. About halfway down the main central corridor, Erasmus found his cabin door, the knob of which was an exaggerated oval for easy turning, even if one's hands were slick with oil. He entered and found a cozy room on the port side, his trunk secured to the wall away from the bed with a long leather belt. On the bed was an invitation for the evening's meal. It indicated that the dinner would be formal. Erasmus opened his trunk to remove his formal dinner waistcoat and jacket. A serious knock on his door interrupted his progress.

Opening the door, Erasmus was met by a well-dressed man in a formal, black, British, military uniform. He stood with an air that suggested he was trying to look informal, but it still looked like he was at attention. His cap was trapped firmly between his hand and elbow, and he was looking straight at Erasmus, waiting for him to start the conversation. So Erasmus did.

"Good evening. I am Chief Inspector Erasmus Drake of Scotland Yard. How may I be of service?"

"Pardon my bluntness. Are you alone?"

"Why, yes. Would you like to talk in my cabin?" Erasmus offered, with a small wave of his hand.

111

"Thank you, yes." The military man took two steps forward, turned quickly, shut and bolted the door, and then turned back as quickly. Snapping a salute, the man rattled off, "Sergeant J.B. Fox of the Her Majesty's Aerial Marines. I must inform you that your mission here is more extensive than you have been told."

"My instructions were to provide guardianship of the crew and passengers. I volunteered to take on this responsibility. Are you sure you have the right man?"

"Chief Inspector, Her Majesty has reason to believe that marauders using fast airships as attack vehicles have a home base somewhere near Vaduz, one of the waypoints in the regatta. A request was made for support from Her Majesty's Aerial Marines, as well as support from Scotland Yard, to investigate the validity of this intelligence, locate the marauders base, if possible, and protect the crew and passengers of the Burke & Hare. Her Majesty has relayed to Her Aerial Marines that cooperation between the nations of Europe is critical at this point in time, and any intelligence we can gather will be used in securing international relationships. I was requested by name by my superiors for this mission. You were also requested by name by Superintendent Horner. We were told that you would not know the full extent of the mission upon arrival, and that you may even have been duped into believing that you volunteered for the mission. Again, I assure you, you were chosen. Scotland Yard gave your name to us last week for this mission. My first responsibility was to brief you on this."

This was more than Erasmus had expected. But what was initially a concern that he was leaving London to go gallivanting around, was now a real opportunity to help the British Empire. *"So, full steam ahead,"* he thought. He bent over, grabbed his best ascot out of his trunk, held it up for mock inspection, and said, "You keep saying 'marauders,' but I keep hearing 'pirates'! I am in. Let us get to this formal dinner, and get the hunt underway."

AU REVOIR, LONDON

BY DR. KATHERINE L. MORSE

McTrowell wiped her hands on a rag and stuffed it in the pocket of her work apron. Her final checks and preparations for the crossing to Paris were complete. She climbed the ladder out of the mechanical compartment up into the bridge and closed the hatch in the floor. The sun was still high in the sky despite the late afternoon hour. She loved being far north as midsummer approached. It gave one the sense that the endless day had endless possibilities, and today was definitely one of those days. She would launch the Burke & Hare just before sunset so the passengers could enjoy the sight of the London gaslights coming on as they sailed southeast toward Brighton. Once they were underway, she would turn command over to her first officer and join Wallace's table for the launch dinner. These dinners were usually dreadfully painful affairs dominated by puffery and bloviating, but there was no getting out of them, and occasionally someone interesting was seated at the table. She scanned the London skyline one last time before heading back to her cabin to clean up and change into dinner attire.

One of the advantages of being the captain on a racing airship like the Burke & Hare was having a proper cabin with a porthole. The rest of the crew was stuck in the sunless gloom of the second deck, but Sparky got the last second-class cabin, number 14, at the back of the ship nearest the engine room. It could be a little loud, but she sometimes found the hum relaxing when she actually got a chance to sleep. Although she doubted there would much of that on this trip once they left Paris.

Knowing that Wallace would wear something ostentatious in eye-assaulting colors, she selected a starkly elegant ensemble in black and cranberry. The John Bull topper was a decidedly masculine and middle-class touch that, no doubt, would get Wallace's attention, but he wouldn't be in a position to comment during dinner. The cranberry cockade picked up the color of her double-breasted velvet jacket. She laced up her black ankle boots snugly, did the best she could to assess her appearance in a hand-held mirror, and headed back to the bridge.

The passengers were on board and getting settled. She heard voices and the bumping of luggage through the walls of the cabins. There was an odd passenger standing in the passage outside cabin seven, a sergeant of Her Majesty's Aerial Marines. The man looked as if he'd been born at attention. She squeezed past him, strode past the remaining second-class cabins, and cast only a glance at the doors of the two first-class cabins opposite each other at the head of the passage before entering the main hall. The galley crew was busily putting the finishing touches on the table settings for dinner. She exchanged nods with the chief steward, Luis-Miguel Sevilla. The fact that Wallace had pulled Sevilla off the Toulouse-Madrid route meant he was pulling out all the stops to make this event perfectly memorable for the select few passengers who had paid the exorbitant price to be on the Burke & Hare during the regatta. The crew would be stripped back to the bare minimum during the regatta and the few remaining would have to be the very best to keep such rarefied customers happy. Sevilla was just the man for the job.

She crossed the main hall and opened the shiny brass door to the bridge. The first officer, Ivan Krasnayarubashka, was already making prelaunch preparations. She had to hand it to Wallace; he had really gone all out to assemble an international crew for the event. She was sure his accounts of the regatta would include copious mention of the uniquely international reach of Western & Transatlantic. Truly the man never missed an opportunity for self-promotion. She snapped out of her reverie to check the pressure gauges. The engine would be up to full power right on time for the launch. The airship port crew was assembling below tower number three to release the tethers. The sun was making its way toward the western horizon. She had the same thought she always had when she watched the sun set in the west, *"When all else fails, the setting sun will lead me home."* She shook her head to clear out the nostalgia and addressed the first officer.

"Gospodin Krasnayarubashka, are you looking forward to the regatta?"

"Da, Gospozha Doctor Lyotcheeka McTrowell. Please to not inform Gospodin Vallace, but dis is my last trip for Vestern & Transatlantic. I am thinking to start, how you say, фабрика, for airship parts in Suzdal."

"Factory. You're a very good pilot. Won't you miss flying?"

"Mozhet buite, but the money vill be much more."

"Yes, you have a point there. I think it's time to go." She signaled through the front window to the port crew to cast off the tether lines. She rang the bell for the engine crew to reel in the aft line while Krasnayarubashka cranked in the fore line. She set the engine to one quarter speed and set a course for Brighton.

"Mr. Krasnayarubashka, keep the engine at one quarter until we clear London and then go to half speed. If I am detained by our glorious leader, go to full speed once we reach the English Channel."

"Aye, aye, empress of the air." She usually tried to keep her actual given name to herself. She wondered if he knew or if he were just being humorously deferential.

She pushed open the bridge door to the main hall and scanned the passengers seated for dinner. When her eyes settled on Wallace's table, she nearly tripped over her own feet in surprise. Chief Inspector Drake was sitting right next to Wallace! He was looking straight at her as if he had been expecting her. She took a deep breath to regain her composure and walked directly toward the table, hoping that her face did not give away her mixed emotions: surprise, delight, trepidation. Drake was up and out of his chair before Wallace. Typical that he would have better manners than Wallace, but Wallace spoke first. Or rather, bellowed.

"If it isn't the illustrious Dr. McTrowell?" As if it were some kind of surprise to discover that she was piloting the Burke & Hare for this historic event! The man had an infinite supply of cheek. "If I'm to believe what they print in The Times, and of course I don't always, you're acquainted with Chief Inspector Drake." He made an oversize, sweeping gesture toward Drake. Like herself and unlike Wallace who, as she had predicted, was dressed garishly, Drake was dressed elegantly and appropriately in black. He pulled out the chair to his right for her. Before she could take the seat, he took her hand and kissed it…again. But this kiss was more intimate and lingering than the last. She suspected that he had been preparing for this moment mentally. She glanced around to see if anyone else noticed, but for once she was grateful for Wallace's personal circus act. Everyone else had their eyes on Wallace, so they missed the intimate moment and the half wink from Drake as he reluctantly released her hand. He deftly slid the chair under her as she swept up her long black skirt to sit down. Wallace plopped his considerable bulk into his beleaguered chair.

Wallace continued, "Chief Inspector Drake is here by special request of Her Majesty."

"I am flattered by such an idea, but I volunteered to participate to observe on behalf of Her Majesty's interests," Drake corrected. His response struck Sparky as uncharacteristically vague and she wondered if there were more to the story. And then she realized that he had admitted that he had volunteered. He knew she was going to be piloting the Burke & Hare; she'd told him. She fixed him with a direct, quizzical look, and she could have sworn that he turned the slightest bit pink before breaking eye contact.

She glanced around the table to ease the tension of the situation. The coveted seat to the left of Wallace was still empty. Surely Wallace hadn't left this seat unassigned! She scanned the rest of the room to see if any guest was still standing. And that's when she got the second big surprise of the evening. The door from the passage to the main hall was opened by Virat who held the door for Jonathan Lord Ashleigh to enter the room after him. As usual, Ashleigh was dressed colorfully, and yet not garishly like Wallace. Perhaps she should suggest that he give lessons in men's fashion to Wallace. She stifled an uncharitable giggle. She was just opening her mouth to greet her friend when he winked at her and gave an imperceptible shake of his head. *"Ah yes, the Machiavellian machinations of Lord Ashleigh. This should be good fun,"* she mused to herself.

Lord Ashleigh strode up to Wallace smartly and shook his hand vigorously. Wallace replied, "Lord Ashleigh, I was beginning to think you wouldn't make it." Yet more Wallace circus. She was quite certain without checking that Ashleigh had been installed in cabin two opposite Wallace in cabin one, and that Sevilla had been given strict orders to notify Wallace the very instant Ashleigh was settled. Perhaps Ashleigh was having his own little bit of theater, making an entrance after everyone else was seated. *"Two can play at that game,"* she thought. Virat held Ashleigh's chair for him and then evaporated to a table in the far corner of the room.

The crew poured champagne for everyone at Wallace's table. Wallace lifted his glass, "To victory in the regatta and success in other ventures." Everyone raised their glasses and drank.

Feeling like having a bit of fun, McTrowell asked, "What other ventures, pray tell?"

"I suppose it's safe to tell you, but I must swear Chief Inspector Drake to secrecy as a man of honor."

"Of course. I have no personal interest in business ventures…so long as they are legal," Drake responded. Wallace roared with laughter as if the Chief Inspector had been joking.

"Lord Ashleigh and I are building a new airship port in his home town of Talkad."

"My older half-brother, Vijay Deva, is the current ruling Maharaja of Talkad. Although I have no official power, I am always working for the benefit of my people. Airship travel is the road to prosperity and I wish to open that road for my people. If Talkad has an airship port before the neighboring principalities, my people will benefit with jobs at the port and in commerce, and the tariffs will enrich my half-brother's exchequer." Sparky smiled. Nowhere in his explanation had he mentioned this enterprise benefiting him directly, although she was sure it would in some way. The generosity of her new friend renewed her faith in humanity. When her attention returned to the conversation, Wallace and Ashleigh had dived into the details of the venture, including the number of towers they would build and how the new roads to the port would need to be paved to support the transport of cargo. The table's occupants were saved from sure boredom by the arrival of the soup course.

Sparky turned her attention to the only other two occupants of the table who seemed a bit out of place. Judging by the similarity of their faces, they were a father and teenage son. Their clothes were of good quality, but all looked absolutely new. And the wearers didn't look particularly comfortable wearing them. They had a slightly awestruck air about them. What were they doing at Wallace's table on such an occasion?

"Welcome aboard the Burke & Hare. Will you be accompanying us during the regatta?" she ventured.

"Um, yes. My name is Aldrich Fremont and this is my son, Jake."

"Pleased to make your acquaintance. Are you racing aficionados?"

"Racing what?" the elder Fremont asked.

"Racing enthusiasts?" Sparky tried again.

"Um, no. This is our first time on an airship," young Jake replied shyly.

"Your first time on an airship and you're participating in an international regatta? Well, that is certainly bold!" Sparky hoped her reply didn't sound as enthusiastically fake to them as it did to her.

"Well, I inherited a large old warehouse and dock on the Tyne from my father and his father before him," Aldrich explained. "They're getting ready to expand the shipyards and they paid me a pretty penny for that rundown bit of Tyneside. No more patching and scraping by for us! Jake and I are having a bit of adventure before he goes off to university." Jake didn't look any too excited about the prospect of advanced schooling. He looked more like the sort of lad whose interests ran to pretty girls and brown ales.

As little as Sparky had in common with them, it provided the opportunity for her to give them an education in airships and racing. They looked genuinely interested and altogether grateful for being rescued from the chore of making interesting conversation themselves. It also kept her from having to listen to Wallace and having to make much effort to avoid any eye contact with Ashleigh, potentially giving away the fact that they knew each other. Drake didn't say a word throughout the meal, only occasionally offering an affirmative sound and nod, but every time she turned to look at him, he met her gaze.

The crew was clearing away the after-dinner port when Wallace stood up without preface and said to Ashleigh, "Shall we go to my cabin to discuss particulars?" And he walked out.

Once again displaying more refined manners, Lord Ashleigh executed a slight bow to the other occupants of the table and said, "Good evening. I look forward to our upcoming adventure." One side of his mouth quirked up in a sly, half smile when he looked directly at Sparky, and his eyes twinkled. He sailed gracefully out of the room.

Aldrich Fremont stood up as well, followed awkwardly by Jake. "I think we'll turn in. Good night."

No sooner had the Fremonts departed than Virat materialized behind Drake and McTrowell. As helpful as the man was, it was unnerving the way he came and went like one of those legendary Japanese ninjas. He produced two identical pieces of Lord Ashleigh's engraved stationery folded crisply in half, one addressed to each of them. They opened them simultaneously. Each one had an identical, one-line request,

Please meet me in my cabin. - JLA

A PRETTY FACE

BY MR. DAVID L. DRAKE

Erasmus looked up from his note and glanced at Sparky's identical note. "May I accompany you to Lord Ashleigh's cabin?" he asked Dr. McTrowell with a slight smile.

"I'd be delighted," Sparky replied.

Erasmus retrieved his cane from the nearby wall where he had left it, and putting a well-mannered crook in his left arm, offered it to Sparky. She slid her right hand in, and they proceeded toward the main passageway, walking a bit slower than they would normally on their own, lingering in the moment.

Once inside the passageway, the 14 doors within the hall faced them. *"But which is Lord Ashleigh's?"* Erasmus wondered. Two steps in and Reginald Wallace's booming voice could be heard emanating from cabin one. He was clearly doing business with Lord Ashleigh by dominating the conversation. Erasmus didn't understand how that worked, precisely, but it seemed to be a universal trait of those in command of industrial endeavors. One more step and Virat opened the door to cabin two in a crisp, but inviting, manner. With a small sweep of his hand, he offered up two cushioned chairs visible from the doorway, both draped in dark green fabric. As they entered the cabin, it became apparent the care Virat had taken to transform the teak and brass cabin into a sitting room worthy of Lord Ashleigh. Virat had converted the day bed into a magnificent couch, decorated with green, mustard and burgundy striped pillows, and the cover was a

119

shiny blue overlay that looked silky and luxurious, complete with braided gold-yellow fringe tassels on its outer edge. Both Sparky and Erasmus raised their eyebrows at the sight. A door in the room apparently led to Lord Ashleigh's private chamber.

They settled into the offered chairs; Erasmus' cane laid once again against the nearby wall. Virat appeared with a steaming silver pot, hovering it over a tea set on the small table between the chairs. The gesture was both an offer and a question. Virat looked first at Sparky, who simply nodded yes. A decisive pour and he filled her cup with the light brown liquid, steamy and creamy. She recognized it as the same formulation of chai she had had before. Virat looked at Erasmus, and he also nodded in approval. Virat dispensed another cup without a word. Virat disappeared into the adjoining room; the door clicking quietly shut.

Sparky and Erasmus lifted their cups and politely raised them to each other before taking sips. Sparky broke the silence. "Are you familiar with Indian chai? It was new to me just a few days ago."

"Actually, no. But I hated the thought of you sitting here sipping it alone. It is a potent brew with these infused spices. I could smell them on the first pour." He was desperately trying not to ask her why Lord Ashleigh might have invited him here, not wanting to look curious or uninformed. Perhaps a different line of conversation would help in getting there. "Have you been working with Mr. Wallace for a long time? He seems quite the character!"

"A number of years. But to be honest, he talked so much about himself throughout dinner, I'm sure he hopes that everyone aboard is discussing him. May I suggest we talk about something else? I'm intrigued by your cane. You obviously don't need it to aid in walking. Does it have sentimental value?"

Erasmus had spent his life giving away very little information about himself, that he felt caught between telling her everything or nothing at all. How did she do that? "Actually, it is just an added bit of protection. I just do not feel fully safe empty-handed. So the cane is something to have in my hands when trouble arises. I hope that is not too ungentlemanly." He looked for a negative reaction that never came, so he continued. "I often deal with the rougher side of society. Having a hand up is important."

"I had assumed as much," she continued in her gentle interrogation. "But it's a bit ornate. I had expected a story along the lines of a present or heirloom."

Erasmus thought that he might as well finally tell this tale. He took a deep breath, and got out two words, "Well, I..."

The cabin door sprang open and Lord Ashleigh glided in. "I'm terribly sorry to have kept you waiting. I'm so pleased to see that you both accepted my invitation." He moved gracefully to the couch and sat gently on it. Just as he sat down, Virat appeared from the other room, poured his master a cup of chai, and disappeared again into the other room. Lord Ashleigh continued, "I have been looking forward to this all week."

Erasmus welcomed the interruption. After years of keeping his past behind him, he couldn't imagine how this young lady from the Americas had him almost blurt it out with not much more than a simple query. Erasmus thought momentarily how a pretty face had come close to loosening his tongue.

BEST LAID PLANS

BY DR. KATHERINE L. MORSE

"And why is that?" McTrowell asked Ashleigh, failing to notice the look of mixed discomfort and relief on Drake's face.

"I always enjoy the company of my dear friend, Dr. McTrowell, and I missed seeing her before her departure from London."

"For which I apologize. Preparing the Burke & Hare for the regatta took considerably more effort than I anticipated," she explained.

"And it was undoubtedly less unnerving than dealing with people after the trials of the preceding week."

"Insightful of you, as always, Lord Ashleigh." She raised her teacup to him.

Lord Ashleigh beamed brightly and turned his attention to Chief Inspector Drake who had regained his composure. "I have been most anxious to make the acquaintance of the illustrious Chief Inspector Erasmus Drake. Each day I look forward to the delivery of the *Times* in anticipation of another story of your derring-do, protecting the citizens of London from nefarious miscreants." Drake fidgeted very slightly in the manner of good men uncomfortable with compliments about their value. "And I am forever in your debt for your part in protecting the life of my dear friend, Dr. McTrowell." The expression on Drake's face turned somber with this last utterance, reflecting his recognition of the fact that Sparky's life had been in clear and terrible danger. He brightened back up right away, and a broad smile turned up the corners of his moustache. Ashleigh continued, "Of course, I'm very excited about the regatta. I believe we will all have an excellent adventure!"

"And what is this venture with Wallace, and why are we pretending not to know each other?" Sparky asked.

"Ah yes, I was certain the very direct Dr. McTrowell would come immediately to this point without beating about the bush." He grinned and winked at Drake as if to say that they both found this quality of McTrowell's charming or amusing. "The business venture is precisely as I explained at dinner. Although my older half-brother, Vijay Deva, is the current ruler of Talkad, he doesn't always act with foresight for the well-being of his subjects. Nor does he understand, or choose to understand, the potential ramifications of their lack of well-being for the throne and its occupant." He cocked his head and smiled archly as if he hadn't just called his brother a selfish, idiotic git. "Talkad Palace is currently serving as a British consulate for the region around Talkad. My brother is less than pleased about having British soldiers billeted in his palace, nor does he care for the rather clownish young officer in charge of the garrison. He takes the short view about the situation and concerns himself only with his personal discomfiture. Having spent much of my life in England, I believe I understand the English better than he does. My apologies, Chief Inspector Drake, if my words offend, but the English are fundamentally businessmen. Aligning one's own interests with the business interests of the English is the surest path to a satisfactory future with them. Denying that such a future will surely exist or fighting their business interests is doomed to failure…for a ruler and for his people. My half-brother won't sit upon the throne forever. Nor do I expect to sit upon it myself. However, whoever sits on the throne will almost certainly be a member of my family and the people he rules will be my people. It is for their future I work." He took a sip of chai while his words sank in. "As for the pretense that we have only just met, Wallace is a man who will use any information to his advantage, an advantage I don't intend to give him. I would appreciate your discretion concerning what I've just told you."

Sparky gaped at Ashleigh for a moment. "I'm looking forward to the day when you don't surprise me. It's a shame for your people that you'll never sit on that throne." And then she too took a sip of her chai because she couldn't think of anything to add.

Lord Ashleigh leapt into the uncomfortable gap in the conversation. "Dr. McTrowell, would you be so kind as to explain the regatta course?" McTrowell relaxed visibly at the mention of a very comfortable topic.

"We will dock in Paris by morning where we will deposit most of our current passengers who booked passage that far. Of course, Wallace wouldn't waste the cabin space just flying the Burke & Hare to the regatta." She and Ashleigh had a chuckle. "We'll pick up a few passengers who are willing to pay a premium to be at the start of the regatta and proceed to Munich. There we'll unload as much excess weight as possible and collect our referee. He'll be a handpicked representative of Maximilian II who will ride on the Burke & Hare for the entire race, ensuring we don't cheat." She scoffed at the implication that she would need to cheat to win the race. "From there, each leg will be a single day. Munich to Salzburg is a flat run, so the crews can learn to work together, and to shake out any pretenders. Salzburg to Innsbruck is the valley run, testing our ability to maneuver the tight confines of the alpine valleys. Then we have the mountain run from Innsbruck to Vaduz. This one has me worried because we'll be climbing and descending at steep angles for which airships are not really intended. The final leg is the downhill run back to Munich. This will be more of a test of the Burke & Hare's speed than the crew's skill. I'm really looking forward to this one because it will take us over the Ludwig South-North railway, a new line being constructed by Royal Bavarian State Railways. Since my piloting duties will be light, I'll have the opportunity to observe the construction from the air, and I do love railroads!"

Just then there was a knock on the cabin door, and they heard Wallace's voice, "Viscount Ashleigh, are you still up?" Drake and McTrowell froze. If Wallace found them here, the secret of their acquaintance with Ashleigh would be revealed. Before they could think what to do, Virat silently opened the door to the other room, stepped out, and waved Drake & McTrowell in. They pulled the door closed behind themselves, and each put an ear to the door, the tips of their noses almost touching. They didn't get to see Virat scoop up their teacups, put them on a side table, and deftly cover them with a cloth before opening the door for Wallace.

Ashleigh stepped in front of the doorway, mostly blocking Wallace's view of the cabin, although it didn't keep Wallace from craning his neck around to try to see into the cabin. "Good evening again, Mr. Wallace. I was just enjoying a cup of tea before retiring." He lifted his teacup from the saucer to his lips to emphasize his point. "How may I be of service?"

"I just wanted to warn you to be careful about our illustrious pilot." He craned his neck around again as if he expected to see her in the cabin. "One can't be certain about the nature of a woman of that age who's not married. And don't get me started on her role in the Pecos Incident!"

With their ears pressed to the cabin door, Drake and McTrowell were able to hear Wallace's words clearly, aided by the inevitable volume of his voice. Drake opened his mouth to defend McTrowell against this slander, but she placed her fingertips over his lips to prevent him from saying a word. She leaned forward to whisper in his ear, her lips so close it made the back of his neck tingle. "*Nemo Me Impune Lacessit*. None shall provoke me with impunity."

LANDING IN PARIS

BY MR. DAVID L. DRAKE

Glued to the door, Sparky and Erasmus stayed there for the duration of Mr. Wallace's interruption. It's seemed that Wallace's jab at Sparky's marital status was just a play to flush her out if she were within earshot. Sparky knew this, and wasn't going to fall for it.

Erasmus could read all of this on her relaxed reaction, and knew that she was not going to join Wallace in this bit of cat-and-mouse.

Ironically, Erasmus didn't do much of this surreptitious snooping in his day-to-day work. So, this felt like juvenile fun, even with Lord Ashleigh's somewhat serious concern that his acquaintance with Sparky might be revealed.

Erasmus suddenly remembered his cane leaning against the wall! Nothing he could do about that now, but he wondered if Wallace would have noticed it with all of the other eye-catching decorations around the sitting room. Erasmus looked around the room quickly and noticed an ornate box on a side table. His curiosity welled up. He glanced quickly back at Sparky to see if she would notice; she was busy listening at the door. Erasmus quietly flipped the lid up, revealing three knives neatly arranged in a red cloth lined tray. Each was nicely made, but more functional than was Lord Ashleigh's usual style. Erasmus quietly closed the lid.

Wallace's hope of finding his pilot in the wrong cabin was dashed, and he bid a good night to Lord Ashleigh. Just as the cabin door clicked shut after Wallace's exit, Virat opened the other door to release Sparky and Erasmus. Sparky and Erasmus stepped through, and Erasmus noticed that his cane was no longer against the wall. He pointed in the general direction of where it had been and just got his mouth open to ask Virat about its disappearance, when Virat produced the cane from behind his back. Erasmus gave a nod of thanks, but had the distinct feeling he was effectively thanking a silent magician who preemptively answered a question about the whereabouts of a rabbit by pulling it out of a top hat. Erasmus replaced the cane in its rightful place against the wall, and he and Sparky retook their seats.

Lord Ashleigh opened with, "I believe your chais are now cold. My apologies! Let me instead offer a taste of port, one that you can compare to that provided after dinner." Virat transferred two small elegant glasses from a tray to the table between Sparky and Erasmus, and filled each halfway from a bottle of port. Then he handed a glass to Lord Ashleigh and poured for him.

Erasmus joined the rest in raising their glasses and taking a sip. *"This is no ordinary port,"* he thought. It wasn't syrupy sweet, nor did it have any bite to it, and provided a more fruitful libation. He instinctively made a humming "yummy" sound acknowledging his approval.

"What I would love to hear is the adventures that you've had this week with the mad scientist and the late Mr. Abusir," Lord Ashleigh requested. "I know the papers had their versions, and I read them all. But I want to hear it from the adventurers themselves!"

Sparky and Erasmus looked at each other to see who should start, and smiles came to them both. "May I suggest that you start, since it was your arrival in London that set much of this in action," Erasmus offered to Sparky.

"I would love to," she replied, and then started the tale. The tale went on for a good bit of time, and Sparky and Erasmus traded off passages that wove an intricate timeline. Lord Ashleigh's enthusiasm was grand and infectious, driving the storytellers on. The port continued to flow, and the time drifted by.

Erasmus only interjected once to ask Sparky about her exclamation after being attacked by Mr. Abusir. "You said, 'Behold, I am become Death.' I have racked my brain, but I cannot place it."

Lord Ashleigh jumped in, "Please allow me to answer this one. It is a translation from Hindu scripture. As the writings reveal, Lord Vishnu is trying to persuade Prince Bhagavad Gita to do his duty. To convince him, Lord Vishnu takes on his many-armed form and says to the prince, 'Now I am become Death, the destroyer of worlds.' There are a number of translations, but this is considered the most poetic. I hope I have done you justice."

Sparky smiled. "You are correct, my dear Lord Ashleigh. Until that final moment with Abusir, I have always tried to do no harm. He forced me to a place I had hoped never to go." The two men nodded in agreement.

Sparky's and Erasmus' syncopated narrative concluded with the boarding of the Burke & Hare, and all sat back and took a final sip of port. Erasmus felt compelled to enquire about their nightcap. "This is head and shoulders above the ports I have had in the past, Lord Ashleigh. Is it just a good bottle?"

"Actually, we have finished two bottles," Lord Ashleigh noted with a chuckle, and added "It's not just a good bottle. Like most ports, it comes from the Douro River Valley in Portugal. I have been investing in a small vineyard about halfway between Serra do Marão mountain range and the Spanish border, overlooking the river itself. The soil there, if you can even call it soil, is harsh, rocky, and steep. The grapes have a very concentrated juice, and my vintner has a special time during the fermentation when he adds the *aguardente*. I like the result a great deal, and wanted to share it with you." Lord Ashleigh's guests raised their eyebrows at this, and looked appreciatively at the empty glasses.

"I could not help but notice your knife set in the other room," Erasmus let slip out.

"Oh, don't misinterpret those! I dabble with knife throwing. More of a minor skill for parlor tricks than an actual sport. I'll demonstrate my dexterity for you someday, I promise."

As the conversation veered toward knives and sport, Sparky inadvertently tugged on the chain and instinctively pulled out her delicate gold woman's pocket watch. She flipped the lid, and glanced down. "2:30!" she shouted, ran to the porthole and looked out. "We are quite a ways over France. Gentlemen, I must part company and get some sleep before I dock the airship in the morning. Lord Ashleigh, it was a great pleasure. And Chief Inspector, I would love to show you my favorite café in the morning if you would like. Until then …" She left in a hurry, leaving the two men in stunned silence.

Erasmus leaned back and grabbed his cane, stating, "Well, sir, I too, must make my leave. I guess I have a breakfast appointment. An exceptional evening. Good night." And with that, Erasmus also left the room.

Morning came early. Paris had its usual grey clouds, but it still seemed bright, and the light streamed in through Erasmus' porthole. From his cabin, the docking seemed to go smoothly. He could hear the shuffling of those passengers who were making their way off the Burke & Hare.

Just as he stepped into the passage outside his cabin, Sparky took up his arm. "I'm in desperate need of a good café au lait. Come with me, my dear sir," and the two of them headed for the docking tower.

Sparky was full of conversational topics as they wound themselves through the streets of Paris. The next thing Erasmus knew, he was seated at an outdoor table at a small café in the Rue du Faubourg Saint-Honoré. She had ordered herself café au lait and a small brioche. Erasmus ordered the pain au chocolat and, taking a cue from Sparky, his own café au lait. He thought that one had to love a city where a grown man could order chocolate for breakfast with a straight face. The food arrived, and they started nibbling and sipping.

The Parisian street was full of the usual urban hustle and bustle, but everyone seemed, well, content. It was a different feel than London teeming with its proper business efficiency. This was more upbeat and cheerful.

Then the oddest thing happened. A man dressed in blue pants, a horizontally striped shirt, and a beret rode by on a unicycle while juggling five red balls. Despite his concentration on his routine, he was glancing around for safety and appreciating crowd reactions.

Then he saw Erasmus. At that moment, he lost all control. Balls flying, he tumbled off his unicycle and ended up sitting on the sidewalk. He looked at Erasmus again and exclaimed, "Drake! Is that really you?"

Erasmus squirmed a bit and slumped in his seat. *"Well,"* he thought, *"perhaps my past will not stay buried."*

Café Au Lait

By Dr. Katherine L. Morse

McTrowell popped up out of her seat, rounded up three of the five balls dropped by the unicyclist, and began performing a simple, but seemingly effortless, three-ball cascade. The prone juggler stared in amazement for a moment before collecting his wits and his unicycle, standing up, and dusting himself off. Sparky passed the balls to him one at a time and he instinctively formed his own cascade with the balls. After a couple of rounds, he stowed them one after the other into a small pouch tucked behind his back. As he bent down to retrieve the final two balls, he doffed his beret, exposing a head of charmingly rumpled hair, and performed an elaborate bow with a flourish of the beret. When he straightened up, he took Sparky's hand and kissed it.

"François LaRue, at your service, mademoiselle…or is it madame?" He winked at Drake. "Is this charming creature your wife?" There was an extended, awkward moment during which Drake and McTrowell exchanged conflicted glances.

"Um, no. We are…" *"Friends, acquaintances, colleagues?"* He pondered. "…having breakfast."

"And where did you find this amazing woman?"

"An inventor's symposium." Sparky opened her mouth to correct him and then cocked her head to fix him with a quizzical look of assessment. They were going to have an interesting conversation about this later. Drake continued, "This is…"

Just before he could say the word "doctor," McTrowell interrupted him, "Miss Czarina Llewellyn. Pleased to make your acquaintance Monsieur LaRue." It was Drake's turn to fix his companion with a quizzical look. Had she made up this name on the spot? How had she known about Llewellyn? And what a peculiar first name to choose! They were going to have an interesting conversation about this later.

McTrowell continued, "And how is it that the esteemed Chief Inspector of Scotland Yard is acquainted with such a gifted *jongleur* in Paris?"

To which LaRue sputtered, "Chief inspector of Scotland Yard?" Drake gave LaRue a very fierce look that suggested the answer to McTrowell's question or further inquiry about Drake's current employment might cost LaRue his life. LaRue demonstrated that he was a skilled manipulator of both small objects and conversation, "Mademoiselle, such a question can only be answered over cassoulet and a bottle of Bordeaux. Meet me at 7 this evening at Chez la Mere Catherine in Montmartre. I imagine you are the sort of woman who knows her way around Paris. And I don't think Drake would dare let you come alone, so I will see both of you this evening." He winked rakishly at Drake, kissed McTrowell's hand again, hopped back up on the unicycle, and rode away, extracting his juggling balls from his pouch and starting a cascade as he went.

Drake and McTrowell stood staring at each other over the table with the cooling café au lait for a full two minutes, neither daring to be the first to speak.

Drake blinked first. "How did you know my middle name was Llewellyn?"

"Are you having a jest at my expense? Surely you know that Llewellyn is my mother's last name and my middle name."

"Your middle name is Llewellyn?"

"Isn't that what I just said?"

"And your mother's last name is Llewellyn?"

"Is there an echo in this café? Yes, that's what I just said."

"But your last name is McTrowell, and you are not married?"

"Chief Inspector Drake, I took you for an intelligent man. Yes, my mother's last name is Llewellyn. My middle name is Llewellyn. My last name is McTrowell. I'm not married. And before you ask, yes, my given name is Czarina." She was red in the face when she finished.

"I beg your pardon, Dr. McTrowell. This is all a bit irregular, although I suppose I should have expected something of the sort from a woman such as yourself."

"A woman such as myself? And what is that supposed to mean?"

Drake had the sinking feeling that his burgeoning relationship with the volatile Dr. McTrowell was about to be over before it started. He took an even breath and tried again. "I did not mean to imply that there is anything inappropriate about you. I am aware that you are an outstanding woman, but you are quite surprising. If you would be so kind, please explain how you came to have a different surname than your mother."

"I'm not much in the habit of explaining about my past. Is your middle name also truly Llewellyn?"

"Yes, on my honor as a gentleman."

"Very well. My father was a charming, but dissipated gambler. Apparently, I get my skill at mathematics from him. Sadly, his recklessness exceeded his mathematical skills, so he lost more than he won, and what he didn't lose, he drank...according to my mother. He abandoned my mother when he found out she was pregnant with me. He drank himself to death shortly after I was born. I never knew the man, not that I consider that a loss. I don't know why she named me after him when she could have just named me Llewellyn and claimed my father died, but there it is. Are you satisfied?"

"Yes, thank you. And the first name?"

"That's a story for another day. I believe you owe me an explanation about your own middle name."

"I suppose that would be a fair exchange. Might we finish our breakfast?" He gestured at their, now lukewarm, bowls of café au lait.

"I think I would like that." She sat down and took a big swallow of her café au lait, hoping her day out with Drake was going to improve. It had been going so well until the mishap with the juggler.

Drake took a small sip of his drink and pondered how to proceed. It was becoming clear he was not going to be able to dodge explanations of his past for much longer, particularly if he wished to continue enjoying the company of Dr. McTrowell. He chose his next words very carefully. "I lived in an orphanage when I was a young lad. I was taken in by an older gentleman, Edwin Llewellyn. In appreciation for his generosity, I assumed his last name as my middle name."

McTrowell smiled enigmatically at him and said, "I see. Thank you." While answering her question directly, he had opened up an entire barrel of questions to which she was quite certain she would not be getting answers any time soon. She made a mental note of these questions and formulated a plan to extract the answers slowly over time. And then she smiled enigmatically back at herself. Executing this plan would require frequent contact with the Chief Inspector over an extended period of time. She didn't mind that idea at all. They finished their breakfast in companionable silence.

Sparky dusted the final bits of brioche off her fingers. "If this is your first trip to Paris, …" She studied his face closely to see if it revealed any information regarding this supposition. "…there's something you really should see." She stood up and waited for him to follow. They walked a few blocks southeast along the Rue and then she turned right. There was a small sign on the side of the building on the corner with an arrow pointing south. Above the arrow, the sign read **Palais du Louvre**.

Dinner in Montmartre

By Mr. David L. Drake

The moonlight on the airship landing grounds was bright, enough so that no additional light was needed to make one's way around the tower to the Burke & Hare, whose cabin portholes leaked light into the night.

The couple walking up the structure were giddy with laughter, arms around each other's waists, and helping hold each other up as they made the trek to the tower. The airship above threw an immense shadow across the field due to the lowness of the moon.

At the tower, the woman took the bottom stair first, spun in place, lifted the gentleman's bowler, and quickly placed a kiss on his forehead. The gentleman took a small step in surprise, and they both laughed out loud again. This scene was taking place well after midnight, and the thought of intrusion into this moment seemed unlikely. However, one of the brightly glowing portholes opened and Lord Ashleigh popped his head out. "You two are in fine spirits! Please join me in my cabin and we can share stories about our day."

"Be right up," Erasmus replied.

The couple made their way up the tower and into the airship with a little teetering in their progress. Lord Ashleigh was in his cabin's sitting room with a glass of port in hand. The door burst open, and the two stumbled in. "I see you're a bit tipsy. Have a seat, you two."

The door to the bedchamber swung open. Virat appeared with two glasses and a bottle of port and served the slightly breathless, smiling guests. He disappeared just as quickly back through the bedchamber door.

"Who would like to start?" asked Lord Ashleigh.

Erasmus cleared his throat, sat up a bit straighter, and started his tale. "At a tasty breakfast of café au lait, brioche, and pain au chocolat, an old friend of mine, François LaRue, happened down the street, juggling. He was actually riding an invention of his at the time. A bizarre single-wheeled contraption that gave him amazing maneuverability combined with the constant prospect of falling down. Which, upon seeing me, he performed the latter with great gusto.

François then invited us to dinner at Chez la Mère Catherine in Montmartre."

While Erasmus caught his breath, Sparky jumped in.

"I wanted to treat Erasmus to one of the great museums of Paris, the Louvre. We went there straight away and spent about four hours walking around the great statues and paintings, all of which I could rhapsodize about for another four hours. The Salle des Sept-Cheminées alone, with copies of Raphael's frescos, are worthy of half an hour of rambling praise."

"We went from there to a small restaurant near the Hôtel de Ville, the City Hall, and split the most tender pastry-wrapped fish complemented with glasses of Chardonnay. We walked that off by crossing the bridge over to the left bank and strolled the Palais et Jardin du Luxembourg, a beautiful garden with wonderful statuary of saints and Greek gods. We also strolled past the marionette theatre and the lovely orange grove."

Sparky paused to take a deep breath. "It was less than two hours until dinner and it was a bit of a trudge to Montmartre, which is just outside of Paris, but we decided that we would see the sites better by foot. We took a few wrong turns along the way, despite our map of the streets. We enjoyed seeing some of the everyday activity of the Parisians as we went."

Erasmus jumped in. "Do you want me to tell the next part?"

Sparky gave Erasmus a knowing glare and said, "Oh, no, this is all mine."

She continued with a considerable amount of pantomime to augment the storytelling. "After exiting a small alleyway near Montmartre, we entered a very small square, not much more than a meeting of alleyways. A rough looking vagabond wearing a white lace kerchief as a mask jumped out in front of us and, in a threatening tone, demanded all goods we possessed, in French, of course. He was hiding some sort of weapon behind himself, adding additional mystery to the threat. Chief Inspector Drake stepped forward, brandishing his cane and, with a commanding voice, demanded that the assailant move along. He made it clear a conflict with him would be foolhardy, all in English, of course. I stuck close to Erasmus, letting him do his commanding voice routine. This didn't go as planned. Instead, the knave laughed, and whistled loudly. Three cohorts appeared from behind, all hiding behind kerchief masks: a red one, a light green one, and, believe it or not, one with dark blue with yellow piping, all preparing themselves for violence.

"The leader took the first swing at Erasmus with the makeshift club he had been hiding. Erasmus deftly stepped back with his right foot and, leaning back, allowed the club to swing past his face with a whooshing sound. Erasmus replied with a potentially crippling swing at his attacker's knee, but his attacker jumped and tucked in his legs and avoided the blow.

"I tried my best to keep my eye on Erasmus' confrontation and on the three attackers to our rear who seemed to be holding back to see what happened in the one-on-one with the leader, White Scarf.

"White Scarf changed his stance, circled, and, using two hands, started using his club as a pointed weapon, preparing to 'stab' Erasmus. Erasmus took a decisively athletic stance and held his cane more like a saber. White Scarf jabbed at his torso, which Erasmus parried easily to the side and struck immediately toward his opponent's head. Then, White Scarf did the most perfect cartwheel to his left, avoiding the riposte, and landed securely on his feet.

"The three from behind must have seen this as a decisive advantage within the battle, and all three took a small step toward us. Yellow Piping grabbed Erasmus' unarmed right arm and tried to pull him off balance. Erasmus slid his cane behind Yellow Piping's back and quite literally flipped him off his feet, causing him to roll into an alleyway. White Scarf stepped into the fray with a kick aimed generally at Erasmus; Erasmus grabbed the foot with his freed right hand and forced it up. White Scarf went with the motion and landed walking on his hands, letting the club skitter away. He pushed off his arm-stand and sprang back onto his feet.

"This is when Light Green Scarf stepped in. I jumped toward him, landing three blows to his chest and one to his face, knocking him down, and advancing on him as I went.

"Light Green Scarf stammered out, in English, 'What?!? ...What was that?'

"Erasmus exclaimed, 'Ho, ho! Everyone break. The fun is over. The lady has some skills that you did not count on.'

"All four of them relaxed, stood up and brushed themselves off. White Scarf actually tugged at his collar and said 'Whew,' bent over, and caught his breath. I turned to Erasmus and sternly asked, 'What was all of this, then?'

"Erasmus answered in a slightly comical tone, 'We were assaulted by these villains. I was in the process of eliminating them, one by one. Then you stepped in and knocked one onto his backside, if I may be so blunt.'

"I turned a bit red and steam may have come out of my ears. I had to ask the obvious: 'Is this another case of your knowing everyone on the street and having a bit of fun? I am not amused.'

"And you know what he said in response? A little sheepishly, I might add. 'Actually, these are our dinner companions. That's François in the red scarf, waiting his turn for the big finish.'

"François pulled down his kerchief, saying, 'Good evening, mademoiselle. You have a most delightful left-left-right combination. I am glad that I'm not Charles, who was on the receiving end of your pummeling. Charles, are you...what is the word...satisfactory?'

"Charles pulled down his scarf and rubbed his chin. He looked between François and me, and all he added was, 'Ow.'"

All three of them laughed and took another sip of port.

"Erasmus, what were you thinking?!" Lord Ashleigh just couldn't believe that Erasmus had set such a thing up.

Erasmus tried to make his response sound official, as if that would give him a stronger defense. "Actually, I did not arrange this, but I did expect it. All four of these gents were my chums in my youth. We practiced this routine as young lads with the intent to impress the ladies. An idea that made sense at the time, when you have no grasp of what women like or dislike. We actually did some public demonstrations of the routine, even earning a few welcome coins of appreciation. But we were using broom handles for 'weapons,' and it was overly extravagant for a realistic fight. We did not figure on the damsel taking out the third attacker, the one who can perform kick-flips on walls."

Another sip of port and Erasmus restarted the story. "Dinner was great and we introduced François, Henri, Charles, and René to Sparky over a delicious five-course meal and one too many bottles of red wine. It was incredible! The cassoulet was superb! We started with these exquisite little..."

Lord Ashleigh cut him off. "My friends! I would love to hear about the meal, but I must tell my tale while I can, since I need your guidance and assistance." They all leaned in slightly. Lord Ashleigh continued, "I have created an unfortunate situation that I must resolve by tomorrow. It involves a young lady. Please, this is not something I can do alone, and my position and status won't aid me!"

Erasmus wondered what trouble Lord Ashleigh could have worked his way into. He mused to himself, *"Oh my dear friend, you may have dug a deep well from which we cannot extricate you."*

MEET CUTE

BY DR. KATHERINE L. MORSE

For once, Lord Ashleigh appeared discomfited, struggling internally with a course of action. Drake and McTrowell waited patiently for their friend to collect his thoughts.

"I had thought to spruce up my wardrobe with the latest fashions since I'm here in Paris." Sparky tried not to smile at the idea of what Lord Ashleigh's "spruced up" wardrobe might look like given his proclivity for bright colors and patterns. She might have taken the opportunity to tease her friend if he weren't in distress.

"A friend in London recommended a high quality, discreet shop on the Rue de Rivoli for shirts and cravats. As I approached the shop door, a gentleman approached from the opposite direction with a haste that suggested urgency. As I was enjoying a leisurely afternoon of diversion, I allowed him to enter the shop ahead of me. He immediately began addressing the shop girl loudly in English without so much as a 'Bon jour.'" Lord Ashleigh continued his story.

The Englishman began pointing to several samples and demanding to know what fabrics were available, how much items cost, and how long it would take to have half a dozen shirts made. The shop girl begged his pardon, in French, and said that she didn't speak

English. The Englishman replied by shouting his demands in English and growing red in the face. The shop girl became even more apologetic and suggested that the gentleman should come back in an hour when the shop owner, who spoke a bit of English, would be returning. Of course, the Englishman didn't understand and only became more irate, shouting insults at the uncomprehending shop girl. At this point, Lord Ashleigh felt it prudent to intervene before the encounter should turn violent. "Sir, perhaps I may be of some assistance. I speak French passably well and would be willing to translate." The suggestion that he might require assistance with someone so inconsequential as a shop girl had exactly the opposite of the desired effect. He rounded on the shop girl and shouted, showering her with spittle, "Do you know who I am? I am Theodore Grossman and my company supplies half the bricks in London. I could buy this shop with the pence in my trouser pockets!" With that he stormed out of the shop with the customary slam of the door, nearly yanking the little brass bell off its string.

Lord Ashleigh and the shop girl stood staring at each other for a moment while the sorely abused bell settled down. The shop girl's face screwed up in a clear indication that she felt like crying, but was trying mightily not to. Lord Ashleigh produced a monogrammed handkerchief with a cheery flourish from inside his frock coat and dabbed the first teardrop before it could roll down her cheek. He addressed her gently in French, "I'm terribly sorry, Mademoiselle…," and then he cocked his head slightly, suggesting she should be forthcoming with her name.

"Gabrielle. Gabrielle Lambert. I'm very sorry I offended your master." She clutched her hands around his handkerchief and the hand holding it.

"My master?"

"Yes, your master, Monsieur Grossman." It was then that Lord Ashleigh realized that his arrival right behind the offensive brick monger had given the lovely Gabrielle the idea that he was Grossman's servant. And, of course, she couldn't understand their conversation in English, so it would have looked like an obedient servant trying to assist his master. The look on her face was one of true gratitude, and her hands around his were invitingly warm. If he told her that he was an English viscount, she would be mortified at her presumptuousness. And that would be the end of that.

"Ah, yes, my master. Perhaps my French is not as good as I thought. I misunderstood you. He does have quite a temper."

Lord Ashleigh paused in his retelling of the story and looked imploringly at his two friends who sat motionless in their chairs. Although Sparky was gaping slightly, she was thinking that, for all his worldliness, her friend was still a young man who didn't realize the implications of starting a love affair on a lie. Drake cleared his throat. "As I feared. You seem to have dug yourself a very deep hole, Lord Ashleigh."

"Yes, and you haven't heard the worst of it," the viscount interjected. Sparky slumped into her chair with a sense of impending doom. Lord Ashleigh continued.

"My master wishes to update his wardrobe with some continental color. I was planning to help him with his selections, but I see I will need to carry out this charge myself." And with that, Lord Ashleigh began buying up two dozen of the shop's most expensive, brightly colored accessories in the finest fabrics, completely without regard for the price. When Gabrielle held up the items in front of Lord Ashleigh, as if he were going to wear them himself and not knowing that he would, she commented how magnificent they would look on him. He mumbled something about this or that being just the thing for Monsieur Grossman, while marveling at the sensation of her fingers brushing against his neck as she held up a golden-brown cravat.

The total came to quite a handsome sum, but paying it wasn't so bad when he touched her gently as she took the money from his hand. She wrapped his purchases slowly, realizing that their encounter was coming to an end. Lord Ashleigh realized it as well. "I should very much like to see you again. Will you be working again tomorrow?"

"No, tomorrow is my day off. I like to stroll around Île de la Cité. I have been watching the work on La Sainte-Chapelle. And then I will visit my grandmother in Montparnasse."

"I have not had the pleasure of seeing the restorations of La Sainte-Chapelle, and I too have my day off tomorrow. Perhaps I should take a stroll as well. When do you think the light would be best?"

"I particularly like it at one o'clock." She smiled, blushed, and continued wrapping.

As she was tying up the last bundle, the shopkeeper returned. Gabrielle's attention turned to him. "Monsieur Girard, this gentleman has just purchased all of this for his master." She smiled and waved her hand over the pile of packages. Although Monsieur Girard smiled at the large purchase, he paused when Gabrielle used the word "master." Monsieur Girard had been in the clothing business his entire life. Gabrielle was mistaken about this man having a master. The young man's ensemble with such perfect tailoring made of exquisitely rich fabrics would have cost as much as a servant earned in a year. Gabrielle had obviously been focusing on the young man's chocolate brown eyes because she had completely overlooked the jeweled dagger and sheath barely hidden by his frock coat. When Lord Ashleigh finally took his eyes off the fetching Mademoiselle Lambert and looked at Monsieur Girard, he realized he was being assessed by a practiced eye and he was in immediate danger of being revealed. He tipped his indigo velvet top hat at Gabrielle and popped it back on his head. "Bon jour, Monsieur Girard. Au revoir, Mademoiselle Lambert." He couldn't help winking slightly at Gabrielle hoping she understood that he really did mean that he would see her again.

He barely noticed the shops as he headed back down Rue de Rivoli, thinking about the next day. Certainly he would have to tell her the truth tomorrow. He must think of just the right thing to say. He ceased his perambulations to consider his approach and gazed distractedly into the window of the shop where he had stopped. Nothing was coming to him. And then he actually noticed the contents of the window. Without giving it another moment's thought, he dashed into the shop, setting the sign hanging over the door to waving to passersby, **Bijouterie**.

MR. WOODHOUSE'S REPLACEMENT

BY MR. DAVID L. DRAKE

After a few minutes in the shop, Lord Ashleigh had picked out a most magnificent necklace with a wonderful display of colored gems surrounded by diamonds. His plan was simple: he would meet Gabrielle during his walk around Île de la Cité, make small talk, confess that he had temporarily gone along with her misunderstanding that he was a servant, produce the necklace, and disclose that he was a viscount. Her good fortune would sweep her off her feet. While finishing his purchase, simultaneously wondering if some part of this plan should occur on bended knee, he heard the shop door close. Thanking the proprietor, he took one last look at his purchase verifying that it was perfect for his intentions.

A commanding voice addressed him from behind, grinding out English smothered in a thick Parisian accent. "Sir, I have seen your type before." Lord Ashleigh spun about and came face to face with Monsieur Girard who must have followed him to the *bijouterie*. Monsieur Girard continued with his monologue. "You have either deceived the shop girl regarding your status, making you a fabricator and false witness, or you are in the process of squandering your employer's money to woo a young lady. Either way, you are a cad. You should know that the young lady is my niece! I have seen that look in a man's eyes before, and I will do whatever it takes to keep you far away from her." The speech came complete with finger-waggles and lip-pouts to illustrate the seriousness of the accusation. The final sentence included a wide-eyed stare for added effect. Monsieur Girard gave a final pout, threw his hands in the air, and stormed out.

Lord Ashleigh was beside himself. His freshly minted plan was deflating like an hour-old soufflé. Now he needed to convince two people that his intensions were honorable if not a bit innocent. But how could he convince anyone of that with a necklace that neither she nor her uncle could ever afford? It did look like he was planning to buy her affections. He also surmised that getting her uncle a gift would not smooth things over either. Nor could he return the necklace, even further convincing Monsieur Girard that it was all a ruse.

He left the shop, necklace properly boxed as a gift and stored in an inner pocket, the parcel of new clothes tucked under his arm. Perhaps there was some other reason that he told the story to Gabrielle. He could be a British detective in disguise! No, that was far too complicated, and he has no credentials to verify that claim. He could be a famous viscount hiding his identity while on travel. But again, to reveal himself, his name would have to be known well enough to justify such an assertion, which it was not.

Lord Ashleigh needed a way out of this predicament. And then it came to him. He needed the ruse to continue. To do that, he needed to find Theodore Grossman, get on his good side, take him into his confidence, and allow the fabricated servant story to continue at least for a day until he could clear up this whole mess.

Since Mr. Grossman was in a hurry to procure his shirts, Lord Ashleigh hoped he could follow his trail by stopping at a number of men's fashion shops near where Gabrielle worked while playing detective. His plan was simple but deceptive. It took a full five shops to succeed and for his patter to sound convincing.

"Bon jour," Lord Ashleigh started, then continued in French, "I'm Ashleigh. My master, Mr. Grossman, has sent me to check on the status of his order he placed this morning. I do hope I have the correct shop since he wasn't clear in his directions."

"Sir, that order was placed just this morning," the proprietor explained. "We haven't even cut the fabric yet."

"Yes, yes. I understand. Mr. Grossman wanted me to verify the quantity of shirts purchased and to make sure they were shipped to the right place." Lord Ashleigh was guessing that Grossman had them shipped to a local address, but it seemed to be a reasonable assumption given Mr. Grossman's haste and level of distrust.

"Mr. Grossman ordered twelve shirts. He selected each of the colors and fabrics himself. Do you want to see them?"

"Yes, please."

The proprietor retrieved a bundle of fabrics carefully bound with ribbon from the back of the shop. He laid the parcel in front of Lord Ashleigh and untied it to reveal a collection of white and off-white fabrics. The proprietor indicated they were all to be made into wing-tip collar dress shirts. They were far too commonplace for Lord Ashleigh's tastes, but that really should not have mattered given his mission here. But it was too tempting not to spice up the lot.

"Mr. Grossman wanted to add a blue and white striped shirt for a night on the town. Can you show me a sample?" It was clear that Mr. Grossman had presented the same disposition here as he had in Gabrielle's shop. The proprietor raised his eyebrows at the suggestion, but retrieved the fabrics just the same.

He laid out the fabric samples on the counter. Lord Ashleigh selected a fine, American cotton, blue with a thin white stripe. He asked for a round-cornered collar with a pleated front, much more fashionable and stylish than its future companions.

"Allow me to pay for this additional shirt now." Lord Ashleigh withdrew the appropriate number of francs from his well-made leather wallet. "Are you shipping the finished shirts to my master's hotel?"

"Yes, of course. We will be hand-delivering them to the Lille et d'Albion at 323 rue St. Honoré. We will have these completed in two days' time. Your business is greatly appreciated."

"Very good. I was concerned that my master might have mispronounced the hotel name, given his difficulty with French. Your establishment has done well. Au revoir."

Lord Ashleigh slipped his hat back onto his head as he left and tried to hide his smile at his good fortune and ability to execute his charade. Wasn't this Erasmus' territory? Comparing stories with him tonight would be entertaining.

The hotel was between rue St. Honoré and rue de Rivoli. Lord Ashleigh glided in with a simple plan: get on Mr. Grossman's good side through mutual business interests, let him know about his predicament, and coax him into playing along with the scheme for a day or two. If all else failed, the promise of future business or some trinket might persuade him. The primary objective was to secure Gabrielle's and her uncle's trust.

A quick conversation at the front desk and Lord Ashleigh was headed to the second floor where Mr. Grossman's party had their accommodations. At the top of the stairs, two men where briskly walking toward Lord Ashleigh with the intent of exiting the building, buttoning their coats as they went. They were engrossed in their conversation and paid no mind to the well-dressed Indian approaching them.

The taller man was speaking in English with indifference to being overheard. "Grossman will skin us alive if we don't fix the EPACTs and get the job finished. The IGC was less than thirty yards away! They could have killed the whole project. Grossman told me we should meet him behind the boulangerie on rue Rémy Dumoncel. They only have about three thousand bricks. We need at least two thousand more." His voice indicated a clear level of concern.

The heavier-set fellow replied, also in English, "I'll grab my extra tool bag out of my carriage house. Fixing the crawlers shouldn't take more than an hour."

"No! Not 'crawlers.' Call them EPACTs. The marketing on this is important."

Just as they passed each other, the taller gentleman suddenly noticed Lord Ashleigh. "Pardon me, are you the shipper? Are you looking for Mr. Grossman?"

Lord Ashleigh thought for only for a split second. This sounded like the perfect way to meet with Mr. Grossman. He deftly turned on his heal and answered nonchalantly. "My name is Mr. Ashleigh. Perhaps I am the shipper you are looking for. Are you going to meet Mr. Grossman?"

The tall man responded with a touch of disapproval. "I'm Mr. Hedgley. This is my employee, Mr. Martin. You are at least three days late, Mr. Ashleigh! Come with us right away. Mr. Grossman is planning to meet us at the site of the excavation. He may not be too pleased, but the fact that you're here means that the entire business deal is recoverable. I suggest we don't discuss anything in public. Come with us."

Rue Rémy Dumoncel was outside Paris on its southwestern side. Lord Ashleigh rode silently in the cabriolet with the two men and their tool bag. The bakery where they stopped was very small and didn't even appear to be open. Mr. Hedgley waved Lord Ashleigh on as they entered a narrow cobble-stoned alley that lead behind the shop, Mr. Martin lugging the tool bag.

Lord Ashleigh simply followed them. He needed to see Mr. Grossman today to make all of his plans work. He rounded the side of the shop to see a dilapidated lot with construction activity and a well-stacked collection of new limestone bricks. The two men went to work pulling on work gloves and laying out mechanic's tools from the bag.

Mr. Grossman wasn't there, so Lord Ashleigh looked about, taking in the scene. Suddenly, a new shining white limestone brick appeared on top of the well-stacked column! It drew Lord Ashleigh's gaze immediately. A small mechanical clicking sound came from the far side of the bricks. It sounded like it was retreating, but ho, now it was getting louder. Two fast-moving mechanical brass arms rapidly stacked another brick on the column. The brick must have been at least 20 pounds in weight and was placed with such dexterity that it hardly made a noise. Trying his best to look unsurprised, Lord Ashleigh walked past the two busy men to get a better view of the far side of the limestone brick stack that was now about four feet high.

The sight took his breath. First was that gaping hole in the ground as if it had been scooped out from below. Perhaps angry devils had dug their way to the surface looking for souls to take. The grass and weeds from the surface curved down into the hole in a manner that made the opening look natural rather than man-made. Out of it scurried eight-legged contraptions hauling limestone bricks on their backs, creating the neatly assembled stack, and then disappearing back into the aperture. The anthropomorphic contraptions were working at such a bristling tempo that it gave Lord Ashleigh an incredible case of apprehension at the thought that the earth was teeming with uncontrollable animated brass spiders. He shivered unceremoniously. This was not the normal way to extract limestone, and it had an incredible creepiness to it. In his best attempt to sound calm, he croaked, "Par...Pardon me, sir, may I ask a question?" He needed to stop himself from asking "what on God's earth is going on here," so he had to think quickly.

"Of course. But make it quick," Mr. Hedgley replied without looking up from his labors.

"How many of these contraptions do you have operating?"

"I thought Mr. Grossman briefed you on all of this. We have 200 Transports and about 50 Cutters. They work as a collective, transmitting task related information using key presses and recognition of specific pitches. They will finish extracting the five thousand bricks you need to ship to England by noon tomorrow."

"So, why the tools?"

"Well, there seems to be something causing breakdowns in the EPACTs under the surface. We need to recover them using re-directed Transports. We would like to get this done before we lose sunlight and before the IGC notices our 'endeavors.'" With his last word, he added a wiggle of his eyebrows to show the task was questionable.

"EPACT? IGC?"

"Good God, man, did you retain nothing? EPACT. Electric-Powered Automated Crawling Transport. Or Cutting Tool. We're still working on the nomenclature. They're similar in structure, but the Cutters have to deal with cutting and extraction, so their legs are much shorter. The IGC is what we're worried about. The Inspection Général des Carrières, or rather the office for General Inspection of the Quarries, verifies the quarries and catacombs for stability. If they found out we were misappropriating limestone from one of the recent cave-ins, the local gendarme would arrest us faster than you could say 'free limestone.'"

"Oh. ... Thank you. Now I remember. Will Mr. Grossman be by soon? I would like discuss the details of my transporting the merchandise with him."

Mr. Hedgley was again indignant. "Discuss it some more? Two months of back and forth and you need some more deliberation? Mr. Grossman warned us you were the weak link in this. He should be by in an hour. I suggest you stand back while we retrieve our lead EPACT."

Lord Ashleigh retreated a number of steps. He wanted nothing to do with these two-foot long crawling monsters. During this entire time, brass creatures were coming and going, stacking up the limestone bricks.

Mr. Martin stood up and, after pulling a whistle out of his pocket, looked at Mr. Hedgley. "Now?" he asked. Mr. Hedgley gave a nod. Mr. Martin took a deep breath, placed the whistle in his mouth and blew hard, producing no discernable sound other than the wind from his lungs passing through the device.

While Lord Ashleigh wondered what that was all about, an EPACT zipped out of the cavity in the earth and scurried crab-like toward Mr. Martin, stopping right at his feet. It was missing two legs on one side, and the unit was clearly doing its best to maneuver with this damage. Mr. Martin gasped and took on the saddest face.

"Oh, my lord! What has happened to you! How are you going to retrieve the other crawlers with this damage! It's going to take hours to fix you."

Mr. Hedgley attempted to keep his employee on task. "Mr. Martin, I suggest you get started. We're losing daylight."

For the next hour, Lord Ashleigh faded into the background while the two men worked on repairing the metallic creature, re-tasking it, and running it through some tests where it appeared to do a mini-version of what it planned to perform under ground.

It was during one of these tests that Mr. Grossman arrived, fully dressed in business attire, and none too happy.

He first looked at the efforts of the workers and sneered in a manner indicating he thought that these mechanical miners were going to be a problem, and then he looked at Lord Ashleigh.

"Why are you here?" he growled.

"He's the shipper," stated Mr. Martin, as if to defend their bringing him to their location.

"I don't think so. This is not Mr. Woodhouse, you bumblers. Did you just bring anyone you found on the street to this location? Have you no sense of propriety?" Mr. Grossman was getting red-faced.

Lord Ashleigh jumped in. "I'm Mr. Ashleigh. Mr. Woodhouse is a colleague of mine and suggested I step in to support your endeavor."

"You don't look, dress, or talk like a shipper. You actually manage a sailing vessel?"

"I have access to a fleet of vessels, both ocean-going and airborne. I am more than capable of transporting your merchandise."

"You've got brass ones, Mr. Ashleigh. I'll say that for you. Simply put, I want you to transport five thousand limestone bricks from this location to the docks in London. Start at noon tomorrow. As I told Mr. Woodhouse, I don't want this shipment to be seen, weighed, tariffed, or seized. And I don't want the IGC nosing around our excavation, so steer clear of them, too. Got it?"

"Well, yes, of course. However, I do want to know …"

"Enough questions. Out of here with you. You're late to the party, and I don't want you to slow down the festivities. Good day."

Lord Ashleigh was doing his best to hide how distraught he was. He mumbled his goodbyes and started his exit without his usual bouncing step and self-assurance. He took one last look at the scene and the stack of limestone bricks that was now well over six feet high from the industry of its scurrying laborers.

He headed back to the Burke & Hare, a gift-wrapped necklace inside his jacket, a bundle of new clothes under his arm, and a head full of concerns.

Lord Ashleigh's story came to its end. Sparky and Erasmus were dumbstruck. Everyone looked around to see who should speak first. Sparky had the first thought.

"Erasmus, you have no jurisdiction here, do you?"

"None. Although I may have easy access to the local constables. But we have a bigger problem. We need to resolve all of this and get Lord Ashleigh to meet Gabrielle."

Sparky's eyes lit up. "I've got it! Listen closely …"

Erasmus smiled and thought to himself, *This must be how Sparky got her title of 'adventuress!'*

THE ESSENCE OF ROMANTIC COMEDY

BY DR. KATHERINE L. MORSE

McTrowell and Ashleigh were already at the gang plank of the Burke & Hare when Drake arrived promptly at 9 AM the next morning as arranged. And they were already engaged in a lively debate, the same one that had resulted in a draw the previous evening.

"I have no need for new clothes."

"You can't be my English aunt in worn riding boots and a gored corduroy skirt stained with machine oil," Lord Ashleigh retorted.

"I could live in the country."

"She does and she rides horses, so I suppose the boots will suffice with a bit of polish, but you must have a more, um, modest dress...and hat..." and then he mumbled "and gloves...and a parasol."

The mumbling failed because Sparky nearly shrieked, "A parasol!?" Drake busied himself with his bowler and then his cravat. And then he wound his pocket watch. And then he refined the waxed curls at the end of his moustache. Anything to stay out of this conversation. Sparky tried the frugal approach. "I'll never wear such clothes again and we're stripping the Burke & Hare of any and all extra weight in Munich for the regatta. What am I supposed to do with them?"

"We'll give them to a women's charity."

"Absolutely new clothes that have only been worn once? That is a complete waste."

"It's my money to waste as I see fit. And I don't see attracting a lovely, charming young lady as a waste of my money. Now, are we off to the dressmaker's? This was, after all, your clever plan."

Drake continued fixing his moustache in order to hide his smile. It was a bit amusing to see Ashleigh get the best of McTrowell with her own plan. He tipped his bowler to them, "Well, now that that is settled, I am off to the IGC. Best of luck to the two of you and I shall see both of you this evening." He marched smartly across the gang plank lest he be caught in another round of their debate. He heard them follow him across the gang plank and imagined he could hear Sparky breathing annoyedly.

It took Drake longer than he had anticipated to locate the offices of the IGC. *"Confounded Parisian streets,"* he thought, *"all alleys and Gordian knots with street names changing every few blocks! The French ought to get themselves some more order to their streets like the English."*

A new challenge presented itself once he located the building and the offices of the IGC. He opened the door expecting to find a duty desk with an officer on duty. Instead, he was confronted by a large room with several desks and chairs, and a handful of ordinary-looking fellows all busily scribbling away at their desks, none of them paying any attention to the door. He stood awkwardly just inside the door for a moment or two, hoping someone would look up, but no one did. He cleared his throat purposefully. A couple of the scribblers raised their eyes slightly, but pretended not to notice him, hoping someone else would risk engaging the stranger whose business would undoubtedly be messy and disruptive. Clearly, they did not understand that Chief Inspector Erasmus Drake was a man of action, not one to be put off by a cold shoulder.

"Bon jour," he ventured loudly, casting a sweeping glance over all the scribblers. *"Je suis Chief Inspector Erasmus Drake du Scotland Yard."* There were a few winces at his accent. And with that he had mostly used up all his French verbs. Fortunately, he had quizzed Lord Ashleigh on some of the critical nouns he needed. *"Clacaire. Malfaiteur. Carte?"* Despite his English pronunciation, the three words "limestone, criminal, and map" seemed to get their attention. A few of them huddled and muttered to each other. One of them pointed at him. Another waved a hand toward a door at the back of the office opposite where Drake had entered. Finally, one of them detached himself from the huddle and approached Drake. He held his hand up, palm out as if he were trying to block Drake's passage, although Drake hadn't moved an inch since entering the office.

"Wait. André speak *anglais*." He waved his upraised hand toward a chair by the door, which Drake interpreted as an invitation to sit down and wait. So he did. The office emissary crossed the office and passed through the door opposite. He returned a moment later without giving any indication of what had transpired and returned to his desk. The scribbling resumed as if Drake had never arrived. Drake waited. And waited. And waited. Although he realized it was rude, he finally gave in to the urge to look at his pocket watch. He had been waiting an hour. His considerable patience was being sorely tested. He stood up. He was considering whether he should attempt to cross the office in search of the illusive André when the door opened and a gentleman older than the ones in the room entered and walked directly up to him.

"Bon jour. I am André Toque."

"Chief Inspector Erasmus Drake of Scotland Yard."

"Scotland Yard? You are outside your ... er ... territory. Yes?"

"If you mean jurisdiction, you are correct. I am here as a private citizen to report a crime."

"We are not the regular police."

"This is not a matter for the regular police. If you have a map, I will show you what I mean." Monsieur Toque disappeared back through the door from whence he had come and didn't return for another fifteen minutes, but at least he had a map. Drake wondered how this agency did its job when everything and everyone moved so slowly and with such apathy. Monsieur Toque unrolled the map which Drake scanned for rue Rémy Dumoncel, following the directions that Lord Ashleigh had given him. Although there were no numbers on the map, he also knew approximately where the boulangerie was located on the street. He pinned the spot on the map with his index finger. "There is a boulangerie here." He tried not to make it sound like a question, but the fact that he had not seen it with his own eyes made his police instincts a bit uneasy.

"Oui, I believe so."

"Behind it is an illegal limestone mining operation. A fellow named Mr. Grossman is using mechanical devices to cut and transport 5,000 bricks of limestone."

"Of course he is using mechanical devices. Do you imagine we cut bricks by hand in France?" He looked indignant at the suggestion that his country was so technically inferior.

"Ah, so you know about this operation?"

A panicked look passed across Toque's face, but then he rapidly regained his composure. "Oh no, of course not. I only meant that limestone cutting requires mechanical devices."

Drake paused for just a moment to consider the answer. But he was running out of time. "These mechanical devices are like spiders or crabs. They crawl into a small hole in the ground to cut and extract the bricks. That is how Mr. Grossman is keeping the operation hidden."

At this declaration, Toque snorted with laughter and no small amount of derision. "Monsieur Drake, perhaps you should not start the day at the cafés that serve absinthe for breakfast. Just because it is available does not mean you should do it. I advise you to return to your quarters, have a bit of a rest, and come back tomorrow when your head is clearer. And, please, only a bit of Bordeaux with dinner and no more absinthe."

Drake blushed slightly, wondering how Toque had known about the absinthe incident back in London. But, no, this business couldn't be a result of any lingering effects of the absinthe since it had been Ashleigh who saw the devices. Toque was just trying to get rid of him. He flipped open his pocket watch again. It was just past 11 AM! Grossman was expecting someone to collect the bricks at noon. One way or another, he was about to get away with this crime.

"Monsieur Toque, I have not been drinking absinthe and time is of the essence. The bricks are scheduled to be moved in less than an hour. If you do not catch Mr. Grossman in the act of committing this crime, you will be unable to prove later that he was the guilty party when rue Rémy Dumoncel collapses, swallowing houses and killing citizens. I believe this is, to use your words, 'your territory.'" The scribblers had been ignoring most of their exchange, but in his aggravation, Drake had raised his voice at this last bit. When he uttered the words "rue Rémy Dumoncel," the scribblers all froze in mid-stroke and exchanged furtive, anxious looks.

The next words out of Monsieur Toque's mouth were delivered with syrupy obsequiousness, "Monsieur Drake, I'm quite certain that this office would be aware of any limestone mining operation right under our own feet. Thank you for taking the time to make us aware of your concern. Bon jour." He placed his hand on the Chief Inspector's shoulder and directed him to the exit, just short of shoving him out the door. Drake was not a man to lose his temper, but something was clearly amiss. Despite the talk of "territory" and "jurisdiction," justice was justice and he would see to it that it was delivered. But, he would need reinforcements.

Sparky was squirming and twitching like a five-year-old at Sunday services as she and Ashleigh exited the dressmaker's shop. She had managed to talk the shopkeeper out of putting her in a corset. One would have thought she had suggested she was going to parade through the streets of Paris like Lady Godiva in riding boots, but sans horse, judging by the horrified look on the shopkeeper's face. However, she had to admit that her favorite boots looked quite spectacular with the polish Lord Ashleigh had arranged while she was being fussed over. On the other hand, the ridiculous little hat would not stay pinned atop her head and trying to juggle the parasol just made matters worse. She hoped Mademoiselle Gabrielle proved to be worth all this discomfort. Under normal circumstances, she would have preferred to walk to La Sainte-Chapelle. However, these were not normal circumstances and she was thankful for the cab that Lord Ashleigh hailed to carry them there in relative comfort.

They disembarked a couple of blocks from their destination. Lord Ashleigh looked up and down the street thoroughly to ensure Gabrielle was not around before stepping out from behind the cab. "I will hide behind the corner of the nearest building, watching closely. You will need to keep her on that same side of the chapel so I don't have to reveal myself to keep you in sight. We need to arrange a signal that it is a good time for me to approach."

"I could throw the parasol in the Seine."

Lord Ashleigh pursed his lips and furrowed his brow to indicate that he didn't share her sense of humor. "Perhaps it would be more appropriate if you just closed the parasol and tapped the point on the ground."

"Very well. I will get in position and keep an eye on you. Give a tip of your hat when she approaches."

Sparky had only just stationed herself in a position where she could pretend to be admiring the stained glass when Lord Ashleigh signaled, or rather waved his top hat frantically. She hoped Gabrielle wouldn't look around and see him or all of Sparky's suffering in these stifling clothes would be for naught. She stole a glance at the approaching young lady. She had to admit that her friend had good taste. The young lady was pretty without being beautiful in that way that could be dangerous. Although her dress was not made of expensive cloth, it was of a flattering and fashionable style and perfectly tailored. Sparky guessed that tailoring ran in the family and Gabrielle had made the dress herself. Sparky waited for Gabrielle to walk around for a few moments. Gabrielle's attention was not particularly on the building, but more on the surrounding streets. She seemed to be looking for someone. Sparky smiled slightly to herself. It was time.

"Bon jour, mademoiselle."

"Bon jour, madame."

Sparky continued in French, hoping Gabrielle wouldn't notice that her accent was American and not English. "I beg your pardon, but I'm new to Paris and my nephew insisted that I should visit Saint Chappelle. I'm unfamiliar with its history. Might you be able to help me?"

"Oh, I would be delighted."

From his hiding place it seemed to Lord Ashleigh that their little costume drama was proceeding well. He was so focused on the action that he didn't hear Drake approaching him from behind. When Drake tapped him on the shoulder, he jumped in surprise and nearly elbowed the Chief Inspector.

"Oh, my goodness, Drake! You gave me quite a start. What are you doing here? Why aren't you helping the IGC arrest Grossman?"

"There is highly suspicious business afoot. They insisted there could not be anything amiss and gave me the brush off, but my instincts tell me that they know more than they admit. I believe we will need to take matters into our own hands."

Lord Ashleigh glanced back and forth between Drake and the conversation transpiring just out of earshot. He wanted to do the right thing, but he was sorely torn because he sensed that Sparky was making good progress. And indeed she was.

"I can understand why my nephew was so adamant that I make this visit. My nephew is a very intelligent and well-mannered young man. One rarely encounters an eligible gentleman of such exceptional qualities. Although he will inherit my father's estate in England, he is studying the law at Oxford as he feels that all men, no matter what class, should have a useful profession."

"He sounds very fine."

Drake continued, "Lord Ashleigh, did you hear what I said?"

"Um, yes, quite so, take matters into our own hands."

"I believe we will also require the able services of Dr. McTrowell." Drake moved as if to interrupt McTrowell and Mademoiselle Lambert, the thought of which considerably pained Ashleigh. Before he could decide how to respond, he heard another voice behind them.

"Drake, is that you again? You are everywhere in Paris this week!"

"Charles, what a surprise! What brings you here?"

McTrowell, sensing interest in the much-celebrated "nephew," pressed forward. "Yes, and did I mention that he is generous? He paid for my passage to Paris and very fine lodgings. It is my dream to find him a suitable wife who will appreciate all of his excellent qualities."

"He does sound like the kind of gentleman who would make a good husband."

Although Charles was usually an animated fellow, he was particularly excited this day. "I'm on my way to meet my sweetheart. I have just come from asking her guardian for her hand in marriage and he has given his blessing!" He produced a ring from his pocket, a very thin gold band with a single, rather small diamond in the setting. One would have thought from the look of delight on his face that the stone was the size of a goose egg.

McTrowell was feeling quite pleased with herself. She had created just the opening she wanted. "Would you like to meet him?"

"Um, yes, I suppose so."

"Well, what good fortune. I'm expecting him to meet me here at any moment." She folded down her parasol, swung it tip down, and tapped it on the paving stones twice sharply.

Ashleigh, who had been following the action near the chapel closely and the conversation between Drake and Charles almost not at all, started when he saw the signal and turned toward the two women. Charles' attention was caught by Ashleigh's sudden movement and turned toward the two women as well.

"Look, there's my nephew now." Sparky waved toward the three gentlemen. Suddenly she hoped that Gabrielle was looking at the men as well so she wouldn't see the look of consternation on Sparky's face. What was Drake doing here? Why wasn't he off foiling the plot to steal the limestone bricks? What was Drake's friend Charles doing here? Had he come for a rematch? Gabrielle, on the other hand, was not the least bit discomfited. She was smiling brightly and waving energetically. *"Well,"* thought Sparky, *"young Jonathan must have made quite an impression on Gabrielle yesterday."*

Lord Ashleigh was having almost exactly the same thought at that moment. He reached up to doff his top hat at the ladies, but Drake stayed his arm. One didn't become a chief inspector at Scotland Yard without having very keen powers of observation. He held fast to Ashleigh's arm for another instant during which Charles bounded across the street, wrapped his arms around Gabrielle's slim waist, spun her around in a circle in the air, and deposited her back onto the cobblestones with a kiss. He dropped to one knee and produced the ring, which he held up to her expectantly. When she clasped her hands over her mouth and began to cry, Lord Ashleigh didn't need to hear their words to know what Charles had asked and what Gabrielle's answer had been.

He turned back toward Drake who tried to comfort him. "I am sorry, my dear friend."

"Thank you for preventing me from making a fool of myself." Lord Ashleigh took a deep breath and let it out. He reached into the inside pocket of his coat and pulled out the neatly wrapped necklace. "The least I can do is make good use of this for your very fortunate friend and his betrothed." He strode toward Charles and the women with Drake a few steps behind him.

Lord Ashleigh walked straight up to Charles and shook his hand, "Congratulations." He kissed Gabrielle chastely on the cheek and handed her the package with the wrapped necklace. "A small wedding gift. May the two of you enjoy a long, prosperous, and happy life together."

Gabrielle was, by now, at a complete loss for words. Charles, on the other hand, was bubbling over with high spirits. "Please, come join us to celebrate this joyous event."

Drake also shook Charles' hand. "I am sure we would all enjoy that very much, old friend, but we have another pressing matter that requires our immediate attention."

"Very well, good luck."

"Thank you. I believe we'll need it." Drake hustled Sparky and Jonathan toward Pont Saint-Michel.

Sparky waited for until they were out of earshot of Charles and Gabrielle before speaking. "Well, that did not go at all as planned."

To which Drake replied, "It was not the only endeavor today that did not go as planned. There is no time to explain, but we need to make haste to rue Rémy Dumoncel to stop the larcenous Mr. Grossman."

"Excellent, an undertaking more to my tastes and skills." With that, she pitched the parasol high over her shoulder and didn't look back as it sailed over a small sign, ***Pas ne natation.***

LIMESTONE PLUNDERERS

By Mr. David L. Drake

Chief Inspector Erasmus Drake switched to his commanding voice. "Follow me or all is lost!" His stride was demanding, headed for

156

the western bridge that lead off Île de la Cité. Sparky and Lord Ashleigh were putting serious effort into staying a step behind the determined law enforcer. Erasmus talked as they walked. "Changing tasks. Here is our status. We are late. The bricks were supposed to be transported from the boulangerie on rue Rémy Dumoncel at noon. That was an hour and 10 minutes ago. We are quite on our own here, unless we can get one or more members of the Parisian police force to accompany us, which may not be easy given the haste we need to get there. Since rue Rémy Dumoncel is just outside of Paris on the southwest side, we should try to secure transportation. There is a cabriolet now! Hurry!"

The three of them rushed across the cobblestone bridge and sped up to the side of the vehicle, Erasmus holding the door for the other two and providing directions to the driver in an earnest voice. Inside the cab the conversation continued.

"What do we have in the way of gaining the upper hand? I do not have my cane, but I do have my revolver. I really do not want to show it, much less use it, for obvious reasons. Your knife, Lord Ashleigh?"

"My *kirpaan*? It's more ceremonial than utilitarian, but it will suffice if necessary."

"Sparky?" Erasmus queried.

"My fists. I didn't prepare for being threatening. Perhaps I should have kept the parasol. I could have frightened the misanthropes by asking them to hold it." She smiled despite the serious demeanor of her male companions who just furrowed their brows at her, each for their own reasons.

The driver did his job well, speeding through the streets of Paris. In the cab, they formulated a plan more or less. At rue Rémy Dumoncel, the vehicle came to a stop and the troop piled out. Lord Ashleigh took the lead since he knew the location and was the person who was expected. They headed down the cobblestoned alley on the side of the closed bakery, Sparky and Erasmus keeping their distance.

Lord Ashleigh rounded the corner and was, as before, quite surprised by the scene. The entire back lot was filled with limestone bricks. Even the back of the bakery, with its door gaping open, was filled with bricks inside the building itself. The skittering of mechanical feet indicated to him that the limestone bricks were still being extracted, even though the neatly stacked columns were now a full twelve feet high. On the side, two men sat on the ground bound and gagged, leaning up against a tree. They were clearly Mr. Hedgley and Mr. Martin. Lord Ashleigh ran over to them, concerned for their well-being. They might be criminals, but this was a beastly state in which to leave one's fellow man. As he approached, he couldn't help but notice that they both were obviously exhausted, perhaps from struggling against their restraints. But given the fact that they were still wearing the same clothes and the state those garments were in, they probably had been toiling all through the night as well. Both men looked up with wild, pleading eyes at Lord Ashleigh's approach. Lord Ashleigh let an "Oh, my goodness" slip out and removed the gag from Mr. Martin, whom Lord Ashleigh thought was the nicer of the two and deserved the initial help.

Mr. Martin took a deep gasp as if he had had trouble breathing. He looked at Lord Ashleigh and said, "Mr. Ashleigh, you have no idea how much I appreciate what you have just done." The twinkle in his eye stood out against his weary appearance.

"Non! Non! Arrêtez de faire ça!" came the shout from within the bakery, and two well-dressed men darted out of the back door. Lord Ashleigh, turned around to see them, but did not understand their concern. At the same time, both Erasmus and Sparky appeared from hiding in the alley, taking in the entire bizarre spectacle. Erasmus recognized one of the gentlemen, Monsieur Andre Toque from the IGC. They simultaneously pointed and said, "What are you doing here?" to each other, but with very different accents.

Mr. Martin took center stage and announced, "It's been lovely, but we must be going!" There was just enough time for Lord Ashleigh, Sparky, and Erasmus to make quizzical faces and for the other IGC agent to yell *"Non!"* again. Mr. Martin pursed his lips and emitted a well-practiced, high-pitched whistle containing an odd pitch variation. It didn't last long, but it didn't need to.

The mechanized bugs erupted out of the mineshaft in a solid wave of clamoring brass, flinging their limestone cargo in every direction except for the source of the whistle. They moved at an incredible speed, over the twelve-foot column of shining white bricks, and down toward Mr. Hedgley and Mr. Martin like a living golden carpet, sentient and purposeful. Mr. Hedgley and Mr. Martin were scooped up onto the backs of the arachnid forerunners that, with pairs of repurposed legs that now acted as carrying arms, rapidly unbound their masters. The men were borne on the metal backs as if they were as light as feathers. Without pause, the entire skittering parade tore down the cobblestone alley. The men had the gall to doff their hats and smile as they rode away. Out in the rue Rémy Dumoncel, women's screams and horses' whinnies erupted, continuing as the mechanical parade retreated into the distance.

The fleeing carpet lasted a while. The last to go were the cutters with radial saw faces and their shorter, dachshund-like legs. Every one of the living kept their distance, plastered to walls to prevent having any one of the bugs even touch them. To a person, the thought of fleeing rats was hard to keep out of their minds, and that instinctual repulsion of amassed vermin was unmistakably present.

Then it was over just as fast as it started with the tail of the gleaming carpet disappearing into the alleyway. Everyone looked around before taking a step forward, inhaling deeply to compensate for the reflex of breath holding during the mechanized exodus.

Erasmus spoke first, directing his question to Monsieur Toque. "What was going on here? This is a highly unusual way to deal with a crime of theft."

"Chief Inspector, I don't know what you are talking about. And here in Paris, I ask the questions, no? What are you and your companions doing here? My assumption is that you are helping these thieves and should be arrested."

Erasmus was starting to get indignant. "Pardon me, my good man, but I was trying to report this theft to you this morning! You pooh-poohed me then. My 'companions' and I had to do something to protect the stability of Parisian firmament, not to mention the theft of the stone itself."

"Pooh-poohed?"

"Yes. Dismissed, rejected, and rebuffed me."

"Rebuffed? Are these English words?" At this point in the conversation, Monsieur Toque smiled, but it was less about unexpected vocabulary and rather was due to the arrival of French workmen with wheelbarrows. The tenor of Monsieur Toque's conversation changed to congeniality as he continued, "Chief Inspector, we at the IGC appreciate you helping in this matter, and I will personally see that this is properly resolved. *Merci et au revoir.*" He shook Erasmus' hand and directed him, Sparky, and Lord Ashleigh toward the alley leading to the street. Slightly befuddled, they single-filed out through the alley as the workmen and wheelbarrows single-filed in.

Sparky was confused as to what had transpired. "Does this make sense to you, Erasm...EEEAAAHHHH!" She jumped to the side when she saw the movement in the shadows under a bit of discarded burlap. Erasmus carefully used the tip of his shoe to flip back the rough cloth scrap to reveal a lone EPACT with only two working legs on its left side and a crippled one on right. The rest had been wrenched off. The machine could only make a sad semicircle and appeared to be out of energy even for that endeavor. Hoping that it didn't have a defensive mechanism, Erasmus slid his left hand under it, placed his right hand on top, and lifted the automaton. It was not light in weight, that was for sure, but not solid metal, either. Erasmus got it high enough in the air to look at the underside where there was a knurled knob in a recessed area of the bottom plate, similar to the setting mechanism on a pocket watch, and a small moveable round handle.

"Sparky, try moving that handle," Erasmus requested, hoping that her original fear had dissipated. She tentatively moved the handle along its path with two fingers. As soon as she managed the full throw of the switch, the legs suddenly went limp and hung loosely from its body.

For whatever reason, the procession of workers paid no heed to all of this and appeared to be more than happy to get to the back of the bakery. Erasmus slipped off his coat, wrapped the brass contraption, and carried it like a heavy parcel under his arm.

Back on the street, they had to walk a good distance to hail another cabriolet. The walk was filled with hushes from Erasmus indicating he wanted to talk only in the privacy of their conveyance.

Once inside, Erasmus was vocal. "Well, does that not just knock the stuffings out of it? They were working both sides."

Lord Ashleigh asked, "Do you think that they were in league with the thieves?"

"No. But I think their goal was to appropriate the bricks after they were illegally mined. You cannot put them back into the ground."

Sparky thought for a second and then countered, "Perhaps they could. Since the IGC is working on retrofitting the parts of the catacombs that are used for the public tours, those bricks could be used to spruce up the visited sections! They probably couldn't safely mine this area themselves, but they could use the product of the limestone plunderers."

"Excellent reasoning! We shall have to see if the newspapers report a grand improvement to the tunnels."

Sparky added, "And see if this region has another cave-in."

Erasmus looked at Lord Ashleigh and gestured to the window. "Would you be so kind? Your French is so much better than mine."

Lord Ashleigh smiled, adding "I would be delighted, my friend. Thank you both for our Parisian adventure!"

Lord Ashleigh stuck his head out of the window, and in his best French, requested transport to the airship port.

Erasmus patted his wrapped parcel and thought to himself, *"Before we leave, I shall send this off to the only man I trust to determine the nature of this contraption, Dr. Edmond Pogue."*

VICTOR AND VANQUISHED

BY DR. KATHERINE L. MORSE

They rode in relative silence for a few blocks, each exhausted and a little disappointed in his or her own way. Sparky was looking forward to getting back to the Burke & Hare, if only to get out of the uncomfortable clothes. But, she was going to miss Paris. She never seemed to get quite enough time in Paris to do everything she wanted. She gazed out the window of the cabriolet in a melancholy state. The cab slowed for another coach stopped in the lane in front of them, and she stared down an alley. She thought she saw something shiny move in the shadows. She blinked and rubbed her tired eyes. She wasn't imagining it. She leaned slightly out the window. There was a pair of the crawlers tussling in the alley.

"Stop the cab! Stop the cab!" She flung open the door of the cab and jumped out even before it had stopped completely. The bustle of the dress made her movements ungainly, and she nearly dumped herself onto her nose.

Drake's eyes followed her trajectory and spotted the wrestling automatons. He thrust his bundled coat into Lord Ashleigh's hands. "Stay here and hold the cab." He leapt out of the cab and followed McTrowell at a sprint. Without the impediment of couture, he caught up to her just as she reached the wrestlers. They were too late to save one of them. The victor snapped off two of the legs of the vanquished and scuttled off down the alley. Drake snatched up the disabled one and held it up for McTrowell to switch off as she had with the first disabled one they had recovered. He set it back down on the ground. "We shall come back for this one."

They dashed after the victor. It scuttled around a corner at the end of the alley and through a hinged flap at the bottom of a much-abused door. Sparky reached for the handle, but Erasmus held an index finger up to his lips. He leaned forward and placed his ear against the door. She followed suit. They could hear muffled voices inside, but it was clear the space behind the door was large and contained many large obstructions, judging by the distortion of the voices. Drake grasped the door handle firmly and gently pushed down the latch, being especially careful to make as little noise as possible. Fortunately, it was dark in the alley, so they wouldn't let in much light. They squeezed through and Erasmus closed the door quietly behind them.

Their eyes took a moment to adjust to the light during which time Sparky realized that Erasmus was actually standing quite close to her. She could feel his warm breath on the back of her neck. When his eyes had adjusted, he tapped her lightly on the shoulder and pointed in the direction of the voices. They inched closer, stopping at the edge of a stack of wooden crates. When they peered around the corner, McTrowell had to slap her hand over her own mouth to keep herself from gasping out loud. Not surprisingly, Mr. Hedgley and Mr. Martin were standing in the middle of the open space. Slightly more surprising was a man neither she nor Drake had seen before. He was little more than a twig of a man with a shock of wild, frizzy brown hair that was not in his eyes only because his eyes were covered by a particularly large and opaque pair of goggles with multiple interchangeable lenses on miniature arms. He looked a bit like a praying mantis. She had an unkind thought about his being devoured, but then she remembered the first part of that scenario and shuddered in revulsion. The sight that had nearly caused her to gasp was the sea of crawlers covering nearly the entirety of the open floor space. The three men were standing around a large worktable, and the crawlers completely surrounded them. It looked almost as if the crawlers had herded the men there and were holding them hostage. Mr. Martin kept looking down at his ankles as if he expected the crawlers to start snapping at him.

Mr. Hedgley was unperturbed by the mechanized horde and was considerably exercised by the bug man. He was stabbing his finger at another dismembered crawler lying immobile on the worktable.

"These bloody things are a lot of work to build and cost dearly! It's your fault they're tearing each other apart! We'll never turn a profit if they keep doing this."

"Now, now, Monsieur Hedgley. Do not worry yourself so much about ze money. You weel take all ze fon out of ze experiment."

"This isn't a bloody experiment! It's a business. You told me you could make our EPACTs work together as a team. Teammates don't go about ripping each other's legs off. It's not very sportsmanlike!"

Sensing that his partner was either going to have a seizure or do some violence to their "colleague," Mr. Martin interjected himself into the conversation, if somewhat timidly. "Well, to be fair, Horace, he did make them work together better. They're a lot easier to control when we don't have to set each one to a single task, what with the good doctor's emergency hive mind."

"Emergent hive mind," Mr. Hedgley correctly.

"Yes, well, they do work together better."

"Right. Right up until one of them decides another's not toeing the line and takes it upon himself to have himself a little swift justice." Hedgley glared at a crawler at the edge of the swarm that was very close to Drake and McTrowell's position. They had to duck back behind the crates before they were spotted. McTrowell realized Hedgley must have been looking at the vicious, fratricidal crawler they had followed into the building. She rather imagined that it had beady, cold eyes, but she knew she was just anthropomorphizing.

"Monsieur Hedgley, soon I weel perfect ze 'ive mind and ze EPACTs weel be fully autonomous. Nothing weel be able to stop zem!" At the sound of excitement in the bug man's voice, the crawlers started humming and hopping back and forth on their sharp, metal feet, making a sound like a swarm of ravenous beetles. McTrowell stepped back in disgust...right onto the hem of her dress. She choked herself with the high, snug collar and let out a gurgling gag. She regained her balance just in time to see the swarm freeze and swivel as one in the direction of their hiding place. The three men stopped and looked around as well. And then the bug man let out a squeal so high pitched it hurt the ears. Neither Drake nor McTrowell needed to wait even a second to know what it meant and that they were in deep trouble.

They turned and fled back the direction they came, slamming open the door, and pounding up the alley. Stealth was a distant dream. Unencumbered as he was, Drake made better time. It only took him a second to snatch up the disabled crawler in the alley as he sprinted to the cab. Ashleigh was leaning out the cab window watching wide-eyed at the pell-mell approach of his friends being chased by an angry swarm of carnivorous devices. With uncharacteristic vigor, Drake shouted, "Drive!" Ashleigh threw open the door of the cab just in time to catch the dismembered crawler Drake threw to him. Drake dove in immediately after. The cab lurched to a start, making it difficult for the two of them to scramble around into position to grab McTrowell's outstretched arms when she finally made it to the cab. A couple of the crawlers had managed to catch hold of the hem of her dress. Drake and Ashleigh kicked them loose and the crawlers took big chunks of the dress with them. Fortunately, the horse needed no encouragement to send it galloping off madly through the streets of Paris, but its flight knocked the three friends into an unceremonious heap on the floor of the cab.

They dragged themselves painfully up off the floor and onto the seats, rubbing sore elbows and knees along the way. Sparky held up the ruined hem of the dress. "Well, I for one am looking forward to a nice quiet, safe activity like an airship regatta."

The cab passed under an elaborate wrought iron archway embellished with **Port du Jean-Marie-Joseph Coutelle**.

TWO CRATES MARKED FRAGILE

BY MR. DAVID L. DRAKE

The interior of the lofty room was round, formed by carved grey-white granite block walls and floor. A wrought iron spiral staircase hugged the side of the room, linking the heavy door halfway up the tower to the floor below. Seven dark-brown tables formed a semi-circle, each one containing the gadgetry of an undertaking: chemistry apparatus on one, another with mechanical parts and tools, and so forth for each of the work surfaces. A man dressed in a heavy white overcoat that showed the signs of scientific toil was moving from table to table: a smear of grease here, a small green splatter there, and minute brown ringlets from microscopic splashes of acid. He busied himself as he flowed from task to task. At one of the tables he pipetted a blue liquid into a jar, noticed a color change, and then jotted down something into a large notebook. Then, moving to the next table, he mated a complex piston assembly with a high-pressure manifold, securing them together with a handful of bolts.

The heavy door opened and a young Asian lady appeared wearing a dark blue, long-sleeved, silk dress. Despite the squeak of the door, the man on the tower floor continued with his labors without even looking up. She looked down on him for a second, watching his uninterrupted industry. She then carefully descended the staircase and walked to his side. In a very practiced movement, she reached out and lightly touched his arm even while he was still collecting the pollen off of the stamens of a large-petaled flower.

He stopped his activity and turned to her. Her petite mouth turned up in a small smile. She gave a small movement of her head that was the remnant of a practiced formal bow that only let a few strands of her shiny, black, straight hair slip from behind her shoulder to the front. He smiled back. "Doctor, you wanted me to let you know when your sister arrived."

From the top of the stairs, a new figure appeared. "Willing to stop to say hello to your sister?" she asked loud enough to be heard throughout the room. Dressed in riding clothes, complete with knee high brown boots, frilly blouse, smartly cut jacket, and a tiny feminine top hat pinned at a jaunty angle, she pranced down the stairs and ran over to the Doctor. "Edmond! How I have missed you! It's been months since we were last together!" She acted as though she wanted to give a grand hug to her brother, but knew better than expose her clothes to whatever was on Edmond's. Instead she stood as close to him as she dared and exuded enthusiasm for their being together.

The doctor replied, "Glad you could make it back to London. Have you been out riding?"

"Oh, no, silly. This is what all the ladies are wearing now! Like it? Oh, I have another great outfit I need to show you."

"Sorry, sis. I have to work until six tonight. I have a couple of clients with deadlines I need to meet. I'll see you upstairs for dinner. Go check out the shops for a few hours."

Edmond's sister made a practiced pouty face, then flashed a smile, and bounded back up the stairs. Edmond turned to his female assistant and requested, "Yin, please see that I have no further visitors for the day. I need to finish a number of these experiments. Thank you so much."

Dr. Yin Young gave her brief bow again, turned, and quietly ascended the stairs.

After carefully pollinating a potted flower, Edmond walked to the last table to his right. On it was a secured wooden crate and a letter. He picked the letter up and scanned it again to make sure he hadn't missed any details. Musing out loud, he said, "So, this is the 'electrical discharge device' seized at the Egyptian Court. Let's see what it looks like."

Obtaining a pry bar from a nearby tool rack, Edmond loosened the crate's top and forced it open against squeaking nails. Peering inside, he saw the gleaming metal of the device. "Ho ho, Chief Inspector, what have you sent me now?!"

Back on the airship, Sparky, Erasmus, and Lord Asheigh sought refuge in Lord Asheigh's improvised sitting room. "Shall it be port, chai, or some other diversion?" their exhausted host offered.

"No port for me," Sparky was quick to answer, "I need to be piloting this airship in a few hours. In fact, I really need to be performing a full ship inspection for airworthiness and evaluate the meteorological state of our route. If you'll please excuse me, I must get to my duties." As she stood, she looked down and quickly realized that she was in a torn dress, totally unfitting for the role she was about to undertake. Sparky added, "Well, first, a costume change is required," and at that, she let herself out of the cabin.

Lord Ashleigh quickly took over the conversation. "Chief Inspector, to whom did you ship those two EPACTs while we were in the terminal?"

"A colleague whom I have known for a few years now, Dr. Pogue. Scotland Yard uses a number of scientific specialists to help with the analysis component of investigations. I have sent some oddities to him over those years, and Dr. Pogue has proven to be top notch! He always comes through. As a matter of fact, I secured his services with regard to one of Professor Farnsworth's electrical discharge contraptions. I am also hoping that he can give us greater insight into the two brass crawlers."

Just as the two men were having their conversation, a porter was wheeling a half dozen wooden crates over to the Western & Transatlantic's Fortis. It was a sizable airship, easily twice the length of the Burke & Hare, and was specifically used for cargo hauling. Nearing the end of his shift, the porter quickly packed the loading platform with the contents of his dolly. Bam! The crate containing 65 pounds of cast iron cookware came down hard. Bam! The 59-pound pallet of French magazines added to the stack. The next two crates were marked **FRAGILE**, so he used a little more care. He placed them side-by-side on top of the magazine pallet. Finally, he added two crates holding flywheels for printing presses to the top. With an arm wave, he signaled his mate to haul the platform up to the floating transport, who tightened the cables as the load was hauled up to the belly of the Fortis. The rocking packages shifted under the weight of the flywheels, and the **FRAGILE** package on the right moved to the side enough to slip off one of its wooden skids. It only dropped an inch. Not even enough for the porter to notice. But inside the crate, it was enough to move a brass lever slightly to one side. The mechanical crawler that it was attached to came to life, albeit a claustrophobic one, and tried to bring its remaining legs into position. Failing that, it made an inaudible whistling sound to see if it had any nearby companions. And then it waited.

Quite unaware of the change in his shipped package, Erasmus chuckled to himself, "I hope Edmond finds this shipment interesting!"

MISS SARAH SLATE

BY DR. KATHERINE L. MORSE

Esmeralda Pogue strode purposefully out of the milliner's shop on the Marylebone High Street, a tiered stack of hatboxes lashed together in each hand. She handed them to her coachman who once again reshuffled her purchases for the afternoon to try to find a secure place for all of them. Fortunately, the shops were closing. Otherwise he was going to have to hire a cab just to deliver her purchases to her brother's "abode" in Shadwell. It was too odd to be called a house, what with the tower sticking out of a building that betrayed its origins as a warehouse. He also found it odd that a person of means such as Dr. Pogue would choose to live in the environs of Shadwell, but then "odd" was a particularly apt word to describe the older brother of Miss Esmeralda Pogue. If the coachman hadn't known their late parents, he wouldn't have believed the siblings to be related.

The coachman had just managed to solve his packing problem when he looked down in horror to see Miss Pogue staring up the street. Surely she hadn't espied another shop still open! No, she was just staring at another young woman on the street who was clearly oblivious to the attention she was drawing. Those people who knew Esmeralda Pogue only from her attendance at teas, balls, and sporting events thought her the usual rich, spoiled, shallow young woman only in search of a husband to continue to finance her taste for frippery. To be fair, she did enjoy the finer things in life and a handsome, wealthy husband (preferably with a minor title) would be a nice acquisition. However, she considered her primary mission in life the care of her brilliant, sweet, but hopelessly distracted older brother. For all his scientific brilliance, he never seemed to be able to quite manage the details of being an adult. So she maintained a close relationship with the solicitor who was the executor of their parents' estate and made regular excuses to visit him near London, shopping admittedly being her favorite excuse.

The sensible Miss Pogue recognized the expression on the face of the other young woman on the street, and it wasn't simply the wide-eyed amazement of a girl newly arrived from the country. She was examining, memorizing, and deconstructing everything she saw, just like dear Edmond. Unfortunately, she was also attracting the attention of the rats of London and not the rodent variety. Esmeralda popped open her pocket watch. Five o'clock. Dear Edmond had said he would work until six, which meant at least seven, which meant dinner couldn't possibly start until eight, plenty of time. She walked directly up to the young woman absorbed in her examination of the fixtures in the window of the watchmaker's shop.

"Good evening. Parseval's makes lovely watches, but they don't keep particularly good time."

The young woman snapped out of her revelry. "Excuse me?"

An American! What an interesting surprise! "Their watches don't keep particularly good time. My name is Miss Esmeralda Pogue." She waited a second or two. "And you are?"

"Oh, I'm terribly sorry. I've forgotten my manners. Miss Sarah Slate of Aspinock, Connecticut."

"A pleasure to make your acquaintance. Do you have tea in Aspinock, Connecticut?"

Miss Slate examined Miss Pogue as if she were a lab specimen. "Yes, of course."

"We like to think that we have excellent tea in London." Again the lab specimen stare. "Perhaps you would care to join me for a cup?" While Esmeralda was well-intentioned, she had never quite grasped the fact that her brother and people like him weren't dim, just chronically distracted by matters so much more fascinating than the prosaic matters of her own concern. Esmeralda turned around, looked both ways along the street lest she be trampled by a carriage, and marched across the street to the nearest tearoom, trusting that Miss

Slate would follow. Years of frustrating conversations with Edmond had taught her that negotiating simple daily tasks was an exercise in supreme frustration; better just to charge forward before he could begin his swirl of deconstruction that would inevitably derail the whole enterprise. By the time Miss Slate had caught on to her role in this pantomime and entered the tearoom, Miss Pogue was already seated and had ordered tea, scones, and clotted cream. She wasn't simply being generous; she was famished from her athletic shopping, and it would be three more hours before dinner with Edmond.

Miss Slate arranged her skirts on the spindly tearoom chair and doffed her unfashionable straw hat. The girl in the striped dress and crisp, white apron that was the uniform of the tearoom arrived with a silver tray, quietly depositing the welcome sustenance on the table that was just barely large enough to hold it all. Esmeralda poured tea for both of them before offering the plate of scones to Miss Slate. "So, what brings you to London, Miss Slate?"

"My grandfather was from England. He left me a small inheritance with the suggestion that I might find it interesting. I have visited the mills of Derbyshire. Quite serviceable, but no more interesting than my grandfather's mills. I had hoped to see more substantial advances. I have come to London in search of the scientific and industrial discoveries about which I have heard so much." The more Sarah spoke, the more she reminded Esmeralda of Edmond.

"London also has many cultural advantages to offer," Esmeralda suggested, hoping to turn the conversation to one in which she could participate.

"Yes, I'm finding the light in London most interesting: the flickering street lamps reflected on the wet cobblestones; the shine of the black lacquer coaches with gleaming brass door pulls; the glittering jewels worn by women such as yourself as you're rushing to the theater. I am considering a study of the effects of soot on the reflectivity of objects in London." Esmeralda sighed into her tea. If she squinted just a bit more so her companion's features didn't look quite so sharp, nor her hair quite so long, she could see Edmond sitting across the table from her.

"I'm sure my brother, Edmond, would have something to offer on the subject."

170

"Edmond? Edmond Pogue? Dr. Edmond Pogue is your brother?!" Somehow Esmeralda had known this was the inevitable conclusion to this encounter. "His work on high-pressure pistons is the best in the field."

What was the use in fighting it? "Miss Slate, do you have dinner plans?"

Sparky wiped her hands on a greasy cloth and stuffed the cloth in the pocket of her favorite blue work trousers. She wiped a few sweaty hairs back from her forehead with the only clean spot on the back of her forearm. She leaned on the bulkhead and stared vacantly out of a porthole. She could see Luis-Miguel Sevilla far below supervising the transfer of the final crates of unnecessary furnishings to a warehouse at the airship port. It was reassuring to know that most of the world had continued on its regularly scheduled rounds while her own life had taken one unexpectedly dramatic turn after another. Although she was exhausted as she trudged back to her cabin, it was the welcome tired of a job well done. She was satisfied that the Burke & Hare was ready for the regatta and there was only the spectacle of the evening's dinner with Wallace, during which he would undoubtedly bloviate about the certainty of Western & Transatlantic's win in the regatta. And then she could get down to the business of actually winning in the regatta. She was sorely looking forward to that! She started stripping off her work clothes as soon as she closed the door of her cabin, hanging them on the hooks behind the door. Dinner wasn't for another half an hour and she felt she deserved a few minutes rest. She spun around to drop herself on her bunk and nearly fell on a package wrapped in cream and pink striped paper tied with a pink satin ribbon. The ribbon was threaded through a hole in a tiny cream-colored card embossed with **Gerard LY, Paris.**

LOOK DOWN

BY MR. DAVID L. DRAKE

The rest of the room faded away as Sparky concentrated on the perfectly wrapped package on the bed. She shook off the obvious guess as to who would have sent it. Perhaps, instead, it was a bon voyage package from Wallace, or a "good luck" gift from the crew for the regatta. But those were remote possibilities. She knew the only way to find out was to open it, but that would also open a place in her heart that she had purposely closed off for quite a while, so she was hesitant.

She picked it up. It was unexpectedly light. Its base was about the size of a shoebox, but the box was considerably flatter. The wrapping gave away that it had been wrapped professionally, most likely by the shop where it was purchased. The wrapping paper was of a fine quality and was completely held in place by the ribbon that fashioned it; not a hint of glue or paste to simplify the wrapping process. She took gentle hold of one of the ribbon ends and held her breath for a couple of seconds. A slow tug and the bow untied, the ribbon sliding off the package as only satin can.

The paper wrapping relaxed about the box and begged to be removed. Sparky carefully reached under the wrapping, cradled the box, and removed the paper. The box was a superb paperboard, white, with a gilt swirl on top. Inside was an envelope and a beautiful, light yellow, silk scarf. Sparky slipped out an "ooo..." and the scarf was around her neck in an instant, the box and envelope left haplessly on the bed as she examined the new adornment in her hand mirror. She thought, *"Not too feminine, but just enough. And so stylish! It will make me want to return to Paris all the more."*

Now to the hard part. She took the small white envelope into her hands. It was tucked rather than glued or sealed. It obviously was written while at the shop of purchase and secured inside the box before wrapping. Inside was a simple, plain card.

Dearest Sparky,
Please accept this small gift as a memento of our outing in Paris, which I have enjoyed immensely.
Erasmus

The history of the package became obvious to Sparky. Erasmus must have slipped into one of the shops while they were walking about Paris on Tuesday, purchased the scarf, written the note, and had the package delivered here to the Burke & Hare. How clever. That way he wouldn't have to carry it around or present it immediately. Actually, with all of the excitement of today, he might have even forgotten that he had it sent.

Sparky spent an extra minute mulling over the details of the present and note. It wasn't too flowery or flattering, but he did use first names, showing a level of familiarity. And despite his claim that it was a small gift, a Parisian silk scarf wasn't a trifle. The intent of the unexpected package was still to be determined by Sparky. She could wear the scarf to dinner tonight to see the man's response, jog his memory of the purchase, and force a bit more reaction. That seemed a bit sneaky, but it would not be too outside her usual manners. Making a plan to do just that, she proceeded with dressing for piloting an airship.

ಹಿಹಿ ಹಿ ಹಿ ಹಿ 🜨 ಲ ಲ ಲ ಲ

Sergeant J.B. Fox was on his third round of walking the entire airship. His plan was simple: memorize the details of the Burke & Hare while all was well so he could spot changes of interest when they arose. He had finished the lower deck and was making his way up to the outer catwalk, hoping to take a last look around before launch.

ಹಿಹಿ ಹಿ ಹಿ ಹಿ 🜨 ಲ ಲ ಲ ಲ

Sparky entered the bridge in her full pilot's uniform. First officer, Ivan Krasnayarubashka, who was already making prelaunch preparations, turned, gave her a polite smile, and turned back to his labors. He was using simple hand gestures to verify with the airfield workman on the tower that all of the lines but one were safely released and the Burke & Hare was close to launch.

Sergeant Fox suddenly appeared on the catwalk on the starboard side of the bridge, rapping anxiously on the window. His face was unusually serious. His shouts were nearly inaudible given the thickness of the glass, and he quickly resorted to simply pointing to something off the starboard bow.

Sparky grabbed her brass telescope and aimed it in the direction of the aerial marine's gesture. Coming through the arched entrance of the airship port was an undulating wave of dust. A shape of golden color was rushing onto the airfield. Through her telescope, Sparky recognized dozens of brass creatures that were scurrying at top speed. She shouted, "EPACTs! Coming this way!"

Her first thought was to wonder how the EPACTs had found them and what destruction they could cause on the Burke & Hare.

Ivan's face screwed up into a quizzical look and said "Vat is dat? Ipecac? You vant to be sick?"

She grabbed the voicepipe that lead to the cabin hallway and shouted, "Drake! Drake! To the starboard side! EPACTs!"

The Chief Inspector was just making his exit from Lord Ashlcigh's cabin when he heard the strangely dampened and echoey plea. He sprinted to the main hall leading to the external door. Outside on the catwalk he quickly joined Sergeant Fox. "Where are they?" Erasmus shouted, the slight breeze of the evening air at this altitude making it hard to hear.

The Sergeant pointed, but followed with his own question, "What are they?"

"Tunneling and excavation contraptions. We not only encountered them just outside Paris, but ended up capturing a couple."

Sergeant Fox raised an eyebrow for an instant, but showed no more surprise than that. The two men looked over the rail to determine how this might play out.

The EPACTs were scurrying in a fashion that actually raised dust despite that the airfield being a well-trimmed lawn. Then, as if flocking birds on the wing, they changed direction in unison and headed for the site where the sizable Fortis was launching. A single remaining rope line was all that was left on the ground from its launch. The EPACTs were headed directly for it.

The five workmen on the port side of the Fortis were oblivious of the scene below as they went about their business of gathering lines and stowing them. The size of the Fortis camouflaged the great distance between the airships. Erasmus instinctively started to wave his arms to get their attention, to no avail.

Sergeant Fox jumped to the small storage compartment on the bulkhead of the Burke & Hare and from it took up the red and yellow semaphore flags stashed within. Bracing himself, he started a series of ridged-armed flag positions as succinctly as if he had practiced them earlier in the day. After 10 positions, he repeated them.

"What are you signaling to them?" Erasmus shouted.

"The easiest thing I could think of," the Sergeant shouted back, "LOOK DOWN!"

The workmen stared at the flags for a few seconds and then looked down as directed. But the EPACTs were at the line. At this point, it was also clear that one of the crawlers had carried a cutter on its back to the scene. The first to the line attempted to climb it, but it wasn't really made for such an endeavor. The best it could do was to trap the rope between three legs and hold on. The next EPACT then scurried over its predecessor and gained a foothold on the line above it. One body length at a time they scurried onto the line. Even from this distance it was clear what the workman did: two ran off to the bridge to request the Fortis get underway, while the others stayed and sawed away at the sizable rope with their pocket knives.

The race was on, EPACTs climbing one at a time, and the workers slicing the rope as fast as they could. Just as the EPACTs made the halfway point, the rope gave way and down came the jumble of brass and hemp. But unlike living entities that would have had to recover from the fall, the EPACTs righted themselves in an instant and headed for the Fortis' tower, climbing up the outside with ease.

The peril was over though. The Fortis had pulled away from the tower before the EPACTs even got to the second floor. The Fortis backed away from the tower slowly, a couple dozen propellers at its aft chopping away at the air. As the massive airship turned to exit the port, the EPACTs did likewise, changed direction, descended the tower and headed back off the airfield at the same clip they arrived.

Sergeant Fox asked the obvious question, "What could have possibly drawn them to that airship? And with that level of resolve?"

Erasmus said, "I'm not sure." Yet to himself he thought, *"but I'm afraid I may have set poor Dr. Pogue up for a surprise."*

PLAY TO WIN

BY DR. KATHERINE L. MORSE

Drake hurried onto the bridge. "How long until we cast off?"

"Only a few more minutes. We need to clear the Paris air space before we lose the rest of the light."

"I need to get back down to the telegraph office to send a message to Dr. Pogue warning him about the nature of the EPACTs."

"You'll never make it in time and I can't hold the Burke & Hare. However, I may have another solution. In his constant efforts to extract yet more money from his customers, Wallace installed an optical telegraph on the Burke & Hare. There is a relay at Calais and another at Dover. Once we're away from the lights of Paris, I can signal to Calais, but we can only hope that Dover isn't fogged over." She handed him her enameled pen and one of her calling cards. "I'm sure I don't need to remind you to be succinct."

Drake quickly scribbled a note on the back of the card:
DR EDMOND POGUE, SHADWELL, LONDON. CRATE ARRIVING SOONEST. EXTREME CAUTION. CI E L DRAKE.

He handed the pen and card back to McTrowell. He seemed on the verge of saying something else, but they were in very close quarters with Mr. Krasnayarubashka. He resigned himself to tipping his bowler and backing out of the bridge.

She inspected the handwriting on the card carefully. She closed her eyes and visualized the handwriting on the small card that had accompanied the scarf. The card in her hand had been written in haste with block letters and only the support of his hand behind the card. The other had been written carefully in script on a proper writing surface. She looked for characteristic similarities, but could find no concrete evidence one way or the other.

Sparky doffed her leather duster as she entered the main hall and handed it to Sevilla. Only one dining table remained in the main hall. Everything save the minimum that Sevilla considered civilized had been removed from the airship. Knowing his exceptional organizational skills, she had no doubt that he had planned the menu for the regatta so as to minimize the necessary crockery and cutlery while still offering a delicious variety of foods. The man was truly a marvel. Such a shame he wasn't an engineer.

She made a bit of a show of untucking and arranging the scarf after she removed her duster, wondering if anyone would notice. If Drake noticed, his expression gave no indication. The extra time it had taken her to calm Mr. Krasnayarubashka's nerves about the EPACTs and to send the telegraph had made her a few minutes late for dinner. There was only one seat left at the table, right between Drake and Wallace and directly across from Lord Ashleigh. She was done for! Wallace would bend her ear incessantly. Drake would sit on the other side, silent as the sphinx, offering no intervention. And Ashleigh would just smile sweetly with only his cheery brown eyes revealing his mirth at her discomfort.

All the gentlemen stood as she approached the table and Sevilla held her chair for her. She wondered why they continued these habits when she was the only woman around, but all previous efforts to change this behavior has come to naught, so she just went along with it. At least this evening it had the benefit of providing noisy cover for her to whisper to Drake as they all sat back down, "I will discover how you managed the purchase and delivery of the gift."

No sooner had they settled than Lord Ashleigh flashed a brilliant, wicked smile at her and commented, "Dr. McTrowell, what a lovely scarf. I believe it's a perfect complement to your hair." So, a co-conspirator was revealed.

"Why thank you. One would hardly have thought I would have had time to shop during all of today's excitement." Of course, the entirety of the true conversation escaped Wallace who thought they were actually discussing a scarf, a topic of absolutely no interest to him.

"Sevilla, champagne to celebrate Western & Transatlantic's glorious finish in the regatta," Wallace boomed. Everyone else at the table looked at each other uncomfortably. Confidence was one thing, but this was just bald-faced arrogance. Sevilla wisely pretended that serving the soup course was an exacting science requiring skills of which a chemist would be proud, thereby delaying any action, or lack thereof, on Wallace's outrageous order. Sparky scanned the faces of her cowardly dinner companions, a task made more challenging by their sudden, intent interest in their dinner napkins and fingernails, giving her a better view of the tops of their heads than their faces. Ah well, once more into the breach.

"Sir, if I may be uncharacteristically cautious and modest; it seems a bit premature to be celebrating. The other pilots are exceptionally qualified, and I would not want to bet against their skills in the treacherous peaks and valleys of the Alps."

"I don't think we have anything to worry about. Luck is for the unprepared."

Up to this point, Sergeant Fox had made almost no impression at all on McTrowell. However, Wallace's last comment made him sit up even straighter in his dress uniform, if such a thing were physically possible, and fix Drake with a stern and meaningful look. At least it appeared to be meaningful to Fox and Drake, but it only served to induce more trepidation in McTrowell. There was another topic on which she would need to buttonhole Drake later, but one problem at a time. She hated to stoop to such a tactic, but it was the only one against which Wallace had no effective defense under the circumstances. She turned to Sevilla and fixed him with the smile her mother referred to, ironically, as "sweet as pie." "Luis-Miguel, surely you acquired some nice Bordeaux while we were in Paris?"

Sevilla was so thankful to McTrowell for throwing him a lifeline that he didn't flinch when she referred to him by his first name. He produced a bottle and opened it so fast that McTrowell wondered if he had been carrying it around in his pocket. He promptly poured her a glass, which she immediately raised, "To the Burke & Hare, the finest ship of the air." She had to hold her arm in the air for an uncomfortable period of time before Sevilla managed to pour a round for the rest of the dinner guests, but it was worth it to forestall any further discussion on Wallace's part.

"To the Burke & Hare," the rest of the guests chimed in. Sevilla had an instant of panic when Wallace took his first sip of wine because the look on his face suggested the Bordeaux was corked. But no, it was only the bitterness of Dr. McTrowell besting him. The rest of the guests smiled when they tasted his selection. Sparky took rather more than a sip.

The rest of dinner passed without incident. Drake, McTrowell, Ashleigh, and Fox seemed to have made a silent pact to discuss neither Wallace's comment nor the multiple EPACT encounters of the day, so dinner conversation was reduced to the Fremonts recounting their "adventures" in Paris, mostly strolling through the Latin Quarter gawking at its colorful denizens. They stayed at the dinner table only as long as polite manners absolutely required.

Lord Ashleigh rose first. "Lady and gentlemen, I find I am quite depleted from today's exertions. Good evening to you all." With that he walked smartly out of the main hall.

Drake, McTrowell, and Fox stood up and said, nearly simultaneously, "Good evening," and marched out as well. When they reached the passage outside the main hall, they found the door to Ashleigh's cabin held open by Virat. They filed into the cabin without question, and Virat closed the cabin door silently behind them.

Virat's hand was still on the knob when Dr. Sparky exploded in the manner that had earned her her unusual moniker, "Did I just hear Wallace admit that he's going to cheat to win the regatta? He may only care about winning, but I have a reputation to maintain! How can I be taken seriously as a pilot if it comes out that the race was fixed? It won't matter that I had nothing to do with it! They'll all say that the only way a woman could have won the regatta was by cheating!" She turned on Drake and Fox. "And what was that look you two exchanged during dinner? What do you know about all this? Out with it!"

Drake cleared his throat. "A woman won the regatta? Now who is celebrating prematurely?"

She scowled back at him. "You know what I mean. I intend to win and I intend to do it fair and square. 'Play to win.' That's my motto." While her personal motto was news to Drake, it certainly wasn't a surprise.

"I can assure you that, if Mr. Wallace intends to cheat, neither Sergeant Fox nor I have any knowledge of it."

Lord Ashleigh piped up, "Nor I."

Drake continued, "Important competitions such as this share similar mechanisms designed to prevent cheating. We will be assigned an unimpeachable referee in Munich, a personal representative of Maximilian II of Bavaria. He will know all the rules without consulting the rulebook. He will be absolutely up to date on all the latest techniques for cheating. He will be unbribeable because his life would be forfeit to the emperor if he were to accept a bribe. In short, Sergeant Fox and I are concerned about the extremity to which Wallace would have to go to cheat." Drake glanced at Fox who, at that moment, was marveling at the fact that Drake had offered up such a plausible explanation without uttering the word, "pirate."

McTrowell let out a weary sigh. "I suppose there's nothing to do but be patient and see what Wallace has planned. Patience is not one of my better qualities. Good evening, gentlemen." Drake and Ashleigh put up a mighty struggle not to chuckle at Sparky's self-assessment as she turned to go. Virat executed an exaggeratedly low bow to hide his face as he held the cabin door for her. Even he had his limits.

Sparky was thankful for turning in at a reasonable hour when the early morning light filtered in through the porthole of her cabin. The last few days had been taxing, and she would need to be at her best for the next week. She rose and dressed quickly. Ivan would be tired and in need of some sleep too. He jerked upright in his chair as she entered the bridge, not a moment too soon. "Mr. Krasnayarubashka, job well done. Go get yourself some sleep."

He mumbled, "Спасибо," and trudged off the bridge. Sevilla caught the bridge door before it closed.

"Buenos dias, Señorita McTrowell."

"Buenos dias, Señor Sevilla." He handed her a steaming mug of café con leche into which he had scooped some cocoa. It was going to be a good day. She could just make out the outskirts of a city up ahead. She pulled out her brass telescope and scanned the countryside. She flipped open her pocket watch and checked the time; Munich, right on time. She scanned to the right, looking for the large open space that would be the airfield. She spotted such an open space. At one end was an inclined embankment with some kind of colored shield on it. It was a hooded monk with outstretched arms made of tiles or paving stones. Written underneath in the same materials was the word **Ludwigsvorstadt**.

FOUR COUNTRIES, FOUR STORIES

BY MR. DAVID L. DRAKE

A small stone building sat near the edge of a rocky cliff on the northern shore of Calais, France. The structure had an odd tower above it, topped with large parabolic dish fashioned from a collection of polished metal plates, pointed out across the English Channel. At the heart of dish was a mirror that was toggling about once per second, flopping this way and that. To the untrained eye, the action looked spastic and random. To the two engineers within the building, it was the lifeblood of the communication system that reached across the English Channel. Although there had been an unsuccessful attempt to lay a wire telegraph cable across the Strait of Dover the year before, it would be months before it was attempted again, and the light telegraph worked properly most of the time.

The night was setting in, cold and damp. Although communication during the day was possible, it was slow enough that waiting until night was commonplace since the signals, a sequence of momentary flashes of light, could be relayed much more quickly. But the night wasn't starting out well; the mist was coming off the channel, causing the 21 miles to the English shore to be unreachable by their light beam. The engineers grumbled. They were looking at a late night or long day tomorrow, and that meant sleeping in one hour shifts to check the on-going conditions. They had a stack of telegrams to relay as quickly as technically possible. Near the bottom of the stack sat a message from Chief Inspector Drake.

The first workmen to approach any landing airship were nicknamed line monkeys, and this was as true at the Ludwigsvorstadt airship landing site as at all other airship ports. These brave men had the very dangerous job of gathering up the lines deployed by the incoming airship, which if mishandled would easily wrap around a limb or torso and do grievous harm if the airship shifted as it came under the influence of the unpredictable air currents near the ground. Even lighter airships, such as racing ones, would be quick to pivot, or come under the effect of a warm bubble of air rising off the airfield, causing a sudden skyward rebound.

As the Burke & Hare descended, four men, quick and strong, grabbed the lines as if they were living vipers and hand-over-hand climbed high enough to force their own body weight to help in the airship's decent. Within an instant they determined the airship was under control and tossed a lead line off the bow of the airship to the fifth man on the tower assigned to the craft. He quickly secured the rope and threaded it through the winch to tow in the vessel for the remaining feet until it safely docked. Additional lines were dropped and secured. The movement of the airship was reduced to a minute quirky sway with the Burke & Hare imitating a fine race horse trying being calmed as it was led to the starting line.

Two other airships were already at the airfield: the entry from Germany, the Iron Eagle, and the entry from France, Le Lapin. Despite the early hour, each had their own flurry of activity: loading fuel and water, inspecting envelopes and the crisscross of lines embracing them, and, in the case of Le Lapin, its crew on rope ladders touching up the colorful paintings of a leaping rabbit on each side.

Sparky snapped her brass telescope out to its full length and peered through it at the Iron Eagle and the activity beneath it. To Sparky, the Iron Eagle had a seriousness to its appearance that was awe inspiring. The envelope was literally bullet-shaped, and the gondola clung closely to it, wrapped in the same material as if hiding the piloting area in an airship marsupial pouch. Sparky's competitiveness kicked in. Quietly to herself she said, "Too long to be as maneuverable as the Burke & Hare, although it will do well in the straight runs. Hmmm."

She was familiar with the exploits of the German racing master, Willy Dampf, and was looking forward to meeting him. In her mind, he was the competitor to beat. She was able to find him easily in the busyness below his craft: a tall, barrel-chested man, wearing a black uniform with ornamental shoulder epaulets and clearly at the hub of activity. What was unexpected was the young gentleman beside him to whom Willy was giving a great deal of attention. The lad looked to be a young teenager. He and Willy were having a very lively conversation, pointing up at their airship's envelope, rudder, propellers and nose, and discussing something where both were listening to the other's ideas. It would have been very advantageous to Sparky if she could overhear that conversation, she thought.

In the middle of Hartford, Connecticut, sat a fairly newly-built factory complete with brick walls, two high smokestacks, and a sign over the front door that read **Colt's Firearms**. Inside the building was a bustling factory floor manufacturing revolvers for the U.S. Army Dragoon Regiments. In the plainly furnished office in the corner of the building sat a slightly confused Samuel Colt. He laid down the letter that he was reading, a lengthy, fifteen-page tome, and wrinkled up his face at what it was describing. Another gentleman walked into Samuel's office and noted the quizzical look.

"What's bothering you Sam?" he asked.

"Ah, Eli, I didn't hear you walk in. It's a letter from a London lawman. He owns one of my '49s. He's quite happy with it, but sent along these detailed notes on how to improve the firing mechanism. It's the idea of using the exhaust gas pressure to expend the spent cartridge and insert the next round in place. It's not a completely unheard of concept, as you know, but his ideas address the manufacturing of the mechanism. His notes read like he has been in the firearms business for a while. At first, I thought he was taking us to court by fooling us into imitating his patented idea. But the end of the letter clearly indicates that he's turning the whole concept over to us to do with as we see fit."

"Does any of it make sense, or is it just another amateur trying his hand at engineering?"

"I have to believe he's studied the craft of arms manufacturing. Look at the details of these drawings! Although they are hand-drawn, he has bore sizings, spring tensioning details, locations of set screws, and three pages of timing illustrations. There are no details on metal hardness, but that could be determined without too much effort."

"Sam, we need to get this order of revolvers out to the Army as soon as we can. Please don't let this distract you. If the orders keep coming in from New Mexico, we'll need to add a new wing to the factory."

"Mr. Blake, you're absolutely correct. I'll set this aside until we have time to look it over."

⊷⧫⊷⧫⊷⧫ ⚙ ⧫⊷⧫⊷⧫⊷

As the morning fog lifted, the London airship port line monkeys could see the immense airship above them; the Fortis was starting its descent toward the airfield. A cadre of eighteen men were needed to bring in the cargo airship and they had to work as a unified team. Their very lives depended upon it. The crew leader started his set of vocalizations that could travel over the field. "Ho. Ho. Gaa. Ho. Now!!" The men rushed in unison to their appointed lines. Inside the cargo area, the very tip of a brass leg jutted out momentarily between two pine boards and then disappeared back into the crate.

⊷⧫⊷⧫⊷⧫ ⚙ ⧫⊷⧫⊷⧫⊷

Erasmus was dressed and preparing to exit his cabin as the Burke & Hare docked. Again, a serious knock came at his door. He recognized it immediately. At the same time as he swung the door open, he said, "Good morning, Sergeant Fox."

The sergeant fired a welcome directly back, "And a good morning to you, Chief Inspector. Our mission truly starts today. I would like to inventory our weapons and, if I may inquire, the mastery we have over each. I don't want to learn this information when it's too late."

Erasmus thought to himself, *"I like this chap's forthrightness and gumption. He'll make a good comrade in arms."*

184

PALL MALL

BY DR. KATHERINE L. MORSE

"Edmond!? Edmond, dearest?! We have company for dinner."

Dr. Edmond Pogue emerged from behind an enormous book that hid his presence in the large and well-used wing chair by the fireplace.

"As you say."

Miss Slate walked right up to Dr. Pogue without introduction, looked him straight in the eye, and stuck out her hand to shake his. Pogue was so unaccustomed to being treated as neither a celebrity nor a curiosity, especially by a young woman, that he returned the gesture unthinkingly. She shook his hand smartly.

"Miss Sarah Slate of Aspinock, Connecticut. I am very pleased to make your acquaintance. I have read your treatises on high-pressure pistons with keen interest. Your sister, Miss Esmeralda Pogue, was kind enough to invite me to meet you and join you for dinner, although I would not presume to intrude upon your private life."

"Um, my private life? Does that mean you would presume to intrude on my professional life?"

"As I said, I have read your treatises on high-pressure pistons with keen interest. My grandfather left me a small inheritance with which to pursue my interests. I am traveling in Britain and the continent examining industrial and scientific works. I consider it very good fortune to have met your sister today as it affords me the opportunity to meet you in person and discuss your work."

Pogue was slightly stunned by Miss Slate's plainspoken manners as years of attempting to communicate with his sister had proven to be an exasperating exercise in feminine prevarication. Little did he know that his sister had much the same feeling about their communications, obscurity being in the ear of the beholder.

"Well then, Miss Slate. Dinner is not quite ready yet. Would you like a tour of my laboratory?"

"Yes, I would like that very much." In years past, Esmeralda would have been peevish about being disregarded as if she were nothing but a small side table, but she had long since realized that there was no interrupting Edmond's brain when it found something more fascinating. She headed out the side door of the drawing room toward the kitchen to check on dinner preparations.

Dr. McTrowell turned her attention to the activity on the ground. Preparations were mostly complete. At the base of the emblazoned embankment was a stage draped in suffocating waves of red and black bunting. The platform was set with a dozen or more baroque chairs dripping with gold leaf and upholstered in red and black, although she wouldn't have gone so far as to describe them as matching the bunting, given the battle of fabric patterns. In the center of the stage was a dais with a podium on top, the sum of which towered over everything else on the stage. Even more gold leaf and bunting! No doubt this was Emperor Maximillian's perch from which to extol the glory of the event to the adoring (or cowering) masses that would assemble in the grandstands arrayed in large U facing the stage. Ah yes, and the arrangement of grandstands left plenty of room for a marching band. Her stomach executed a little churn when she realized that she was probably expected to occupy one of those baroque chairs for the entirety of the opening ceremonies, feigning interest and gratitude. She hoped that Sevilla hadn't offloaded all the good port in Paris.

There was a great deal of activity near the base of one of the unoccupied towers. Shipping pallets and crates lay strewn around the ground, but in an elliptical shape where the inside area of the ellipse was clear and about the size of a small airship. Even from the air she could see big yellow circles painted on many of the crates with large blue numbers painted inside them. The crates seemed to be arranged in sequential, clockwise order. She pulled out her telescope again. She could make out dozens of workmen pulling metal beams and wooden slats out of the crates. Other men were rushing around holding sheets of paper with diagrams on them, small boxes of screws, and bent rods of various sizes. They were examining the diagrams, fishing screws out of the boxes, and using the bent rods to fasten the beams and slats together. Although the whole activity appeared completely chaotic, by the time the line monkeys had the Burke & Hare safely anchored, the men on the ground had assembled something that looked remarkably like the gondola of a small airship.

Sparky put away her telescope and made a complete circuit of the Burke & Hare's catwalks, double checking the security of the mooring lines and ensuring everything was in good order. When she returned to the airship in a few hours, she would be accompanied by the Emperor's referee. Despite his supposed objectivity, his first impression of the ship would color all his subsequent judgments of the crew. She intended to run a clean race, but she wanted the referee to be favorably disposed should circumstances call for a little "latitude." Satisfied that the Burke & Hare was in a state of complete preparation, she marched across the gangplank to the scaffolding that served as a temporary mooring tower. The tails of her leather duster flapped wildly behind her as she bounded down the stairs of the tower. The first smells of summer swept down from the Alps, lifting her spirits. She was really looking forward to the regatta!

Half an hour later, her spirits were in the doldrums again. She had arrived a few minutes early at the judges' station and collected a copy of the rules printed in English. There was a lot of superfluous text, but the rules were the obvious ones:

- No drafting
- No intentionally forcing an opponent down or into a mountainside
- Minimum and maximum altitudes for each of the legs of the race
- No dropping ballast after a leg had begun
- Additional equipment and devices not inspected by the referees prior to the start of the race was strictly forbidden

- The decisions of the referees and judge were final

It had taken her less than five minutes to read and absorb the rules. And then the referees, judge, and other pilots arrived. The judge welcomed each pilot personally, showing off that he could greet each of them in their native language. "Guten tag, Herr Dampf. Bon jour, Monsieur du Garde. Buenos dias, Señor Garza. God dag, Herr Swenson. Good morning, Miss Dr. McTrowell." Oh well, at least he was trying. "Ich bin Herrn Zimmermann."

He then proceeded to make some sort of speech in German, in very slow, sonorous tones, punctuating his monolog with grandiose hand gestures. This went on for several minutes during which she thought she would nod off despite a good night's sleep. Then he switched to Swedish and, after another minute, she realized she was seeing the same hand gestures again. She was shifting from foot to foot to stay awake by the time he got around to English. And then she discovered that he wasn't even saying anything of substance! Glorious Bavarian Alps, magnanimity of the Emperor in hosting the regatta, the honor of good sportsmanship… Only the risk of incurring the disfavor of the referees kept her from pulling faces at the judge. Although, truth be told, a few of the referees were struggling to maintain their carefully constructed façades of professional decorum, and she was sure she caught one of them rolling his eyes. The judge finally finished his human marionette show in all five languages. He picked up a copy of the rules printed in German and handed it to Captain Dampf. He picked up another copy for himself and began reading them out loud! Was there going to be no end to this torture?

Just as she felt her brain actually getting numb, she heard the level of noise on the field behind her rise above the usual hum and clatter. She heard rowdy shouting. She was dying to turn around and see what was causing the commotion, but she wasn't going to be the first. The revelry was getting louder and closer. It finally disrupted the judge's droning, and he now wore an expression of umbrage that suggested he felt this interruption warranted a martial response. One of the referees turned toward the noise, and Sparky seized the opportunity to do likewise. A dozen or so gentlemen dressed entirely in white were gamboling across the airfield shouting, "Hup, hup, hup," in cheerful unison. Their sprightliness was remarkable considering the fact that they were loaded down with picnic hampers, folding chairs and a table, umbrellas, and two sets of brightly colored mallets and matching balls. When the white-clad swarm reached the middle of the field, they spread out. Despite their disorganized appearance, it only took them just moments to set up a picnic table covered with white linen and loaded down with mouthwatering picnic fare and champagne! Everyone on the field stood in stunned silence. And then, in a twinkling, the cohort had laid out two perfectly straight pitches of iron arches without any measuring!

Sparky heard a string of invectives coming from behind her. While she didn't speak German, she was pretty sure she recognized the sound of cursing in any language. The judge was so infuriated by the intrusion into his moment in the sun that he was spitting as he cursed. Little droplets of spittle clung to the bottom of his moustache. Although there were a couple of sympathetic looks among the referees and pilots, they were mostly captivated by the spectacle in the middle of the field. The judge stormed off toward the entrance of the airfield, probably in search of enforcements. Ah well, nothing to do but pass the time until this little disruption sorted itself out. Her curiosity got the best of her, as usual. She picked out the tallish fellow who seemed to be directing the improvisational fête and walked straight up to him.

"Guten tag."

"Guten tag. You're not German."

"Nor are you." But the accent was neither quite British nor quite French.

"Breton. Marius Hinault, at your service." And he doffed his hat with several extraneous and extravagant flourishes.

"Dr. Sparky McTrowell, pleased to meet you. What is this?"

"Pall mall, a game of skill. Mark my words; it will be all the fashion quite shortly. Would you care to join us in a match?" He followed this by a sweep of his arm as exaggerated as the hat salute to indicate the pitch.

"I don't believe I know this game. And Herr Zimmermann will undoubtedly return with the *Wachtmeister* in short order."

"On this I depend!"

"Excuse me? You'll be arrested."

"Oh, most certainly not. Maximillian will never permit his grand event to be spoiled thus. Merely we will be asked to leave and so it will be in all the broadsheets. And thus shall I make my great fortune." His head bobbled enthusiastically. He raised his arm above his head, made a couple of swiveling motions of his hand, and snapped his fingers twice. One of his compatriots dashed over and handed him two glasses of champagne, one of which he extended to Sparky.

Caution was not generally in her nature, but she hesitated before she took it from his hand. "You say 'thus' quite a lot. How will you 'thus' make your great fortune?"

"In my family are carpenters for generations. When my father dies, I look for new ventures. We play this game and I think it needs more color. So, I make these." This time his sweeping arm motion took in the rack of painted, matching mallets and balls. "The dilettantes will thus read about our party in the broadsheets and they must buy a set. I am making the only ones like this, which they must have!" He threw his arms up in the air, nearly spilling his champagne. "Oops." He took a sip of his champagne, selected a bright blue mallet and matching ball, and marched onto the pitch.

Sparky abandoned her unaccustomed attempt at caution, took a sip of her champagne, grabbed the matching yellow set, and followed. A few of Hinault's partners in mischief joined them on the pitch as Hinault explained the rules. He took the first stroke, but missed the first arch. Someone helpfully took her champagne glass out of her hand so she could take her shot. It went in generally the right direction, but was a little short. She turned back around to discover her glass in the hand of Willy Dampf. He had a glass and matching mallet and ball set of his own. "Zis looks like fun, ja?" He held out the glasses, so she returned the favor and held both their glasses while he took his shot.

As Hinault had expected, a crowd gathered, including a few reporters. Since the *Wachtmeister* had not yet arrived and the mischief seemed contained to the pitch, no one concerned themselves enough to intervene. The fact that one of the Bretons was passing through the crowd handing out glasses of champagne and small plates of cheese and charcuterie probably placated the crowd as well. Although the contestants all started off pretty well, it became clear on the second turn that Hinault had had quite a bit more practice than everyone else, including the other Bretons. He beat them all on only his third and very timely turn. Herr Zimmermann had returned at the head of a small troop of *Wachtmeister*.

Sparky stepped backward into the crowd, slowly and nonchalantly. One of the Bretons threaded his way through the crowd, relieving the spectators and Sparky of their champagne glasses while another zipped about the pitch, snatching up the iron arches, and a third collected and racked the balls and mallets. Marius Hinault strolled up to Herr Zimmermann with his hands clasped prayerfully under his chin, a smile on his face, the very picture of serene good cheer. Needless to say, Herr Zimmermann's expression bore nothing in common with Hinault's. Sparky couldn't hear their exchange because she took advantage of the diversion to return to the judge's table at a smart clip before Herr Zimmermann noticed that she had been an accomplice to the unauthorized frivolity. Captain Dampf rejoined her a moment later, striding up as if he had been away on important business. He winked and smiled conspiratorially at her, but didn't say anything.

The pilots watched the spat from a distance for a few more minutes. The reporters stood just out of range and scribbled frantically. Despite the waving, pointing exhortations of Herr Zimmermann, the Wachtmeister seemed disinclined to take punitive action. The instant that the judge's hands came to a rest, Hinault grabbed his right hand and gave it a firm, warm shake, smiling broadly. He turned and waved to the reporters and crowd. And he simply walked off the field, having been safely preceded by his brothers in arms with all their gear.

Willy Dampf turned to her and smiled again. "Neffer or alvays do business vis zat mon."

ALL IN GOOD TIME

BY MR. DAVID L. DRAKE

The morning fog was lifting off the streets of London. Dew, which is beautiful as it settles over an English meadow, had a different effect on limestone city buildings: it made them slick to the touch and added a slight shine. Within minutes, the condensation formed rivulets on the stone walls, gathering the previous day's soot as it trickled down in minute, running-mascara tears. Dr. Edmond Pogue took note of this, as he often did, as he made his way back home from his morning constitutional. What intrigued him was the competition between order and chaos, and how the simple reaction to temperature changes of the buildings and air, and the relationship of humidity and gravity, caused the building walls to self-clean. Well, to some extent. But, over time, the cycle of night and day, cooling and heating, caused the buildings to become cleaner, less chaotic. Interesting and strange.

As Edmond neared the repurposed warehouse, he saw a figure standing near the entrance. As he approached, it became clear that it was Miss Sarah Slate, returned from dinner and the tour of the laboratory the night before. She was staring at the granite stone of the building, completely obsessed with what she was studying. She was dressed as simply as the previous day, a light woman's jacket over a checked cotton dress. She wasn't wearing one of those fashionable hoop skirts, thank goodness, since it was clear that she wanted to re-visit the laboratory. She was using her finger to dam up a rivulet of condensation, then reroute it to another path. Was she thinking of the struggle between order and chaos, Edmond wondered, or was she off on some other tangent completely?

"Good morning, Miss Slate."

She simply turned without hesitation and replied, "Dr. Pogue, last night at dinner you offered a continued discussion on piston compression and the theory of multi-stage steam engines. I am here for that discussion."

Normally, one would be taken back by such brusqueness, but just one dinner with Miss Slate was all it took for Edmond to learn her ways. He was neither surprised nor put off.

"Now would be excellent. I am expecting to complete some analysis today and start some new work, but that can wait for a short time. Allow me to let you in."

At that, Edmond produced a sizable key ring covered with a jumble of keys of varying proportions. He guided one of the largest into the door lock and turned. The two of them were greeted with a most satisfying sound of turning tumblers and sliding latches. With a push, the heavy wooden door groaned on its iron hinges as it swung open.

"After you," Edmond offered, and Sarah walked in without hesitation.

Sarah entered the granite-walled hallway that ran for approximately one hundred feet straight ahead from the entrance. On its right side were a number of archway openings for domestic rooms, such as a kitchen and a sitting room. But the prize for Sarah was at the end of the hallway, the door leading to the well-publicized tower laboratory. She could not hold back her enthusiasm, and walked as quickly as she could without running to the far door. There, she opened the door herself and stepped out onto the landing within the tower. The look on her face was if she had found a new home. She surveyed the tower laboratory, and it was all she could do not to sprint down the stairs. Despite her being there just the night before, her eyes grew large, and she just took it all in as Dr. Pogue caught up to her.

"Grand, isn't it?" Edmond asked, seeing it through her eyes. "Go on down, I'll be right with you."

As Sarah descended the stairs, Edmond turned; as expected, Yin was quietly waiting behind him holding a rosewood serving tray bearing a silver tea set and a china cup.

She smiled delicately. "I have your Earl Grey, Doctor. The usual: two lumps and a splash of milk?"

"Thank you. Yin, that would be perfect." After a slight pause, he added, "You may want to ask Miss Slate if she would like something."

Yin nodded acceptance of the request, backed away a step, and turned toward the kitchen to retrieve a second teacup.

Edmond gave Sarah a greater amount of his morning time than he had originally intended. As with most conversations regarding high pressure systems, the mathematics were straightforward enough, and he covered them in the first half hour or so. But the comparison of the theoretical and the practical was the fascinating part for both of them. What caused pressure leakage, mechanical failure, long-term corrosion? How can engine dimension scaling, multi-piston staging, dry-steam reciprocation, and any other consideration be employed to maximize temperature energy conversion into mechanical energy?

How do the materials used for the boiler, engine, and drive chain effect output? Now those topics were interesting and entertaining.

Near 10 AM, Yin descended the stairway and approached Edmond, even though he and Sarah were deep in conversation and layering pencil mark mathematics over pencil mark mechanical drawings on a stack of paper that they slid back and forth between the two of them.

"Doctor?"

"Yes, Yin."

"I wanted to tell you that two delivery men are here with two crates. Should I have them brought down?"

"Odd. I wasn't expecting any deliveries. Yes, please have them brought down."

In a few minutes, Edmond and Sarah cleared one of the laboratory tables. The delivery men placed the two crates on it and withdrew after Yin provided them a nice compensation for their efforts.

One of the crates looked slightly damaged in transit. On top of it were the shipping instructions and an attached letter. Dr. Pogue removed and open the letter, punctuating his reading of the complete letter silently by reading key phrases out loud.

"Delightful! It is from Chief Inspector Erasmus Drake! ...Contents are mechanized mining tools. ...Interesting. ...EPACTs. Electric-Powered Automated Crawling Transport. Two crates containing..."

In her enthusiasm, both to help Edmond and through her own curiosity, while Edmond was reading, Sarah took up a nearby pry bar and started to open the top of the slightly damaged crate. One corner came up.

Yin appeared at the top of the stairs again and swept smoothly down the stairs. "Doctor! A telegram has arrived." She handed the envelope to Edmond. Edmond ripped open the envelope without hesitation knowing that in his business, telegrams were only sent if there was an urgent communication. Unfortunately, the top line of the telegram was a formally-worded expression of regret and defense from the transmission conglomerate.

PARTIAL OR GARBLED TRANSMISSION AT
CALAIS-DOVER TRANSFER LINK.
RETRANSMITTING AT EARLIEST OPPORTUNITY.

"Curious," he said. "I love puzzles. I bet I can make a good guess at the original transmission." And he read out loud the miscommunication.

DR EDMOND POGUE, SHADWELL, LOND -- ATE
ARRIS NEST. TREMEN --- L DRAKE.

"Well, it's also from the Chief Inspector. And it's particularly garbled. Let's see..." Edmond turned his back to Sarah and ran his left-hand fingers through his brown hair while staring at the telegram.

Sarah was not interested in jumbled word games. Pry bar in hand, she returned to the task of opening the crate. She took on a second top corner. Pry bar in place, she pulled down using her weight to force the corner up. In an instant, the EPACT inside muscled its way out, being even scarier by being crippled. It crawled out like a ghoul from the grave, its broken legs working spasmodically while its two good legs dragged it forward, as if going for its liberator. Sarah didn't scream, but instead stood catatonically at the sight of the diminutive brass monster. Edmond spun around in time to see Yin grab the empty crate, flip it upside down, and slap it over the crawling EPACT just inches from the feet of Miss Slate. Then, just as quickly, she jumped onto the box, standing, to hold it prisoner again. The EPACT reacted to being caught again and began poking holes through the side of the crate with its two good legs.

It took quite a while for Edmond to capture the EPACT, calm down Sarah who didn't like being startled, and realize that Erasmus was trying to warn Edmond of "extreme danger," or something of that nature, with the telegram. However, Edmond did note Yin's quick response and cool demeanor. Perhaps there was more to Yin than he had previously suspected.

The rest of the letter, which Edmond read out loud for Sarah, explained what Erasmus knew of the switch on the base of the EPACTs and the Chief Inspector's desire to understand how such a small mechanism could do so much autonomously with such strength and endurance. Sarah and Edmond looked at each other and knew they had a shared interest.

"Miss Slate, would you care to be in my employ to investigate this mystery?"

"But of course. Can we start today?"

"Delightful! Just delightful!"

On the Burke & Hare, Erasmus and Sergeant J.B. Fox agreed that the limited size of Erasmus' cabin room was too confining to properly display their various martial skills, both with and without weapons. With swords and pistols tucked under their arms and stuffed in their jacket pockets, they exited the Burke & Hare and found a cleared quiet corner of the airship landing grounds.

For the next hour, they both demonstrated their shadow fencing skills, hand-to-hand combat, and pistol handling. Styles were compared, and in general admired, although they both agreed that the Chief Inspector had a good deal of room for improvement regarding his pistol handling capabilities. The final exchange had the men stripped to the waist, illustrating the pugilistic techniques that they preferred.

Gathering their shirts and vests, J.B. said, "That was very instructive. I have enough particulars to proceed forward with planning against the marauders."

"All due respect, my dear man, but how can you have enough to make plans? Do you have additional information on how these pirates operate? Or their strategy? Can you share with me what kind of battle preparations would make sense?"

J.B. smiled. "All in good time. It will be revealed all in good time."

Erasmus uncomfortably accepted this answer, but tucked this issue in the back of his mind to think upon later.

The two men returned to the Burke & Hare to store their armaments. While in the sergeant's cabin, J.B. commented, "My good man, I do believe you didn't reveal everything either. All of your defensive sword postures show a slight squaring of your hips and shoulders, indicating that you are used to having a second sword or staff in your right hand. You didn't show a two-sword technique. Are you planning to share that with me?"

It was Erasmus' turn to smile. "You are very observant. All will be revealed in good time."

They both understood the symmetry of the information that they withheld and the understanding of men who highly regard their privacy. At that point, J.B. opened his trunk to place in his sword and Erasmus spied a complicated wooden slat and canvas mechanism stashed within. *"Ah ha,"* thought Erasmus, *"this military man has even more tricks up his sleeve."*

AUGUSTINER KELLER

BY DR. KATHERINE L. MORSE

What was it with all these infernal headaches? Sparky felt like she had a fence post sticking out of the back of her head. She gingerly opened her eyes one at a time, wincing as the light coming in through the porthole assaulted her light-starved pupils. Things were not yet in focus when she heard Drake's voice off to her left, "You are awake!" For a man usually so reserved, he managed to pack quite a lot of relief and concern into four syllables.

"Yes, and you're quite loud." She hadn't meant to sound quite so surly.

"I am terribly sorry, Dr. McTrowell. I am exceedingly relieved that you appear to be on the mend. What is the last thing you remember?"

"What?" Her surroundings were now in focus. The sun was setting. On the wrong side of the ship. And she was in the wrong cabin. "Who moved the Burke & Hare and what am I doing in Lord Ashleigh's bed?"

"No one moved the Burke & Hare since you docked it three days ago. I am endeavoring to explain why you are in this cabin."

"Three days ago!? What day is it and why is the sun setting off the port side?" Her raised voice must have penetrated the walls of the cabin because Lord Ashleigh dashed into the room followed closely into the cramped space by Virat.

"Oh, my dear friend, I feared the worst!" Ashleigh exclaimed. "I haven't slept for two nights!" Virat simply proffered a hot cup of chai, but the smile in eyes conveyed his own sense of happy relief. McTrowell took a long, grateful swallow of the steamy, sweat, spicy drink that miraculously dulled the throbbing in the back of her head.

"Obviously something momentous has happened and I'm the last to know."

Drake returned to his questioning, not entirely successfully resisting his natural tendencies to make it an interrogation. "The sun is not setting; it is rising. It is," he snapped open his pocket watch, "8:15 AM, Saturday, May 31st. If you will tell me what you remember of the events of Thursday, May 29th, I will fill in everything else."

Drake and McTrowell were passing the tower dock for The Iron Eagle, heading for the exit from the airfield, when Captain Dampf exited the tower.

"Und vot mischief are you zeeking today, Captain McTrowell?"

"My colleague, Chief Inspector Drake, and I are going to sample the local beer about which we have heard so much."

"Hm, an excellent idea. Und vere vill you be performing zis sampling?"

"We have heard a great deal about the Hofbräuhaus."

"Hm, yes, zis is ze ushual choice."

"But, undoubtedly you have a better suggestion?"

"Ze Augustiner Keller is not so vell known, but I zink it is more…agreeable. Und not zo many drunk visitors."

"And where would we find the Augustiner Keller?"

"You haf only to vollow me. I vas chust on my vay dere."

McTrowell winked at Drake as if to say, "Yes, I'll bet he was."

For all her suspicions about Captain Dampf's nefarious intentions, he didn't seem to be trying to ply her for information about the capabilities of the Burke & Hare or her strategy for the regatta. The barmaid in the dirndl greeted him by name and he ordered their first round of beers before they even found a table. As promised, the patrons seemed to be mostly locals drinking beer with their friends. There was an occasional burst of loud laughter, but no real rowdiness, and no one seemed to be embarrassingly drunk, but then it was still the middle of the afternoon.

When the barmaid brought the beer, Sparky's first impression was that she could stick her entire head into the stein. She would have to pace herself. Both of her drinking companions weighed half again what she did. The other delightful revelation was the delivery of a basket of pastries or rolls twisted into the shape of loose knots. They were chewy and an excellent complement to the beer. The fact that she hadn't eaten a proper breakfast made them all the more delicious. And maybe the lack of breakfast was making the beer go to her head even faster. She gnawed the second loop of the treat and waved the remainder at Willy Dampf.

"These are delicious! What are they?"

"*Brezel.*"

"They remind me of sourdough from home."

"Zour dough? Zis does not zound tasty."

"It loses something in translation. It's really good and so are these." She wolfed down the last third and washed it down with a healthy swallow of beer. She peered down into the stein. Despite her efforts, it was still frightfully full.

She lost track of time as they swapped stories of daring airships landings in treacherous weather. Drake acquiesced to retelling the story of his literally hair-raising capture of Professor Farnsworth. Dampf regaled them with the virtues of the sheepherding dogs he bred at his family farm in the Bavarian countryside. More honest and trustworthy than the "dogs" one encounters in the city he opined. They all drank a toast to that. The light was cutting a very sharp angle across the table and McTrowell couldn't remember if she had drunk three or four of the head-swallowing steins of beer. She'd eaten so many of the *brezels* that, despite the lack of breakfast, she was not going to need dinner.

"Gentlemen, I declare that I can drink no more beer nor eat any more of these." She waved the last little bit of a pretzel. "Shall we return to the airfield?"

Drake stood up crisply, "A capital idea." McTrowell looked him up and down. Apparently one of the Chief Inspector's many excellent qualities was his capacity for drink. As she stood up a bit unsteadily, she assessed the contents of his stein. About an inch of liquid remained in the bottom and it appeared quite flat. She could only recall the barmaid delivering a single stein to him when they first arrived. No, that couldn't be correct. She must have not noticed during all the collegial storytelling.

Captain Dampf waved across the hall to get the barmaid's attention and then made a loose circling motion in the air with his fingers pointing upwards. He walked toward the door, more steadily than McTrowell as she noticed.

"Um, shouldn't we pay for the beer?"

"I haf made arrangements."

She smiled at him. "The French have a term: bon vivant. Do you know it?" He smiled broadly and slapped her warmly on the back, nearly knocking her off her feet.

The streets were more crowded in the evening than they had been at midafternoon. The regatta was intended to draw spectators to Munich and, on that point, it was succeeding. The streets were packed with out of town visitors in search of dinner and entertainment to accompany the festival atmosphere of the regatta. In an attempt to escape the press, Willy Dampf led them down a narrow side street heading more toward the Marienplatz, but away from the crowds. They had only gone a few meters down the street when a band of gypsies entered behind them, making quite a racket and moving with remarkable haste. As they were in no particular hurry, the three of them moved to the side, single file along the wall of a building to allow the gypsies to pass. It seemed not to be enough because the gypsy band expanded to fill all the space between the encroaching walls. And they were making quite a ruckus. Sparky scanned around herself for her companions, but there seemed to be gypsies everywhere. Being pressed this closely by other human beings had always had an unpleasant, disorienting effect on her. She only needed to calm herself for a few moments until the gypsies passed. She took a deep breath, stopped where she stood, closed her eyes, bowed her head, and placed her hands over her ears.

"And that's the last thing I remember."

"You could not possibly be expected to remember any more. The 'gypsies' used a 'picking' technique I have observed the gangs of pickpockets in London using. They approach in a tight, loud group to the discomfort of their target, forcing the target into a corner. As they get closer, they spread out to block the target's passage and separate the target from the rest of their party. And then they close back in on the target. It is not unlike packs of lions on the veldt in Africa. The chief distinction in this case is that their intended prize was not your money; it was you." The expression on his face was as grave as she had yet seen. "To be more precise, you and Captain Dampf. As soon as I recognized the tactic, I came to your aid. Unfortunately, I was not fast enough to prevent the felons from striking a foul blow to your head, knocking you unconscious." She could see on his face that he was mentally flogging himself for not being more alert or faster in his response to the danger. "I must say, however, that I left an 'impression' on one of them that he will almost certainly never forget." She wasn't entirely sure what kind of impression he meant, but she had the distinct feeling that it was of the irreparably physical variety. This seemed to bring Drake a bit of cheer.

"What about Captain Dampf?"

"I could only reach one of you in time." Her eyes opened wide and she gasped in distress. "However, it appears that Sergeant Fox has been keeping close watch on us. By this I mean that he apparently followed us all afternoon. When he observed me coming to your defense, he executed a flanking maneuver from the back of the pack of gypsies and came to the aid of Captain Dampf. Although I must say that Captain Dampf acquitted himself admirably and Sergeant Fox probably did more of a service to the gypsies than to Captain Dampf who gave three of them a proper thrashing before Fox reached him." And now Drake seemed considerably cheered. Sparky smiled as well, not only to know that Dampf was unharmed, but because she knew that Drake had not had a moment's hesitation when faced with the choice of whom to defend.

"Why would a band of gypsies try to abduct me and Captain Dampf?"

"Ah, well that's an interesting question, the answer to which lies in the Marienplatz."

THE MARIENPLATZ CONFRONTATION

BY MR. DAVID L. DRAKE

Erasmus pulled a chair up next to the lushly made bed that cocooned Sparky. Sparky needed to hear the rest of the story. Erasmus cleared his throat to begin the remainder of the tale, but word that Sparky had come to was making its way around the airship, and Erasmus would just have to wait. First was Luis-Miguel Sevilla, carrying a platter of breakfast pastries and a small glass of fresh apple juice. The platter was presented as if it were an offering for this wondrous turn of events. He looked incredibly relieved at Sparky's ability to sit up and talk.

Reginald Wallace made his entrance as Luis-Miguel left. He started his monologue as he stepped through the door. "Doctor McTrowell! You've awakened! What a relief. Now I don't have to have another racing pilot flown in! Ha, ha!" His fake laughter at his own self-centered humor put a strange hush over the room. "Well, now I'll need to run out to let the press know about the good health of my pilot. Can't wait to see you back at the helm." He left as abruptly as he came.

J.B. Fox had been standing guard at the door to make sure that Sparky was protected. He slipped into the room and simply asked one question, although his tone hinted at it being heartfelt.

"Are you back with us, Doctor?"

His eyes softened, to hear Sparky reply, "I'm back. But still groggy. Thank you for asking."

He nodded and smiled, but stayed in the room with Sparky, Lord Ashleigh, and Erasmus.

This ended the small parade of well-wishers. J.B. turned and locked the door for privacy. Erasmus again quietly cleared his throat to finally tell the remainder of the tale of what happened.

"Willy Dampf stayed back to guard you, Sparky. J.B. and I followed the gypsies that attacked you to the Marienplatz, which is an open area in the center of town. There, we were able to corner one of them who was wearing a bright blue tunic. We lost the other two in the crowd, unfortunately. He was a scrappy sort. He pulled a pair of knives out to do us harm, spitting and cursing as he jabbed at us. We kept our distance, of course, while trying to keep him cornered. You probably do not remember that I had my cane with me. Well, to be honest, Doctor, it is a sword stick."

"Did you really think I didn't notice that when I first inspected it in Lord Ashleigh's sitting room? Really, Chief Inspector. I'm an inventor. The locking mechanism near the handle is beautifully made and subtle, but I am observant. Please, continue."

Erasmus' eyebrows raised, but then came back down to hide his surprise. He always thought he had kept this secret well, but between Sparky's and Alistair Bennington Rutherford's ability to spot the sword stick, he now wondered how many people had known and not told him. Well, back to his story.

"The sergeant spotted it first: the man we cornered was cursing in German. So he asked *'Ne rakesa tu Romanes?'* Do you speak Romani? The fellow responded with a very confused look. That meant he was not a true gypsy and was using it as a guise. Perhaps in reaction to this, he made a break for it and I was forced to unsheathe the live blade of my sword stick. I used the scabbard to hit the outside of his knee and the back of the blade to 'tap' his collarbone. This was not intended as a killing cut, but instead to arrest his motion, which it did admirably. It also cleanly removed the top two ties on the impostor's shirt, unveiling the scoundrel's chest. There both J.B. and I saw the tattoo of an anchor piercing a skull. Not one suited for land dwellers, but rather for rough men that sail either the ocean or sky."

"What would sailors be doing here? And why would they want to attack me and Willy?"

Erasmus looked at J.B., who responded with a "continue your story" nod.

"It has become clear that pirates were using gypsy disguises to get near the two of you and the other airship pilots. But to finish, three or four additional counterfeit gypsies threatened the two of us from behind, just long enough to allow our cornered pirate to escape. Then the rest of them disappeared into the crowd. We then got you back to the Burke & Hare safely, summoned a local German doctor to examine you. He put some salve on your head and instructed us to apply ice chips on and off to reduce the swelling. It looks like it was a successful process, but you had us mightily worried, if I do say so myself."

The men in the room gave Sparky plaintive facial expressions that showed agreement with Erasmus' last point.

Erasmus continued. "After confirming our concerns, J.B. and I went to check on the whereabouts of the other regatta pilots. All the others had not left their craft or crew, except Pierre, who was not to be found. Later that night, the story got back to us that Pierre was, if I may be so blunt, looking for evening companionship, as he often does. He ran into two sham gypsies, but fended for himself with his well-known knife skills. Apparently, his attackers did not expect such a fight. Still, it was a close call. He ended up with some minor cuts near his left wrist and a sizable bruise on his right shoulder. Sergeant, should I continue?"

"Please do, Chief Inspector," the Aerial Marine replied.

"Sparky, J.B. warned me that we may have to deal with pirates at some point in the regatta. But the Sergeant was not expecting such an early confrontation, particularly in the city. The Aerial Marines had not briefed him that the problem was worsening, so we were taken by surprise. J.B. has agreed to let you and Lord Ashleigh be briefed on the situation, since our lives may be at stake."

J.B. then proceeded to explain that multiple countries, including Great Britain, were concerned over the loss of safe air space for commercialization due to airship pirates who had started to drive craft away. Part of the reason that Bavaria was holding the regatta was to map the location of the pirates, allow a team to go in and remove them, and for international travelers (and investors) to feel safe about traveling the Bavarian skies. J.B. added, "Any part of this trip may be thwarted by pirates. But we are prepared."

Sparky rubbed her head. "May I be led to my cabin? I could use a change of clothes and a restorative drink of birch bark tea." The men agreed and moved to help her to her feet. During this activity, J.

B. requested that all of this be kept secret, since non-crew passengers might panic, or leak the situation to the reporters. They all agreed to do so. Erasmus promised himself, *"No additional harm will come to this woman while I'm on this assignment."*

AIR WINCH CANNONS

BY DR. KATHERINE L. MORSE

Since she was still a bit wobbly, Sparky spent the rest of Saturday on the Burke & Hare, checking and rechecking its state of preparedness. She was grateful for the lack of public duties and not just because she was a tad unsteady.

Unfortunately, Sunday was quite different. McTrowell and Luis-Miguel Sevilla scoured the airship for any additional extraneous ballast that could be offloaded in Munich and collected at the end of the regatta. She knew they would need to lighten the load as much as possible if they were to have a fighting chance against the sleeker Iron Eagle. She mentally cursed Wallace for taking on paying passengers. That man's greed vastly exceeded his sense. And then she had a truly uncharitable thought about Wallace's personal girth and momentarily entertained a wish that surely violated her Hippocratic oath.

Distracted as she was by her daydreaming, she was nearly knocked off her feet by Herr Fenstermacher, the referee, who was climbing up out of the mechanical compartment under the bridge.

"Guten tag, Herr Fenstermacher."

"Guten tag, Dr. McTrowell. You feelink better, ja? You are not zo goot vis ze deutsches bier, no?" His obsequious smile dared her to cross him.

"No, I suppose French wine is more agreeable to me." She smiled back smugly. Two could play at that game.

"I haf finished my inspegshun. You vill meet at za judges station in von hour." He marched off of the bridge without another word, nearly colliding with Ivan Krasnayarubashka who was entering.

"Is very unpleasant man!"

"Indeed, Mr. Krasnayarubashka. I want to thank you for managing preparations so expertly while I was…indisposed. I'm going to head down for a spot of breakfast before the meeting with the judge and referees. Let us hope the ballast allocation for the Iron Eagle is fair."

She looked across to the tower where El Toro Rojo had anchored while she was unconscious. Its yellow envelope with a rampaging red bull was certainly eye-catching, even headache inducing one might say. But that wasn't the most unusual thing about it. There was a metal scaffolding ring that ran from the top of the gondola around the entire circumference of the center of the envelope. There was a large bronze cylinder mounted on the top of the scaffolding pointing fore and aft, and a matching one about two thirds of the way down to the gondola. Presumably there was a third one mounted on the port side that was out of view. She wondered what it could possibly be. It must have some very valuable function to warrant the considerable extra weight.

When she reached the gangplank, Drake was standing at the railing scanning the skies apprehensively. "Good morning, Dr. McTrowell."

"Good morning to you, Chief Inspector." Without even asking or indicating what he was doing, he preceded her across the gangplank and down the tower. As she made the turn at the first landing, a shadow flickered overhead. She looked up just in time to catch a glimpse of a black shape moving quickly off the gangplank. She could hear footsteps above her all the way down the tower, but couldn't see their source. She had her second near miss of the morning at the bottom of the tower when Drake stopped crisply and surveyed the surrounding area before stepping aside to allow her to exit the tower. He was nattering inanely about the weather. How very unlike him! She stole a look over her shoulder and the mysterious shadowy specter was revealed to be Sergeant Fox in his black combat fatigues. She and Drake were strolling at a relatively leisurely pace, but Fox wasn't closing the distance. She glanced back twice more between the base of the tower and the teahouse next to the parade ground; Fox was always five seconds behind them. Drake repeated his maneuver from the bottom of the stairs when they entered the teahouse, but this time Sparky was prepared. She started counting to herself 1-2-3-4-5, but no Fox. She turned back to Drake. "You and Sergeant Fox are not very stealthy."

"One is not subtle when one wishes to deliver a message of deliberation."

She took a slow breath. "I see." She spotted Willy Dampf across the room and waved at him. He looked quite pleased to see her and immediately headed toward her and Drake. He was obviously unaccompanied. "The other pilots don't appear to be under surveillance."

"Protection. Surveillance is for suspects. Their protection is not my concern." It was at that moment that McTrowell realized that he was a different person when he was "on duty" and she was very glad to be under his protection and not his surveillance.

"Guten tag, Dr. McTrowell. How vunderful zat you are recovered!" He looked as though he wanted to embrace her, but thought better of it at the last minute and shook her hand vigorously. "Guten tag, Herr Inspector Drake." Sparky wouldn't have thought it physically possible, but he shook Drake's hand even more vigorously.

"Thank you. I'm relieved to be recovered and ready for the race." Dampf didn't strike her as the kind of man to be intimidated by a little posturing by a competitor, but it didn't hurt to let him know that she wasn't going to be deterred by little misfortune and a bump on the head. Drake entertained her throughout their brief breakfast with the history of sword sticks, which was pleasantly diverting. She didn't need to look back to detect the shield of Sergeant Fox reattaching himself as she and Drake exited the teahouse.

Drake dropped back when she got up to the judge's table. He took up a position equidistant from the table, but opposite Fox. They walked in a circle around the table and the pilots. If they were attempting to appear nonchalant, they were failing miserably, but perhaps this was more deliberation. While all the pilots were present, neither the judge nor the referees were anywhere in sight. She flipped open her pocket watch. It had been an hour and five minutes since she and Herr Fenstermacher had parted company. All the officials were late. How very un-German! She and the other pilots discussed the weather conditions and the topography of the course. She checked her watch again. The officials were half an hour late. What was keeping them? Drake and Fox had come together on their perimeter and were talking quietly but purposefully. When they resumed their patrol, the perimeter was smaller. Drake had his sword stick out and his thumb on the release; Fox's hand was on his pistol. The conversation between the pilots dwindled down to nothing and they all began looking around nervously.

It was very nearly an hour past the designated meeting time when Herr Zimmermann hastened up to the table trailed by a phalanx of referees. He was quite red in the face and obviously perturbed. He launched immediately into a diatribe in rapid fire German. McTrowell, Pierre du Guarde, and Björn Swenson exchanged bewildered looks. Although Felipe Garza didn't seem to understand what was being said, he looked quite anxious. Of course Dampf understood every word, each of which contributed incrementally to the expression of astonishment and indignation on his face.

Before Zimmermann could launch into his customary translation into multiple languages, Dampf turned to McTrowell and exclaimed, "Ze judges haf approved ze Ret Bull's use of air vinch cannons!"

Felipe Garza lost his composure and triumphantly shouted, "Olé!"

POMP AND PREPARATIONS

BY MR. DAVID L. DRAKE

The first reaction to the announcement regarding the air winch cannons was stunned silence by the other pilots at the table. If they didn't understand Herr Zimmermann's German, they apparently caught the gist of Willy Dampf's English explanation. Suddenly, the table was all abuzz with pilots speaking in their native language to no one in general and exclaiming how incredulous they were. The exception of course was Felipe Garza, who couldn't help himself, but sat there smugly grinning at the news. Willy stood and showed a side of himself that he hadn't revealed to Sparky yet, which was indignance. He bellowed out in German some unkind words, turned as if he were going to storm off, thought better of it, and sat down.

Sparky realized that she might the only person at the table who was not familiar with this technology. Rather than reveal her ignorance, she asked Herr Zimmermann, "Could you please explain how you came to the approval of the air winch cannons?"

Herr Zimmermann made an interesting request, "If I may, my technical English iz not so good. Iz there zumone who can translate into English for me?"

Sergeant Fox approached the table. In German, he stated that he'd be willing to translate. His accent was very good and, to Sparky's ear, he sounded like he had grown up in Munich.

Herr Zimmermann rattled out five or six German sentences, then nodded to Fox that he could translate those. Sergeant Fox began his translation.

"The judges have discretion as to what constitutes a legal means for propelling the airship through the air, be it forward, up, or down. Obvious illegal means include pushing off the ground, pushing off or bumping other airships, and drafting competitors. Obviously, any help from support vehicles to propel an airship is also illegal. Using rising warm air bubbles, including tacking through them, is legal. Throwing off ballast is illegal, and therefore the firing of cannonballs rearward to gain speed would also be illegal. Similarly, using 'extraordinary means,' such as firing compressed steam or air off the back of the airship is just as illegal. Setting specialty sails is perfectly legal, since it takes advantage of the atmospheric conditions."

Herr Zimmermann again rattled out a long string of German and nodded to Sergeant Fox to restart his translation.

"What El Toro Rojo is being allowed to do is fire specialty sails out of 'cannons' to take advantage of atmospheric conditions near their airship, but not normally reachable by fixed sails. If extraordinary means were used to fire off the sails, such as gunpowder or compressed air from their steam engines, then the judges would have ruled them an illegal aid to flying. But their cannons are set through man-power, like a crossbow. After the specialty sails are fired out of the air winch cannons, they deploy in a similar manner to an umbrella. They are immediately hauled back in, pulling the airship forward. Because of the manner they are deployed and utilized, they have been deemed legal for this regatta."

Sparky was aghast. "How is the Burke & Hare supposed to compete with that?" She looked around for support, but it was clear that the judges were holding fast to their decision. Her concern was that the regatta was going to be a test of technology rather than skill. She always knew that the shape and the design of each racing craft played a key role, but that was a known part of the competition. This ruling could change everything and make it more of a sprint to deploy specialty sails.

One by one, the pilots stood and begrudgingly headed to their airships, undoubtedly not looking forward to telling their crew about the final judges' decision. This was true for all of the pilots, save Felipe Garza, who still had his unstoppable grin and a twinkle in his eye. Even Willy Dampf left without so much as a "goodbye." Sparky also stood, made a sour face, and left the table with her two protectors trailing behind her.

The remainder of Sunday night was spent checking and rechecking the various systems of the Burke & Hare. This was an arduous task since it was critical for both success in the regatta and for the safety of the craft and its crew. To add to this, the airship had to be prepared for two hours of regatta enthusiasts walking through the Burke & Hare. Any piece of equipment that wasn't permanently fixed onto the vessel had to be stowed or risk being taken as a keepsake.

The crew had a difficult schedule in the morning. From the completion of the parade of airship crews at 10:30 AM, if all went according to plan, until noon, they had to have the airship ready for a fast-paced sprint from Munich to Salzburg, a little over 70 miles. The Burke & Hare could travel that distance in about an hour and fifteen minutes, given fair weather and favorable winds, but any misstep in preparation could easily add ten minutes to the time, which would mean a sure loss on that leg. For that reason, the Burke & Hare crew was triple checking the boilers, steam engine, power train, propeller, cabling systems, fuel load, water level, accuracy of gauges, envelope pressure, safety equipment, emergency lines, auxiliary sails, and pre-race food quality and quantity.

One by one, the lights went out on the five moored airships as the crews attempted to get some sleep. The loud party on El Toro Rojo finally stopped around midnight. The glittering of the few scattered lanterns on the airfield was all that could be seen as the night came to a close.

Monday sunrise came all too soon for the airship crews. But by eight o'clock, they were in their finest regatta uniforms, ready to receive the expectant crowds gathered outside the airships. The Burke & Hare, just like the other airships, had set up a series of rope passageways to lead the spectators in one side of the airship, down the stairwell to the engine control room, back up another set of stairs, through the cabin hallway, out onto the catwalk, and return the viewers to the tower where the airship was tethered. At each major turn within this labyrinth stood one of the crew members to help guide the gawking populace. The two hours of showing the Burke & Hare went by at a glacial pace. Many inane questions were asked in broken English, or were not in English at all, about every shiny doodad on the airship. The one positive side to this parade of humanity was the wide-eyed children who fancied themselves as future airship pilots. The youngsters viewed the airship as the world's largest walk-in wooden toy, and every brass fixture and rope knot as a wonder to enjoy.

When ten o'clock arrived, there was a silent sigh of relief by the Burke & Hare crew as they persuaded the last of the looky-loos to exit the airship.

Erasmus and J.B. muttered as they squeezed into borrowed crew outfits, J.B.'s chest being of greater size than anyone else on the airship and Erasmus' thighs having a similar problem as he tried to put on a pair of the official trousers. This was a mandatory concession if they were to participate in the parade with Sparky. Well, technically they were guarding her as she played her part as a carefree racing pilot, but the two of them had to look like they were members of the airship crew to provide her protection during the procession.

It was possible that the grinding of Sparky's teeth was actually audible as she waited in marching line for the parade to start. "Not exactly your cup of tea, is it?" asked J.B., in one of the few times to date that he broke out of his military veneer. An answer from Sparky was not necessary, given that her body language indicated she'd rather be taking a barefoot stroll on hot coals.

The parade itself was uneventful. Everyone, in both the parade and in the crowds, impulsively waved at each other. Brass bands played oompa polkas and swaggering military-themed marching tunes. When it was over, it all seemed mercifully short in duration. At the conclusion of the parade, Erasmus and J.B. stayed close to Sparky as they endured the pomposity of the address by Maximilian II, King of Bavaria.

The applause rose for the finale of the speech right on time, eleven o'clock. Erasmus, J.B., and Sparky all made a beeline for the Burke & Hare to rejoin the crew and get their craft aloft. When they reached the top of their docking tower, they noticed an odd formation of non-racing airships gathered around the starting point in the sky. There must've been 30 or 40 small airships, probably privately owned, all wanting a better view of the regatta's start. Sparky had never seen such a show of wealth and interest at an airship race and was stunned into silence for more than a few seconds.

When Sparky had finished her gaping, the three of them hustled inside the Burke & Hare, disappearing into their respective cabins to change into more appropriate clothing. Sparky emerged first, now in full pilot's uniform, and took her rightful place at the helm of the airship. As Erasmus and J.B. reentered the hallway, Sparky's voice could be heard over the voicepipe, "Casting off! Take your stations! Let's get this race underway!" Erasmus thought to himself, *"What a grand adventure I happened upon in the service of Queen and country!"*

The Flat Run

By Dr. Katherine L. Morse

McTrowell's heels snapped out the staccato rhythm of her excitement as she shifted from foot to foot on the bridge. Although she heard the echo of her footsteps, she felt like she was actually floating over the deck. She shook Mr. Krasnayarubashka's hand crisply and snapped her goggles down over her eyes as the Burke & Hare floated free of its moorings. She wanted a good starting position, preferably where she could grab an early lead over El Toro Rojo. She scanned the pennants flying over the parade grounds and navigated toward the windward side of the rampant bull. She had just positioned the Burke & Hare slightly below the Spanish ship when she noticed The Iron Eagle performing a similar maneuver, but slightly above.

"Great minds think alike," she thought to herself. Du Guarde and Swenson weren't as nimble lining up, so Le Lapin and The North Wind were at a slight disadvantage on the leeward side of Garza. McTrowell placed her pocket watch open on the console in front of her so she could keep an eye on it as she feathered the engine and reversed the propeller to keep the Burke & Hare from crossing the start line before noon, even sliding back from the line several meters. She held her left hand lightly on the controls while watching the line judge on the ground through the telescope in her right hand. He faced the cannoneer and raised his hand. McTrowell reversed the propeller again. He dropped his hand and the cannoneer lit the cannon. McTrowell opened the throttle all the way. The Burke & Hare crossed the start line just as the sound of the cannon reached the ship and exactly at the same instant as The Iron Eagle.

As she had expected, Dampf used his greater speed and the wind to come up under Garza, arriving ahead and to the Spanish ship's leeward side. With the advantages of surprise and a bit of the same wind on her side, McTrowell brought the Burke & Hare to a position forward and windward of El Toro Rojo. She glanced over toward The Iron Eagle and could have sworn she saw Dampf wink at her. They both backed off their engines once they secured their flying blockade.

"Mr. Krasnayarubashka, I can manage the bridge for this flat run. Please get to the voicepipe on the aft catwalk and keep me apprised of any and all maneuvers by El Toro Rojo. If Dampf and I don't keep that ship contained and their air winch cannons out of play, this race will be over before it's started."

"Da, gospozha doktor lyotchika." She saw the first mate of The Iron Eagle depart its bridge just moments after Ivan. Most of an hour passed fairly uneventfully except for the occasional blocking maneuver in response to Mr. Krasnayarubashka's reports from aft about the actions of El Toro Rojo. Although about half of his reports became unnecessary after only a short while because Dampf's first mate was doing an equally competent job of informing his captain, so

McTrowell could follow the lead of The Iron Eagle when Dampf got his report before she got hers. She relished the vision of Garza's frustrated face she was conjuring in her head. She hadn't had so much as a glimpse of Le Lapin or The North Wind since the opening cannon, but she imagined the blocking was having an equally aggravating effect on the other two ships as well.

In addition to its superior speed, The Iron Eagle had the advantage that its captain knew the countryside passing below better than any other competitor. Sparky couldn't recognize any of the villages passing beneath the Burke & Hare, so she was restricted to estimating the race's progress by her stopwatch. Then she spotted a large body of water, the Chiemsee. That meant they were approximately two thirds of the way to Salzburg. That meant she had less than twenty-five minutes to figure out how she was going to beat The Iron Eagle at the finish line without giving El Toro Rojo an opening to fire the air winch cannons. She tried several scenarios in her head, playing them out and weighing their advantages, disadvantages, and particularly their risks. When she could see Hohensalzburg Castle in the distance, she called Krasnayarubashka back to the bridge.

"Ivan, we only have one chance to win this leg. The Iron Eagle is faster, so we have to take away its wind while continuing to block El Toro Rojo from using its air winches. The warm air will cause an updraft as we approach the bluff on which Hohensalzburg Castle stands. We need to drop down, catch that wind, and rise in front of the Iron Eagle without dropping so far that we give Garza an opening to fire. Is that clear?"

"Da, gospozha doktor lyotchika."

She grabbed the voicepipe. "Stoke the boilers, gentlemen. We're making a run for it."

McTrowell wouldn't have been entirely surprised to see the frantic activity in the engine room of the Spanish ship at that moment, but it was still a sight to behold. It was equally obvious to Garza that he could only hope to get one chance to engage the technical superiority of the air winch cannons, and he wanted to be prepared to use them to maximum effect. Crammed into the same space as the steam engine powering El Toro Rojo were three leather sling seats with iron hand rails in front of three identical sets of pedals. A lean, sinewy, and very sweaty Spaniard sat in each seat, stripped to the waist in a vain attempt to mitigate the stifling heat and barely managing to hang onto the hand rails from the sweat running down their arms. They were cranking the air winch cannons like they were crossbows, and all three of them were now straining with their last bit of strength to tighten the cables and locking gears one or two more notches.

McTrowell kept an eye on the cockpit of The Iron Eagle, waiting to see the increase in activity that would presage its run for the finish line. She saw the first mate return from his aft position.

"Flaps up, Mr. Krasnayarubashka."

"Flaps up."

She gave it as much left rudder as she could, blocking as much of the Iron Eagle's wind as possible. She counted to herself, estimating how low they could drop without unblocking El Toro Rojo...six, seven, eight. "Flaps down!"

"Flaps down," Krasnayarubashka responded. McTrowell opened the throttle all the way and the Burke & Hare lurched upward. Sparky's stomach was left behind. Not because she was unused to the sudden, steep climb, but because The Iron Eagle had surged ahead despite being deprived of its wind. Not only would it win the leg, but it had opened a hole for Garza!

"Disparen!" Garza screamed. Fortunately, his first mate was a cooler head and he only fired the top and starboard air winch cannons. The port cannon would have gutted the Burke & Hare. Unfortunately, the cannons were designed to be fired in unison, so when the pedalers reversed the gearing and pedaled frantically to haul the canopies back in, it dragged the ship wildly off course. The Burke & Hare sailed easily

past in the draft of The Iron Eagle. And then Le Lapin snuck by as well. The Burke & Hare was so close behind The Iron Eagle at the finish, Sparky thought she felt the wake of its propeller buffeting her face, but it was only her bitter imagination.

Krasnayarubashka slammed his fist down onto the console. "Черт возьми!"

THE VALLEY RUN

BY MR. DAVID L. DRAKE

Like many of the non-crew, Chief Inspector Erasmus Drake had been watching the race from the common room that was the dining area just the evening before. At Krasnayarubashka's outcry, he realized the race was over and sprinted to the outside door leading to the catwalk. Overlooking the railing, he peered down at the excited crowd just a few hundred feet below. The racing official with a large flag started waving it wildly, signaling completion of the leg. The crowd, pressed in tight, shoulder-to-shoulder, all raised their arms and shouted in victory. Erasmus thought, *"Even with their political differences, the people of Salzburg must see themselves as Bavarians, so the Iron Eagle winning this leg is a huge win for them."*

Lord Ashleigh and J.B. Fox soon arrived by his side, also leaning over the rail to see the reaction of the townsfolk. Before either of them had an opportunity to comment, Sparky's voice could be heard over the voicepipe. All three men retreated back into the airship common room to hear her announcement.

"...and given the challenges of the course and the competitors, placing a close second is an excellent start to the regatta. I understand, as well as all of you, that this race is far from over. Please be aware that we have followers in the crowd down there in Salzburg, as well as the press, and they will see each and every one of us as members of our crew. When you are on the ground, please take care to always show your great enthusiasm for our finishing in second place. The Western & Transatlantic Airship Lines appreciate your cooperation. Personally, I'm looking forward to the opportunity to take the lead tomorrow! I hope you all are with me in this endeavor. Thank you."

Erasmus looked around the room expecting to see surprised expressions from those who knew Sparky, but there weren't any. He realized that a side of her he had not previously seen had just been exposed; she had a great amount of discipline when under pressure and realized that childish emotions do not a great leader make.

Lord Ashleigh turned to Erasmus and flatly stated, "That was far too exciting. I'm stepping into my cabin for a spot of chai. Care to join me?" Erasmus wasn't really in the mood for the hot beverage and instead thought he might see if he could spend a moment with Sparky. "I much appreciate the offer, my good friend, but I'm going to tend to my duties to make sure that the crew stays safe during our docking." Lord Ashleigh smiled politely, executed a small bow, and retreated to his cabin. Erasmus was sure that his excuse did not fool his friend who knew the true reason.

As it turned out, the finish line was on the front edge of the airfield of Salzburg. To the port side of the Burke & Hare was the Salzach River, and in front of them on the starboard side was Mönchsberg Mountain topped by Festung Hohensalzburg, the grand Hohensalzburg Castle, a very impressive sight, particularly when viewed from the sky at eye level. Beyond the airfield were the town cathedrals.

The airfield in front of them had only been made to accommodate one airship at a time on a permanent basis. However, four additional towers had been temporarily erected to accommodate the regatta competitors. The Iron Eagle was being flagged toward the permanent tower; perhaps due to their placement in the first leg of the regatta, or perhaps because they were the Bavarian entry. Either way, they had earned their place of honor. The rest of the ships followed the waving of their associated country's flag at the top of their temporary wooden towers. As the airships carefully descended to moor, the crowd rushed over to meet them.

By the time the crew of the Burke & Hare descended their tower, the crowd of well-wishers was so thick that they couldn't descend the final steps and were halted on the stairwell, waving to the throng. It had become clear that every resident of Salzburg had come out to see the conclusion of the first regatta leg, and they had been joined by others who had gotten there by other means. The majority of the shouts from the audience were a mishmash of incomprehensible German to the ears of Erasmus.

A brass band struck up in the distance and the crowd seemed to ease back a bit. This allowed the English-speaking newspaper reporters to come to the fore, pencils in hand, shouting questions to Sparky. It suddenly occurred to Erasmus that the fact that Sparky was the only female pilot in the regatta made her an instant celebrity. Sparky handled each of their questions as she slowly descended the staircase, allowing her crew to get by.

Erasmus and J.B. were surreptitiously armed to the teeth. It was somewhat amazing they didn't clank as they walked, given the revolvers, swords, and knives they each had hidden in various locations on their person.

Erasmus and J.B. scanned the crowd, but didn't see any immediate danger. One unexpected incident happened, though. When Jake entered the throng, he was approached by an enthusiastic young lady who asked him in broken English if he had just disembarked from the Burke & Hare. He innocently replied "yes," to which she threw her arms around him and gave him an incredibly forceful kiss, followed by, "Mine parents are from England land, they live here, yes, we cheer for you! So proud!" She followed this proclamation with an excited little hop followed by another big hug, which actually picked Jake off the ground by a few inches. Jake was, as expected, speechless. After a few seconds of silence, she said, "Please me by staying here. I get parents of mine. Please stay!" She then turned and burrowed her way through the crowd. Jake turned to his father. He just smiled at him and slowly shook his head.

Sparky was just finishing up with one of the reporters. "I thought it was a fair race. The Iron Eagle did well on defense throughout the leg and made a clean break for the finish line. My only regret is that in our final maneuver we should have zigged when we zagged, leaving us at a close second. We're looking forward to the remainder of the regatta."

"Thank you, Dr. McTrowell." The reporter seemed pleased with this, scribbling quickly, dynamically finishing with a period, and disappearing into the crowd to probably send in his article by telegraph.

The band suddenly changed tunes and, at a central podium, Herr Zimmermann called for the pilots to approach. Erasmus and J.B. followed Sparky. The podium was set up in a classic tiered pyramid for awards with five locations for the five pilots. The front of the podium had the Salzburg crest on the front.

Herr Zimmermann announced the names of the airships and pilots, starting with the fifth-place finisher, The North Wind piloted by Björn Swenson. The tall, blond Swede proudly took the podium, waving wildly at the crowd. Despite coming in last in the first leg, the crowd roared with enthusiasm. Herr Zimmermann then called for Pierre du Guarde of Le Lapin to take his rightful place on the podium. Again the crowd cheered. Felipe Garza of El Toro Rojo was called up to take the third position, and he humbly ascended the podium and bowed to the crowd. Again, a cheer went up. Sparky did her best to hide the rolling of her eyes.

"Finishing a close second, the Burke & Hare, piloted by none other than the illustrious Dr. Sparky McTrowell!" Again the crowd roared, but with the interesting distinction that the ladies' voices could clearly be heard. As Sparky turned to face the crowd, she removed her signature airship pilot's headgear and waved it in the air, smiling broadly to the crowd.

"And in first place, our very own Captain Willy Dampf piloting the Iron Eagle!" Willy took half a step toward the podium, but then two large members of his own crew hoisted him up onto their shoulders and carried him to the high central position of the pyramid-shaped podium. He turned and smiled brightly waving his arms. The crowd roared ecstatically.

Each competitor was handed a rolled up colored flag to add to the back of their airship to indicate their position in the regatta. The pilots tucked their flags underneath their arms and waved to the crowd for the last time while on the podium. The band struck up a lively tune that clearly indicated to everyone that the festivities had concluded, and it was time for all good citizens to seek their dinner and discuss the intricacies of the regatta.

A dinner for the airship crews had been prepared in the oldest part of town at the Stiftskeller St. Peter. Each airship crew was provided a large table and a suitable Bavarian feast was brought out, starting with garlic and goulash soup, the main course being pig shank with sauerkraut, and finishing with *Wiener apfelstrudel*.

Erasmus noticed that Reginald Wallace had not joined the crew at the table. He was less concerned about the political shenanigans that Wallace was probably involved in while he was out and about, and more concerned about his safety. The owner of an airship line would be an excellent high-profile target to someone who wanted to interfere with the regatta or who was planning to kidnap him for ransom. But Erasmus' priority was to stay here and protect those from the Burke & Hare who had joined in for dinner. Aldrich and Jake Fremont were there. Lord Ashleigh was also there. Much to the surprise of Erasmus, Virat was seated as a guest. It was interesting to see someone else serving Virat. He was exceedingly polite and was able to get through the meal without uttering a sound save a few hummings of approval.

The talk during the meal at the Burke & Hare table was jovial, but not high-spirited. Jake was able to add to the tales told by saying that when the father of the lass met him, she was more subdued in her excitement, but still gave the impression that Jake was the prize at the end of the race. In comparison, the conversation at El Toro Rojo table was bordering on secretive, with all of their conspiratorial whispering. At the Iron Eagle table, it was clear to even Erasmus' untrained ear that the final seconds of the first leg was being told and retold many times, with crew members trading off tales of their expertise, patting each other on the back, and pouring goblets of wine for each other.

To close the evening out, a quartet played Mozart pieces during dessert, starting with the quiet and sweet Aria from Don Giovanni, followed by a livelier tune from The Magic Flute, and finishing with the rousing Piano Concerto Number 5 in D, Movement 1.

Sparky walked around the table while the men had seconds of *apfelstrudel*, thanking the crew and making small talk. She bent down to ear level with Erasmus and J.B. and whispered, "I see that neither of you touched your drinks tonight. Taking your jobs seriously, I see."

She followed it with a polite smile, which the two men mirrored back. *"Kid all she wants,"* Erasmus thought, *"but we will not have another incident here in Salzburg."*

As the music ended, the crews started shuffling out to get a good night's sleep. Willy Dampf approached Sparky and offered getting a nightcap at the Stieglkeller. He said it was a bit of a walk up the hill to the fortress, but worth the effort.

"When you say nightcap, don't you really mean beer?" she retorted.

He smiled and said, "Uf course! Chust a small one," and held his thumb and index finger to indicate a tiny thimble of brew. They both chuckled. Willy added, "I vould like to haf vun uf my crew come vith us. Her von Zeppelin." A very young, serious-looking and well-dressed man stood up from the Iron Eagle's table and bowed to Sparky. Willy patted him on the back, saying, "He is a very promising young engineer. Well virth the extra veight on der airship! Ha!"

Sparky replied, "Well, of course," while wondering if a "man" of the age of thirteen should be going to the Stieglkeller after dinner.

J.B. turned to Erasmus. "I'll shadow the crew back to the airship."

"I'll watch Sparky," and then Erasmus added, "Stay safe."

The parties went their separate ways. After a climb up the twisting footpath to the fortress, Erasmus found himself seated in a large beer hall with long running communal tables and a sizable stein of beer in front of him. Sparky, Willy, and von Zeppelin went deep into conversation about airship piloting, defensive strategies, design tradeoffs, and the topography of tomorrow's run. While Willy enjoyed a couple of steins, Sparky nursed a glass, and von Zeppelin had a low-alcohol variant of the local beer. Erasmus had plenty of time to look around the brew house.

Two tables over, he spotted Krasnayarubashka talking to someone, perhaps a local of Salzburg. They must have been friends from before, given the animated conversation and how exhilarated they were to see each other. They spoke Russian quickly and enthusiastically while toasting frequently. Erasmus continued scanning the room, keeping an eye on Sparky and Krasnayarubashka, but the evening continued to be uneventful.

When Sparky finally drained her glass, she and Willy stood. She extended her hand for shaking, but Willy took it for kissing. Sparky quickly looked toward Erasmus, concerned about his reaction. She saw a raised eyebrow for a split second, then the solemn face of the man protecting her.

All four of them proceeded back down the path away from the Hohensalzburg Castle and to the airship grounds. They parted company quickly, given the hour and von Zeppelin's best attempts to appear a mature adult and not an utterly exhausted boy. Neither Sparky nor Erasmus mentioned the hand-kissing incident during the ascent of the Burke & Hare's tower, although they were both thinking about it.

The singing of the early-rising birds made sure that no one in any of the airship slept past daybreak. Despite the best efforts of Luis-Miguel, few of the Burke & Hare crew were interested in breakfast given the size of the meal the previous night. By nine o'clock, most of the carefully-made mushroom and cheese omelets had been tossed to the same birds that woke the crew.

The crew readied the airship for the second leg. J.B. and Erasmus traded tasks; J.B. followed Sparky and Krasnayarubashka to the pre-race rituals, and Erasmus stayed to guard the crew. Was he avoiding Sparky due to a polite hand kiss? He didn't want to ponder that too long. He had a crew to watch over.

Erasmus first verified that everyone was on board, even Reginald Wallace. Reginald had retired directly back to his cabin after his light breakfast of tea and toast, and seemed to be nursing a hangover. Perhaps he was more worried about the outcome of this regatta than Erasmus would have expected. But it was not for Erasmus to worry about, or care about, for that matter. Owners of businesses seemed to worry about everything all the time, so Erasmus figured that Reginald was just sleeping in the bed that he had made for himself.

Erasmus had taken most of the morning watching six crew members hard at work on the preparation of the boilers and steam engine. There were the usual activities of lubricating everything and verifying that the water taken on board was as pure as possible so as not to clog the tubes between the boilers and engine while under seam.

Erasmus learned about the Burke & Hare's unique two-boiler system. To maximize the power output, spherical boilers were used with high-temperature coal that was packed over three-quarters of the boilers surface area. This provided a very fast-heating boiler, allowing the Burke & Hare to provide sudden bursts of speed, sprinting, if you will. But due to the size of the boiler, it would require more than one boiler's worth of steam to make it through a leg of the regatta. For this reason, a two-boiler system was used; as soon as the second boiler was up to pressure, a steam transference switch could be thrown, allowing the steam engine a new power source in the blink of an eye. It also meant that new water could be introduced into the system without loss of pressure by pouring it into the standby boiler. Spherical boilers also reduced the chance of a boiler explosion.

Erasmus marveled at the complexity of the system. Heat vents from the boilers directed wasted heat to the air in the envelopes, maintaining the heated, and therefore expanded, air in the gargantuan balloon that gave lift to the airship. The steam engine was a two-stage, piston-style mechanism that allowed the steam that exited the first set of pistons to be used to power a second set, taking full advantage of the power left in the steam. The ability to collect the steam and send it back to the boilers was a possibility, but the additional tubes and coolers were too much additional weight for a racing vessel. To add to that reasoning, a closed-pressure system required too much care and raised the risk of something going wrong. The waste steam from the engine was released into a special rubber lined envelope that was allowed to fill, removed by hand, and cooled; the condensed water was poured into the standby boiler. Keeping all of the power system working was a full-time job for three or four of the crew and for all six when they planned a boiler switch-over.

Just over the roar of the boiler fires, Erasmus could hear the bass drum and brass horns of the band outside kick into a rousing march. He heard the scuffling of feet as Sparky, Krasnayarubashka, and J.B. return to the ship to prepare for launch. Erasmus left the engine compartment and went upstairs to check in with J.B. and snoop on Sparky.

She had the look of a woman who desperately wanted to transition to a useful task. She had attended the pre-launch activities in her pilot's uniform so she wouldn't have to change clothes. She immediately took the helm and rattled off a list of pre-launch instructions to Krasnayarubashka who did his best to keep up with her. J.B. gave a full and overly formal report to Erasmus in about twenty-five seconds that boiled down to nothing of interest happening.

In twenty short minutes, the Burke & Hare was on the starting line, carefully controlling its position. The common room directly behind the bridge held most of the non-crewing passengers: Wallace, J.B., Aldrich and Jake Fremont, the referee Herr Fenstermacher, Lord Ashleigh and, taking a rare break from the galley, Luis-Miguel Sevilla. The only non-crew missing was Virat who was no doubt in one of Lord Ashleigh's cabin rooms performing the never-ending undertakings to keep his master's world in exemplary condition.

The flurry of activity on the bridge was incredible. No fewer than six topographic charts lay on sideboards, held in place by clamps. Between the rapid conversations on the voicepipes to the engine room and the fast exchanges between Sparky and Krasnayarubashka, it was clear to Erasmus that the intensity would be far greater for this run. From the bits and pieces of concentrated technical dialogue and complex gestures toward the various charts, Erasmus was able to gather that the airships had a good deal of freedom as to how they could get from the Salzburg starting line to the Innsbruck finish line. However, it would be foolish to fly high and suffer the fickle mountain gales. It would be wiser to stay in the valleys where the winds were more predictable in both strength and direction. For this reason, all of the airships were initially headed north. Sparky's strategy was to turn hard to port as soon as they cleared Mönchsberg Mountain and head west to cross over the town of Bad Reichenhall. From there, it would be rough going over hilly terrain until passing over Kiefersfeldon. That was the eastern end of the remaining valley run to Innsbruck. There were a number of route choices over the hilly area, but it came down to choosing between sprinting ahead or defensively blocking opponents from gaining a lead. The plan also rested on seeing what the other airships were going to do tactically, so planning only allowed the Burke & Here pilots an understanding of their options. Erasmus was startled out of his contemplation by the starting cannon. The steam engine roar, the thrust from the propeller, and the shouts from the crowd meant the race was on.

Erasmus went back down to the engine room to see the activity that kept full power to a sprinting airship. It was inspirational to see the back-breaking effort to keep the muscles of such an athletic vessel running smoothly. Coal was shoveled. Water levels and pressures were checked every few seconds. Joints were lubricated. Vibrations were controlled. Steam exhaust bags were changed. Flap cables were checked for tension. Air flow ribbons were examined and reported back to the helm. Envelope pressure and stress were verified and compensated for. The six crew members were drenched in sweat, laboring to make sure that the craft literally flew off the starting line. Erasmus imagined that the crowd was staring up, pop-eyed, as the flying behemoths achieved top speed in a matter of minutes, and their shouts turned to gasps of disbelief.

Erasmus knew from the regatta briefs that this run was about 85 miles long, a good 14 miles longer than the flat run from Munich to Salzburg. That meant more water, coal, time, and stress. This was going to be a true test of the crew and vessel.

It was only minutes later that the Burke & Hare banked around the Mönchsberg Mountain. Erasmus lost his balance and grabbed for the nearest rope hold. The crew all made a simple weight shift in their stance and continued their whirl of activity. Erasmus smiled at their talent and headed back upstairs to the common room.

The airships had spread out as they headed across the flat plain to Bad Reichenhall. Despite the Burke & Hare's best effort, it was still nose-to-nose with the other airships. They all had chosen the same altitude, approximately 200 feet up, where the winds were most favorable. Looking forward, El Toro Rojo had taken the rightmost position, neighbored by Le Lapin, the Burke & Hare in the middle, then the Iron Eagle, and on the far left was the North Wind. From a race perspective, the Burke & Hare was in a favorable position. To make headway on her required not only gaining ground, but also clearing enough to cut in front. And since she was in the middle, where she went the others had to follow or change altitude, or be disqualified by bumping airships. With all the airships under full-steam, they sky-wrote a musical staff across the sky with their trails of water vapor at just under 80 miles per hour.

Looming ahead past Bad Reichenhall were three side-by-side mountains, each of their peaks standing about 3,000 feet above the plain floor. Sparky's plan was to follow the Saalach River to the valley between the left of the middle mountain, limiting the amount of climbing required. The danger was that her plan would allow El Toro Rojo to take the rightmost valley and use their air winch cannons without interference from the other airships. But at this clip and given the upcoming terrain, the Burke & Hare would be foolish to change to defense now. So on she pushed, toward the leftmost valley.

Just over Bad Reichenhall, Sparky saw El Toro Rojo fire its air winch cannons. The three bundled sails sprang out ahead trailing their lines behind them. The initial effect was to cause El Toro Rojo to lose about 15 feet off the rest of the pack from the force of firing the sails forward. All three lines suddenly went taut, and the umbrella-shaped sails opened fully. They must have changed the size of their sails overnight, since they were visibly larger than the day before. They were hauled back in at an astounding speed, thrusting El Toro Rojo forward. When the maneuver was completed, El Toro Rojo had gained half of a ship length on the rest of the airships.

Sparky's initial impression was that it was a great deal of effort for such a small gain. But if properly timed, half an airship's length is the difference between a win and an also-ran. It was clear that El Toro Rojo wanted to get into that valley first, so they must have been shooting for the same valley as the Burke & Hare. Sparky grabbed the voicepipe. "I need a high-head sprint! Double-up on the boilers if you must! On my count. Three...two...one...now!"

Erasmus saw both Sparky and Krasnayarubashka grab for handholds, so he leapt to do the same. As fast as he thought the Burke & Hare was going, the airship lurched forward, and Sparky dropped the nose to gain some additional speed through gravity. Although Erasmus had been standing, everyone else in the common room was sitting except Wallace, who landed on his rump. He was up fast enough, but with his hangover eliminated and his dignity slightly bruised.

Although 30 feet lower than before, the Burke & Hare was ten feet in front of El Toro Rojo. Over the voicepipe, the echoey shouts from the engine room could be heard, "High-head sprint over in three...two...one...done!" The airship slowed back to the previous race speed, but she was in an excellent position.

Transitioning into the valley was claustrophobic. Due to the close conditions, both Le Lapin and the Iron Eagle dropped back so as not to collide. Due to Sparky's maneuver, the Burke & Hare's envelope was now at the same altitude as El Toro Rojo's gondola, forcing it to have to gain altitude and lose a bit of speed. The North Wind tried to stay abreast of the Burke & Hare as long as possible, but when its envelope was within three feet of the Burke & Hare's, Herr Fenstermacher stood bravely on the port-side catwalk and blew his whistle and waved off the encroaching North Wind. Since the Burke & Hare had the lead, they had priority to proceed and the other airships had to give way.

Sparky smiled at their well-timed maneuver and let out a very American "Woo-hoo!" Even with their lead, Sparky turned to Krasnayarubashka and stated, "The fact that the Iron Eagle didn't try to use their raw speed to take the lead means they must be purposely letting us do the rough front work while they wait to come from behind. We need to watch them when the valley opens up."

The formation remained through the narrow valley with the Burke & Hare in the lead, El Toro Rojo and the North Wind side-by-side behind, trailed by the Iron Eagle alongside of Le Lapin. Sparky pushed the tempo of the race since the Burke & Hare was rather maneuverable. Krasnayarubashka found a very favorable wind at 180 feet, which was dangerously close to the minimum altitude for the leg of 150 feet above the ground. However, all of the ships were following her lead, as close as they could without being called for drafting. The sharp right turn at the town of Lofer that went through the narrow pass made the Burke & Hare's gondola swing out to the port side eliciting audible gasps from the common room. It was possible to see the individual goats grazing on the mountainsides, and that just seemed all too close for those who hadn't raced before.

Sparky executed another hard right at Kirchdorf in Tirol, entering an even narrower valley to negotiate. The train of high-speed airships whipped thorough the passage, not a single one of them having the room to perform a pass. A hard left at Kössen and the valley began to open up, given breathing room to the brisk race.

The town of Kiefersfelden was ahead, nestled at the junction of three major valleys. It was a major decision point for Sparky since she had to decide whether to stay low and follow the prevailing current, or hug the mountains on her left and head into the next valley while forcing the North Wind over and crowding out EL Toro Rojo. It was riskier, but she decided to hug the mountains.

Over the voicepipe she asked, "Can I get another sprint here and save one for the finish?"

"Not possible given the coal and water. Only one push left," was all the answer she got.

"Krasnayarubashka, do you think we can hug that hillside and catch a favorable updraft?"

"Eta big reesk. But I vill try." At that, Krasnayarubashka tightened his chin strap and rushed out onto the catwalk on the port side, holding on with one hand, and sticking his other out over the side into the wind, feeling for a minor change while the airship flew ahead. Sparky leaned the ship over toward the hillside. The rules were clear on this, she could only fly so low, but she could get as close to the mountainside as she wished, as long as they didn't hit anything. Erasmus held his breath as they leaned closer and closer. Trees flew past. Sparky made the Burke & Hare climb a bit. The other airships weren't willing to go that close and were maneuvering around the mountain at a safer distance.

Suddenly, Krasnayarubashka gave a thumb's up. Sparky tipped the nose of the Burke & Hare up and pulled the release for the horizontal sail. The Burke & Hare sprouted wings on each side that caught the updraft that was riding over the sides of the mountain and lifted the ship. It felt like the airship was in another sprint, but it was gaining altitude, and the pitch of the engine noise hadn't changed. It had the feeling of falling up and gaining forward speed.

The pack of airships responded as Sparky had hoped. The North Wind gave the mountain more room, forcing El Toro Rojo to swing wide around the turn. Le Lepin and the Iron Eagle did likewise. Krasnayarubashka fought his way back into the airship and retook his place at the helm, looking amazingly wind-worn. With another release pull, the horizontal wing sails collapsed, retracted, and fastened to the sides of the airship's envelope.

Coming into the final valley run, the Burke & Hare was an airship and half ahead of the North Wind, which was now leading El Toro Rojo. Le Lapin and the Iron Eagle were neck and neck, but bringing up the rear.

There were only two more locations where the valley widened for the remainder of the route: at the town of Kirchbichl and at Innsbruck itself. Erasmus thought that if Sparky could maintain her lead through Kirchbichl, she could sprint her way to the finish.

Within a minute of gaining the lead on the corner, the town of Kirchbichl came into view. That's when it happened. The Iron Eagle turned up its engines and flanked El Toro Rojo, obviously with the plan to not only gain the lead, but also to block another use of their air winch cannons. El Toro Rojo responded by dropping down quickly to keep a clear passage ahead. With the Iron Eagle out of the way and El Toro Rojo dropped down, Le Lapin earned its name in a half-minute dash that gained a 50-foot climb and a sprint over the top of El Toro Rojo. They gained a full half airship length and legally began their descent side-by-side with the Burke & Hare. But it was too late. The command to fire the air winch cannons had already been given.

The top middle cannon shot its umbrella sail into the back of Le Lapin, ripping a giant hole in the back of its envelope, deploying the canopy inside Le Lapin's envelope, and tangling the attached rope into the French airship's series of three propellers. At first the spinning propeller pulled El Toro Rojo toward the entangled airship. As soon as the rope went fully taut, Le Lapin's main propeller suddenly stopped rotating, its steam engine seized, and a loud popping echoed throughout the valley. All of the racing crews knew that noise; it was the breaking of mechanical components under high pressure. A specialty release valve instantly fired within the heart of Le Lapin, and scalding steam billowed out of the sides of the damaged airship.

With the steam from Le Lapin pouring over the sides of the Burke & Hare, Sparky took the airship hard to port to escape damage. But for the rest of the regatta, with the disabled Le Lapin in front of them, this created an instant airship traffic jam. The Iron Eagle had to climb rapidly over Le Lapin, while the North Wind turned sideways to attempt to stop as quickly as possible, swinging their gondola back and forth in a manner that would have made a strong man's stomach flip over. But El Toro Rojo got the worst of it. The ropes from the cannons were made to be reeled back in, but there was no easy way to cut them loose. With the top cannon line attached to an airship that had a punctured envelope, they both lost altitude quickly.

Erasmus knew that it would be foolish for the envelopes to be one giant bag of hot air. Ironically, this accident was an interesting way to learn how these structures were segmented. Apparently, Le Lapin used a three-segment approach that allowed for one of the segments to be completely pierced and the other two to gently lower it to the ground. That is, unless it was tethered to another airship.

Le Lapin hung by its tail, tipped at a thirty-degree angle, nose down. El Toro Rojo was now supporting a heavier-than-air object by a line connected to the top of its envelope, twisting El Toro Rojo sideways and forcing its gondola up to the starboard side.

But no whistles were blown, so the Burke & Hare rushed on. The Iron Eagle had slowed its progress, but then rushed forward at full speed. The North Wind was less fortunate. It had to come to a full stop, gain altitude, which was very time-consuming given that they were in a regatta, and then restart their race to the finish.

The regatta was now quite spread out through the final valley run. The Burke & Hare was two airship lengths ahead of the Iron Eagle, and the North Wind trailed by half a mile.

Sparky shouted back to Erasmus, "Is everyone on board safe and sound?" J.B. and Erasmus sprinted off to check on those who weren't in plain sight. J.B. ran to Lord Ashleigh's cabin to verify that Virat was not injured, and Erasmus sprinted downstairs. Both returned reporting no casualties, although the sudden turn to avoid disaster surprised even the veteran crew.

By the time Innsbruck was in sight, The Iron Eagle had gained on the Burke & Hare and was one airship length behind. The anticipation was Sparky's enemy. She didn't want to lose another leg to bad timing after leading most of the race.

"Gospodin Krasnayarubashka, you choose the time for the sprint."

"Me, Gospozha Doctor Lyotcheeka McTrowell? If you order it so, I vill do."

The co-pilot took a mental triangulation on the nearby landmarks of mountains, steeples, and the finish line flags. He knew the Burke & Hare had about twenty seconds of sprint in her.

Over the voicepipe he shouted, "I please need high-head sprint! On my count. Tree...two...one...now!"

Sparky hung on to the pilot's handholds, but looked out the starboard side window to see the Iron Eagle's sprint that brought the nose of their ship up even to the window of the Burke & Hare's bridge, and she smiled.

The Burke & Hare lunged forward, and the nose of the Iron Eagle retreated as a band below struck up a lively tune, marking the finish of the second leg. The Burke & Hare had finished first.

Reginald Wallace let out a "Woo-hoo," but everyone knew he was just not doing it right. But that was okay; it was for all the right reasons.

Erasmus looked at Sparky and she at him, and they smiled. He thought, *"What a woman. What a woman."*

THE MOUNTAIN RUN

BY DR. KATHERINE L. MORSE

Captain Dampf's spirits were not quite as high as usual that night in Innsbruck as they sat drinking lagers at Bierwirt. Despite the Burke & Hare's win that day, the Iron Eagle was still leading, but by a maddeningly thin margin of 47 seconds. Although Dampf had managed to hang on to the first place flag, it was McTrowell's hand Emperor Franz Josef had shaken first. And it would be her picture on the front page of the broadsheets the next day. It was not a particularly proud day for the German Confederation.

However, by comparison to the Spanish and French situation, it was positively festive. Of course Le Lapin was out of the race, being damaged beyond repair. The only saving grace was the drag of El Toro Rojo had slowed its descent sufficiently that no one had been injured … unless one counted Pierre du Guarde's pride. He had screamed to the judge and referees for a full twenty minutes about the "scandal" of the whole thing, but there was really no point. His ship was ruined. Señor Garza had screamed for another twenty minutes about the gross unfairness of being disqualified since du Guarde had "obviously" caused the incident. There was really no point to his display either because everyone else had clearly seen that it was his fault. Honor, sportsmanship, and international relations left no room for any action besides the Spanish entry's complete disqualification.

Drake sat at Sparky's elbow performing his beer sipping charade and paying more attention to the crowd around them than the conversation. Sergeant Fox sat by himself near the door performing the same act, but somehow sitting at attention. Although they were now well out of Munich, they were taking no chances given the boldness of the "gypsies." Between the sentry duty and Dampf's doldrums, their evening out didn't last long nor did Dampf do his usual damage to the establishment's stores of beer. Sparky suspected that, like herself, he was planning for the next day's leg to Vaduz, Liechtenstein, for which he wanted to be fresh and rested. It was barely dark when they all headed back to their respective ships.

Drake and McTrowell strolled back to the airship field with Sergeant Fox trailing behind like a Chinese wife, but with his head held high, on the alert for any danger. As they approached the mooring tower, a figure separated from the shadow.

"Dr. McTrowell…" was all the figure managed to utter before Drake tackled it and Fox cinched it into a headlock. In the earnest wrestling that ensued, the would-be assailant's face flashed under the light of the lantern mounted on the tower and McTrowell recognized him.

"Mr. Fremont!" Drake and Fox stopped in the middle of pinning Aldrich Fremont with his hands behind his back.

"Bloody hell! What's the meaning of this insult?" Fremont struggled to his feet and straightened his clothes with umbrage. Drake dusted himself off and replaced his bowler firmly on his head.

"I am terribly sorry, Mr. Fremont. We mistook you for a miscreant who intended to do violence to Dr. McTrowell. Please accept my apologies," Drake offered.

"I only wished to congratulate the good doctor on her brilliant win today." He huffed and glared at Drake and Fox.

"Thank you, Mr. Fremont, although it was a testament to the ability of the entire crew to work together. I'm hoping tomorrow will be just as successful. To that end, I think all of us could use a good night's sleep." She fixed Drake and Fox with a meaningfully stony stare before heading up the tower.

McTrowell was making her way to the bridge the next morning when Aldrich approached her again, looking around cautiously for her guard dogs before getting close.

"Hello again, Dr. McTrowell."

"Good morning, Mr. Fremont." She dearly hoped he would get to the point quickly because she hadn't much time to finish preparations for the day's leg. She gave him her best "I'm in a hurry so get on with it look."

"That Chief Inspector."

"Yes?" Clearly she needed to spend time brushing up on her repertoire of meaningful looks.

"He's quite prickly."

"Excuse me?"

"Quite stuffy and full of himself."

"Um."

"I can't imagine why that good Mr. Wallace allows his presence on this airship. Don't you agree?"

"Un-huh. I really must get to work." She tried her "aren't you lucky you inherited something valuable because you haven't the wits to come in from the rain" look. It had no more discernable effect than the "get on with it" look. Yes, when this was over, she really needed to find a good mirror and put in some practice time.

"Доброе утро, Mr. Krasnayarubashka. Are you ready for another day of adventure?"

"Da, da, Gospozha Doctor Lyotcheeka McTrowell. Flying vit you is always beeg excitement."

"This mountain run is going to be tricky because I don't know where the updrafts will be and we'll be going over too many peaks to risk making a critically wrong guess on them. It's valley from here over Zirl to Telfs. My plan is to tail the Iron Eagle as closely as possible without getting penalized for drafting. Dampf knows these mountains, so he'll make good decisions almost everywhere and we'll follow his lead…closely. When he makes a mistake, we'll correct course before we make the same one."

"But, Gospozha Doctor Lyotcheeka McTrowell, how vill ve vin if vc follow all de vay?"

"We will conserve fuel by staying on the optimal course. When we get over Bludenz, we'll make an all-out run for it."

"Are you sure you are not descended from Genghis Khan or Ivan Grozny?" She only smiled at him.

When the starting gun fired, Sparky counted slowly to five before opening the throttle gently while Krasnayarubashka lifted the flaps to fall in behind the Iron Eagle. She rested her hand lightly on the throttle, carefully keeping the Burke & Hare out of the turbulence of the Iron Eagle. As Zirl came into view below, she spotted the first mate of the Iron Eagle making his way around the outside of its gondola. He glanced up at the North Wind that was taking the "high road," but obviously Dampf was no more worried about it than Sparky was. The first mate glared at the Burke & Hare in the Iron Eagle's wake and scurried back toward the bridge. No sooner than he disappeared from view than Herr Fenstermacher appeared on the bridge of the Burke & Hare. He pulled out his telescope, studied each edge of the envelope of the Iron Eagle, made some numerical notes and calculations in his notebook, and checked the time on his pocket watch. But he said nothing.

After a period of time that Sparky estimated to be 10 minutes, Fenstermacher pulled out his pocket watch and stared at it for several seconds. He snapped it shut, pulled out his telescope, and repeated his scanning, note taking, and calculation activity. But this time he said something.

"Fraulein McTrowell, you are dancherously close to being called drahfting."

"How dangerously close?" She never took her eyes off the Iron Eagle.

"Sree point fife yards too close."

Sparky closed the throttle very slowly to back off from the Iron Eagle before establishing a position she judged to be four yards farther behind it. Fenstermacher remained on the bridge for a few more minutes before departing without a word. The door clicked closed and Sparky opened up the throttle very slowly, making sure as to maintain this distance. When she returned to her previous established speed behind the Iron Eagle, she heard Krasnayarubashka chuckle softly.

"Play to win," she smiled back.

No sooner had they passed over Telfs than the Iron Eagle began to take evasive maneuvers, trying to shake the Burke & Hare off its tail. McTrowell remained steadfast without wasting fuel to follow Dampf's contortions. The dance became more frantic as they passed Lech. Both McTrowell and Dampf knew there was less than an hour left in the leg and letting the more maneuverable Burke & Hare pass would give away the lead. As a result, the stretch between Lech and Bludenz was uneventful while Dampf attempted to conserve fuel. McTrowell sent Krasnayarubashka aft to check the progress of the North Wind. By blazing his own path, Swenson had put himself at sufficient disadvantage to not be a contender in the mountain leg.

"Coming up on him from below didn't work last time, Mr. Krasnayarubashka. We're going to come down on him from above this time." She grabbed the voicepipe. "Gentlemen, double-up the boilers. We're about to burn up all the fuel we've saved." She turned to her co-pilot. "Flaps up, Mr. Krasnayarubashka."

"Flaps up."

She opened up the throttle three-quarters of the way, angling the Burke & Hare upward at a precarious angle amusingly similar to the broadsheet Wallace had shown her the day he finagled her into this mess. She opened up the throttle the rest of the way, shooting over the top of the Iron Eagle. She knew she was counting on the element of surprise because her faster opponent would win if she didn't get ahead of him before he saw it coming.

"Flaps down, Mr. Krasnayarubashka."

"Flaps down."

They cut in front of the Iron Eagle as closely as possible without bumping and Sparky held the throttle wide open. She wondered if the Iron Eagle's referee was lecturing Captain Dampf about drafting. Vaduz Castle rose into view. It was a straight shot and the throttle was wide open, so there was nothing for Sparky to do but keep an eye out and take deep breaths to calm her jangling nerves. Suddenly out of the corner of her eye she spotted the tip of the Iron Eagle's envelope coming up on the starboard side. *"Damn!"* she thought. The engines couldn't put out any more and the finish line was from the ground to the stars, so climbing or descending would only contribute to a greater loss. It was all over except for the sulking and second-guessing. She glanced at Ivan who was also looking starboard and whose expression was as disappointed as hers. The two of them scanned back and forth sullenly between the advancing Iron Eagle and the finish line.

On her fourth or fifth check on the Iron Eagle she thought it looked like it had receded. Ivan had a look of surprise on his face that suggested he had seen the same thing. They both registered the shared hope on their faces. They stared to the starboard. They watched the tip of the Iron Eagle disappear out of view behind them. It was quite literally running out of steam!

"It vorked!" Krasnayarubashka yelped. He slapped Sparky hard on the shoulder.

"Throttle, Ivan. Throttle."

"Oh, da," he replied sheepishly as she steadied her shaking hand.

She was holding her breath as they crossed the finish line. A cheer went up in the common room and she let out her breath. She turned and shook Krasnayarubashka's hand vigorously. "Please take her down, Ivan."

THE DOWNHILL RUN

BY MR. DAVID L. DRAKE

Erasmus, J.B., and Lord Ashleigh had been silently watching the final minutes of the regatta leg into Vaduz from the main hall. They saw the Iron Eagle's nose retreat from the Burke & Hare's final sprint, but when they heard the shouts of the crowd, they knew they had taken the leg. They quietly uttered manly "harrumphs" and "well, of course" and shook hands around the small circle, as if they had contributed to the triumph through their mental cheerleading as opposed to just adding weight to the vessel.

Even Wallace walked over and joined the small circle and added his hand to the ritual, but he was more subdued than the other three men. Wallace flatly added, "This is a proud day for the Western & Transatlantic Airship Lines," with the passion traditionally reserved for "I think I got mud on my shoe."

Erasmus was surprised that Wallace joined them, since he had been solitary throughout the trip and regatta, but also that he wasn't pumping the room full of false enthusiasm. *"Something for me to ponder about later,"* he thought.

Over the voicepipe, one of the crew members in the lower deck requested, "Dr. McTrowell! Please meet with us in the boiler room." This announcement was loud enough that the common room congregation heard it. The timing of the request, right at the finish of the leg, concerned Erasmus. Sparky answered in the affirmative and turned the helm over to her able co-pilot to bring the airship into port.

"May I accompany you?" Erasmus enquired of Sparky while she smartly rounded the corner to head down the flight of stairs to the mechanicals.

"Certainly, but...," she trailed off for a second, as if pondering whether she should finish the thought. "...I don't believe I'll need protection for this little outing."

Erasmus smiled. "I understand. You should know then that I am no longer concerned with the hand kissing you received from Herr Dampf. It seems your response was to whip his backside. Twice. My

237

interest is why the engine crew solicited you. Just appeasing my curiosity."

"Very well." With that, Sparky hurried down the stairs while waving Erasmus on to follow.

In the boiler room, three crew members in oil- and soot-stained overalls were standing around the two spherical boilers. Sparky joined them.

"Excellent work, gentleman. We won the leg! Now, how can I help you?"

"During me last hourly inspection, I found t'is little beauty. Boiler number two 'as a 'airline fracture," the tallest of them declared, emphasizing with a point of a finger, adding, "'ere." Sparky leaned in a bit to see the nearly undetectable line. The boilers were still incredibly hot from propelling the airship into port. The line was faintly redder than the surrounding iron.

"What is your assessment? Will it hold through the next leg?"

"Given its size, it may just be superficial and doesn't go through to 'ta water chamber. On the other 'and, it could burst if 'ta pressure gets 'igh enough. We 'ave a couple of choices..."

"One choice is obvious: run on only one boiler. Not a good choice for a race."

"Rather, the blokes and I figure our first choice is 'ta run t'is boiler at 80% maximum, and use it only as needed for 'ta final leg."

"And the second choice?"

"Well...we know we cannot replace it 'ere in Vaduz. It's a very unique boiler. Any replacement t'at could be found is going to weigh 'undreds of pounds more than t'is one. We can't drill or replace any parts without making it weaker. Me'n 'ta lads t'ink we can wrap it wit' an additional iron band to keep the crack from getting worse."

"How long will that take?"

"Most of 'ta night. And we'll need to buy a barrel ring or two."

"You have yourselves a job for the night. But even with the wrapping, let's plan to run number two at 80% tomorrow. A boiler explosion would ruin everybody's day. We'll get a replacement in Munich. And lads, good job spotting this. You may have saved us from a rough patch."

The crew responded with three broad smiles and a couple of tugs on the brims of their caps. Erasmus was impressed that Sparky handled the situation so well, but the idea of a potential boiler explosion would clearly counter his goal of keeping everyone on the Burke & Hare safe. He decided to check frequently on the status of the boilers the next day. It might save a life or two.

Vaduz was a smallish city and the gathered crowd was justifiably meager compared to Munich and Salzburg. But their spirits were high and all wanted to meet the famed "lady pilot from the Americas." Confetti rained down on the Burke & Hare crew as they descended their tower stairs, Sparky leading the way with her hands in the air, waving to the shouts of "Spar-Key! Spar-Key! ..." Erasmus and J.B. brought up the rear, clanking a bit from their weaponry. Erasmus ran through his mental checklist: sword, check; loaded revolver, check; knives, check; truncheon, check; and sword stick, check. It seemed odd to be hauling this amount of armament into this placid town with its rolling green hills, old stone Vaduz Castle, and majestic Saint Florin cathedral steeple. But he was thinking this was the last evening that he was truly concerned about the safety of the Burke & Hare crew and passengers, and he wanted to be prepared.

The ceremonies were on a smaller scale than the last two, but the merriment of the participants was much greater. Rather than receiving the trophies for the leg on a specialized platform, the three airship pilots stood at different heights on a stone staircase leading to the castle. Sparky stood a head or so higher than her competitors and beamed at the crowd. A trio of German-style accordion players squeezed out exuberant music while backed by booming tubas and bass drums. Sparky pulled off her pilot's headgear and waved it in one hand, while in the other waving a miniature handheld flag bearing the Vaduz Coat of Arms. The crowd danced and hooted and returned the wave with their own handheld flags. The pilots were mobbed as they descended and treated as ambassadors of modern technology and exploration.

J.B. agreed to watch the high-profile entourage through the traditional banquet and whatever after-supper festivities they would participate in, while Erasmus agreed to guard the boiler room crew.

The day passed into night too quickly for the lads. With a deep-pit fire raging a safe distance from the airship, they alternately heated and hammered two thin iron rails into the correct circumference for wrapping boiler number two. The borrowed anvil got a full workout that night. Erasmus knew that the blaze and clamor might draw in curious townsfolk or worse, nosy regatta competitors, so he cooked up a story about adding support braces to the airship in case someone came around. It wasn't good practice having the opposition knowing that the Burke & Hare couldn't withstand a prolonged sprint. But the effort was for naught; all of the celebrities and their associated festivities were in town, which was much more interesting than noisy craftsmen. They were left alone to work late into the night with the exception of one lone figure, who approached using a military stride as if reporting for duty.

"J.B., all goes well, I assume."

"You are correct, Chief Inspector. Everyone is safely back on the Burke & Hare except for Mr. Reginald Wallace. He stayed on board when the rest of us disembarked, and he wasn't there when we returned. Do you think we should search the town for him?"

Erasmus thought for a few seconds. "I do not believe so. Drawing us away to search for one person and leaving the rest of the airship unguarded is a poor plan. I also believe that our crew, particularly the pilots, are the ones most in danger, and they are safely aboard. Mr. Wallace has returned on his own before. The lads here are nearly finished with this part of the task and will soon be moving to finish in the boiler room. I am hoping for everyone's sake the remainder of this job is quieter."

"Agreed, regarding both Mr. Wallace and the noise. Are you planning to stay up with them, or get some sleep?"

"I shall see this through. You should get some sleep so that one of us is fresh for tomorrow."

"A sound plan. Good evening, Chief Inspector." With that, J.B. turned and headed straight back to the tower stairs, striding militarily.

The lads deemed the two bands to be properly hoop shaped and finished by drilling three holes at each of the hoops' ends. Afterward, they doused the fire and gathered their tools to move the activity into the boiler room. Erasmus helped by carrying one of the bands. The actual banding of the number two boiler took less time than expected, but it did require a great deal of exertion to get the first band on tight enough to have a positive effect on the boiler. Three rivets were banged into place to retain the tension, but the racket was over in just a few minutes.

"What are you going to do with the second band?" Erasmus asked.

The tallest replied, "If we only shaped one, then it would 'ave broke when we tensioned it. If we shaped two, then the first one will 'old fast. It's 'ta nature of the beast." He added a toothy grin that indicated that he was both half kidding and half truthful. Erasmus shook his head in mock disbelief. He knew that if something were to go wrong with the first band tomorrow, the second would be there to replace it. But that story was less colorful.

Now well past midnight, the band on tightly, the lads called it a day. Erasmus, fatigued, headed up to the cabin hallway to get some needed sleep. As hc passed cabin number one's open door, Erasmus noticed a lit candle on the bed stand and the silhouette of Mr. Wallace sitting on the bed, his head buried in his hands. Erasmus politely knocked on the door, but the shadowed figure didn't react.

"I thought I would just see if you are doing well, Mr. Wallace."

Reginald stood slowly and took a few shuffled steps to round the bed toward Erasmus. The man was still fully clothed for the evening, complete with jacket. He listed a bit to the left, then caught himself, and continued his shuffle. That was when the smell of whiskey hit Erasmus. It was the smell of a man who had been drinking for hours, letting the spirits seep into his very soul until his clothes had the aroma of the drink.

Erasmus took a step toward Reginald, fearing that Reginald would fall, and he would need to catch him. Instead, Reginald wrapped both his arms heavily around Erasmus' arms in a sloppy drunken bear hug, placing his head on Erasmus' shoulder.

"Waa shed leeb mem? Waa?"

"Reginald, I am afraid I cannot understand you. Are you hurt?"

Reginald raised his head and looked straight at Erasmus as best he could, given the effort it took to prevent his head from wobbling. Fresh tears streamed down his face over the tracks of previously dried tears. Reginald managed an overemphasized head shake that indicated that, no, he wasn't hurt. Then he attempted his question again.

"Why did she leeb me? I loved her."

"Who left you, Reginald?"

"My wife! Just before we left London. Gone."

Erasmus considered his predicament. He was effectively slow dancing in the middle of the night with an unsteady drunk who reeked of alcohol with every exhalation, who had finally confessed to a progressing marital difficulty. But since he owned the airship on which Erasmus stood, just dumping him in his bed to sleep it off might not be the best diplomatic tactic. Erasmus hadn't predicted this situation when he signed on to the Burke & Hare outing.

Erasmus thought hard for a couple of seconds about the best approach to get out of this situation and to his cabin's bed without endangering his assignment. The two extremes were spending the next hour listening to the man's matrimonial issues, or telling him to be the man he needed to be and leaving him wallowing in his own sorrows. Erasmus decided to split the two and still be able to get to bed as quickly as possible.

"I can see she means the world to you. You should sleep on it, and you can tell me about it in the morning. We shall put together a plan, you and I. Agreed?"

"Thatz a GREAT idea! Oh, thank you. You're my best friend on this trip!"

"I suggest you prepare for bed now. We will talk tomorrow."

Reginald nodded his understanding and with an uncoordinated twist, let go of Erasmus and fell backwards into his bed, feet still on the floor. In seconds he was drunk-snoring, fully clothed. Erasmus moved is legs, his shoes still on, onto the bed so that he would at least be horizontal throughout the night. Determining that his job was done here, Erasmus snuffed out the candle, closed Reginald's cabin door, and retired for the evening.

Erasmus played unintentionally with his spoon at the breakfast table. He had arrived a few minutes late, and he needed his morning cup of Earl Grey to get himself fully awake. Luis-Miguel was busy serving the crew that had made it up to the common room on time. Erasmus became aware of the fact that it was nice to be waited upon, but he missed just making his own morning tea.

Reginald sat down beside Erasmus. Erasmus gave him a quick look over and determined that the man had an incredible capability to hide a hangover. Erasmus wanted to appear sensitive to Reginald's plight.

"Mr. Wallace, a good morning to you. Would you like to set aside some time today to chat?"

"And a good morning to you, Chief Inspector. That would be fine. What would you like to discuss?"

"The matter we spoke of last night."

"We spoke last night? I'm afraid I don't recall our discussion. Was it business?"

Erasmus was greatly relieved that Reginald actually didn't remember or pretended not to remember the discussion. Either way, he was off the hook from listening to a problem for which he probably wasn't the best advisor. Now he needed to politely back out of this conversation and he would be liberated from the whole affair.

"It was a trivial matter about the repair of one of the boilers I observed last night. I just wanted to say that I thought the crew did a superb job of completing the task, on time and with minimal supplies."

"Oh, wonderful. I'm not concerned with the details of the day-to-day activities, just the big picture. Like winning this regatta! Today's the big day, is it not? Is there anything else you wanted to discuss?"

"No, no. I am also looking forward to the day's events. Ah! Breakfast has arrived."

Erasmus' steaming cup of Earl Grey arrived accompanied by a laden serving plate, and the men dug into their morning eggs and sausage.

After breakfast, Herr Fenstermacher asked the entire Burke & Hare crew to stay seated in the main hall. He stood to make an announcement.

"Guten tag. Vith da final lek of da regatta today, I want to announce da standings of each airship. Deez times are ovicial. Da airship Le Lapin has been eliminated due to damage. Da airship El Toro Rojo has been eliminated due to illegal action."

A couple of the boiler crew pumped their fists in delight and loudly said, "Yes!" Although this outburst was frowned upon by the remaining polite assemblage, its sentiment was secretly shared. Someone fake-whispered, "First time a rabbit stopped a bull!" Tittered chuckles went around. Herr Fenstermacher ignored the interruption and continued.

"In third place, 13 minutes und 46 seconds behind, is da airship Da North Wind. In second place, 3 seconds behind, is da airship Da Iron Eagle. In the lead is da airship Da Burke und Hare. Da objective for overall victory is to have da least overall flyink time. Best of luck! *Danke schön.*"

After Herr Fenstermacher left to perform his usual pre-race airship inspection, Sparky signaled for the team that did the repairs to join her on the bridge. Erasmus figured he was "part of the team," and added himself to the group.

"Good morning. I trust you all got sufficient sleep for the final leg. Are you satisfied with the repairs? Do you have any concerns?"

The three workmen looked at each other to see who had any concerns and, after a few shrugs, looked around to determine who was going to make the report. Finally, the tallest lad piped up.

244

"All went well, Dr. Sparky, except for taking a good deal of 'ta night. We made two bands in case we need a replacement during 'ta run. 'Ope 'ta not be needing it, we do." With that, the lads all nodded approval of the summary.

"Tell me more about the repair."

"'Ta band runs perpendicular to the 'airline fracture. 'Ta lads and I will need to keep a sharp eye out to see if the fracture spreads outside of the band. We 'ad to guess at the amount of tension. We settled for just using all of our might. Well, two of us pulling with leavers and 'ta other 'ammering three rivets home. It's a clean fix, Dr."

Again a round of approving nods. Sparky seemed satisfied.

"Well, I'd still like to run number two at 80%. Our race is with the Iron Eagle, and it's a fast airship. I'd like to have just one sprint today to stay safe, but properly timed to win the regatta. So please stay alert for instructions from the helm."

"Of course. 'Ta lads and I'll prep 'ta boilers and engine now. Godspeed."

The three of them hustled out to the main hall and downstairs. Sparky turned to Erasmus and flatly stated, "Let's finish this race."

One of the castle's cannons sounded the start of the final leg. Sparky knew the real race was between the Burke & Hare and the Iron Eagle. Her plan was to stay side-by-side with the German airship and then sprint at the end. It was a fairly straight-forward plan, but it had worked for many racers.

The North Wind took off like a shot, as if they wanted to sprint the entire distance.

To Krasnayarubashka, Sparky strategized, "I know their plan. They want us to chase them and make some tactical error. I'm not going to take that bait. Let's see what the Iron Eagle will do."

"Da, I agree. Let them run ahead."

The run was out through the valley, bear to the right, and make a straight run to Munich. As predicted, the Iron Eagle made the run at a more reasonable pace. Sparky stayed close, and the two airships were side-by-side through most of the valley. Twenty minutes into the race, Sparky was looking at the final valley between two peaks. As before, the airships were staying low to avoid the high air currents.

Sparky crinkled her brow and strained to see the obstruction ahead. "What is that?"

Krasnayarubashka replied, "Is not look good..."

Sparky's snapped open her spyglass and put it up to her eye in an instant. She gasped. The North Wind was lower than the Burke & Hare, but more than three airship lengths ahead, steaming forward at full speed. Beyond that in the narrowed valley pass were three giant black hot air balloons supporting a net that hung all of the way to the ground. Above the balloons were three small, sleekly-shaped airships with multiple propellers on each. All of their envelopes were jet black, save for the nose of each ship, which displayed a white rough-hewn rendering of a human skull.

"*How uninventive,*" thought Sparky. Were they really pirates of the air? What could they possibly want from three stripped down racing vessels? But more importantly, why haven't any of the officials of the race sounded their whistles indicating that the race is delayed due to obstruction?

The North Wind had no choice but to stop, climb up to the altitude of the sinister balloons, or turn and run. Either way, it had to slow down significantly. It only took seconds for Sparky to determine Swenson's decision. The speed of The North Wind dropped off as they diverted their heat to the envelope, causing it to distend slightly, resulting in the ship rising quickly.

Watching this development, Sparky slowed the forward thrust of The Burke & Hare to see what would befall The North Wind and to keep her own airship away from harm. The two pirate airships on the outside of their formation sprouted glider wings and nose-dived off their positions, propellers spinning wildly. In synchronization, they both leveled off to rapidly pass by The North Wind where they both fired a single cannon round into the side of the entrapped racing vessel. Both Sparky and Krasnayarubashka cried out at the report of the guns. Two gray puffs of smoke hung in the air, pinpointing the three-dimensional location of the assault. Both projectiles hit the lower fore compartment, just under the ship's bridge. The North

Wind stopped its ascent, debris falling from the punctured sides of the craft. What is that falling out, wondered Sparky, pots and cooking apparatus? They must have perforated the galley on both sides of the gondola.

Sparky grabbed the voicepipe. "We're under attack! Repeat! We're under attack! Bring number two boiler up to 100%. Stand by to take evasive maneuvers."

The two swooping pirate ships nosed up and climbed back higher, close to their original height. They were now above the Burke & Hare and the nearby Iron Eagle. The wounded North Wind continued forward toward the gigantic net, just being pushed by the ambient wind. On her decks and visible through her port holes, her crew was running every which way, perhaps preparing for another attack, putting out a galley fire, or addressing the fundamental concern that the North Wind could plummet into the valley because of its damage. Still no whistles from the officials!

Sparky shouted out a set of orders to Krasnayarubashka that detailed a plan to climb as quickly as possible and get out of the valley. Krasnayarubashka reacted by grabbing a set of lever releases that diverted the steam from the engine to the envelope from boiler number one, since it was already at 100% pressure and could spare the heat. If Sparky timed it right, both boilers could be back to 100% when they got to the altitude above the barricade. The Burke & Hare might be able to sprint out of the valley confines.

The door of the bridge flew open, and Erasmus and J.B. leapt through in their best heroic crouches, each with a revolver in one hand and a sword in the other.

Erasmus spoke up. "We shall prepare the passengers and then position ourselves if boarded. Any special orders?"

With her eyes fixed on the instruments and the chaos external to the airship, Sparky replied, "Please find out why Herr Fenstermacher has not blown his whistle! The airships need to retreat to safety!"

"Understood!"

They shut the door just as quickly, and off they went. The plan that Erasmus and J.B. had worked out back in Munich was that they would each take one side of the ship; Erasmus would take the starboard side and J.B. would take the port side. Their first order of business was to order each passenger to take up arms or take cover, depending on the nature of the attack and the constitution of the passenger. The next was to position themselves along the outside of the airship and defend it as needed with the help of the passengers with the stomach for combat. Erasmus entered cabin number one belonging to Reginald Wallace. J.B. went unannounced into cabin number two, which contained Lord Ashleigh and Virat.

The voicepipe in the bridge came alive with an otherworldly echoey British voice tinged with grave concern. "Bridge, diversion of the steam to 'ta envelope was successful but 'ta envelope is not 'olding the pressure load. We probably 'ave a leak! We don't 'ave a spare man down 'ere. Can someone else 'andle it?"

Krasnayarubashka instinctively reached under the console and pulled out a rectangular green bag marked **Emergency Envelope Repair Kit**. "I vill fix," is all he said as he ran out through the common room and through the external door to the starboard side catwalk. Krasnayarubashka threw the strap of his bag over this head and shoulder, messenger bag style, and climbed the ropes toward the top of the envelope. To the untrained person, the only way to spot a leak was to either see the hole or to feel the softness of the exterior of the envelope due to the loss of pressure. But Krasnayarubashka could just look out across the vastness of the envelope and see where the skin was not tight enough. This skill made patching holes a much quicker task while aloft. What he didn't realize as he inspected the envelope was that pirates were descending from lines dangling from the menacing airship above.

Cabin number one was darkened to the point that Erasmus had to wait for his eyes to adjust to see shapes in the room. The curtains were drawn, and not a single lamp was lit. "Reginald?" Erasmus queried into the darkness.

A grunt issued from the corner, and Erasmus could finally make out Reginald sitting quietly in a chair. Erasmus pulled back the drapes, pouring some much-needed light into the room. Reginald winced and grunted at the change in his surroundings. What Erasmus discovered was Reginald sitting in his undergarments, an open bottle of whiskey in one hand and a cork in the other. Reginald looked up and sleepily asked, "I thought you were going to help me with my wife. You never came back to talk to me. Why?"

Erasmus didn't have time for this. "Stay here and do not leave your room. We are under attack. We can deal with these other issues when this is over."

Leaving the room, Erasmus shut the door and proceeded to cabin number three. He figured he only had a few moments to get through the odd numbered cabins and secure his team. By the time he had finished with cabin five, he had Luis-Miguel armed with a small single shot pistol and a butcher knife. Cabin seven was Erasmus' own cabin. Aldrich Fremont was in cabin number nine with his son, Jake.

"We're under attack by foreign airships! Do you have any weapons to defend yourself?"

Aldrich looked nonplussed. "We are on a pleasure ride. I don't plan to get involved with a scuffle."

"Then take cover and stay quiet. Lock your door after I leave."

Jake chimed in. "I will help. What can I do?"

Aldrich was initially dumbfounded, then incensed. "What are you saying, boy?! Let these men do their jobs to defend us. It is none of our concern."

"Father, I'd rather stand and fight than cower. Chief Inspector, do you have a weapon I can wield?"

"Of course. There is a trunk in my cabin, number seven. Out of it grab a truncheon and a knife. Join me and Luis-Miguel on the starboard catwalk. Aldrich, stay here and stay safe."

"Jake!"

"Sorry, father. This is too important to quarrel about."

With that, the two of them left the room.

In cabin fifteen, Erasmus found Herr Fenstermacher cringing in the corner of his room, his whistle buried in his hands, clutched to his chest. He was literally sitting on the floor scrunched into the intersection of the two walls and the floor. Erasmus opened with,

"Herr Fenstermacher, why have you not called off the race? We need your assistance in this matter!"

"Day vill kill me! I vas told not to stop the race. Leave me be!"

"What do you mean? Have you made a deal with these devils?"

"Dey vere paid to permit da race to pass drough da valley! Dey veren't supposed to attack. Dis is not supposed to happen! I do not vant to die!"

"None of us do. Give me your whistle so I can end this."

"NOOOooo!" Herr Fenstermacher clutched his whistle tighter to his chest. Of all of the items that Erasmus didn't bring on this trip, why did it have to be his policeman's whistle? He wasn't about to wrestle with this man when an attack could rain down on them at any point. Time was too precious.

"Very well. I will deal with you later. I have an airship to defend." Erasmus slammed the door as he left.

Krasnayarubashka found the offending puncture in the envelope. This feat was akin to finding a coin in an airfield. It was almost on the top of the envelope, so the surface was not too sloped. The puncture was small enough that the envelope was still helping support his body weight, but the surrounding surface was very soft, and he had to stick to hanging onto the support ropes to make sure that he didn't cave in the surrounding airbag. The Burke & Hare had twenty-four chambers allowing for multiple perforations before a catastrophic failure. After belting himself and the repair bag to one of the support ropes, he freed up his two hands to perform the repair.

Air was escaping from the hole. There was no whistle since the hole was a ragged thick cloth, but the rate of loss was significant. The repair tool allowed a small umbrella-like tool to hold a round piece of cloth. Glue was placed on the underside of the small umbrella, which was pushed through the hole, opened, and then allowed to stick to the inside of the envelope, held there by the air pressure. The flat tines of the umbrella were left in place, and the umbrella shaft was removed to allow other repairs. It wasn't perfect, but it would save the craft from deflation. A real repair could be done while docked, where a gummed patch would be sewn into place. A large rip or a sizable hole couldn't be repaired this way, but it would do a fine job for this size leak.

As Krasnayarubashka put the finishing touches on the task, he noticed that the edges of the hole looked slightly burnt. *"A bullet hole,"* he thought, *"it must have been fired from above."* He instinctively craned his neck to look up. That's when two black boots landed on the envelope next to his face.

Over the bridge voicepipe came, "Bridge, 'ta pressure in 'ta envelope is 'olding again. Pressure is building in bot' boilers. One is at 70%; two is at 90%; wit' bot' rising."

"Prepare to ascend," Sparky barked into the voicepipe.

Erasmus joined Luis-Miguel and Jake on the starboard catwalk. "All looks clear from here," Jake offered as a report, sounding concerned that the call to arms was unwarranted.

The rotundness of the envelope prevented them from looking straight up, but they could see the disabled North Wind drifting toward the suspended net. At that moment, one of the North Wind's crew members was leaning out of the splintered hole on its port side, surveying the airship's damage.

The Burke & Hare suddenly, but gracefully, started to ascend. Unlike most of its upward movements, this was forceful and continuously accelerating. Erasmus grabbed tighter to the rail and felt it in his legs. His companions did likewise and looked at Erasmus with a "wow, that was unexpected" look.

Suddenly a man's scream rang out from above, followed by the thud of a heavy weight bouncing off the side of the envelope, and finally by an upside-down human body plummeting over the edge of the envelope overhead. The scream continued as he fell. In the split second that Erasmus saw the falling silhouette against the bright blue sky, he also saw that it was struggling with a rope wrapped loosely around its leg.

The rope went taut, whipping the arms and head downward, bouncing the living marionette once, then settling at suspending him by one ankle.

"Ivan!" yelled Luis-Miguel. From his actions, it was clear to Erasmus that the rope was not tied to him, simply entangled. Krasnayarubashka carefully but quickly climbed up his own leg to get to the little bit of rope wrapped near his left foot. The airship continued its ascension, making Krasnayarubashka appear to descend, but more importantly, the rope to visibly vibrate as it rubbed against the airship's envelope.

In an instant, the rope gave up its hold, Krasnayarubashka cried out, and the three men helplessly watched as their co-pilot fell.

Jake, his mouth frozen in a silent scream, leaned hard over the railing, as if wishing to grow impossibly long arms and catch Ivan.

"Jake, don't look down. Stay on task. We need to deal with whoever is above us."

Jake looked up, bent on retaliation. Luis-Miguel held his weapons all the tighter and mumbled a Spanish phrase that was not for the faint of heart to hear.

"Luis-Miguel, run and tell Sparky about Ivan. Then on the port side, tell Sergeant Fox the same. Join Jake back here and make good our defense. I am going up to the top. Neither of you follow. I need you here."

Sparky manually inventoried her three challenges: ascend to clear the curtain-like net; avoid the three smaller, faster and armed airships; and have the resources and the head of steam to sprint away without causing a boiler explosion. She saw the two attacking airships disappear from above her. So she was ascending as hard and fast as possible to get above them, bump them, or scare them out of the way. Hopefully, this action wouldn't rip an unrecoverable gash in the envelope.

Then she saw the net part like the curtains of a stage. *"How odd,"* she thought. The North Wind was going to drift through the barrier's opening, allowing them access to the other side. Sparky's speculation continued. Were the pirates letting the Swedes pass to win the race? Had they taken enough damage that they were no longer considered a threat? Or were the pirates separating the regatta participants with the remaining pirate airship above the net planning to attack The North Wind separately? But she realized that she had plenty to worry about right here on her own vessel, and she needed her co-pilot back.

The door flew open. Sparky turned to see who it was, and a breathless Spanish messenger relayed the sad news. Sparky straightened her stance, held her breath for a second, and tears sprouted from her eyes. She couldn't help it. She wanted to be strong, but this was truly unfair. She quickly pulled a handkerchief from within her jacket, wiped her eyes and nose, nodded her understanding of the message to Luis-Miguel, and turned back to her controls. Luis-Miguel solemnly closed the door and rushed on to complete his task.

Erasmus stashed his revolver in a pocket inside his leather cape coat and secured the saber into his belt. His hands free, he started the climb that took him up the outside of the envelope, rounding the bottom of the inflated sausage that held the Burke & Hare aloft. He was not unfamiliar with climbing up such ropes. His attention was not on the hazardous climb, but on the unknown dangers ahead.

Erasmus crested the envelope crawling, even though the slope was minor enough that he could stand. The scene was not quite as he had expected. Two smaller airships were about fifty feet above the Burke & Hare, both of which must have been rising at the same pace, since the distances didn't seem to be changing. Three lines were hanging down onto the top of the Burke & Hare's envelope. A fourth line limply ran off and over the starboard side, posthumously indicating the path that Ivan had taken on his descent. In front of him, Erasmus saw five-darkly clothed figures wearing dirty-black tricornered hats. Four of them were facing away from Erasmus toward the port side. One was looking around to make sure no one snuck up on them from their rear. Due to the curvature of the envelope, it was difficult to see who or what the four were looking at. Erasmus crept closer.

"We not be needing more lives lost, my friend. Surrendering your ship is the wisest of choices."

"They speak English?" wondered Erasmus. After covering a few more yards, Erasmus could see the full setting. Standing on the far side of the pirates were Lord Ashleigh, J.B., and Virat, in that order. J.B. was also wearing some complicated harness and backpack, with some type of stakes and canvas jutting up out of the backpack behind his head. Pistols were leveled, and a standoff was in progress. But a five-to-three standoff meant that the pirates really had no interest in just killing everyone or they would have discharged their weapons already.

Sergeant Fox replied, with a tone of voice reserved for clear, fearless intent. "Leave. Now. We are commanded to guard this airship, and I have no plans to fail in that duty. Again, leave now."

"If it is a standoff," Erasmus reasoned, *"then joining the fray will only help sway the pirates to our side of the argument."* With that, Erasmus slipped the revolver out of his cape coat, put it into his right hand to leave his left free, and carefully stood on the envelope.

The pirate lookout noticed him. "There be one more of them," he stated quietly, indicating Erasmus' direction with a well-aimed point of this pistol. Then the lookout squinted and smiled. "Drake? Drake! How ye be?"

The hoarse voice was familiar to Erasmus, but who could it be? His face was weathered and old...

"Tobias?"

"Have not seen ye for...what?...twenty or twenty-five years! Still go by 'Drake?'"

"Yes. Yes, I do. Why are you with this crew? You were a first-rate lieutenant."

"Ahh, you poor lad. You still be ignorant of the truth." Tobias shook his head and laughed. "These be my people, all along."

Erasmus came to a sudden realization. A pure clarity came over him that flipped over his childhood beliefs and showed the slimy creatures that lived under it. His stomach twisted.

"Not one of you told me. I thought we..."

Turning fast to face Erasmus, the coattails of the center pirate flew out, and a commanding female voice added, "Well this is good. We have a reasonable man aboard." She started the long walk over toward Erasmus. The other pirates cowered slightly when she spoke, hinting that they were not looking forward to where she was taking the conversation. She added, "Please to be making your acquaintance, Drake. Let us come to some mutual understanding to put this all to an end."

As she approached, Erasmus saw her scandalous outfit. She was primarily in black, with a few hints of dark purple. Her open frock coat revealed a leather corset worn on the outside of her black blouse, a brace of pistols crisscrossing her torso, and a skirt raggedly ending above her knee. Her tricornered hat looked like it had been used to beat a rat to death and then fastened with gold trinkets to hide its disreputable state. Her black boots were almost knee-high and their leather untended. Although she might have been considered handsome by some when unmarred, she had two facial scars: one that ran diagonally from her left forehead to the bridge of her nose and the other drawing a line from her right earlobe halfway to her chin.

She forced a quick smile, and sheathed her sword as she replaced her pistol back into the brace. "No one needs to get hurt here," she stated flatly as she advanced.

"Unfortunately, it is too late for that. We lost our co-pilot when he fell off the starboard side."

She stopped in front of Erasmus, right hand extended. He noticed that she also blocked his aim at the four others. Being left-handed himself, he willingly slid his revolver back into his coat and extended his right hand for the ceremonious handshake.

She replied, "An unfavorable loss. When we landed, we spooked him. He lost his balance and fell overboard."

She took Erasmus' hand firmly and slowly, as if she wanted the moment to last.

Erasmus retorted, "I do not believe it was an accident. He was a very accomplished airship engineer. He would have tethered himself. And that remaining half of a cut tether that I see over there flapping in the wind means that he had help going over the side."

She screamed, "Now!!" and all hell broke loose. She squeezed Erasmus' hand with the grip of someone who climbs mast lines with ease and, within the blink of an eye, drew her sword out of its scabbard with her left hand, upside down and edge-side outward. Erasmus twisted to avoid the initial upward cut, but it still sliced his face just between his right eye and temple. In the same motion, he drew his sword, pulled it back in preparation for thrusting, but at the same time, pulled hard on her right hand to avoid the reach of her oddly-armed left hand. Erasmus' thrust hit her square in the midriff, but the corset turned aside the point as it was apparently metal-lined body armor.

Neither was willing to let go, figuring that the close-range tussle was to their advantage. She punched her rounded hand-guard into Erasmus' side and flipped the blade up to prepare to drive the pommel into his hipbone. Erasmus countered by dropping his tip and driving the sword into her thigh a few inches above her right knee. *"That should slow her down,"* he thought.

Shots rang out as two of the other pirates took fast, poorly aimed shots at J.B. and Lord Ashleigh. Tobias ran to the lines with that hunched-over run reserved for running from gunfire. He obviously didn't want any part of this.

As if orchestrated, Lord Ashleigh dove to his right and Virat to his left. Before either of them hit the envelope, they had each drawn, thrown, and buried a throwing knife into the chest of a pirate. It happened so quickly that both pirates looked down in unison to see the fatal throws, before collapsing into the canvas. Erasmus saw this out of the corner of his eye and thought, *"Ahh, they have been secretly practicing together."*

But the hellcat that Erasmus had skewered wasn't ready to quit. She let out a bloodcurdling scream, her eyes grew large, and she clenched her grip down all the more. Despite the wound that went both in and out of her leg, she bellguarded Erasmus in the same location as the cut, just inside his right temple. The splash of blood blinded his right eye. She pulled back to repeat the blow. Erasmus withdrew the sword and sliced down on her right wrist, again meeting metal hidden under her frock coat. The second blow to his right temple was hard and all the more vicious. Erasmus reeled and was kicked in the chest by the remaining pirate who came to aid his queen. She finally let go of Erasmus and stumbled on her wounded leg.

Erasmus stumbled back, blind, trying to stay on his feet. He waved his sword to find his attackers, but with no success. He reached up to clear his eyes, but only found warm wetness. With a bloodied right hand, he grabbed his revolver, leveled it, but then realized that he had a greater chance of shooting the airship's canopy than any of the pirates. Wait! That's it. He pointed his revolver skyward and fired off six shots into the general vicinity of the two airships above. The screams of pirates rang out, indicating he had hit his mark.

An incredibly hard punch, or was it a kick?, walloped his stomach and Erasmus staggered back once again. But this was no ordinary stagger. It was that gut-wrenching, unstoppable stagger off the side of a mountain where the more you try to right yourself, the faster you backpedal. He fell. He rolled and then bounced. He let go of the sword and the revolver; there was no reason to hang on to them. Flashes of sky and darkness went zipping past. He reached out for...well...anything. Then, the hardest jerk on his right arm he had ever felt, followed by his right hand finding a rough-hewn hemp rope. Instinctively he grabbed it for all he was worth.

Despite the fact that he was hanging by one hand, he stopped and let his head clear. What had happened? It was apparent he had fallen near the edge of the airship envelope. With his free left hand, he wiped his left eye. He spotted a lone coil of rope, most likely used for mooring the vessel, perhaps in high winds or bad weather. He jammed his left arm through it and lassoed it. He realized it was a miracle he was still attached, albeit tentatively, to the Burke & Hare. He was not all the way to the envelope's edge, but he was close. He quickly came to grips with the fact that he was lying on the very lip of the canopy. His right arm hurt like it had been pulled out of the shoulder.

He heard more gun shots and more scuffling. The lasso of mooring rope was attached to another rope that ran down the side of the envelope. Erasmus knew he couldn't stay there; he had to climb down to safety. He slipped his left hand around the vertical rope and tested his strength. His grip felt strong enough. He let go with his right to start the climb down.

Lord Ashleigh landed on the port side catwalk, ran into the main hall, and over to the bridge. He flung the door open and shouted, "Stop the ascent! The two airships above us are damaged and descending!"

Sparky adjusted two floor mounted levers, and the upward movement of the airship slowed. "Is it safe to flee the area?"

"Stay in the vicinity! Virat and J.B. scaled the lines to the pirate ship. They are in the process of further disabling it."

"Is everyone else safe?"

"Erasmus took a tumble off of the starboard side. You didn't see him fall?"

"No!"

With that, they both sprinted to the starboard side catwalk.

Sparky shouted, "Look for Erasmus!" And she took the remainder of the team, Jake, Lord Ashleigh, and Luis-Miguel, and spread out along the catwalk to look up to search for the Chief Inspector.

The lone, undamaged pirate ship swooped down, headed for the Iron Eagle. The Iron Eagle's envelope opened a large vent from the top and descended 100 feet in the wink of an eye, spoiling the pirate ship's shot at the Iron Eagle. The pirates swooped back up to hold the high ground.

Erasmus' feet dangled over the side of the envelope. Sparky shouted for him to hang on. Exhausted and weak, he responded by rapidly going hand over hand to get to safety. He put a single foot onto the railing and leaned in, reaching for any handhold. His foot slipped on the rail and he fell to his chest, bouncing unceremoniously, catching the rail with only his bloody right hand.

"Sparky?" he gasped.

And his grasp slipped to his fingertips.

|SHILD

BY DR. KATHERINE L. MORSE

Sparky threw her body on the railing, grasping for Erasmus' hand. Her hand came away slick and sticky with his blood. *"No,"* she thought, *"do not let it end before it has even begun!"* She searched frantically for somewhere to wipe the blood off so she could get a better grip when the wind whipped her new, "lucky," yellow silk scarf into her face. The scarf! She whipped off the scarf, not bothering to wipe her hands, and wrapped it quickly around his right wrist. "Give me your other wrist!" Weakly, he reached up in the direction of her voice. She was nothing more than a blonde blur through the blood in his eyes. She whipped the now-bloody scarf around his left wrist and rotated her own wrists, reeling in the slack across the palms of both hands. She bent her elbows, pressed the flats of her fists to her clavicle, and braced her feet against the base of two rail posts. This was going to hurt…both of them. She tightened up all her muscles and threw her body backwards. Drake screamed in pain as his bruised and bloodied body was dragged over the railing. He landed squarely on top of Sparky, all elbows and knees and 50 pounds heavier than her. She exhaled a grunt of pain.

When the realization of their success hit them a second later, they smiled slightly to each other and she whispered in his ear, "Silk is like true love, beautiful to behold, soft to the touch, but strong when tested."

"You are truly a remarkable woman."

Lord Ashleigh reached them first and helped Drake to his feet. "My dear friend, you gave us a terrible scare."

"I fear the worst of today's horror is not yet over."

Luis-Miguel reached down to help McTrowell off the catwalk. When he took her hands and began to pull, she winced in pain and grabbed her right shoulder.

"Augh! As if the situation weren't bad enough already!" She got her feet under herself and rose on her own. "Luis-Miguel, please see to cleaning up Chief Inspector Drake and try to stop the bleeding. I'll sew him up properly later. Mr. Fremont, you're with me."

"But, ma'am, I want to defend the ship."

"Jake, the best way to defend this ship is to get her out of harm's way. She needs four strong arms and with the loss of the brave Mr. Krasnayarubashka, I'm down to one. Your two will have to make up for three. Now, will you help me save the lives of everyone aboard her?"

"Yes, ma'am!" He fairly ran after her as she made as much haste to the bridge as she was able.

Aboard the pirate ship, Sergeant Fox was marveling at the stealth of Virat and his ability to understand what Fox wanted him to do with just minimal hand signs. Under cover of the panic caused by the unexpected defense mounted by the Burke & Hare, the two of them had managed to climb to one of the pirate ships and sneak into the engine room, which the pirates had left woefully undermanned. There was only one "engineer" and he was running about like a rat trapped in a rapidly filling bilge. Fox and Virat were conferring silently about their next move when Fox accidentally dropped a grenade he had been hoping to use on the mission. It was a small device, but it hit the wood deck with an echoing thud. Despite his attention on the mechanics of the ship, the sound got the engineer's attention. He whirled around to face its source in time to see the sergeant vault a steam pipe; no small trick given the leather, wood, and canvas contraption strapped to his back. Fox wrapped his muscular arms deftly around the pirate's throat and choked him out before he could raise the alarm. By the time Fox turned back around, Virat had snatched up the grenade, lit it from the steam engine's furnace and wedged it firmly under a boiler mount. They didn't need hand signs to communicate the urgent need to get off the pirate ship.

They scrambled up the ladder out of the engine room and onto the tight catwalk, headed directly for the lines leading back down to the Burke & Hare. And came face to face with four angry, cutlass-wielding pirates hell-bent on mayhem. They were well and truly done in. Retreating would send them to a fiery death in the engine room. Even if they could defend themselves against the pirates, though they were outnumbered two-to-one and in such tight quarters as to make it almost impossible to wield their weapons, they surely could not dispatch the pirates before the boiler blew. Fiery death again! Virat had just an instant to spare for a sad wistful thought of the beautiful, deep eyes he would never see again and the small, gentle hands he would never hold again. He braced himself to fight to an honorable end, taking as many of his foe with him as possible. He was jerked off his feet by one of those muscular arms that were such a prominent feature of Her Majesty's Aerial Marine.

"Hang on tight to me!" J.B. shouted right into his ear. Then the fool leapt over the railing out into open space. This was not an honorable death. They would plummet to the earth, their bodies becoming food for scavengers. And yet, a lifetime of servitude made Virat reflexively follow the direct order shouted at him. He clung to Fox with his arms and legs. Fox worked an arm between himself and Virat and yanked on a handle in the middle of the harness crossing his chest. The mysterious, cumbersome device on Fox's back transformed into the most miraculous thing Virat had seen in his long, eventful life. They became the outstretched wings of a roc.

Virat was still marveling at the device when their trajectory was rocked by the explosion of the pirate ship above them. Drake and Ashleigh saw and felt the explosion from the catwalk of the Burke & Hare. Drake watched helplessly as Ashleigh's face turned gray. He had never known a life without Virat. When Virat wasn't right at his elbow, he was no more than a bell ring away. Jonathan was suddenly a boy again, a boy who had just lost his father. His chest hurt. Drake grasped him firmly by the shoulders.

"My dear friend, I cannot imagine the pain you are suffering, but we must fight on if Virat's death is not to be in vain. He has sacrificed himself to give us this advantage. Let us seize it." And then he saw something over Ashleigh's shoulder than his brain could not make sense of. It looked like a giant bird with a huge, lumpy body. It was making straight for the Burke & Hare. *"Oh dear,"* he thought, *"let this not be some new treachery."* He was trying to decide what defense might possibly succeed when the lumpy body of the flying predator resolved itself into Sergeant Fox with Virat clinging to his neck and legs. Drake let out an uncharacteristic whoop of joy and spun Ashleigh around.

Drake called to the chief steward, "Sevilla, step up here on the rail with me!" Drake climbed up on the railing and held his arms out wide, gesturing for Luis-Miguel to do likewise. Fox slowed his approach by tipping the wings up slightly. The wings filled the field of view of the three men on the catwalk. Fox grasped Virat around the waist and said to him, "Prepare to let go on my mark… Now!" He flung Virat away from his body and into the waiting hands of Drake and Sevilla who more or less caught him. Mostly they stopped his forward trajectory, and the three of them landed in a heap on the catwalk. Drake thought to himself, *"I have had quite enough of this maneuver for today."*

Relieved from the awkward burden of a passenger for which his wings were not designed, Fox swooped away toward the net blocking the valley. Ashleigh quickly wiped a tear from his eye before the pile of his comrades on the catwalk could see it. He glanced out into the open space left by Fox's departure, trying to think of the right thing to say when one of the two remaining pirate ships rounded the back of the Burke & Hare. He found himself staring right down the barrel of a cannon preparing to broadside the Burke & Hare. It was so close he could see the cannoneer touching his glowing linstock to the fuse. With barely a thought, he reached up to his brace and unleashed a single knife in one smooth, continuous motion. It snipped off the smoldering tip of the fuse and lodged into the throat of the cannoneer. The look of glee on the pirate's face evaporated into one of utter astonishment before he keeled over in a gurgling mess. Feeling that he had sufficiently regained his composure, Lord Ashleigh turned to aid his comrades.

On the bridge, Sparky and Jake were watching the third pirate ship harry the Iron Eagle. The marauders couldn't get close enough to fire their cannon or board because the Iron Eagle was armed with Potzdam muskets and several crewmembers who knew how to use them. Neither had the crew of the Iron Eagle succeeded in damaging the pirate ship, but a couple of the pirates would undoubtedly be looking for a new line of work if they survived their injuries. The two racing airships really needed to work together if they were going to put a stop to this attack without more casualties. She needed one more good idea. Drake opened the door. She barely glanced at him before returning her attention to the Iron Eagle.

"You're still bleeding."

"Thank you for your concern. Virat and Sergeant Fox returned safely. Fox has departed again."

"Yes, I saw his dramatic leave-taking. A truly marvelous invention those extensible wings; I wish I had invented them. I believe he's trying to make a passage for us." She snapped the cover off her telescope, handed it to Drake, and pointed ahead at the net. Drake opened the telescope and focused on the net. Fox had landed on the net and was climbing up it toward the middle balloon. Fox had made the hard decision to relieve himself of the wings, probably because they were too great a burden to make the climb possible. There was the bravest of them all. If he succeeded in his mission of bringing down the net, he would probably go down with it.

"Courageous Sergeant Fox may be in need of rescue," Drake remarked.

"Yes, I've added it to my list of miracles to perform today. Do you still have a bladed weapon?"

"Yes, I have my sword stick."

"Are you still physically able to wield it under duress?"

"Yes, why?"

"I have an idea." She breathed warm air onto the brass cover of the telescope and polished it on her corduroy skirt. She waved frantically across at Willy Dampf until she caught his attention. "I hope he is current with his signaling." She played with the telescope cover until she caught the light and then began flashing the reflection toward Dampf.

Dot-dot-dot-dot dot-dash dot-dot-dot-dash dot pause dash-dash-dot-dot dot-dash-dot-dot-dot dot-dot-dash-dash pause dot-dash pause dot-dot-dot dash dot-dash-dot dot-dash-dot-dot-dot dash-dot dash-dash-dot pause dot-dash-dot-dot-dot dot-dot dash-dot dot

She could barely make out the perplexed expression on his face, but he nodded. She gave the telescope cover another burnish.

Dash dot-dot-dot-dot dot-dash-dot dot-dash-dot-dot-dot dot-dash-dash pause dot-dash-dot-dot-dot dot-dot-dot-dash dot dot-dash-dot

Again the perplexed expression, but this time followed by a gesture of exasperation with his arms in the air, but finally a head nod. Sparky turned to the two other occupants of the bridge.

"Mr. Fremont, fetch Mr. Sevilla and double time it to the starboard catwalk. Prepare to catch a line that will be cast from the

Iron Eagle. Once you have secured the line, leave Mr. Sevilla there and return here. Chief Inspector, please fetch your sword stick and meet Fremont and Sevilla on the starboard side." She grabbed the voicepipe. "Mr. Wilkinson, have the spare boiler band carried to the starboard side. Grab your tools and meet me on the bridge." As everyone hurried off to carry out her mystifying set of orders, she thought to herself, *"This had better work and that boiler had better hold, because there's no hope without the spare."*

Wilkinson arrived on the bridge promptly, clanking in his full tool belt. He received his orders in absolute bafflement. He had never flown with the peculiar American woman pilot before, but he had heard some truly outrageous stories. He had always imagined these stories to be drunken embellishments, but now he wasn't so sure. On the other hand, all his mates who had regaled him with such epic yarns had all lived to tell the tale, so he too headed dutifully to the starboard side.

As soon as the pirate ship made its most recent pass at the Iron Eagle, a huge crewmember dashed out onto the port side catwalk carrying an enormous armload of rope that he dumped unceremoniously. The two other crewmembers laid down their rifles and helped unwind the rope. The big fellow snatched up a large iron bar with a lightweight line tied to it. With a mighty grunt, he hurled the iron bar across the open space between the two ships. Jake and Luis-Miguel stood ready to catch it. At the last instant they thought better of standing in the path of a flying iron bar and jumped back. It struck the side of the Burke & Hare's gondola, leaving a nasty dent. Wilkinson commented, "At's gonna need fixin'." Sevilla and Fremont sprang forward to grab the lightweight line. Wilkinson slipped a pulley over the line before helping the other two haul in the heavy line attached to it. They tied the line securely to the railing as the crew of the Iron Eagle did likewise on their side. Wilkinson commented again, "Make it fast, boys. A man's life depends on it." The newly minted first mate and the chief steward looked at Wilkinson quizzically, but considering the events of the day, neither of them could work himself up to a real sense of surprise. They tied off the line solidly and gave the thumbs up to the Iron Eagle crew who returned their affirmation.

Having successfully executed his ordered task, Jake hurried back to the bridge wondering what was coming next.

Wilkinson set to work immediately, pulling a length of chain and a pair of mated nuts and bolts out of his kit. "Keep a lookout there will ya, Sevilla?" He worked quickly, threading the chain through the eye attached to the axle. "Inspector, 'and up that boiler stay, will ya?" Despite his fatigued arms, Drake picked up the stay and propped it on the rail. Wilkinson deftly fastened the two ends of the chain to the bolt holes in the opposite ends of the stay, pulling the right wrenches from his tool belt without even looking. He gave a good tug to each junction to ensure it was fast. He slapped Drake on the shoulder, "Good luck to ya, man." And he headed back to the engine room.

Erasmus turned to Luis-Miguel. "Are you strong enough to steady the sling? I'm putting my life in your hands."

"Sí, Señor Drake. Vaya con dios."

When Jake returned to the bridge, Sparky was signaling the Iron Eagle again.

Dot-dot-dot-dot   dot-dash-dot-dot-dot   dot-dash-dot-dot pause dot-dot-dash-dot dot-dash dot-dot-dot dash

Willy Dampf saluted her.

"What do we do now ma'am?" the young man asked.

"Now I need your two strong arms. When the pirate ship comes around again, I'm going to pull hard aport until that line you tied draws taut."

"And the pirates will run right into it?"

"I'm hoping they will think that's our plan. If I give you the signal, I want you to push forward on both of those levers with all your strength. Our gambit depends on you. Are you ready?"

"Yes, ma'am!"

She spoke into the voicepipe in what she hoped was a calm, reassuring voice, "Mr. Wilkinson, how is that repair holding."

"She's sound."

"I fear I may be about to test the quality of your repair. Give me full power."

"Aye, aye, captain."

She saw the pirate ship round the front of the Iron Eagle. Just as she had explained to Jake and warned Wilkinson, she opened up the throttle and steered sharply to the port side. The tether between the Burke & Hare and the Iron Eagle snapped straight and she felt the ship jerk like a dog on a leash, but she held the Burke & Hare straining to the port side. Dampf held the Iron Eagle hard to starboard. She tried not to listen to her heart pounding in her ears as the approaching vessel seemed to slow to a drift.

Outside on the starboard catwalk, Sevilla removed his waistcoat, wrapped it around his hands and leaned over the railing to hold the pulley a couple of feet away from the railing. Drake climbed shakily over the railing, grasping the sword stick in his right hand. He sat down in the sling, slid the sword stick down the front of his waistcoat, and extracted just the blade. Drake and Sevilla waited for the signal. Sevilla began to tremble and sweat from the exertion of holding Drake and the sling against the side of the ship that vibrated frantically from the tension on the line. He didn't want to think about the possibility of the line or a railing giving way because there would be no way to save Drake. He would be lucky not to be pulled overboard himself.

On the bridge, Sparky whispered to herself, "Go on, take the bait." She saw the pirate ship's flaps lower before the ship itself changed course. "Now, Mr. Fremont! Push for all you're worth!" The Burke & Hare shot up, stressing the engines so hard Sparky could hear the keening through the ship. The pirate ship nosed under the line. Out on the catwalk, Drake and Sevilla watched the prow of the pirate ship pass right under them.

"Bueña suerte, Señor Drake," and Sevilla let go of the pulley. Wilkinson's maintenance of his pulleys in tip top form revealed itself as they zipped right along the line while Drake clung fast to the sling with his right hand. He stuck his feet out in front of himself to counter balance so he could lay back and reach down with his left arm. He steeled the muscles in his neck, arms, and back. He felt the blade of his sword make contact with the envelope, and every fiber of his being shook with the effort of holding steady, an effort made even harder by the air geysering up from the newly-opened slash in the envelope. He felt the blade skip over three seams in the envelope, which meant he had punctured at least four separate pockets.

He didn't have a chance to admire his handiwork because the railing of the Iron Eagle was coming up fast and he was closing on the Iron Eagle's crewmembers who were there to stop his traversal. One of them was the size of a Black Forest oak. Drake's ride was getting more precarious because the tension between the ships was lessening, causing the rope to slacken. The oak tree pulled the rope up from the railing and held it above his head, removing the slack and aiming Drake right at his chest. Drake suddenly realized he still had his sword stick in his hand. He hated to lose the lovely blade, but couldn't very well land safely without risking self-injury or stabbing his rescuer, so he pitched his blade toward the catwalk as best he could. He was too early with his throw. The gleaming blade disappeared as Drake careened toward the German airship, hopping up slightly just before he made contact. And make contact he did. He bounced squarely off the tree's chest and landed at his feet on the catwalk. Drake thought to himself, *"Yes, indeed, I have had quite enough of this maneuver for the rest of my life."* He struggled to his feet once more. *"Danke schön,"* he said to no crewmember in particular.

The oak tree chuckled at their new visitor. "Velcome aboard!" he offered in his best English.

Erasmus allowed himself a peek over the railing. He had to admit to himself that he felt a touch of pride at his excellent work as the pirate ship sank like a rock into a very deep crevasse. Two down, one to go. One of the German crewmembers signaled for Drake to follow him to the bridge where he was greeted warmly by Dampf, despite the seriousness of the situation.

"You und your frent, Dr. Sparky, make quite a gud team, Herr Drake."

"Thank you, Captain Dampf, but we must still deal with the remaining ship and find a way to recover Sergeant Fox, assuming he does not give his life in the line of duty opening the net." Although he was first and foremost a man of duty, Drake still wished fervently for Sparky to win the race. As nonchalantly as he could manage, he continued, "Herr Fenstermacher has refused to stop the race despite the attack. Has your referee also refused?"

Being likewise a keen competitor, Dampf paused a moment before answering as he recognized Drake's motive. "Ja, und I haf srown him in za brig." Drake momentarily lost his composure and his eyebrows shot up at the revelation that the Iron Eagle had a brig.

Before the two of them could confer further on a plan, the third and final pirate ship dove, nose-down, in front of them from the cover of a cloud, then abruptly leveled out a few hundred feet above the racers and approached very slowly. They were too high to fire their cannons on either regatta competitor at their current altitude. They couldn't be planning to ram because they were too high, moving too slowly, and their vessel was too small to have any effect. Then they started to climb still higher and move toward the Iron Eagle's port side. What could they possibly be doing? They dropped three lines just as they were moving out of view of the Iron Eagle's cockpit and Drake's stomach sank.

"I have to get back to the Burke & Hare."

"Herr Holzfäller, sent Herr Drake bek ze vay he came!"

True to his name, Herr Holzfäller literally lumbered as he ran down the port side catwalk. Drake felt like he was running downhill and uphill all at once as Dampf set the Iron Eagle on a steep climb. By the time they reached the line between the two ships, the Iron Eagle was higher than the Burke & Hare. Drake was looking straight across at the pirate ship as the Pirate Queen disembarked from one of the dangling lines and slid over the far side of the Burke & Hare's envelope. Before he could step up on the railing, Holzfäller snatched him up like he was a ragdoll, swung him over the railing, and stuffed him into the sling. He barely had time to grasp the slides of the sling before Holzfäller gave him a hearty shove off while holding the line taut. At least Sevilla hadn't abandoned his post at the far end. As Drake stuck out his feet to brace for impact, he realized what would immediately follow. He wondered if there were airships with padded catwalks. To be fair, Sevilla himself provided quite a bit of padding, and they would have lots of bruises to compare if they got out of this predicament alive.

"The pirates have boarded."

"Sí, Señor Drake, I know. I am not the fighting man you are, so I was staying out of sight waiting for an idea. Do you have one?"

"Only that we have the element of surprise on our side. I expect they will focus their attention on the bridge and the engine room. I see you still have the butcher knife. Do you still have the single shot pistol?"

"Sí."

"It requires a very steady hand to use as an offensive weapon." This statement only served to cause Sevilla more consternation that showed visibly on his face. It was clear to Drake that Sevilla could not use the pistol to shoot an enemy, even if his life were in danger. "Now I have an idea. Boiler number two is in a fragile state. As quietly as possible, sneak into the engine room. If it is occupied and Mr. Wilkinson and his crew are not there, shoot the boiler. I do not believe it will fail completely, but it may spring a leak sufficient to fill the engine room with scalding steam. Retreat to a safe distance as quickly as possible and defend yourself with the knife if necessary. Can you do that?"

"Sí, I think so."

"Good man. I am heading to the bridge." But he didn't make it all the way to the bridge. As he attempted to open the door to the main hall stealthily, he spied the back of a pirate guarding the door. He could see Sparky facing a little to his left, toward someone he couldn't see through the crack. Why was she just standing there? He'd seen the results of her handiwork against the Duke of Milton and Abusir. She wasn't entirely overmatched. And then he remembered young Mr. Fremont whom he couldn't see or hear. He must still be on the bridge under guard and she wasn't willing to risk his life. Then he heard that terrible icy voice again.

"I suppose you thought you could just sail right into Melköde and steal my throne because you are the great Dr. Sparky McTrowell."

"Miss Ishild…"

"Queen Ishild!"

"Queen Ishild, I fear that you have read too many penny dreadfuls. I'm here to fly a race, no more no less."

"If that is so, why did you bring the famous Aerial Marine Sergeant Fox and that traitor, Drake?"

Sparky made a mental note of the adjective "famous" and the noun "traitor" for later research. "I did not bring them. They were sent by Her Majesty who does not confide her motives to me."

"Her Majesty," Ishild fairly spit out the title. "It is easy to be a queen when someone has already built you castles and you have thousands to protect you while you drink tea. I must defend my people from her treachery with my own sword!"

"Technically, I believe she's an empress. However, this is not as germane as this alleged act of treachery. As I said, Her Majesty does not confide her motives to me, but I believe she is generally regarded as an honest monarch."

"Then why, after twenty-five years, does she build railroads and send airships?"

"In addition to fewer penny dreadfuls, I also recommend an up to date atlas. This is Bavaria. Railroads and regattas are arranged at the behest of King Maximilian." Drake winced at Sparky's condescending tone. He feared it would only further enrage the pirate queen, whose name was apparently Ishild, and indeed it did. The next words out of her mouth were nearly a scream.

"He is just a lap dog for her! I know this Ludwig-Süd-Nord-Bahn is all her idea and I will put a stop to it like I put a stop to your first mate!" Erasmus could see Sparky's jaw muscles clench and relax.

"What do you mean 'put a stop to my first mate?'"

"Surely you don't imagine he just fell?" Ishild jeered nastily. And then to emphasize her point she made a swift, downward slicing arc with her sword. The flash of the tip revealed to Drake how close she was standing to Sparky, too close for him to get to her before she got to Sparky. "And then I will finish making your Drake not so handsome."

Erasmus saw a look cross Sparky's face that he had not yet seen. It was as cold and still as a frozen lake. The intonation of her next words was so flat, he couldn't tell if they were a question or a statement. "That was you ..." Sparky gritted her teeth to hold back her visceral response to the murder of her friend and co-pilot. She changed her focus back to the present, pretending she was referring to Drake. "...who nearly blinded him."

"What if it was? What do you care for him? I owe him for what he did to me. And what he did to my father."

Erasmus saw Sparky's shoulders bunch up and then a small wince. He'd forgotten about her shoulder. No wonder the pirates had gotten the drop on her! Then her shoulders relaxed again, and she drew her right hand up in a fist.

"Ha! You think you can stop me with that?" The last word wasn't out of her mouth before Sparky threw a roundhouse punch with her left hand, knocking out the pirate queen whose body fell into view.

Seizing the element of surprise, Erasmus cranked the handle and threw his entire body weight against the door, fetching up a good knock on the back of the head of the pirate standing guard, knocking him out cold. Drake smiled at her, "We shall make a southpaw of you yet."

They both heard a loud thud from the other side of the cockpit door. Sparky whirled toward the sound, yelling "Jake!" Sparky snatched open the door, and the inert form of yet another pirate fell onto her boots. Jake was standing there with the truncheon in his hand and a look of jubilant amazement on his face.

"I hid it in my coat and waited for a diversion," he waved the truncheon in illustration.

Drake fairly glowed, "Well done, lad. Can you keep an eye on these three, and if needed, give them another clout while I go fetch my manacles and rope?"

"Yes, sir!"

When Sevilla reached the engine room, he found a less menacing standoff. Wilkinson and the pirate Tobias were dancing around the boilers, Wilkinson with a spanner in his hand and Tobias with a cutlass. Tobias was no longer young or nimble, and Wilkinson didn't want to risk damaging his precious engine, so neither was much of a threat to the other. Wilkinson spotted Luis-Miguel out of the corner of his eye. "Sevilla, what are you doing 'ere?"

Sevilla drew the pistol, struggling to steady it in his sweaty, jerky hand. "Chief Inspector Drake says I should shoot boiler number two, but you will need to get out of here first."

"Ye'll do no such bloody thing to me boiler!"

"Those were the Chief Inspector's orders."

271

"Well this is me engine room and I give tha orders 'ere!" Wilkinson had stopped stalking Tobias during this exchange and Tobias took the opportunity to catch his breath.

Just then the captain's familiar voice came over the voicepipe. "The bridge is secure. The pirate queen has been taken captive."

With that, Tobias sighed, "Hallelujah," and sat down on the greasy floor.

"Wha in bloody 'ell are ye doing?" Wilkinson shouted.

"I'm too old for this nonsense. Now that the Valkyrie is finished, I'm going back to my quiet farm and my old lady."

"What are ye blubberin' about?"

"The lot of us got tired of pirating twenty-five years ago and settled in quiet, little Melköde. We mostly minded our own business, married the steadier of our wenches, and sent the troublemakers away. It was all going just lovely, except that old Captain Benjamin Tuttleford III just couldn't resist telling his daughter, Ishild, grand tales of the old days, filling her head with the glories of pirating days. Well that one, she has a temper like her mother. When 'Tuttle' died, she decided that being the king or queen of the pirates was like being king or queen of a proper country, which it ain't, and so she decreed herself the pirate queen inherited from her father. We mostly put up with it seeing as how there weren't any more ships, and we were mostly too old for such flights of fancy. But she got the other younguns all fired up to play 'pirates' again. When King Ludwig decided to build his railroad, she decided that he was invading our sovereign domain." He stopped, took a breath, and wiped his sweaty forehead with a threadbare old handkerchief. Wilkinson and Sevilla just stood there staring at the old pirate, dumfounded.

"Now, where was I? Oh yes, the railroad. So she goes a recruiting a right nasty bunch of layabouts from around about the area that are all out of sorts about the unfairness of their station, and they start thieving their way to fortune, raiding airships and railroad construction sites. So, then she sends a fellow to parlay with our new King Maximilian to demand he stop with his railroad. Now, being a real king, he's used to getting his way and he knows how to go about it. So he offers up good money for us to keep out of it. When we all hear this news, we think, 'Right, that's marvelous. The barn needs fixing and the missus would love some fabric for some Spring dresses.' But, no, her highness wasn't having nothing to do with old Maximilian's generous offer and she declared that it was war, and she sent her fellow back to Maximilian to say as much. Like I said, Maximilian's a proper king and he's used to getting his way, one way or 'tother. 'Tother way was sending back a message, but not all the bits of the messenger, if you get my meaning." Sevilla swallowed hard and tried not to "get too much" of the meaning.

"Then Maximilian must have figured he needed his message to be absolutely plain, so he planned this regatta to show who was sovereign of this bit of land. Some of us old hands who know something about pirating thought we should sign on to keep her from complete catastrophe, but I don't see that this plan was any better than the rest of 'em. And I think you fellas can figure out the rest." He picked up his cutlass, turned it around hilt first, and offered it to Wilkinson. "If you would be so kind as to tell Drake that I've surrendered and lock me in some quiet little cabin until the rest of this flapping is over, I'd be much obliged."

Wilkinson took the cutlass, turned to Sevilla, and said, "You tell the Chief Inspector. This makes my head hurt."

For all the pulling and maneuvering, neither the Burke & Hare nor the Iron Eagle had made much forward progress, but they were drifting inexorably toward the net. Because the net was meant to catch something the size of an airship, the mesh was very widely spaced, making Sergeant Fox's climb long and strenuous since he had to climb the individual lines rather than climbing it like a ladder. However, he was persevering and McTrowell could see that he was reaching the center balloon. With the prisoners securely bound in the main hall and within sight, Drake opened the door to the cockpit to confer with McTrowell.

He opined, "Sergeant Fox is a brave and direct man. I do not believe he will have considered his own rescue, but only the target of his mission."

"I was just having the same thought. I'm also quite concerned that we have seen neither Lord Ashleigh nor Virat in some time."

"Right you are. I shall look for them while you think on Sergeant Fox's dilemma."

Drake found Ashleigh and Virat the first place he looked, in Ashleigh's cabin, or at least behind the door of what had been his cabin. The interior looked as if the pirates had ransacked it, but there was no sign of pirates. Little bits of silk were everywhere, but mostly it looked as if every silk throw and coverlet in the cabin was in a motley pile in the middle of the floor. Completely uncharacteristically, Lord Ashleigh himself was sitting on the floor next to the pile, rapidly, although not entirely deftly, wielding a needle and thread. Drake heard hammering sounds from the bedroom. Virat was hammering the planks from the bed frame into another type of open frame with a chair seat nailed to one of the planks. It looked somewhat like a catapult, but somewhat cockeyed.

Without looking up from his sewing, Lord Ashleigh said, "I understand that the ship is secure."

"Yes, that is correct."

"And how is Sergeant Fox proceeding."

"He has very nearly reached the central balloon."

"Very good. If you would be so kind as to help Virat carry the components of the frame to the starboard side, I believe we have a method for recovering Sergeant Fox, or at least ensuring his safe extraction. I certainly hope the good sergeant is as clever and informed about the machinery of aerial combat as I think he is."

Drake, unaccustomed to having no clue as to how to resolve the situation himself, felt obliged to do as Ashleigh asked. When they reached the catwalk, Virat began securing the frame to the railing.

Ashleigh continued, "Please tell the good Dr. McTrowell that she should get as close to the net as she feels is safe. The instant she sees any sign that Fox has succeeded, she should proceed with all haste, keeping the Burke & Hare as steady as possible given the difficult circumstances." Without reply, Drake headed straight to the bridge and delivered the message.

"What is he about?" McTrowell asked.

"I have not the faintest idea."

"Nor have I, but I'm quite happy for someone else to give the orders for a bit. Tell Lord Ashleigh that I have understood his instructions and will execute them to the best of my abilities."

Drake returned to the catwalk where Virat had finished stabilizing the framework. Ashleigh was rolling his motley, silk quilt into a tight log. At the end, it was sewn to the back of one of his straight, silk, traditional Indian tunics. He tied the log securely with a silk sash. "Virat, I believe we're ready for the spring." Virat extracted a throwing knife from his jacket and threw it directly at the Iron Eagle, or rather the railing where the tether between the two ships was still tied. The far end of the line fell away, unceremoniously dumping the iron hoop sling into the valley below. Drake was none too sorry to see it go. He didn't care to experience that ride ever again. Ashleigh cut the near end of the rope, threaded it across the frame and back, and tied it off. He and Virat picked up two lengths of wood, inserted them between the two lengths of rope and twisted. When the rope was twisted as tightly as they could manage, Lord Ashleigh jabbed his head toward the plank with the chair seat nailed to it. "Drake, would you be so kind as to pick that up and insert it between these two levers with the chair seat pointing upward?" When he did so, the chair seat leaned over the railing. Virat took hold of the seat and held it as far down as the railing would allow. Lord Ashleigh picked up the silk bundle, and both he and Virat turned their attention to the net and the balloon.

Drake could stand the suspense no longer. "Pray tell, what is the bundle?"

"Why, my curious Chief Inspector Drake, it's a parachute. I'm trusting that Sergeant Fox will recognize it as such despite its colorful nature." Drake could think of nothing further to add to the conversation, so he turned his attention to the net as well.

J.B. Fox paused underneath the balloon to catch his breath. He would need to be fully prepared when he boarded. He looked up at the bottom of the basket where the two halves of the net connected. The lines of the net were as thick as his forearm. They fed up through the floor of the basket. There was no way to hack through the lines from below because he was only carrying a boot knife, and there was no way to brace himself to get enough leverage. He would have to storm the basket. He grasped the lip of the basket in both hands and pulled himself up, hopping between his hands to land on his feet in the basket with his hands free. These pirates clearly were unschooled in close quarters combat because the lone defender of the balloon was armed with a musket. Fox performed a sweeping block with his right arm, disarming the pirate and knocking the musket free. He performed a swift chop upward at the pirate's Adam's apple, instantly disabling the guard.

Unfortunately, the musket discharged when its stock struck the floor of the basket, firing straight up into the canopy. Fox leapt from the lip of the basket and caught the top edge of the net. He hoped that the balloon was only slightly damaged and would drag the net and the other two balloons to the valley floor slowly enough that he would survive the fall. Within five seconds he realized that hope was futile. The crown of the balloon was shredding and he would soon be in free fall. Well then, Queen and country.

On the bridge of the Burke & Hare, McTrowell was watching the center balloon intently through her telescope. She saw it wobble during Fox's brief tussle with the balloon's defender. And then she saw a small puff as the crown of the balloon blew out from the musket blast. That was the sign! She opened the throttle all the way. When Fox made his flying exit from the basket, she turned to Jake Fremont. "Mr. Fremont, steer so that Sergeant Fox is as close to the starboard side as possible without hitting him. You will have to adjust your course to match his trajectory." She watched through the telescope while gently adjusting the throttle and giving Jake instructions for small course corrections. She hoped desperately that Lord Ashleigh knew what he was about, because they were swiftly approaching the net and Sergeant Fox was dropping precipitously. She clenched her hand on the throttle, preparing to shut it off lest the Burke & Hare collide with the still-suspended net, obviating the Aerial Marine's sacrifice when she spotted a large, brightly colored projectile not unlike a large chaise cushion sailing up in an arc from the starboard side of the ship. It was aimed right at the sergeant. Why were they firing on him?

Fox spotted the airborne upholstery at nearly the last possible instant, barely snagging the silk sash of the bundle with one hand while hanging on with the other. His catch pulled the sash loose and the bundle started to unfurl. He let go with his other hand, executing a graceful back flip and catching the jacket with his other hand. He snagged the next rung of the net with the backs of his knees. No sooner had he opened the jacket than he realized what a gift Lord Ashleigh had sent him. He struggled into the jacket that was, not surprisingly, a bit snug. But better tight than loose enough to be pulled off. From his bat-like perch he watched the Burke & Hare pass closely overhead, or rather, underfoot. He let go with his knees, letting the breeze fill the parachute and carry him downwind toward Munich.

Drake, Ashleigh, and Virat held their breath, watching the arc of the package and Fox's aerial calisthenics. They dashed to the railing to look down as the airship passed over the sinking net. Even Virat shouted and danced with joy as their acrobatic brother in arms floated safely free.

Sparky and Jake could hear their jubilation on the bridge, even over the noise of the engine. She turned to the young Fremont. "Mr. Fremont, what do you say that we win this thing?"

To Munich!

By Mr. David L. Drake

Herr Axel Richter's feet dangled, wishing to touch the floor. He was a slight, bookish man, with wisps of grey in his hair and small round glasses. Björn Swenson, the Swedish airship captain, was pinning him against a support column, his two meaty fists clutching Herr Richter's jacket lapels, the waistcoat and shirt underneath, and a good bit of the man's armpit skin. Their eyes were at the same level, despite that Captain Swenson would normally tower over the German.

"Answer me!" the Swede boomed in his native language, into Herr Richter's face.

"Which question?" Herr Richter weakly responded. His Swedish was passable. Even though Captain Swenson, as well as the rest of his crew, knew German, the Captain made it clear that Swedish, and only Swedish, was to be spoken on The North Wind.

"All of them! Are we still racing? Are we in danger if we continue? Why haven't you called off the race?"

Herr Richter swallowed hard and looked around using only his eyeballs. What a sight to see! The North Wind's boiler room was larger than most racing airship's and was normally better lit than most, given its series of square windows that ran the length of both sides of the craft. But right now, additional light was flooding in from where the very tidy galley used to be, which was now a jumble of birch planks, cooking utensils, and broken stone- and glassware, all covered with a light dusting of flour. He saw the crew hard at work trying to clear the area in hopes of patching the breaches on the port and starboard side.

"I had no idea...," Herr Richter stammered out. "King Maximilian's men said they would leave us be! You must understand that we were told that the regatta was safe to pass over Melköde. I was told...not to stop the race."

Captain Swenson made a face that clearly indicated his questions were still not being answered directly, and he slid Herr Richter a couple of inches higher.

"It's safe! It's safe! Continue to Munich as fast as you can. I'm not calling off the race!" Herr Richter squealed, kicking his feet uselessly around.

Captain Swenson's shouted his commands into the face of the official even though they were meant for the crew. "Bring up the boiler to full! Clear the galley debris. Use the broken planks to feed the firebox! Re-plank the hull from interior walls, and make her fair as best you can! Flank speed, boys! Flank speed!"

The twelve-man crew redoubled their activity. They tossed splintered boards from the galley area toward the boiler room. They shoved the planks whole into the secondary stage firebox to heat the boiler tubes to red-hot. Captain Swenson slid the official down to his feet and left him standing, alone and unimportant. The Swede turned and clambered up the ladder to the bridge, while Herr Richter sheepishly adjusted his glasses.

Captain Swenson yelled to his co-pilot, "We must fly! I don't know if it is safe here, and the race is still in progress. Spare nothing! To Munich!"

The North Wind had been designed and constructed by Captain Swenson so that its birch planks were of uniform size and fastened together in a regular manner. His primary reason for this painstaking process was to allow for easy configuration at the start of a regatta and to reduce the difficulty of obtaining replacement planks. He had never thought that he would be reconfiguring his airship during an actual race. But a captain has to do what a captain has to do. Rather than using bulky nuts and bolts, the North Wind used small threaded fasteners that could be loosened with a handheld L-shaped hexagonal-sided bar. One or two quick twists and interior walls planks popped free from their supports, ready for hull repair.

Behind the North Wind, a musket shot sounded, and the middle of the three black balloons suddenly stopped supporting the center of the substantial rope net. As the structure started to collapse, the figure of a man leapt off of the top of the net, significantly slowing his fall with a bright patchwork of cloth puffed out above him.

The North Wind's bank of propellers whirled to a frightening speed, and the airship sprinted forward.

To Sparky, watching the North Wind as it rushed away, it appeared as if unpainted birch planks were magically materializing from within, healing the craft's wounds, and the ship was galloping away as a healthy beast. Her competitive drive kicked in. In a flurry of activity, she and Jake on the Burke & Hare's bridge maneuvered their vessel, adjusting to a steeper angle of climb to avoid the descending net. While the Burke & Hare was effectively stalled in mid-air, the Iron Eagle shot past the Burke & Hare's starboard side at an abrupt angle, breaching over the rope webbing, clearly in hot pursuit of the North Wind. Sparky yelled a few choice words, nothing that Jake hadn't heard before down at the docks, but not from a woman.

She grabbed the voicepipe. "The race is on, lads. Give me all you can! Take boiler number two up to 90%, and keep an eye on her."

Sparky knew her best strategy was not to try to catch up with the North Wind. The true race was with the Iron Eagle. That was, of course, if the North Wind didn't get too far ahead. Due to a slight head wind, she wanted to actually stay behind the Iron Eagle, let it do the work, and then come from behind. But as before, she couldn't directly draft. They had to stay back enough to be legal, but close enough to take advantage of the Iron Eagle blocking the current.

Out of the starboard side, Sparky could see the tail of the Iron Eagle as it continued to increase its speed, still tipped. Sparky feathered the controls to sneak in behind the German airship. Unexpectedly, the Iron Eagle nosed up even farther. Sparky muttered, "That doesn't make a good deal of racing sense..."

Jake gasped and pointed at the figure of a man, clearly a pirate from his garb, tumble spread-eagle off the back of the Iron Eagle's envelope. If it was any consolation, the man just barely missed the whirling propeller before he plunged into the valley below. Jake watched, open-mouthed, as the man dropped. "Don't watch...," Sparky offered, but Jake didn't heed her advice. The Iron Eagle leveled off. There was a small band of her crew on the aft catwalk that had been watching to verify that they had rid the airship of its unwanted passenger. They let out a whoop when they confirmed the desired outcome.

Sparky was unsure if this was the right thing for a young man to see. "I wish I could have spared you that," she said quietly.

Jake worked hard to get the words out. "I...I appreciate that. But this was a fight, and...I am here to do my part. I just didn't expect to see another man...die..."

Erasmus appeared at the bridge's doorway. His crimson hand was pressed hard against his right temple to staunch the bleeding, but it was failing. Fresh blood was dripping from between his fingers, staining the front and sleeve of his jacket. His voice was steady, but somber. "Doctor, this may not be the best time, but I could use your assistance in securing my wound."

Sparky turned to Jake, inquiring about his confidence, "Can you hold her steady right here at the tail of the Iron Eagle? Be honest with me."

"I believe so."

"It will only be for a few minutes. I'll get one of the boiler room lads up give you a hand, but I must mend our Chief Inspector."

Sparky grabbed the voicepipe once again and requested Mr. Wilkinson come to the bridge to stand in for her.

She turned and grabbed Erasmus by the arm. "Come with me. I have a kit in my cabin."

"Much obliged," he replied. But on the way to the cabin, he found himself with the odd feeling that he was assigned to the Burke & Hare to protect the passengers and was now dependent on others to put him right. He understood teamwork, but this was, well, different. He was supposed to be the one fighting the good fight, not amplifying the problem.

Sparky stated flatly, "I know what you're thinking. Stop it. You did a great deed in confronting and resisting the marauders. Let me patch you up."

"Is my stoicism showing? I had hoped to conceal that affliction."

"If I have time, I'll lance that delightful masculine virtue."

Erasmus managed a smile.

Inside Sparky's cabin, she led Erasmus to a chair, retrieved her medical kit, a bottle of alcohol, and a clean cloth, and sat down in a chair facing him.

"On my command, remove your hand. I'll wipe the area once, see the extent of the damage, and then I want to you pinch the wound closed with both your hands. Then I will sew you back together as best I can. I will fix you up properly in Munich, assuming we get there safe and sound. This will hurt, if that makes you feel better." She smiled at him quickly, immediately followed by her serious doctor expression. "Ready? Now!"

The door of the bridge flew open. Mr. Wilkinson took a quick step in and surveyed the situation. The Burke & Hare was a tad over 50 yards away from the back of the Iron Eagle, a safe distance, but proceeding at close to full speed. Jake was at the co-pilot's helm with one hand on the rudder control and the other on the throttle. He was white as a sheet. He didn't want to make a single mistake. A trickle of sweat dripped from his forehead and landed on his left eyelash, but he didn't move a muscle or even blink.

"Steady, lad. I am 'ere to 'elp ye." Mr. Wilkinson stepped up to the pilot's controls and took them softly. "Ye can relax now, I got 'er."

Jake forced his hands off of the levers and took a small, unsteady step backwards. Snapping out of his stupor, he blinked hard twice, wiped his forehead with his sleeve, and took hold of the handhold to steady himself.

Jake's voice faltered through his confession. "I've piloted a few boats on the Thames and ridden my share of horses. This was like directing a flatboat with an elephant on it through a flood. Every touch made the whole airship move! I just wanted to hold it steady."

"You did fine, lad. Take a breather." Mr. Wilkinson smiled to himself. He was used to minor docking maneuvers, and he had handled this size craft in moderate winds, but under near full speed, the Burke & Hare was no easy piloting task. Jake's labors at the helm put him at ease a bit, knowing that he would have an easier time of it. Still, he looked forward to Dr. McTrowell's return, allowing him to retreat to his sanctuary below.

The bridge door opened a second time, and Herr Fenstermacher marched in. He had gotten his confidence back as if he had not personally caused anything of consequence. "Dis is quite unusual to switch pilots. Do you gentleman know vat you are doing'k?" he queried.

Dr. McTrowell knotted off the stitches, retrieved a pair of small scissors, and cut the thread. "I had no catgut available, so I used silk. I'm afraid that we will most likely need to re-open the wound and re-suture it when we have the time and facilities. 'Queen' Ishild did you the disservice of adding an extra jab at the end of her cut. The wound is deeper than it appears. My handy work will keep you from bleeding externally, however you will be developing a serious bruise. I'm afraid this may leave your countenance quite rakish and dashing."

"Just what I need," Erasmus joked. Then he became serious again. "I must let you get back to the bridge. Without Sergeant Fox, I need to verify the safety of the vessel myself." He started to stand.

"Not so fast! I need to wrap a bandage on your head to keep this clean. It will only take a minute." She produced a spool of gauze that she wrapped over his eyebrows, across the wound site, and around the back of his head. Three times she circled his head before deftly knotting it in the back. While Sparky was performing this action, she added, "You were lucky. It appears that she was taking aim at your right eye."

"I think that was her second choice, actually. If I had not dodged most of her initial cut, she would sliced me from neck to crown, if I may be so blunt."

Sparky winced at the thought. She stood up, wiped her hands on a clean cloth, and proclaimed, "You'll hold, my dear Chief Inspector. Now I do need to return to the bridge." With that, she tossed the cloth to Erasmus, turned and left, leaving the door open for Erasmus' exit.

Erasmus cleaned himself up as much as he saw fit. The blood on his clothes would just have to be addressed later. He found a hand mirror on a side table and held it up to survey the bandage. The silk thread was black and he could make it out through the three layers of gauze. Sparky's work was a row of tidy x's on a hillside of unhappy skin that was already distended and angry. He reached up and lightly touched the bandage that was over the wound, causing himself to flinch. *"Well,"* he thought, *"no wearing my bowler any time soon."*

As he left the cabin, he mentally checked off the things he wanted to do in priority order. He needed to check on the prisoners to make sure that they were still secured, check on the status of boiler number two, and then go room to room to verify that they didn't have any unexpected guests aboard and that the crew and passengers were safe. And, finally he needed to check the exterior locations where someone could be hiding. That included the top of the envelope, despite his shoulder injury and a touch of anxiety about returning to the site of his near-death. Perhaps he could get some aid in that pursuit.

Erasmus proceeded directly to cabin number two. He knocked loudly to make sure that he would be heard over the engines, which seemed to roar more than usual. Ironically, the door to cabin one opened. There stood Reginald Wallace, still in his undergarments, a near-empty bottle of whisky in his hand.

"Did you want to see me?" Reginald slurred. "Have we finished the race? Did we win?"

"Not quite. But I do suggest you get fully dressed for the ceremony," Erasmus teased.

"Capital idea! We can talk about my wife at that time." Without waiting for Erasmus' answer, Reginald closed the door. Erasmus immediately heard some shuffling from within cabin one when the door of cabin two opened. Lord Ashleigh had opened his own door, and it was clear that he and Virat had been busy putting the cabin into some semblance of organization after the removal of most of the silk cloth. They had made good progress, but cushion padding and cotton wads were still scattered about. Virat was still scooping up the fluffy masses and stuffing them into a cotton pillowcase. "Erasmus! Nice bandage. No doubt Dr. McTrowell's efforts. How can I be of service?"

"I need to secure the vessel, but my right shoulder is quite impaired. Can you and Virat verify that the top of the envelope is secure?"

Lord Ashleigh glanced quickly in Virat's direction and received a nod of approval.

"Why, of course! We'll be right on it. We just need to stock up on throwing knives. We'll see you as soon as we get back."

"Thank you, my dear friend."

Erasmus turned and headed to the common room where Queen Ishild and her two confederates were secured. They were seated on the floor, leaning back on the aft wall of the chamber. They were not happy. Erasmus gave them a good look over. Not only were they manacled behind their backs, but they were also tied about the arms and ankles. To add a measure of security, the ropes about their arms were also secured to a rope handhold that was affixed waist-high on the wall. It allowed them enough slack to sit on the floor. This was to allow the Queen to keep weight off of her leg, which was still weeping a dark stain onto her black stockings and skirt.

Ishild was glaring at Erasmus. "My leg needs attention. Fetch a physician."

Erasmus thought for a second and replied unsympathetically, "I think not." He punctuated the response with a light kick to the sole of her right boot, causing her to wince in pain. She snarled at him and grimaced for a second with the continued pain of the wound.

Erasmus offered his reasoning, "My blade was thin and sharp, not like your meat-chopper of a cutlass. You see; you are hardly bleeding. Our doctor is busy, and you will live until Munich. It will help if you hold still. I would hate to have them amputate. It would be a waste of a perfectly good boot."

The pirate next to her could not sit idly by any longer. "Cut ye tongue out meself, I will, talking like that to me Queen," he hissed out between his too few teeth.

Erasmus smiled. "Love to stay and chat, but I have a vessel to secure. Just stay here in our sitting room. We shall be arriving at your jailhouse before you know it." He headed down the stairs to check on boiler number two. Halfway down he met Luis-Miguel, who was carrying a cutlass, followed by Tobias. "Er, Hello. Luis-Miguel, what are you doing?"

"Taking this prisoner to a cabin for locking up."

"Then why is he behind you? Tobias, did you surrender?"

"Aye," Tobias sighed, and he told Erasmus the shortened version of how he didn't want to be involved in this raid in the first place. He just wanted to go home.

"Luis-Miguel, hand me the cutlass, place Tobias in cabin number nine, and tell Aldrich Fremont to watch him. It will make Aldrich useful. And serve him right."

As he passed, Erasmus patted his old friend Tobias on the back, and Tobias responded in kind.

Sparky entered the bridge, saw the three men, and felt the tension in the air. She didn't have time for this.

"Good job, men. I'll take it from here. Herr Fenstermacher, if you have something to say, say it to me."

Mr. Wilkinson relinquished the helm to Sparky with a tip of his workman's cap and made a hasty exit out of the bridge door.

"Not'ing at zis time, Doctor." Herr Fenstermacher followed this with an unpleasant smile, but he held his ground and stayed on the bridge, as if he were waiting for some racing violation that he could use against the crew.

Sparky ignored him. "Mr. Fremont, let's finish this race."

Erasmus continued his tour. Boiler number two was holding steady at 90%. None of the cabins had any issues, although Reginald was truly struggling to get himself fully dressed. Aldrich did not like his assignment, but grudgingly accepted it.

Lord Ashleigh and Virat returned to proclaim that, not only was the envelope clear of marauders, but they had crawled the length of the envelope and miraculously didn't find any punctures in the envelope surface. The three of them together verified that the catwalk was clear of interlopers, and Erasmus reported to Sparky the security of the Burke & Hare.

Björn Swenson could see the steeples of Munich in the distance. "Good, good," he said out loud in Swedish.

The first mate stepped onto the bridge. "Captain Swenson. To maintain flank speed, we have used all of the broken planks as fuel. We will be switching back to coal."

"No. Start removing the interior walls and burn them, too. We must increase our lead as best we can. The removed walls will also lighten our load. Keep the boilers at 120% or higher."

"Aye, aye."

The first mate disappeared, and the sound of industry continued as the interior walls came down, and the engine roared on.

Willy Dampf knew he had a fast airship, but with the Burke & Hare as close as legally possible, it would still come down to a sprint. Willy conferred with his co-pilot, young Herr von Zeppelin, "Ve haf tried going faster zan ze Burke & Hare, und ve haf tried changing altitude. Zo far Doctor McTrowell has out-maneuvered us tvice. How about ve fake our final sprint early?"

"Ja, that may work. Or you can do the opposite. While they are following, slow down slightly a good distance from the finish. They will either slow down themselves, or they'll swing alongside of us to pass. Either way, we are free to sprint to the finish. We have the faster vessel, even if they have more fuel."

"A zound plan, but it must be done at just ze right time. We need to be ahead by more zan 3 seconds."

The young co-pilot grabbed a compass, scale, and pencil out of his tool pouch and turned to the detailed chart of Munich, already marked with the visual points for dead-reckoning. With a quick calculation in the margin and two swings of his compass he marked one point along their trajectory. "Here is ze optimal point for ze start of zeir sprint." A couple of more calculations and a pair of compass movements, and he marked another location. "Here is our best deceleration point to force zem out too soon. Zen we sprint to ze finish. I vill check with ze crew on fuel levels to verify ze plan."

"Egzellent. I vill check on ze points of visualization," Willy added. At that, his co-pilot ran out to check with their crew.

⊱⊱⊰⊱⊰⊰ ⚙ ⊰⊱⊰⊱⊰⊱⊰

Sparky was worried about her strategy. Ivan had been a good sounding board. Losing him made this task all the harder. She decided that, to get past those thoughts, she would walk through her plan out loud, letting both Jake and herself hear it.

"At this speed, we're traveling about 90 feet per second. The Iron Eagle is about 400 feet long, and we are about another 150 feet behind her. So we are currently a little over 6 seconds behind them. We need to be less than 270 feet from the Iron Eagle's nose to win the regatta. That's two thirds of her length. To be safe, we need to be less than half of her length away when it crosses the finish line."

She and Jake looked at each other. The last two victories were well-timed sprints. A two-boiler sprint now might endanger the crew, not to mention the crowd in Munich. Sparky swallowed hard.

Captain Swenson looked at his watch. At this speed, they should cross the finish line in about eight minutes. Neither of his opponents were in sight. He silently congratulated himself on the modularity and composability of his airship design. He smiled, nodded to himself, and pictured the podium at the finish line, with a tall Swede at...

A loud whooshing sound followed by a hiss, and the deceleration of the North Wind sent the crew off-balance, grabbing for the nearest brass handholds.

"Status!" the captain cried.

The gold-blond first mate anxiously reported, "Sir! Some of the secondary heating pipes have melted! We are losing steam into the firebox. We can only give you about one quarter power now, and we cannot add more fuel to the secondaries at this time."

"*Helvete*! What's our alternative?"

"We can seal off the secondary firebox, allow it to pressurize, and keep going. However, we may foul the engine if we do."

"Damn the engine! Seal off the secondary, and give me ten more minutes of steam!"

"Aye, aye!"

Four of the Swedish crew grabbed their thick heat-protecting gloves and scrambled through the toolbox for the right wrenches. They cranked down the seals on the secondary heating unit despite the water vapor that was spurting out in sticky-hot swirling clouds. The fire within died with a horrible sound, and the whole unit trembled under the shock of being pressurized. The propellers grudgingly continued to turn, and the airship went from locomotive speed to penny-farthing speed.

The crowd at the Ludwigsvorstadt field gasped as the North Wind's venting tubes suddenly gushed black smoke, and the airship slowed. The steam engine, which was audible, lost its high pitch. The whoosh of the high-speed propellers stopped even though the devices continued to turn. The individual blades were now visible as they swung through their arcs.

The race became watching an ailing floating sausage drift toward the finish line. The crowd was consumed by their singular desire for the sound of the cannon signaling the race's conclusion. The minutes went by in agony, and the low murmur of "come on" and "you can do it" in German turned into a rolling chant. At the apex of the incantations, the cannon sounded, the crowd cheered, jumped up and down, laughed, and threw their Bavarian alpine hats into the air.

After the initial excitement died down, the other two ships popped over the horizon, the Iron Eagle in the lead, the Burke & Hare alongside. The crowd was back to cheering again with the race reborn.

To watch the behemoths at top speed was breathtaking. The nose of the Burke & Hare was near the middle of the Iron Eagle, but the Iron Eagle appeared to be gaining on her. Everyone spun around in unison to watch them pass by overhead. The cannon didn't report again, since the first airship had already crossed over the finish line. The spectators on the finish line cried out when the Iron Eagle crossed, and the wave of cheers emanated from there.

The docking of the airships went smoothly, despite the acrid smoke still coming from the North Wind. The crews descended their towers to the rambunctious applauding and hooting of the throng. Brass bands struck up, and the celebration was underway, even though the ground officials were still huddled and studying their watches.

Erasmus mixed into the crowd, carrying the scabbard of his walking stick, not sure what to do with it. He had lost his policeman's sword, his revolver, and his sword cane blade. "Yours," a deep resonating voice from behind him said. Erasmus turned and saw Herr Holzfäller, the massive German who had broken his fall. He was holding out Erasmus' sword cane! "Stick in hull of airship. Yours!" Erasmus lovingly took back his weapon and slid it back into its scabbard, where it clicked into place. *"Danke schön. Danke schön."*

Finally, the officials walked in unison to the grandstand and made their announcement. "Coming in third place, twenty-three seconds behind the winner is the North Wind!" the lead official boomed. Cheers went up; applause rang out. Björn Swenson jogged up to the podium on the stage of the grandstand. He waved a Swedish flag in one hand and his hexagonal wrench in the other. The Swedish ground crew started a bouncy chant in Swedish that Björn swayed to while he enjoyed the attention.

"Coming in second place, one second behind the winner, is the Iron Eagle!" the official bellowed. The crew picked Willy Dampf up onto their shoulders and carried him to the grandstand. On the podium, Willy took a deep bow and waved his hands at the cheering crowd.

"In first place is...the Burke & Hare!"

Sparky proudly took the top tier of the podium. She raised her pilot's headgear and her two crossed flags of the Americas and Great Britain. Confetti rained down on the three pilots, and she smiled her biggest, trying to hide the emotional pain of losing her co-pilot.

Erasmus could tell, even though he was a dozen rows back in the crowd. He wanted to hold her and tell her that it was acceptable to celebrate the victory now and grieve later.

Suddenly above, in the crewless Burke & Hare, a hissing sound erupted over the crowd. Steam poured out of the port-side emergency release pipe.

Mr. Wilkinson's voice rang out, "We just lost boiler number two!" and Sparky joined the crowd in a laugh.

Erasmus felt a tap on his shoulder. He turned and saw a young man dressed in the uniform of Her Majesty's Aerial Marines, the same that J.B. had worn when they first met.

"May I help you?" Erasmus enquired.

"Sir, I'm here to escort you to an important meeting. Please follow me."

Erasmus knew better than to ask questions as to the nature of the meeting or where it was going to be held. All the information this Marine was going to relay to Erasmus had already been said. The young man turned crisply and marched off toward an ordinary brick townhouse; Erasmus was right behind him. At the door, the Marine knocked twice, the door was opened from within, and two more Marines crisply waved them in. Erasmus couldn't help but notice that they had revolvers in their right hands, both kept surreptitiously by the side of their legs, but ready for use if needed. *"Must be an important meeting,"* Erasmus thought.

It was a plain entryway for an urban household with a small foyer for the removal of jackets and boots and a plain stairway leading to an upper floor. One of the door guards flatly stated, "Chief Inspector Drake, your sword stick, please," and held out a hand to receive it. Erasmus surrendered the newly regained weapon. "Please proceed up the staircase. Thank you."

Erasmus nodded his understanding, replying, "You are welcome." Erasmus took the first few steps upstairs. All three Marines stayed at the entryway. Erasmus continued his mysterious climb.

At the top of the stairs was a short landing and an open door leading to a small, carpeted room with comfortable furniture circled around a lit fireplace on the far side of the room. Another Marine gestured him to enter the room. Erasmus stepped in, and the Marine stepped out onto the landing, closing the door behind himself. The fire crackled, and the logs shifted a bit, changing the way the light played throughout the room.

A woman's voice came from one of the chairs facing away from Erasmus, strong and clear. "Chief Inspector, please pardon the secrecy and the urgency of this meeting. Come forward so we can see you." Erasmus proceeded around the chair and turned to face the handsome woman who sat very erect, wearing brocade and velvet.

"Your Majesty!" Erasmus immediately knelt to one knee and bowed his head.

"You may stand," she said in an authoritative voice. Erasmus did as requested. His head was swimming with numerous questions, which he was trying to silence so he could give his full attention. He also became very aware that his head was bandaged, and how odd he must look to her.

She continued. "Since you are here, we take it that you were able to suppress Ishild Tuttleford's attack. Are we correct that you have her in custody?"

"Yes, your majesty. She and two of her marauders."

"Sergeant Fox is not here with you. Did he survive?"

"Yes, to the best of my knowledge. He was gliding to the valley floor near Melköde when I last saw him. The three attacking airships were disabled, so I believe that he is out of harm's way."

"Good. We want to inform you about this assignment on which we sent you. Listen carefully. We are not given to repeating ourselves. As you were informed by Sergeant Fox, we are trying to secure alliances with other heads of state. One of our goals was to strengthen our association with King Maximilian as he addresses a strenuous internal conflict within Bavaria. As part of that, we offered to help clear the routes of the Ludwig-Süd-Nord-Bahn railroad, which involved quelling the upstart Ishild Tuttleford, who has threatened us personally in missives in her own hand. We agreed to hold this international regatta directly over the area that Ishild Tuttleford claimed to control, to show that it is a safe passage. From our reports, it was not clear if Ishild Tuttleford would stand down or attack. Britain sent you on a perilous mission, and you persevered." She paused, but her eyes indicated that she was not finished speaking.

"As you now understand, the other airships were not aware of the probable attack since King Maximilian thought the route had been secured. The attacks are not to be discussed. Any errors in judgment by the officials should be overlooked. There is nothing to be gained by humbling the Bavarians. With Ishild Tuttleford captured, the Bavarians can proceed with the railroad as planned, and King Maximilian will be grateful for our support." She paused again, eyes fixed on Erasmus.

"Given what we have seen from this assignment and knowing your background..." Erasmus' eyebrows raised, and he opened his mouth to speak. "Shush! we have ten thousand eyes and ten thousand ears! Of course we know!" She paused for only a split second and then restarted. "Knowing your background, and given what we have seen from this assignment, we are offering you an opportunity to join the ranks of a newly formed agency that will work to secure my international interests. This agency will remain entirely secretive, reporting exclusively to us. Sergeant Fox has already agreed to be part of that agency. May we have your allegiance on this endeavor?"

Erasmus blinked twice as he processed the offer.

"Yes, your majesty."

"As we had hoped. You will retain your employment at Scotland Yard. You will be requested for assignments in a similar manner as before. Your loyalty to Britain is recognized and appreciated. That is all. You are dismissed."

Erasmus bowed deeply and started to exit the room.

"One more thing. Please give this to the Burke & Hare pilot."

She handed Erasmus a purple envelope with the name "C. Llewellyn McTrowell" written on it in perfect script, which he slipped into his interior jacket pocket.

In the street, he distantly remembered descending the stairs, getting his swordstick back, and leaving the building. He wasn't sure if he wandered the streets of Munich for a while or not, but he found himself back in the celebrating crowd.

"Erasmus?"

He looked up to see Sparky, full of life and enjoying the moment, standing right in front of him. Without hesitation, he leaned over and kissed her, square on the lips. They both pulled back an inch, shocked that it had happened. Sparky grasped his injured face gently with both her hands, pulled him close, and kissed him hard.

An Honorable Endeavor

By Dr. Katherine L. Morse

"Dies ist nicht Paris. Holen Sie sich ein Zimmer."

Drake and McTrowell unlocked from their kiss and looked around sheepishly to see a policeman making a good show of indignance at their public display of affection. He didn't seem terribly serious about his order, probably owing to the jubilant atmosphere of the street. Drake instinctively reached up to tip his bowler at the cop, but wound up flapping his hand around his temple in the absence of his customary cover. To save Drake any more discomfort, Sparky saluted the policeman smartly and, taking Drake by the hand, headed back in the direction of the airfield.

There was too much commotion to talk for most of their walk. It didn't help that Sparky was immediately recognizable in her leather duster and aviator's cap. Despite Drake's injuries, exhaustion, and general disorientation from his meeting with the Queen, he had to extricate Sparky a couple of times from overzealous fans and well-wishers. When they reached a calm spot at the bottom of the docking tower and out of the maelstrom, they said at the same time, "Are you all right?"

They both paused for a beat, and Sparky got her bearings first. "It still hasn't fully sunk in that Ivan is gone. This was supposed to be his last flight, but not like this. I'm beginning to feel like my life is one crisis after another, punctuated by writing letters of condolences. He had such big plans for returning home and starting a new life. What am I going to tell his family?"

"Ah yes, about that. I am afraid you will have to be a bit creative. You may not tell them about the pirates."

"What? Why can't I tell them the truth? On whose orders?"

"Her Majesty's."

"Her Majesty? Her Majesty Queen Victoria? And how did Her Majesty come to convey these orders to you?" She grasped his wrist surreptitiously while looking closely into his eyes. She moved her head back and forth slightly to determine if his eyes were tracking. His pulse was strong and his breathing slightly elevated, but no more than would be warranted by the walking and recent "excitement."

"She spoke them to me directly just a few moments before I met you on the street just now."

"Let's find a place to sit down. You may have lost more blood than I realized. Are you feeling at all dizzy?"

"I believe there is no part of my person that does not hurt at this moment…except perhaps my lips." He paused a bit awkwardly. "However, I am quite lucid. Her Majesty is here in Munich. She summoned me and provided some explanation for today's events that I may share with you later. I believe her presence is a secret, as is the pirate attack."

She looked directly into his face, vacillating between pursuing the line of questioning about Queen Victoria and further exploring the state of his lips.

"I had almost forgotten. Her Majesty has a missive for you as well." He reached for the inside pocket of his jacket. Before he could retrieve the purple envelope, their attention was diverted by a farm wagon rattling onto the airfield. It was driven by an older woman neither of them recognized. From her dress and demeanor, she appeared to be a farm wife. Seated next to her on the plain wooden bench was none other than Sergeant J.B. Fox, considerably the worse for wear, but essentially intact. They ran to meet him, or at least moved as quickly as they could manage in their present state.

By the time Drake and McTrowell reached the wagon, Fox had managed to climb down. Sparky threw her arms around his neck and gave him a big hug. She was rewarded with a response that consisted mostly of "oo" and "ouch."

"I'm sorry. I'm just so glad to see you alive! Are you injured? Do you require medical attention?"

"It's nothing that a hot bath and several pints of stout beer won't cure." He indicated the woman sitting on the wagon's bench. "This is Frau Fitzpatrick. She was watching today from the ground. She's looking for her husband." Drake and McTrowell stared blankly at him. "A certain Tobias."

Realization dawned on Drake's face. He had forgotten all about the prisoners on the Burke & Hare! He had no idea whether the local authorities had taken them into custody. He turned to Frau Fitzpatrick. "Please wait here." He headed up the docking tower without considering whether she understood a single word of English. Fortunately, farm wives are a patient lot by necessity.

Fox turned to McTrowell. The look on his face was very grave. "Ma'am, we have a motto in Her Majesty's Aerial Marines: no man left behind." She looked at him evenly, hoping further explanation would be forthcoming. When he walked around to the back of the wagon, she followed. "Normally I wouldn't show a woman a sight like this, but you're a medical doctor and as stalwart as any Marine I've ever known." She nodded slightly at the compliment. He pulled back the corner of a tarp lying across the bed of the wagon to reveal the pulverized body of Ivan Krasnayarubashka. In spite of her medical training and stalwartness, she gasped. It was different when it was a friend.

He replaced the temporary shroud. She took a slow breath in an out. "Thank you, Sergeant Fox. You have done a fine service to his family today. I hope it will bring them some small amount of comfort."

Drake crossed the gangplank onto the Burke & Hare and dashed into the main hall. There was no one there. He poked his head into the cockpit. No one there either. He had a very bad feeling about this. He was heading out of the main hall to search the rest of the ship when he encountered Wilkinson coming in.

"Wilkinson, do you know where the prisoners are?"

"Why, yes. Ole' Maximillian's troops come and 'auled 'em away."

"All of them?"

"Yeah, all three. That one, she spat an 'issed like a rabid cat. Wouldn't want to be meetin' 'er in no dark alley."

"Three, you say?"

"Beg pardon?"

"Oh, nothing. Thank you." Wilkinson continued on his path to the cockpit and Drake headed down the passageway to cabin nine. He rapped once on the door and opened it. Tobias was lying on the bottom bunk, snoring softly. Aldrich Fremont was nowhere to be seen. Drake shook Tobias slightly and held a finger to his lips.

When Tobias stirred, Drake asked in a whisper, "Where is Fremont?"

"Don't know. He was complaining about needing to use the head before I nodded off."

Drake stepped back out into the passageway and looked around. No sign of Fremont. He leaned back into the cabin. Still speaking softly, he said archly, "I am surprised you did not escape." He jerked his head back over his shoulder slightly.

Tobias just rubbed his eyes and replied sleepily, "Huh?"

"I said, 'I am surprised you did not escape.'" He enunciated each word clearly and gestured more strenuously backward with his head, also engaging his shoulder this time.

"Oh, yes, right." Tobias shambled off the bunk and out of the cabin, patting Drake on the shoulder as he went past.

He was just nipping into the main hall when he heard Drake's voice raised in reproach, "Fremont, where is your prisoner?"

"I left him sleeping in my cabin."

"Unsecured? Do you not understand the meaning of the word 'prisoner'?" Tobias was out of earshot before Fremont could muster a reply.

By the time Drake had finished remonstrating Aldrich Fremont and returned to the base of the tower, Tobias, his wife, his wagon, and Fox were gone. Sparky was leaning against the tower with a bundle rolled up in canvas at her feet.

"I believe one of your prisoners escaped," she quipped.

"Most unfortunate. It seems Mr. Fremont is no better a guard than a defender. What is that?" He indicated the roll at her feet.

"Don't look. It's Ivan's body. Sergeant Fox was considerate enough to return it. I've sent him to determine if any of the Krasnayarubashkas traveled to Munich for the conclusion of the race."

He wrapped his arms around her shoulders and she rested her head on his collarbone. Neither of them said anything for a few minutes. When she regained her composure somewhat, she said, "Would you please stand guard over Ivan? I should get to the purser's office and make arrangements for a coffin. It would not be respectful to return Mr. Krasnayarubashka to his family wrapped in an old tarp smelling of hay and pigs." He just nodded and she trudged off across the airfield.

Not surprisingly, the purser was very efficient at his job. He had carpenters assembling a plain pine box within the hour. Sparky retrieved some sheets from the Burke & Hare. She and Drake had Ivan neatly wrapped in the sheets and nailed into the coffin by the time dusk was setting in. Fox returned to the airfield in the company of the man Drake had seen drinking with Krasnayarubashka in Salzburg. Sparky saw him glance at the rapidly assembled coffin. She walked toward him, extending her hand. "Здравствуйте, меня зовут Спарки МкТровелл."

"Здравствуйте, меня зовут Юрий Краснаярубашка."

She continued in Russian. "You're related to Ivan?"

"He is my cousin." He eyed the coffin again. "What happened?"

"There was…an accident. A crew member failed to secure your cousin's safety line when he went out to perform a repair. I am very sorry for your loss. Your cousin was an excellent pilot and it was an honor to fly with him."

"Thank you."

"Western & Transatlantic Airship Lines will make all the arrangements to send his body home and pay for everything."

He thanked her again, but he was no longer really engaged in the conversation. He was just staring at the coffin. Drake waited for McTrowell to precede him up the stairs to the Burke & Hare. Fox trailed behind them. She commented, mostly to the air, "I am sorely in need of several days of sleep."

Unfortunately, she could not afford several days of sleep. By the time she awoke in the morning and crawled achingly out of her bunk, Wilkinson and Sevilla were already well underway making the Burke & Hare ready for the return journey, including disconnecting the disabled boiler. She encountered Jake Fremont in the passageway. He was attempting nonchalance with zero success.

"Good morning, Mr. Fremont."

"Good morning, Captain." Ah, so that was what this was about.

"Mr. Fremont, as you well know, we are tragically without a first mate and must make haste back to Paris and London. Are you willing and able to serve?"

"Yes, ma'am!"

"Meet me in the cockpit in twenty-five minutes." He fairly scampered toward the main hall. She expected he would be in the cockpit in less than one. She nearly bumped into Drake as he came in from the catwalk. The dressings on his head looked fresh and his bowler was back on his head, albeit tipped back somewhat to avoid too much contact with the bandage.

"I would have changed the bandage for you when I changed the sutures."

"Um, that will not be necessary."

She looked at him quizzically for a moment. "Why not?"

"Her Majesty sent her physician to examine me."

"And what did he say?"

"How do know Her Majesty's physician is a man?"

"They always are."

"Yes, well, he said that he could not do a better job than had already been done, and that I should return to the physician who performed the original suturing when my face healed and have 'him' remove them."

"I'm sure 'he' would be happy to do so and to change the bandage as it heals." She wasn't sure whether to smile or scowl at the exchange and so just settled on getting to the bridge. She turned on her toes to leave.

"The letter from Her Majesty?"

"I beg your pardon," She said, stopping mid turn.

"Her Majesty sent a message for you last night, but I failed to deliver it amidst the arrangements for Mr. Krasnayarubashka."

"Oh, yes, I'd forgotten as well."

He handed her the envelope and stepped into the gondola on the way to his next mission of the day. She read the address on the outside of the envelope and felt like she was being choked.

Drake stepped up to the door of cabin one and knocked smartly. He heard a mumble from inside that he chose to interpret as an invitation to enter. Wallace was still in bed and looking like he'd been ridden hard and put away wet. Drake entered and closed the door smartly.

"Mr. Wallace, it is past time to face your situation like a man and take action to correct it. Why did she leave you?"

"My wife? I don't know."

"Every investigation must begin with facts. What did she say when she left?"

"She said she was bored and that she wanted to 'do something.'"

"Did she indicate what she meant by 'something?'"

"Some business thing. Why would she want to do that? I bought her a beautiful new townhouse in Belgrave Square and gave her an unlimited budget to decorate it any way she wants. She travels to Bath every summer for the waters. She lunches every day with her lady friends. We have a Christmas Ball every year that everyone wants to attend. What more could she want?" He practically sobbed the question.

"Do these activities sound interesting to you?"

"Well, of course not! I'm not a woman."

"Nor am I. Nor do I claim to be an expert on women." *"Neither,"* he thought to himself, *"do I wish to become an expert on such women."* He continued, "But these activities do seem repetitive and tedious to me."

"What is your bloody point, Drake?"

"As I said, every investigation must begin with facts. The only fact in evidence at this time is that she has stated that she is bored. I recommend pursuing this line of questioning with her when you return to London." Drake stood up crisply to leave. "One more thing. I strongly advise listening to her answers to your questions." He exited the cabin without waiting to hear Wallace's reply that seemed to be forming, slowly and incoherently, on his lips. Drake was sure he didn't want to hear it, nor would it be further illuminating.

Standing alone on the catwalk, Sparky swallowed hard. There was no avoiding the letter. Drake had delivered it, and one didn't forget or lose a letter from a queen, even if it wasn't her queen.

Dr. McTrowell,

We have ten thousand eyes and ten thousand ears. Do not mistake a lack of action on our part for a lack of knowledge. Soon you will be called

upon to further aid Chief Inspector Drake, a commission in which we believe you will be strongly invested. Endeavor to honor the memory of your grandfather in this task.
Victoria Regina

BACK TO PARIS

BY MR. DAVID L. DRAKE

Sparky read the letter from the Queen a couple more times, both to extract every possible meaning that the Queen might have placed in her words and also to memorize the letter. She proceeded directly to the boiler room and secretly deposited the letter into the glowing coals of the boiler fire. No good could come of retaining the letter. She took a good deep breath and let it out slowly. She realized that she had drawn the attention, even for a moment, of a very powerful woman. After watching the last remnants of the letter disappear into ash and smoke, she turned and proceeded to the Burke & Hare's helm to make their way to Paris.

Erasmus and J.B. sat across from each other at their table in the common room as Luis-Miguel served them breakfast. They had the appearance of patients at an infirmary. They did their best to look stout-hearted, but no reasonable person would have bought the fraudulent demeanor. J.B. had newly-applied gauze wrapped about his hands, both of which apparently took a dreadful beating the previous day when he landed in a spruce tree, clawing as he descended to get a hand hold. Erasmus' head was still swollen, his bandages adding to its girth. They didn't speak much, avoiding the obvious conversation regarding their level of discomfort.

The airship moved gently under them as it was released from its moorings. The quietness of the engine was noticeable to Erasmus, compared to the roar of the last four days.

At the next table, Reginald Wallace held court with a few new passengers who wanted the privilege of flying to Paris on the regatta-winning airship, paying handsomely for the pleasure. He elaborated on beautifully embellished tales of the regatta, stringing together narratives of high-speed heats and break-neck maneuvers, midnight engine overhauls, scheming pilots, and grand racing strategies and tactics. It wasn't that the stories were incorrect, for there was more than a drop of truth in each bit of it, but rather that each had been fluffed up like an oversized pillow until it was soft and safe for the public to ease back into.

A few times, Erasmus and J.B. responded to Reginald's patter by rolling their eyes and giving each other an "I can't believe he just said that" look.

After finishing their meals, J.B. stood and signaled Erasmus to follow him. Erasmus wiped his mouth on his napkin, stood, and followed J.B. Just within his cabin, Sergeant Fox picked up two items that were secreted under his bed and held them out for Erasmus. "I recovered these from the fields of Melköde. The locals saw them fall and gave them to me when they saw that I survived my descent. I placed them in the cart and pulled them out last night while you were looking for Tobias." The items were both dirty, and J.B. handled them with just his fingertips to try to keep his bandages clean. The Colt 1849 revolver looked like it had landed in the dirt, barrel first. The dirt was packed hard into it, and it was obvious that J.B. had knocked off and brushed off as much as he could. The saber hadn't fared as well. It was irreparably contorted in the middle of the blade. "I wasn't sure if the blade was important in some way, so I retrieved it. The revolver looks like it doesn't have a scratch. Even the wooden handle is unbroken." Erasmus accepted the lost items with acknowledgment of his gratitude and appreciation that J.B. was thinking of more than just himself after his rough landing.

Erasmus placed the items in his cabin, planning to clean them later that evening while docked in Paris. He proceeded on to visit cabin number two to see in what activity Lord Ashleigh was engaged. After his knock, Virat opened the door to reveal that the sitting room was magically transformed into a homey suite with standard issue blankets used as throws over the sofa and footstools. There was not a silk pillow in sight, not surprising given that they all had given their exterior fabric to save J.B.'s life.

Lord Ashleigh was sitting quietly and reading the morning papers from Munich, which he set aside at seeing Erasmus' smiling face.

"Come in! Come in! Can we get you anything, my friend?"

"Señor Sevilla's breakfast was more than enough. However, I would like to talk to you about the fine art of throwing knives..."

The Paris airship field was busy that day, with the Western and Transatlantic Airship's Fidelis preparing to leave for London, freeing up docking tower number eight for the incoming Burke & Hare. The Fidelis was a commuter airship, with nothing more than rows of seats in the passenger hall. The well-attired steward was making his rounds, checking on the comfort of his travelers.

He proceeded to the next row of three seats. "I pray that you are comfortable. May I see your tickets?"

A twig of a man with a shock of wild, frizzy brown hair looked up from a notebook covered with drawings and notes. He produced three postcard-sized tickets from his jacket's breast pocket and held them out for the steward.

"Welcome aboard, Monsieur, and your companions, Mr. Hedgley and Mr. Martin. If you need anything during your trip, please let me know." He moved on to the next row of passengers, unaware of the danger that was about to be transported to London.

Erasmus watched the Fidelis gracefully leave the airfield from the window of the Burke & Hare common room, glad to be back in Paris. *"I wonder if Sparky knows how she got that scarf,"* he chuckled to himself.

THE PECOS INCIDENT

BY DR. KATHERINE L. MORSE

Considering the unfortunate outcome of the regatta from the perspective of the French, Wallace didn't object to Sparky's request to stay on the Burke & Hare throughout the day, allegedly supervising repairs while Luis-Miguel Sevilla put the passenger cabins back in order. In truth, Wilkinson had the whole matter completely under control. Sparky spent the day wandering aimlessly around the ship, catching up on some technical reading, and trying with little success to get the blood out of her lovely new yellow scarf. Not that she objected to the reminder of its critical role in saving Drake's life, but wearing a bloody scarf in public was, at best, in bad taste and, at worst, ghoulish. It still had some faintly rusty stains when it came time for dinner, but she chose to wear it anyway. When she took her seat at dinner, the seat she had come to consider her "usual" seat in just the last few days, Lord Ashleigh noticed the state of her scarf.

"It's a shame that such a lovely item should get damaged so soon. Especially considering how fond of it you seem to have become." He winked at Drake and none too subtly.

"Yes, and it's not as if I haven't really tried to get it clean." A dejected expression settled on her face. Despite everything that had happened this week, the stains on the scarf just seemed to be one thing too many.

"Among his other considerably impressive skills, Virat has a method for cleaning silk that is unmatched. In fact, I believe it saved his life once." He flashed his broadest, warmest smile at Sparky, hoping to cheer her up. And it did. "Come by my cabin after dinner and we'll see if he can affect a rescue. And maybe we can persuade Chief Inspector Drake to join us for a spot of port at the same time." And then he invoked that smile again. It occurred to Drake that such a smile was a dangerous weapon, not that he minded having it wielded against him at the moment. Some port and some time relatively alone with Sparky would be a delightful close to the day.

By the time Sparky arrived at Lord Ashleigh's cabin, Erasmus was already seated comfortably. No sooner had Virat opened the door for her than he held out his hand for the scarf. Obviously Lord Ashleigh had already apprised him of the situation. She handed over the scarf and Virat disappeared into the bedchamber to work his magic. Sparky took the third seat with a glass of port in front of it.

Ashleigh raised his glass in toast, "To the amazing events of this week, may we never see their like again."

"Here, here," Drake chimed in enthusiastically.

Ashleigh continued, "My dear friend, Dr. McTrowell. Mr. Wallace tells me that this is not your first eventful voyage. He referred to it another adventure as 'The Pecos Incident.' I am in the mood for a story about anything other than this week's trials. If it would not be too taxing, would you be willing to relate the tale?"

Sparky thought about it for a moment, took a somewhat generous swallow of her port, and began, "As you probably all know, the Treaty of Guadalupe Hidalgo, ending the Mexican-American war, was signed on February 2, 1848 in Mexico City."

Lord Ashleigh smiled and nodded. "Yes, it was in all the newspapers."

THE EMANCIPATOR

A correspondent of the North American writes from Washington on Monday: "It is quite currently reported here — with what plausibility you may judge — that the Administration has received the basis of a treaty made between Mr. Trist and Herrera. By it, Upper California and the entire country east of the Bravo are to be ceded to us for fifteen millions of dollars."

February 2, 1948

"Ah, yes, the newspapers. You can't believe everything you read in the newspapers." She rolled her eyes.

"There was an attempt to sign the treaty in December 1847 in Santa Fe. I was the first mate on a small ship that was secretly taking the Mexican ambassador to Santa Fe for the signing. His name was Don Raul Ascencio Archuleta Pacheco de Fuerte y Calvados, but he preferred to be called Jorge. He spoke perfect English, but he tended to lapse back and forth when he got excited, which he did quite a bit.

"Little did we know that Don Jorge had a beautiful, high-maintenance, mestiza mistress, Catalina, in Albuquerque. We were forced to make an unannounced stop to collect her. The woman brought on a dozen heavy steamer trunks full of dresses, jewelry, lotions and potions, and different shoes for every dress. She had two dozen mantillas!"

"Lace doesn't take up that much space," the viscount quipped.

"I think you're missing the point," she retorted and launched back into her story.

I warned the pilot, Captain Burrows, that the extra weight would make it difficult to maintain the elevation necessary to get to Santa Fe safely. As we approached La Bajada, it became clear that my dire prediction was going to be realized. Burrows kept insisting we could make it, but I knew we were going to slam into the precipice. If we crashed into the cliff face, the gondola would tip backward, upsetting the engines, setting the ship on fire, and sending us all plummeting to the base of the cliff in a ball of fire.

Captain Burrows realized too late that I was right. He screamed and covered his face with his hands. I spotted a culvert in the cliff face off to the port side that was wide enough for the gondola and I drove straight into it, shouting back to the engine room to shut down the engines. We slammed into the culvert, wedging the gondola tightly. The envelope jerked back and forth on its tethers, but it held. The walls of the gondola groaned. Glass popped out of portholes, shattering and tinkling strangely musically to the bottom of the cliff. Captain Burrows slammed his head into the console, knocking himself out cold. It was probably a blessing in disguise because I expect his leadership in the subsequent misadventures would have resulted in an even greater debacle. I heard Don Jorge's mistress scream all the way up on the bridge.

ALBUQUERQUE DAILY
Brave Captain Burrows Saves the Day

The quick thinking of heroic local airship Captain Maynard Burrows saved the lives of the passengers on his three-hour site-seeing tour of the Indian pueblos. When his airship suffered an unexpected mechanical failure, Captain Burrows piloted his airship with breathtaking precision into a culver in the face of La Bajada, cleverly "docking" his ship safely so his passengers could disembark in comfort and safety.

December 1847

I turned my head just in time for my leather cap to deflect the flying glass of the cockpit window that couldn't flex as readily as the wooden gondola. Fortunately, it mostly popped out and showered across the prow that was skewering the pumice. I had just verified that Burrows was unconscious rather than dead when the entirety of the crew, Enrique and Filiberto, tumbled into the cockpit cursing and crossing themselves repeatedly.

"*Madre de dios*, what happened?" blurted Enrique.

"We didn't die. Let's see if we can keep it that way. Haul Captain Burrows onto solid land. I'll get the ambassador and his trollop."

Of course she was still screaming despite Don Jorge's attempts to calm her. I wondered whom his family had bribed to secure his diplomatic post.

"If you're quite through watering the deck with your crocodile tears, I suggest we abandon ship before it abandons us." I marched back to the bridge without awaiting her answer. It only took a couple of moments for them to join me on the bridge.

"Don Jorge, help me give her a hand up. Señorita Catalina, crawl to Enrique and Filiberto." I pointed.

"*No, no, no. ¡Me voy a morir!*"

"Yes, probably, possibly by my own hand." The ship creaked obligingly to emphasize my point. She shrieked and scrambled across the prow into the able hands of Enrique and Filiberto. Don Jorge followed her. The look on his face suggested he was even more terrified than she was, but at least he opted for maintaining his manly composure without whimpering. Which is not to say that he wasn't trembling like a half-drowned cat when I reached the cliff top, and I really didn't think it was that cold.

Having secured the crew and passengers, I surveyed the area in hopes of spotting signs of habitation rather than having to perform more complex navigation. And that's when I spotted the old Indian with the donkey, both standing perfectly still at a short distance, watching our unintentional circus. He was probably from Cochiti. Sadly, my knowledge of Keres was completely non-existent beyond the single fact that I knew the name of the language itself. Hoping that he spoke at least a little Spanish, I shouted, *"¿Puedo comprar el burro?"*

Don Jorge shook his head, mystified. "Why do you want to buy the burro?"

The old Indian slowly shook his head.

I turned back to Don Jorge. "Because you still need to get to Santa Fe to sign that treaty."

"¿Y yo qué?" Señorita Catalina demanded. Ah, so she did actually understand English and it was, once again, all about her.

"¿Puedo contratar a el burro?" I shouted. The old Indian stared blankly at me, so I waved him over.

"We almost died and you still want me to go to Santa Fe to sign the treaty?" Don Jorge whined.

"If you don't sign the treaty, all of this," I waved my arm at the entombed ship, "was for nothing."

"Este hombre necesita ir a Santa Fe," I explained to the Indian. He held out his hand. Ah yes, some things are universal in all languages. "Don Jorge, give him some money and explain that you'll give him some more when he gets you to Santa Fe."

"I am not going with this dangerous *indio*. He'll probably kill me the minute you're not looking and steal all my money. And why should I pay? *Yo soy* a guest of the gobernment of Los Estados Unidos. My government already paid your company to take me to Santa Fe. So, take me to Santa Fe." And then he crossed his arms over his belly like a spoiled four-year-old. One wonders how someone so spoiled and lazy got to be so rich, but then it was his family's money and they probably got it oppressing peasants like me. I considered throwing in with the "dangerous *indio*" on the murder and theft plan, but my conscience got the best of me. I fished a half dime out of the pouch on my tool belt and handed it to the Indian.

"Enrique and Filiberto, start a fire and keep the captain warm. As soon as I get to some kind of settlement, I'll send help. Don Jorge, get on the donkey."

"El burro duerme," the Indian said. I looked at the donkey. He seemed to be awake. Not really wide awake, but obviously not asleep. I didn't know what to say in response, so I just pointed in the general direction of Santa Fe and we set off. Since the Indian and I were walking, it was slow going. Don Jorge complained that the blanket over the donkey's back wasn't a proper saddle, completely ignoring the fact that he was riding while we were walking. I was about to offer to switch places with him when the donkey stopped in his tracks, locked his knees, and keeled over toward me. I jumped back just in time to avoid being flattened. Don Jorge wasn't so lucky. Not only did he hit the ground, but he landed right on a cholla cactus. I stifled a giggle.

"El burro duerme," the Indian repeated. Even Don Jorge's shrieking wasn't enough to wake the donkey. The Indian reached under his *zarape* and came back with a handful of salt that he held under the nose of the somnolent pack animal. It snuffled a couple of times, opencd one eye, and hungrily lapped up the salt. The donkey was narcoleptic!

I pulled a pair of tweezers out of my tool pouch. "Hold still." I started removing cactus spines from Don Jorge's tender hide, each extraction being accompanied by an "ouch" or an *"hijole."*

"I'm not getting back on that treacherous beast."

"Very well, I'll send them on their way."

The reality of walking the rest of Santa Fe must have dawned on him because he changed his mind instantaneously. We trudged along for another half an hour during which Don Jorge grew more impatient...and cold. I offered that the walking was keeping me warm and I would be happy to switch places with him. Failing to appreciate the generosity of my offer, he decided to put heel to the donkey to motivate him. It served only to motivate the donkey to fall asleep again. I saw its knees lock up, which was enough warning for me to assist Don Jorge this time. Maybe it was the cold, but I was just not quick enough to catch him. There was no cactus this time, but he was still sporting a few small stickers from his previous encounter with the succulent's self-defenses and he got to relive some of the suffering. I also shan't repeat what he said about the snoozing creature, but it did involve the animal's name in the vernacular.

"Sin sal más," the Indian said after he resuscitated the burro the second time.

"At the rate we're going, we won't make it to Santa Fe without more salt. *¿Dónde está el pueblo más cercano?"*

"Agua Fria."

"Yes, some cold water would be very refreshing right now!" Don Jorge screamed. "Where is the nearest village?!"

I pointed to a wisp of smoke about a mile ahead of us. "He meant that we're near the village of Agua Fria."

He huffed at me rather than admit his lack of knowledge of the local area. "I do not trust that animal. I will walk." And so we did, with Don Jorge wincing every step of the way like a debutante who has worn a pair of shoes too small to the cotillion.

Agua Fria was not more than a couple of small adobes with adjacent corrals and kitchen gardens reduced to twigs and shreds by the dry autumn and winter frost except for the dried hollyhock stalks standing sentry. The only color other than earth was the partially used *ristras* hanging under the protection of the tiny porches.

"¿Hola? ¿Hola? Hay alguien en casa?" I hollered, but there was no reply. "No one seems to be home." I walked around the back of the house and peered in a window. I saw a neat little kitchen that looked like it had been recently used, but no one was home.

"Now what are you going to do?"

"I think I'll just sit down on the ground and cry."

Don Jorge was absolutely stunned. "Really?"

"No, now that you've cheered me up, I think I'll go see if there are any salt licks in that tack box by the corral."

"Oh, good idea." Apparently, irony was not part of his formal education.

No horseman who wanted to stay a horseman in this climate would have been without a salt lick, but I didn't expect the really excellent good fortune that lurked in the tack box. Rather than a huge block that would have required chipping, there was a bag of fist-sized licks. I guess it made sense that you might need to take one with you just as we needed to at that moment. I looked around again, but no one had returned and we couldn't afford to keep waiting. I grabbed the smallest one from the bag and closed the tack box. I pulled a half cent out of my tool pouch and placed it right in the middle of the lid where the owner would be sure to see it the next time he opened the box.

Don Jorge trailed me back to the front of the house where the Indian and the donkey were waiting patiently, or at least the Indian was waiting patiently. The donkey was making hors d'oeuvres of the hollyhock seed pods still clinging to the stalks. I nudged the salt lick under its nose to lure it away from its snack and also to make sure it got a bit more salt before we trekked the last few miles to Santa Fe. Once he got bored with the salt, I handed the rest to the Indian and wiped the donkey slobber off my hand.

Scientific American.

THE ADVOCATE OF INDUSTRY, AND JOURNAL OF SCIENTIFIC, MECHANICAL AND OTHER IMPROVEMENTS.

| Vol. 5. | New York, September 23, 1848. | No. 1. |

THE
SCIENTIFIC AMERICAN:
CIRCULATION 11,000.
PUBLISHED WEEKLY.
At 128 Fulton Street, New York (Sun Building,) and
13 Court Street, Boston, Mass.
By Munn & Company.
The Principal Office being at New York.

TERMS—$2 a year—$1 in advance, and
the remainder in 6 months.
See advertisement on last page.

Poetry.

EFFICACY OF SODIUM CHLORIDE
IN THE
TREATMENT OF NARCOLEPSY
IN
EQUUS AFRICANUS ASINUS

BY C. L. McTROWELL, M.D.

RAIL ROAD NEWS.

The Ogdensburg Railroad.—
This road is in such a state of forwardness that it is expected will be ready for travel in the fall of 1849. The engines and cars, of the most approved kind, are in the hands of the makers. The distance between the lake and the river St. Lawrence is 118 miles; the rails are of the same description as those on the Portland road, and the cars will be enabled to pass over them with great rapidity.— Before long this road will be linked with others now in progress, and form an uninterrupted chain to the city of New York.

When we finally arrived at La Fonda on the plaza, I told Don Jorge to pay the Indian for all the extra fuss he'd caused. I glared at him meaningfully before he could start his "*Yo soy* a guest..." tune again. When he pulled out his purse, one of the coins in it was a half cent. Now why would a Mexican ambassador have an American half cent? So, I asked him, "Where did you get that coin?"

And he replied, "Oh, I just found it lying around."

"Lying around? I left it to pay for that salt lick. We've stolen a salt lick!"

"You should mind your tongue. *Yo soy* a guest of the gobernment of Los Estados Unidos and an ambassador de Mexico. And I'm not the one who took it." I wanted to smack the smug smile right off his face.

We went inside to wait for Lieutenant Colonel Edwin Sumner to arrive from Fort Marcy. Someone in a nearby kitchen was simmering a pot of pozole, which made my mouth water. I hadn't had a bite to eat since our stop in Albuquerque early that morning. Don Jorge went up to the desk and demanded a bath so he could soak out the rest of the cholla spines. There was a very beautiful young woman also waiting in the lobby. Although I'm far from an expert on women's fashions, I believe the clothes she was wearing would be described as tasteful and expensive. This detail seemed to escape the esteemed ambassador because he invited her to come help him in his "time of need." As you have probably come to realize, I'm no more of an expert on diplomacy than I am on fashion, but I was certainly not surprised when she slapped him, lucky her. I was preparing a face-saving apology for my tactless ward when the Territorial Governor, Donaciano Vigil, entered. Consistent with our "luck" that day, the young lady proceeded to complain about Don Jorge to Vigil. Her uncle. The beautiful, refined young lady was his favorite niece who was engaged to be married the next week at Mission San Miguel to Vigil's military aide. I began inspecting the floorboards for a crack large enough through which to crawl. Don Jorge then proceeded to suggest that a young woman so near her nuptials should not be so free with her favors, which motivated the territorial governor to slap Don Jorge on the other cheek.

Don y Doña Alejandro Mondragón
solicitar el honor de su presencia en la boda de su hija

Doña Felicidad
Al
Capitán Francisco San Diego
en la
Misión de San Miguel
Sábado, 06 de diciembre 1847

Fiesta de recepción seguirá en el Palacio de los Gobernadores

I was assessing the availability of exit routes when Lieutenant Sumner arrived just in time to hear Don Jorge challenge Vigil to a duel. And blast the luck, but Sumner was standing between me and the door. Vigil proceeded to relate the exchange so far and, to his credit, his account was unflinchingly fair and accurate. Sumner listened to Vigil's story without interrupting. He thought for a moment and then said, "Very well. I will serve as your second if that will suit you."

Completely nonplussed, Don Jorge replied, "As my other retainers are regrettably indisposed, Dr. McTrowell will serve as my second." You know that I'm rarely at a loss for words, but I was struck dumb at the horror of being involved in a duel. It was way past time to take matters into my own hands. I realized that the least disastrous outcome would be to get Don Jorge out of Santa Fe before the duel, but I needed an excuse to just get out of the room.

"Gentlemen, I failed to anticipate the need to bring my dueling pistols, so I will need to go purchase replacements. If you'll excuse us." I marched Don Jorge back out onto the Santa Fe Trail. As soon as we were out of earshot of Vigil and Sumner, I explained to Don Jorge that our only hope was to flee.

"But, Señorita McTrowell, that would stain my honor and endanger the treaty."

"At this point your honor is as stained as your *chaqueta* and the treaty is as endangered as the dodo. And more than your honor is likely to get damaged in a duel with a man who was raised in the dangerous environs around Santa Fe and a lieutenant colonel of the US Army. Discretion is the better part of valor. We need to get out of town."

I dragged Don Jorge pouting to the stables where we picked out horses and had them saddled. I told him I'd ride out and scout around a bit to make sure we could get away without being seen. And I expressly told him to pay for the horses. I had just determined that neither Vigil, nor Sumner, nor any of their aides were about when Don Jorge came riding up almost at a gallop, yelping *"Estupido cholla, estupido cholla."*

"Don Jorge, we'll attract less attention if we ride at a pace more suitable for town." He glanced nervously over his shoulder when I caught sight of the stable boy running around the corner waving and shouting, "Horse thieves!"

I glared at Don Jorge ferociously. "Horse thieves!? Didn't you pay him?"

"*Yo soy* a guest of the gobernment of Los Estados Unidos."

"Horse thieving is a hanging offense, you spoiled, pompous *calabaza*! Ride like your life depends on it…because it does!"

Fortunately, we still had the element of surprise on our side, more or less, as we rode southwest out of town, back toward La Bajada. Unfortunately, our path would take us right by Agua Fria again. We weren't three minutes into the return trip when I saw a cloud of dust rise behind us; we were being chased as I had expected. We rode by the same little adobe farmhouse where I had "provisioned" the salt lick. My stomach sank as I realized that the woman of the house was standing outside with two men. She was gesticulating at the box where the salt lick had been. She held up her hand three times to indicate the heights of the three recent, unwelcome visitors. She pointed meaningfully toward Santa Fe. When the threesome looked toward Santa Fe, they spotted me and Don Jorge bearing down on them. That's when both of her hands went into action. I won't describe her hand gestures, nor will I repeat the colorful terms in which she described us, but she left no doubt that she had seen us pilfer the precious salt and expected satisfaction. Her two male benefactors scrambled in the direction of the corral. They were saddled up and on their mounts in time to join the posse from Santa Fe. The rising cloud of dust behind us grew larger and more menacing.

As if we didn't already have enough problems, I realized the dust cloud was not the only ominous harbinger in the sky. The clouds ahead of us were low, gray, and opaque. And then the wind picked up. And then it started blowing wet flakes of snow the size of silver dollars. I pulled down my goggles to keep the flakes out of my eyes. I could barely see where the horse was taking me. That's when I realized that the blizzard was obscuring our path not only from us, but also from our pursuers. I wrestled my compass out of my belt and took a bearing back toward the ship. I shouted to Don Jorge, "Fall in behind me and stay close!" I took a sharp turn to the west and rode for what I judged to be about two minutes before pulling up sharply on the reins, bringing my steed to an abrupt halt. Needless to say, our two horses almost had an unpleasantly personal encounter.

"Médico estúpido," Don Jorge spat at me.

"Shhhhh!"

"What are you doing?"

"If you want to live to see your annoying mistress again, you'll shut up now," I hissed. I continued in a whisper, "The blizzard is holding down the dust and obscuring our tracks. The posse doesn't know where we're going. I have taken a bearing toward the ship. So long as we ride slowly, and in silence, we can get back to the ship without being discovered."

"And what will we do once we get back to the ship?"

"I only perform one miracle at a time. Now be quiet."

If we had continued at a gallop, we could have been back to the ship in ten minutes, but at a slow walk in the blizzard, it took thirty. We had to stop a couple of times because we heard the posse in the distance. I was sure the stamping of the freezing horses would give us away, or maybe it was just the pounding of my heart. At one point I thought I heard a scream and another sound like an avalanche. This was followed by considerable shouting and the sound of receding hoof beats. That was the last we heard of them.

SANTA FE CHRONICLE
Unexpected Blizzard Thwarts Posse

A posse chasing a pair of horse thieves from the notorious Manzana gang was thwarted by an unexpected blizzard on Wednesday. The miscreants sorely abused a stable hand at La Fonda and made off with two fine steeds. Such was the heinousness of the crime that Lieutenant Sumner himself joined the posse. The lawmen were close on the heels of the fleeing felons when the aforementioned blizzard dashed their plans. Sadly, a posse member, Señor Juan Camisaroja, came to an untimely end when he rode off La Bajada while blinded by the storm.

December 1847

The ship and the crew made for a pretty forlorn sight when we found them, a task made easier by the waning blizzard and the way that Señorita Catalina's shrill voice carried. She had obviously forced Enrique and Filiberto to unload her trunks, but now she was berating them because the trunks were getting snow on them and the dirt was turning to mud. They had obviously given up caring because they were huddled around a tiny, hissing campfire that the snow was striving mightily to extinguish. Captain Burrows was conscious, but both of his eyes were blackened and he was staring in fascination at the snowflakes. I didn't need to examine him more closely to know that he had a concussion, but that would have to wait until we got back to the safety of Albuquerque. The ship's gondola looked like a crushed almond shell and the cockpit window was now completely broken out, but the ship was still wedged firmly in the cliff face and the envelope was still inflated. There were long scrape marks on the prow of the gondola. I envisioned poor Enrique and Filiberto dragging the trunks out through the broken window. Perhaps I hadn't gotten entirely the worst of the day.

Enrique leapt to his feet. "Señorita McTrowell, you are alive!"

"Barely, and thank you for sounding so surprised." He looked a little sheepish.

"Capitan Burrows is not so well."

"I can see that. Please take charge of the horses and see that they don't get away. We may need them."

"How are we going to get back to Albuquerque?"

"Miracle number two, coming right up."

I walked up to the edge of the cliff and along the starboard side, checking the contact of the ship with the cliff. I repeated the process on the port side, my inspections accompanied by the alternating expressions of affection and threats of disembowelment from Señorita Catalina toward Don Jorge.

"Enrique, is the engine still operating?"

"Sí, but the mounts are a little loose."

"That will have to do. Fetch me as much spare line as there is on the ship. Filiberto, get everyone on the ship and start up the engine." I took the reins of the horses and loosened up their flank cinches just enough to slip out their saddle blankets before re-cinching their saddles.

Señorita Catalina turned to Filiberto and said something to him in Spanish. I didn't hear all of what she said, but the tone of her voice and the way she pointed toward her trunks and the ship made it clear that she was ordering him to put her trunks back on the ship. Before Filiberto had to face her wrath or disobey a direct order, I said to her, "Your trunks are staying here." As I expected, she started screaming, stamping her feet, and saying some very unflattering things about me. "Or you can stay here with them and die in this snow storm."

Sensing it was time to engage his diplomatic skills, finally, Don Jorge said, *"Mi palomita, te voy a comprar ropa nueva."* Apparently, the only thing better than a dozen steamer trunks filled with expensive, fashionable clothing is the promise of a dozen new steamer trunks with new, more expensive, more fashionable clothing. She still retrieved her mantillas before allowing Filiberto to help her across the prow and through the broken cockpit window.

Enrique returned with about a hundred feet of line. I handed him one end of the rope. "Hold on to this and don't let go, no matter what." I walked to the prow of the ship and laid down on the edge of the cliff with just the top half of my body resting on the prow and my arms draped around its sides. I lowered a few yards of the other end of the rope down with my right hand and started swinging it back and forth. I banged my right hand on the rocks a few times before I managed to catch the other end in my left hand. I threaded several more yards through my left hand before scooting most ungracefully back onto the cliff top. My mother would have fainted in horror if she had seen my contortions, all while Enrique was watching my backside in stunned silence. I continued threading until half the rope was on either side of the prow, at which point I tied a fairly snug loop. Then I slipped one of the horse blankets between the rope and the prow to even out the pressure.

I rolled up the other horse blanket and threw it through the cockpit window to Filiberto. "Filiberto, knock off all of the broken glass you can and drape this over the edge of the window. Enrique, tie that end of the rope to the saddle horn of the roan." I tied the other end to the saddle horn of the appaloosa. They both looked perplexed and dismayed.

"Here's the plan. Pay close attention because we're only going to get one shot at this and if we fail, some or all of us are going to come to a messy end, including the horses. Enrique and I are going to lead the horses down the opposite sides of the culvert until the rope is taut. Filiberto is going to put the engine on full reverse. Once the gondola starts to pull loose, I'll give the signal and we'll spook the horses toward the edge of La Bajada. The horses should provide enough muscle to pull the ship loose. You and I will only have a few seconds to run back to the top of the culvert and jump through the cockpit window." I tried smiling nonchalantly as if I hadn't just suggested diving off a thousand-foot cliff after a receding, and mostly unpiloted, airship. They were clearly not fooled.

I tried to breathe evenly as I led the appaloosa along the cliff edge. I could hear the engine turning and rattling on its loose mounts.

It hadn't occurred to me that the ship might just tear itself apart once relieved of the compression of the culvert. I stroked the horse soothingly while I waited for the engine to build up enough steam. And then the gondola gave a creek and a crack, sending tiny bits of pumice down the cliff face. "Now!" I yelled. I slapped the appaloosa as hard as I could on the rump and sprinted back to the head of the culvert.

The prow was still touching the cliff face, but it pulled free just as I got there. I managed to take two skittering steps on it before unceremoniously flopping torso first through the window. I allowed myself an instant to congratulate myself for the foresight to have Filiberto put down the horse blanket. Enrique had a harder go of it because he was a few steps behind me. He fell forward on his first step but managed to get a grip on the window frame. I grabbed the inside edge of the blanket and rolled away from the window, dragging Enrique into the cabin with it. He rolled over me and wound up in a tangled bundle with the blanket on the deck. There was no time to worry about him. I grabbed the helm and shouted back to Filiberto, "Full ahead."

The ship convulsed and shuddered, but it turned and headed in the direction of Albuquerque. I just had time to look back for the horses. Sensible creatures that they are, they had stopped at the cliff edge. They tugged back and forth on the rope a couple of times before walking back toward the top of the culvert. If they kept going the same direction, someone in Agua Fria was going to get a couple of nice horses. Maybe it would make them forget about the salt lick. Señorita Catalina cried at the receding view of her trunks of dresses and shoes.

SANTA FE CHRONICLE
Fancy Dress Blessing on Cochiti Pueblo
The inhabitants of nearby Cochiti Indian awoke Thursday morning to an unexpected gift from "Mother Earth." Several trunks of clothing, much of it of the fancy dress variety, were discovered unattended near La Bajada. As no one has stepped forward to claim the items,

the clothing was distributed to the women and
girls of the pueblo.

December 1847

There wasn't a proper airship port in Albuquerque, just a dusty field with a few rails sunk in the ground. It was more like an airship hitching post. I brought the ship in as low as possible and threw a line overboard. I slid down the line as fast as I could without burning through my gloves or boots, although my hands and feet were still so frozen I probably wouldn't have noticed. I'd just finished lashing up the ship when Don Jorge stuck his head overboard.

"Señorita McTrowell, how am I supposed to get down?"

"You're no longer my problem, but I suggest the rope ladder rolled up by your feet."

"Oh, sí."

I was almost away from the field when I heard his squeak. Apparently, he hadn't accounted for the fact that the ladder, like everything else on the ship, was wet from the snow. I turned around in time to have the pleasure of seeing him fall the last four feet to the ground, or rather the mud. Did I mention he hadn't yet had time to remove the rest of the cholla stickers? I quick marched to the tanner and ordered the warmest, sturdiest leather duster they made.

C. de Baca Tanning

Finest Leather Goods in Albuquerque!

"Until last Thursday, it was the longest day of my life."

The cabin echoed with Jonathan Lord Ashleigh's baritone laugh. "My dear friend, you become more colorful with each passing day. But, I'm curious. Why does Mr. Wallace refer to this as 'The Pecos Incident?'"

Before Sparky could finish her sip of port, Chief Inspector Drake spoke up. "I believe I have solved that mystery. You have not mentioned the name of the small airship."

"Bravo, Erasmus. It was Los Pecos."

THE PARISIAN PARTY

BY MR. DAVID L. DRAKE

With a break in the narrative, Erasmus, Sparky, and Lord Ashleigh took a few seconds to stop and sip their port. Without warning, but with perfect timing, the bedchamber door swung open and Virat appeared, a perfectly clean yellow scarf draped over his forearm.

"You got it clean! I could kiss you!" Sparky exclaimed and jumped up from her chair. Virat simply scooped it off his arm and holding it with both hands, offered it to Sparky with a slight bow. She accepted it, exuding delight in the miracle he had performed, and flipped the middle of her prized possession to the back of her neck. Virat simply retreated back into the bedroom with a very slight smile.

Sparky's face suddenly went serious. She looked from Erasmus back to Lord Ashleigh and back to Erasmus. "Erasmus, how did you obtain this scarf? And get it wrapped in time for me to get it before we left Paris?"

Erasmus smiled broadly, making the curls in the ends of his moustache climb slightly higher on his cheeks. His eyes twinkled, and he glanced quickly at Lord Ashleigh who echoed his grin. There was a perceivable pause as the two men were stalled in a standoff to see who would offer an explanation first.

Sparky's patience wore thin in a second and a half, and she coaxed them again. "Well?" She dragged the word out a bit in an accusatory tone.

A small knock came from the door to the hallway. It was the type of knock made by a diminutive hand trying its best to be loud enough. Virat was in the room and answering the door faster than any of the three could stand up, demonstrating a precision of movement that made Erasmus think that Virat must practice this feat on his own to execute it so effortlessly. When the door swung open, a boy in his early teens dressed smartly as a messenger stood in the doorway, holding a few small, bright blue envelopes. Virat politely gestured for him to announce himself.

"Chief Inspector Drake, I am here to deliver your invitations." His voice gave away his French accent, but his English was perfect. Everyone in the room instantly understood that this young man had delivered messages to many people visiting from many countries during his tenure as a messenger, and he could have spoken Italian or German just as well as English.

Erasmus stood and replied, "Excellent! Please come in."

The lad stepped into the room with confidence and handed invitations to each person, including Virat. Erasmus, who received his invitation last, asked, "Are all of the arrangements set?"

"Yes, sir. Precisely as you requested. It was a pleasure doing business with you." With that, the young man extended his hand for shaking, which Erasmus took and shook heartily. The lad stepped back, took the door handle, bowed deeply, and closed the door as he backed into the hallway.

It seemed that everyone except Erasmus had been infected with a look of puzzlement. They looked at Erasmus, then at their envelopes, and then slowly ran fingers under the flaps to open them. The card inside was simple and elegant.

Sparky broke the silence first. "Erasmus! This is rather..." She trailed off, realizing that if she stated that this seemed unusually formal for him, it might be off-putting after the work that he had put into organizing the get-together. And if she suggested that it was astoundingly unanticipated, it might sound like she thought he was stodgy. Instead, Lord Ashleigh helped finish her languishing sentence with "...intriguing."

"Friends," Erasmus started, "I know this is unexpected. As it turns out, I recently came into some money and I thought our last evening in Paris should not be spent sitting on an airship. I have made arrangements, using the services of the young gentleman that you just met, to treat us to one of Paris' finest dining establishments. At least that is what I have been informed. I could not get a supper arranged in time, but I thought this would make a great ending to the evening."

Lord Ashleigh was delighted. "Jolly good! I'll get out my top hat and jacket. Will it be just the four of us?"

"Oh, no. There will be a few more." Erasmus opened the door to the hallway, and there was a line of passengers waiting to disembark, all dressed in their fineries.

Lord Ashleigh turned to his manservant. "We haven't a moment to lose! Virat, my friend, please find us sufficient garments of fashion and finish. We are going out!"

Erasmus formed a crook in his arm, which Sparky took without hesitation. "Come, my dear. I will guide you all the way to your cabin door. We have a party to attend."

When Sparky rejoined Erasmus in the hallway, she had on a white blouse subtly fringed in lace, a gold necklace with a feminine brooch, a mustard-colored skirt, and a jaunty brown jacket with smart lapels. He was dressed in his black frock coat, a waistcoat of striking blue, and a black cravat that Sparky hadn't seen before. She had changed Erasmus' bandages and dressing earlier that evening, so he still had a gauze halo that didn't quite fit into the rest of his ensemble. He was holding a black top hat.

Sparky enquired, "How do you plan to wear that?" gesturing at the top hat.

"It is borrowed from Jonathan. His head is...well, I shall show you." Erasmus placed the hat on his head. It easily fit over his bandages and came to rest on his ears. Sparky attempted to hide her snicker, but failed. Erasmus stood firm. "A gentleman needs a proper hat, especially if he is accompanying a lady."

Sparky thought of firing back a retort about her being a "lady," but instead did her best curtsy with a touch of sarcasm. Erasmus stood tall and offered his crooked arm again, which she took.

Eight cabriolets waited near the base of tower number twelve where the Burke & Hare was moored. They were glossy black and had the shine of recent polishing. Passengers were still boarding when

Erasmus and Sparky descended the stairs of the tower. By the demeanor of the driver of the closest cabriolet, it was clearly reserved. He stood, guard-like, in front of the door, waving others past.

"This one is for us," Erasmus said.

The driver stepped to the side and opened the door to the vehicle. "Evening, Doctor. Evening, Chief Inspector." Erasmus guided Sparky up the step and into the conveyance, removed his borrowed hat, handed it in to her, and climbed in. They were soon joined by Lord Ashleigh and Virat, both dressed handsomely. Lord Ashleigh sported a midnight blue jacket and top hat complemented with a royal blue tie. Virat's gold and burgundy sherwani was beautifully embroidered with swirls and detailed designs. The door closed and the clacking of horseshoes commenced; the coach got underway with a slight lurch just as Lord Ashleigh was tipping his hat to Sparky.

The procession of cabriolets through the streets made a unique sound. With all of the horses going at the same speed and separated by the same distances, they proceeded train-like through the cobbled avenues. Knowing who was paying for this expedition, the young organizer had staged Erasmus' coach to be last in the line, so that he would be the man joining the ongoing party.

The conversation in the carriage was lively and animated, and the travel time went by quickly. Soon, it seemed, they slowed their pace and took over the avenue in front of the restaurant Les Trois Frères Provençaux. The cabriolets deposited their passengers as efficiently as they had picked them up. The driver lent a hand to Sparky as she descended the coach, and the men stepped out. Sparky tried her best to stay demure, but her entire disposition was oozing "Ooo, fun!" Once they had all exited, Erasmus adjusted his top hat to sit a bit straighter and offered his arm once more, with a cheerful, "Shall we...?"

Sparky took his arm again, and Lord Ashleigh responded with a soft "Yes, yes, yes," and his customary grin. They all proceeded inside.

It was a party atmosphere. The large, beautifully-appointed hall had been rearranged to have table after table, each with its own special offering: one crowded with glasses of champagne, another with chocolate desserts of varying shapes and sizes, one with digestifs, one with ramekins of crème brûlée and similar custards, and, of course, a table of cakes, tarts, and pastries. To a person, everyone in the room was milling about, and pointing out and discussing the latest offering that caught their eye. Everyone from the Burke & Hare was there.

Erasmus started to make a few mental notes. Luis-Miguel looked like he was memorizing some presentation tricks. Reginald had his pants on, thank goodness. Jake took on a schoolboy look. Somewhat retrograde from the maturing he had done over the course of the regatta, but perfectly acceptable for the evening. Mr. Wilkinson apparently had an unexpected weakness for bon-bons. Slightly out of character, but it made the engineer seem all the more human. Ahh, and Aldrich Fremont was having a good time. Erasmus thought, *"Perhaps he will change his mind about me a little, ... just a wee bit."*

Sparky leaned in toward Erasmus, whispering, "That's enough, you can stop scrutinizing the room. This looks impressive and...expensive. How did you recently come into money, if I may ask?"

"Indirectly through the Queen. King Maximilian had a price on Ishild's head. It was known throughout his military and security force, but apparently not outside of that circle. He paid it through to Queen Victoria since it was her countrymen who brought Ishild to them. The reward was passed on to me. It was delivered by Her Majesty's physician when he saw me, although I do not think that he realized he was passing an envelope full of gulden notes to me. I thought that this was a pleasant way to repay everyone involved."

"This is very...nice of you. Let's go over there and get some champagne!" She dashed ahead to scoop up a glass.

The festivities carried on until well past midnight without slowing down, except when the chocolate soufflé came out, and everyone hushed for the cutting. The night ended with the final bottle of champagne being sabered and everyone giving the Chief Inspector a toast for his generosity.

The party-goers slowly exited to the awaiting carriages. The chill of the Parisian night had settled in, and the party-goers pulled their jackets close as each of them patiently lined up to get back into their vehicles.

When all four companions were back in their seats, Erasmus had a wry smile. Lord Ashleigh couldn't ignore it for long. "My dear Mr. Cat, I think you have a bit of canary feather on your lip. Would you like to tell us what's on your mind? Great party, by the way."

"Why, thank you, my good friend. As for my story, I think I have had enough bubbly and sweets to loosen my tongue. I want to tell my tale."

Sparky chimed in, "Your tale?" She had a fairly good idea of what he was about to explain, but wanted to feign some polite ignorance.

"Yes, my tale. The whole Ishild-Tobias-Tuttle story. I shall see if I can finish it before we arrive back at the Burke & Hare. I have only been able to put it all together with the addition of a few of the things that Tobias and Ishild said during the last few days. And I have been keeping this story rather quiet for fear that I might lose my position at Scotland Yard if it got out. I no longer have that fear."

"Pray, go on. You have my ear," Lord Ashleigh coaxed.

"This tale starts, simply enough, as early as one can: my very first memories. I was brought up on a sailing vessel that navigated the oceans of the North and South Atlantic. We were on the mercenary ship the Fearless, a wooden, 240-foot vessel made for speed. She counted on wind and sails for most her power, but we had a crude steam engine and screw propeller in case of dead calm. I was told since my earliest memories that I was the son of the captain, the proud Benjamin Tuttleford III. Although he treated me as such, I could tell that many of the other lads he called 'son' were from many a country and race, that I was just another of a collection of children that ended up on the ship. Around the age of eight, I witnessed a new boy being brought on to the ship and was told that he was Tuttle's son, so I just figured that this was how I had come aboard.

"A bit of history now. Slavery had been outlawed in England since early in the twelfth century, and western Europe had given it up long before that. But it was still a raging trade between Africa, the Caribbean, and the Americas. The ship's mission was simple enough. We sailed under the English flag and stopped as many of the slaver ships as we could, returning their captives back to their native countries. We had papers for our privateering, signed by King William himself, which were posted outside of the captain's quarters. I learned my letters and how to read from those papers.

"I mastered the ropes and could climb like a chimp. I spent many days in the crow's nest looking for our next target. As with all on board, I learned how to wield a sword and knife and how to fire a cannon. The crew also knew a number of other beneficial arts. A Portuguese sailor, unfortunately no longer with us, taught us lads his country's form of stick fighting, which was as beautiful as it was deadly. I was planning to get a brace of pistols when I turned fourteen, but I did not get the chance, as you will soon learn. Oh, yes. Tobias was our cook. He held his own in hand-to-hand, but the man could turn any exotic meat or fruit into a gourmet meal. He had an astounding collection of dried spices. He gave me the privilege of learning each by its appearance and aroma.

"I could ramble on for a long time, but here is the crux of the story. The Americans saw our activity as pirating and took steps to stop us in the Caribbean. We took serious damage and limped back to England, pumping all the way. There was a bit of a scuffle as soon as we docked, and everyone on board was separated by the local navy personnel. All of us children were placed in an orphanage. Four of my best friends were there. Within a year and a half, we escaped, and I do not think the orphanage wardens tried too hard to find us. We lived as entertainers on the street for a while. During that time, I helped an older gentleman who was in a scuffle with a robber, and he took me in. My friends, François, Henri, Charles, and René, left to go back to France, their native country.

"After that, I attended classes in the British school system, but the truth is that my time on the Fearless taught me more about geography, maths, history, and languages than I ever would have learned in a classroom.

"What I learned from Tobias a couple of days ago was that England had rescinded our papers while we were at sea. We were actually operating as pirates without our knowledge. The King wanted to make amends with the Americans and see if they could help resolve their slavery issues politically. We were caught in the middle of that transition. Tobias said that while the crew was on bond awaiting trial for our 'crimes at sea,' they hopped the next ship to Europe and settled the Town of Melköde. Tuttle got married and had a daughter, Ishild."

Lord Ashleigh wrinkled his nose. "So Ishild is, in a way, your sister?"

"In a way," Erasmus chuckled. "Because she heard stories about me, she must have thought that I was the older brother who abandoned the family, a traitor of sorts. The one who stayed in England, the country that turned its back on their brave sailors."

Sparky chimed in. "So, what is your real name?"

"Good question. I was always called 'Drake' while on the Fearless. It means 'dragon' and that is a whole story in itself. The orphanage would not let me have only a single name, so they called me 'Erasmus,' which ironically means 'beloved,' which is not quite the way they treated me. The man who took me in was Edwin Llewellyn. For all that I owe him, I took his last name as my middle name."

The carriage slowed. "Ahh, we are here! I hope you have enjoyed my little story. You can see why I was concerned if Scotland Yard found out. I am a criminal of the high seas. It is not something that looks good on one's CV."

Lord Ashleigh smiled and winked, adding, "Your story is safe with us."

As they piled out, Erasmus thought, *My friends are in good company, since the Queen also seems to think I am worthy enough.*

Home Again, Home Again, Jiggity Jig

By Dr. Katherine L. Morse

"Mr. Wilkinson, shut down the engines."

Sparky gently steered the Burke & Hare toward tower number three as the lack of power caused the air ship to lose momentum. The ship's crew threw the mooring lines down to the tower crew who efficiently lashed them down. She waited for the slight tug back against the mooring lines that would tell her that the ship was held fast. The ship gradually inched closer to the tower as the tower crew winched in the mooring lines so the gangplank would reach. She would rather have slept after Drake's delightful soiree, but Jake Fremont was not ready to handle the ship alone at night crossing the English Channel and docking in London was not for the faint of heart.

"Mr. Fremont, I am forever indebted to you for your valor and steadfastness. Although we can never speak of the events of the last few days publicly, always remember that everyone on this ship owes you their life. If you will accompany me, I believe I can repay you in some small way."

Not knowing what else to do, Jake merely nodded, said, "Yes, ma'am," and followed her off the bridge.

McTrowell marched straight to the office of Western & Transatlantic Airship Lines. She had the vague sense that something was amiss or a little different when she walked through the door, but she was tired and intent on her task, so she dismissed it out of hand. Without waiting for the civil pleasantries of a greeting, she said directly to the office manager, "Mr. Littleton, this is Mr. Jake Fremont. Young Mr. Fremont has shown a preternatural talent for airship piloting. Please see to it that he is sent to the pilot training school at Wiltshire with the highest recommendation from Western & Transatlantic, and provide him with a guarantee of employment when he successfully completes the course." She turned to shake the hand of the dumbfounded young man. "Mr. Fremont, I look forward to flying with you again. Please contact me as soon as you have completed your training. Mr. Littleton here always knows how to reach me, regardless of where I am."

He repeated, "Yes, ma'am," in the same tone as earlier and shook her hand. And then the two of them stood there awkwardly because the office had gone silent and everyone was staring at them. Sparky looked around and realized, much to her embarrassment, that she must have just interrupted a conversation and a lively one at that. There was another woman in the room, a formidably proper Victorian woman who probably would have stood as straight as an iron rod even without her corset, Annabelle Wallace. Although no one in this office would have dared to refer to her thusly. She might be only half the mass of her husband and admirably trim for her age, but everyone knew Mrs. Reginald Wallace to be the equal, or perhaps superior, of her husband when it came to will.

"Mrs. Wallace, what a surprise to find you here. I apologize for interrupting." No sense antagonizing the owner's wife, regardless of their marital situation. The look on Annabelle Wallace's face was more intimidating than anything Ishild could have mustered.

"Mr. Littleton and I were just reviewing the improvements I have made in the efficient operation of this office." McTrowell hazarded a quick glance about. If pressed, she would have to have admitted there was markedly less clutter and chaos about the place. And that Mr. Littleton looked quite discomfited about the situation. But Mr. Littleton was no fool; he took advantage of the diversion to usher Jake Fremont into a side room where he could afford himself the relief of executing Sparky's orders and extricate himself from further "review" with Mrs. Wallace.

Mrs. Wallace continued, "I would like your opinion as another woman who engages in airship travel. I find the enterprise to be unsuitable for women of quality and station. Women of means in these times are considerably interested in enlightening travel and providing the benefits of an experiential education to their offspring. However, they require comforts and security that are not currently offered by my husband's enterprise. He must add educational, sightseeing tours for women of quality that include suitable comforts, and reliable, trustworthy chaperones and tour guides."

Although it wasn't, strictly speaking, a question, McTrowell felt obliged to offer some reply, so she said, "Indeed," and hoped that would be sufficient to keep the conversation moving.

"This will be a boon to his business." Mrs. Wallace was no longer speaking hypothetically, and Sparky felt an uncharacteristic sympathy for Mr. Littleton and, at the same time, some antipathy for his having escaped and left her with no exit. Mrs. Wallace had paused in her proclamation, obviously waiting for an affirmative reply. Why was there no pirate attack when you needed one? She was on the verge of actually stammering when the door opened and Wallace himself entered, followed closely by Drake.

"Annabelle, my darling, to what do I owe this unexpected pleasure?" Sparky's eyebrows shot up in astonishment. Who was this man and what had he done with Reginald Wallace? From behind Wallace's back so that only Sparky could see, Drake made a motion of passing his hand down in front of his face, leaving his face an emotionless mask.

Thankful for the warning, Sparky settled her expression before Wallace saw it. She saw her escape route. "Mr. Wallace, your clever and enterprising wife has identified a new business opportunity for you: educational, sightseeing tours for women of means and their children. No doubt she has already identified several customers for this offering from among her estimable friends."

Quickly taking his cue in this little pantomime, Drake chimed in, "What a capital idea. Reginald, you are a fortunate man to have married a woman with such keen business acumen and an eye for new opportunities." And then he gave Wallace a little nudge in the back for good measure. Sparky ducked around the couple to follow Drake who headed toward the side offices the instant it looked like their little improvisational drama was working.

Before they could congratulate themselves on their handiwork, they heard shouting in the adjacent side office. They opened the adjoining door to find the elder Fremont shouting at Littleton, who was obviously bewildered about the source of Fremont's acrimony. They entered just in time to hear the unhappy traveler shout, "This was supposed to be a pleasure cruise. I was assaulted by one of your buffoons, pressed into service as a jailer, and nearly killed. I demand a refund in full!" Given the secrecy of the week's events, Mr. Littleton had no idea what Fremont was going on about, and it showed clearly on his face.

McTrowell entered, followed by Drake. "Mr. Littleton, may I be of assistance?"

Before Littleton could muster a sensible reply, Fremont pointed a finger at Drake and barked out, "That buffoon!" Of course, Wallace could also hear the tirade from the adjoining office and came to investigate the source of the confrontation. He had an uncharacteristically serene composure.

"Mr. Fremont, what seems to be the trouble?"

"I demand a refund! I am never doing business with this company again!"

Wallace smiled. "It is my fondest wish. Please see the cashier in the front office who will provide your refund. In the future, might

I suggest the services of Occidental and Oriental Travel Lines." And he stepped back out without another word. Sparky had to slap her hand over her mouth not to laugh out loud to hear Wallace recommend the services of his chief competitor. Apparently, she and Drake were not the only ones who had had quite enough of Aldrich Fremont. Littleton just threw up his hands and dropped his head on the desk. It had all just been too much for him.

Virat was loading the last of Lord Ashleigh's belongings onto his coach by the time Drake and McTrowell returned to tower number three. Ashleigh greeted them with his usual warmth, "Well, my good friends, it has certainly been an eventful week. What are you planning next?"

"I have a meeting first thing in the morning with Sergeant Fox at which my future will become more clearly defined," Drake replied. Ashleigh and McTrowell exchanged a look of curiosity at the vagueness of this answer.

"I have well and truly burnt my bridges with Mrs. McCreary, so my most urgent business is to find new lodgings until my next assignment," Sparky interjected. Ashleigh and Drake exchanged meaningful and awkward looks. The silence stretched. Even Virat stopped his packing duties to hear what would transpire next.

Drake opened his mouth to speak, but Ashleigh deftly cut him off. "My good Dr. McTrowell, as I have a commodious residence and a female servant who may serve as an appropriate chaperone, might I offer you my hospitality?" He waited for her answer. Sensing that she might be wavering, he added, "And Virat would be able to prepare chai for you at any time."

She smiled back at him. He was dangerously clever and insightful. "You are too kind, but this time I think I shall accept your generous offer."

"Excellent! Chief Inspector Drake, would you care to join us for dinner this evening, at say six? I trust that will give you sufficient time to resettle yourself and report in."

"Yes, thank you. I look forward to seeing the both of you then." He tipped his hat to both of them, but it was clear to all of them which of the two he was most looking forward to seeing.

No sooner had the coach lurched to a start than McTrowell looked Ashleigh straight in the eye and said, "All right, no more stalling. Tell me about the scarf."

"It's quite lovely and complements your hair color nicely."

"That is not what I meant and you know it. Where did that scarf come from and how did it get on my bunk?"

"I might have been meddling…or matchmaking a bit."

"Go on."

"It seemed to me that you and the good Chief Inspector had an affinity for each other, but I feared the reticence for commitment that you two share would prevent you from taking action in time." She nodded, not giving him the respite of a conversational interruption. "I bought the scarf during my shopping excursion our first day in Paris. I wrote the note and had it wrapped. When I saw you kiss Drake on the forehead that night, I knew I was right about the two of you."

"You saw that?"

"It's amazing what you see when you look. I gave the wrapped package to Drake the next day and bet him a good bottle of port that, if he gave it to you, you would kiss him on the lips before the trip was over. He's a logical man. Either a kiss from you or a bottle of port. He couldn't lose."

"You troublemaker, I ought to flatten you like the Duke of Milton the day we met," but she was smiling nevertheless.

He winked and smiled, "Was the kiss not to your liking?"

ABOUT THE AUTHORS

David L. Drake and Katherine L. Morse are the award-winning, San Diego-based authors of "The Adventures of Drake and McTrowell – Perils in a Postulated Past," a serialized steampunk tale detailing the adventures of Chief Inspector Erasmus Drake and Dr. "Sparky" McTrowell. The duo's many adventures are provided in penny dreadful-style episodes on the web (www.DrakeAndMcTrowell.com). They have produced four novels since 2010: "London, Where it All Began," "The Bavarian Airship Regatta," "Her Majesty's Eyes and Ears," and "The Hawaiian Triple Cross." Drake and Morse won a Starburner Award for the radio show based on "London, Where it All Began," which has run multiple times on Krypton Radio.

When not cosplaying their alter egos at conventions all over the West, they are both research computer scientists specializing in distributed modeling and simulation. Mr. Drake is a nationally ranked foil fencer. Dr. Morse is an internationally respected expert on standards, but prefers to be recognized for her cookie baking skills. They throw awesome parties if they do say so themselves.

Made in the USA
Columbia, SC
15 February 2020